The Rebirth of Her

Also by Gertrude T.

Random Attachment

The Rebirth of Henry Whittle ©2020 by Alison Murphy (writing as Gertrude T. Kitty) All Rights Reserved.

Edited by Caitlan Murphy and Grace Murphy
Cover designed by Grace Murphy

The Rebirth of Henry Whittle is fiction. Some locations are loosely based on reality. The names, characters and events in this book exist only in my imagination.

THE REBIRTH OF HENRY WHITTLE

By

Gertrude T. Kitty

The Rebirth of Henry Whittle

To those I love unconditionally,
I will always have your backs:
Tommy, Paddy, Caitlan, Grace, Tink, Alan, Mum
Kay and Martin
Grace, Sam
My loveliest friends Sharon and Paula
You all give me so much more than you receive

Diane Faulls, my friend and punctuation queen

My friends, the beautiful ladies of the BB Book Club:
Jennifer, Sue, Imeda, Wendy, Francis, Jessica, Diane, Karen, Debbie,
Fiona, Michelle, Vanessa, Cathie

Patisserie Brione, Eastcote,
Ahimsa theVegancafé, Pinner
The Red Onion, Ruislip High Street

To every girl and boy
being yourself is freedom.
It's your beauty,
Your strength,
Your character.
Your honesty.
Your chemistry.
Your heart.
Your bravery.
Your kindness to yourself.
And kindness is everything.

Dear reader.
I very much hope
you enjoy.
Happy reading and
best wishes
Gertrude T. Kitty

The Rebirth of Henry Whittle

IT BEGINS WITH MURDER

It's embarrassingly simple. I begin with blunt force trauma. Followed by a swift injection of Vecuronium and his muscles are rendered flaccid. His wrists I bind with electrical ties; purely precautionary – the paralysing agent has a habit of unexpectedly wearing off, and Whittle is accustomed to some heavy shit.

I'm tempted to use a knife – there's something cleansing and biblical about washing enemy blood from your hands, but it's drama I don't need – dead will suffice.

I never prolong the inevitable, unless information needs to be extracted. With Whittle, sure, there's an element of gratification.

Steadily inhaling, I place a hand under his chin, the other on his temple, before twisting gradually. I've broken necks innumerable times, in a split second; this needs to be a moment. Exerting pressure, his neck turns unnaturally, his face contorting as his cervical vertebrae twists, compromising his fragile spinal cord. It's untrue a victim dies immediately from a broken neck. When the spinal cord severs: the brain separates from the body, the respiratory muscles paralyse, breathing is impossible and blood vessels relax, then dilate, forcing a fatal drop in blood pressure. This takes a few excruciating, terrifying minutes. I watch Whittle's life falter. Then, increasing the pressure between my hand and his skull, I finish off.

CRACK.

Whittle is dead.

HENRY WHITTLE

My reflection is pale-skinned and dark-eyed. I see an emptiness in my expression, as if tragedy has flattened my features, but not my unruly hair. My lips are dry; I moisten them with my tongue, but I know they'll swell and be split tomorrow. Standing naked, my eyes shift to the sink's plughole, clogged with hair from numerous scalps. I'm repulsed, but still I catch it up in toilet paper and flush it. The sink surround is no better; congealed toothpaste and foundation cake the china surface, filling in its cracks. I look down at my bare feet on the one lino square that hasn't lifted from damp. This communal bathroom is one of the many joys of Greenmead; home for the criminally insane – backspace – children. I laugh at the irony; I'm a week short of adulthood.

"Sparrow, stop crying in the bog like a loser and let me in."

"Mercy stop pounding on the door! Jesus! And I'm not crying!"

It's not kids or shitty rules doing my head in, it's the lack of privacy - I can't be alone...I can't have one uninterrupted moment.

Greenmead is my recurring nightmare. I'd bounced between here and foster parents until my Aunt Trish, weak from liver cancer, finally conceded and took me in. She'd needed a carer and I'd needed a home. It was a fair exchange, though part of me resented her rejection when my parents died – a very large part of me! But I had to get over it, considering she was in intense pain and dying.

"Spa-rowwwwww!"

"Give me five and I'm done - no make it ten. Actually, make it never."

I'm sick of it all. Being nice, getting trampled on, being shunted around...being abused at the fucking graveyard!

I eye my clothes sprawled across the floor; their heavy stench polluting the air. Who the fuck shakes a can of beer and sprays it at a random person in a cemetery?

For a slight second I tremble from the memory.

"Phewwwww."

I sink onto the loo, resting my head against the cold, tiled wall.

I'd seen them before, outside the parade of shops on Whitby Road, getting off their faces, looking for easy targets, verbally abusing everyone whilst making it personal: packy, faggot, bitch, tranny. The blond boy is pure, uncut evil; nose to nose he'd spat abuse: slag, slut, slit. When an enemy's angry breath dampens your skin and their eyes roam around their sockets like they're having a seizure; it's more than unpleasant – it's an attack.

Panicked, I'd searched anxiously for help, my eyes darting across row upon row of graves, until spotting a man, semi-concealed by an angel headstone. He was observing, like we were some kind of social experiment. Silently, I'd pleaded for help. The man momentarily leaned forward, as if to take a step towards us, before turning away, no longer entertained.

Even here, safe, fear clings to me. I can't shake it off.

"Crap!"

As if the blood on the tissue isn't evidence enough, I look between my legs into the toilet basin, at red droplets, fading quickly as they dilute. At least I'm not pregnant. My inner optimist smiles.

"Sparrow, hurry up!"

"Mercy, call me Phoenix otherwise I'll be in here forever."

"Phoenix hurry the fuck up."

"Mers, not cool sis."

Luke's voice, deep and smooth, is a welcome intrusion.

"Like I care!" shrieks Mercy, her footsteps thudding off; her feet reinforced with resentment.

"Hey Phe."

"Hi Luke."

Silence.

"You doin' ok?"

"Fine, I'll be out in a tick."

"Bless."

"Kk."

"Sweet."

I'm awkward; it sounds like a brush off, like I'm not bothered; I am; Luke and I go way back. Irritated, I turn the shower's thermostat up, letting hot water pulse over me.

"Aahh!"

"Phoenix?"

"It's ok Luke, the temperature plummeted, taps must be running downstairs or Mercy flushing the loo on purpose!"

"I'll check it out bae."

"Thanks, and stop calling me bae!"

"My mouth's on predictive text bae."

I smile. I could dwell on how challenging my life is, but the optimist in me brushes negative thoughts aside. Instead, I scrub my skin with value shower gel, wash my hair with value shampoo, wrap myself in a value towel and open the bathroom door to continue my value life.

About to turn into my room, the door opens and there stands Luke. I don't want to chat, not even to Luke, but I smile weakly, securing the towel that barely reaches my mid-thigh. Luke leans leisurely against the doorframe, his bright eyes working hard not to look me over.

After our sad search for comfort, under the quilt, a few years ago, I imagined an awkwardness between us, but we'd easily slipped back into the friends' domain.

"I've made a cuppa; it won't happen again Phe and no comment on how well you wear your towel. Not a word bae; promise."

Luke's broad shoulders fill the doorway. His white t-shirt fits tightly across his pecs; he makes Donnay look like Ralph Lauren – only a buff six pack achieves that.

It's hard to ignore the pale pink scar on his forearm that contrasts distinctly with his smooth black skin. It's also hard not to experience a shortness of breath in his company, because Luke Lawrence is w.ellllll fit.

I elbow him gently in the ribs.

"The more you hurt me, the more you want me. My psychologist explained how you channel your passion through acts of violence."

"You're such a knob," I say cracking a smile; enjoying how it relaxes my facial muscles.

"Umm, you, me, knob, in the same sentence...I like it Whittle."

Luke steps forward; raising his hand then looking a little flustered as to what he should do with it considering I'm in a towel.

"Phoenix sorry you're back in this shithole."

"I'm sorry for me too."

"We could be sorry together."

How I wish it were that simple.

"Tomorrow I'd like that, but today I need to be sorry alone."

"Safe," he smiles.

His smile is gorgeous; it's the first thing I noticed about him. Way back when we were both eleven, both new to Greenmead, both traumatised.

Turning, Luke walks casually down the corridor; his shape becoming less distinct in the shadows of the dark hallway.

In the room allocated to me and IT, I slump onto the padded chair at my desk. My fingers pick bits of foam from beneath the ripped plastic. It's petty vandalism, but rolling and squashing foam between my fingers is strangely soothing. Drinking my cuppa, I think about this morning, before the funeral. Claire Evans aka Cow Evil, the social worker from hell, dropped a humongous bombshell on me; Henry Whittle. My uncle. Even saying that in my head is weird.

Swinging around in my chair I try to escape a burst of anger that is furious yet heavy and burdensome. How do I not know this? Why had Dad and Mum not told me? Trish never mentioned him either. Why? Especially towards the end when she knew I'd technically be homeless? It's bizarre. It's difficult enough adjusting to Trish being gone - I hadn't said goodbye; I'd been collecting her pension and buying prunes. Was it awful I kept it? The pension, not the prunes?

"I've committed benefit fraud," I confess solemnly, blowing out.

I thought of Trish's purse; how she'd emptied it into mine on her last evening. Like she knew Death was coming for her. We'd become close quickly, terminal illness does that. She'd sorted out my driving lessons, insurance and registered her Daewoo Matiz in my name, so I could drive her around, mainly to the hospital.

Why withhold something so significant? I mean we'd watched Pointless together; I'd read Mills and Boon to her for God'sake; there'd been countless opportunities to tell me about an uncle. So why fucking not?

I sooth my disgruntled grief with warming tea. Only to ignite it again when I think of this morning and how insensitive Cow Evil was. She should have told me about Henry yesterday or tomorrow. She'd delivered the dramatic headline of the day and purposely left me hanging. God she's sly and mean...and fucking enormous.

My conscience pricks. It's wrong to judge people on appearance, I know that, and there's beauty in all shapes and sizes, but according to Phoenix Whittle's Guide to Survival, there is an exception...the person is a total bitch and has it coming.

Pellets of rain belt against the windowpane; so hard I think the glass might crack...or me. I want to cry but my reservoir of tears is dry. It's not an endless well; there are only so many tears a broken person can shed.

The burial was traumatic, and memories of my parents' funeral seized me, twisting me inside out. When a child knows only happiness and kindness trauma and grief kick in hard. It didn't sweep or drift it catapulted me into darkness. It sounds clichéd, but I was entrenched in sadness, it was so much a part of my makeup until Trish's. She'd been harsh, snappy, racist, and homophobic, but she'd given me a home. I'd been lucky, unlike the lifers at Greenmead.

People adopting like the concept of turning a troubled kid's life around. But, it's too real, too street, too demanding; leading to multiple rejections, like Luke.

Luke's sound; a good friend and a good laugh; not because he takes the piss, but because his sense of humour is wicked. He's tough; it isn't something he puts out there like a lot of boys, it's low key. He's also flirty, but not vulgar.

When I think of Luke, I think of Priti; my best friend since year seven; unpopular via association. It's so undeserving because Priti never badmouths anyone without good reason – she's above petty bitchiness without being judgy of it.

Suddenly, I'm agitated. That's how anxiety works - for me anyway. I'm in a good space one minute, then from nowhere comes an overwhelming sense of dread and hopelessness. It's like being turned inside out - everything that's fragile and susceptible is revealed and there's no reverse switch; I'm totally exposed.

Lifting myself off the chair is a monumental effort. I climb up the metal bunk ladder, squashing the duvet around me, smothering myself with negativity.

Although I sometimes paddle in the pool of self-pity, it's hard when I'm in rough seas, drowning.

Totally drained, I'm too empty to sleep. Both my history and future unsettle me: my parents not breathing; the abusive graveyard boy; the mysterious Uncle Henry...and everything in between. As exhaustion dominates anxiety, I drift off...an image of Dracula manifesting in my subconscious. I want him to be real. Not in a gooey, eternal, romancey way. I need the secret to immortality, to raise my parents from their graves, but I'm nearly eighteen; old enough to know...dead is dead.

As expected, I sleep badly. I wake at midnight, then again at six am-ish. The metal bunk bed squeaks as I shift my weight attempting to find a comfy position. I lay transfixed by the mould above. Mould gets me thinking about poisonous spores migrating into the air, perhaps I'm breathing them in now and they're killing me.

"Stop squeaking Sparra. It's too bloody early for that shit!"

"Then stop kicking my mattress!" I retort.

Searching under my pillow for my portable CD player, untangling the earphones, I lay back on my flat pillows. How many kids have rested their heads here? Washing powder only eliminates ninety-nine-point-nine percent of germs. So, am I breathing in a fraction of a germ belonging to the last unwanted kid? I press play; the battery sign flashes. Fucking typical. I lower my lids, squeezing so tight, the skin surrounding my eyes folds into crow's feet. I think about Henry; he's probably comfortably tucked up in bed. He most likely has a job. What does a marine do after the Navy?

***

Dragging his body down the stairs, Whittle's head lollops back and forth, leaving a thin trail of blood on the uncarpeted surface. Tossing him on the sofa, I sit on a chair opposite. Pulling a cider from my rucksack I crack it open. Sitting legs outstretched, leaning back, I enjoy the scene. I swallow a mouthful of cider, the acid sweetness of the alcohol hitting the spot. I relax a while and enjoy Whittle. It's true. Revenge tastes sweet.

Refreshed, I stretch and walk towards the window, downing a mouthful. I regard the external environment; the acres of woods, farmland and fields. This house truly is off the beaten track; giving me privacy and seclusion. No one will knock on my door trying to sell me double glazing or asking if I'm worried about the future.

I take my last swig of cider.

Back to business...in this case pleasure. From my tool bag I set out a few, shiny instruments. Swiftly I remove all traces of Whittle's identity; a clean operation as dead bodies don't bleed.

I make a call.

The Cleaner comes under darkness. In a van with untraceable plates. By then, rigor has passed and Whittle is a bag of bones. It's a memory I'll savour for some time; the end of the Whittle line.

MENTAL HEALTH

Sitting with Mercy at the kitchen table, eating supermarket brand cereal, I'm confused by the chaos. Bodies, pushes, insults and spilt milk are a collage of breakfast at Greenmead. I'd forgotten how hard being around people is. At home I'd had Trish and at school I have Priti. Here, it's a conveyor belt of damaged teens; the unwantables.

"Sparrow, what you up to?"

I glance at Mercy: she's reed-thin, her long hair, with its split ends, needs washing and she's beyond pale.

"Eating cornflakes."

"I mean later."

Her tone is sharp. An insult only a syllable away, but I detect a trace of mateyness.

"Swimming then counselling. You?"

"Hangin' with my mum," she mumbles, chewing on her hair.

"Great. How's that working out?"

Mercy stares at me long and hard; a mirror would crack.

"Her pimp jacked her and she's making snow angels."

"Mercy, I'm genuinely asking."

"You're a bitch, Sparra."

"Mers, don't be like that."

"Whatever," she says sulkily.

I wash up and grab my swim bag.

Driving to the baths, I think of Mercy. Was my tone bitchy? Was I critical?

I pull into the remaining bay of Highgrove's carpark, by the blue roof estate. Tension rises on queue. On the grassy mount, in front of the estate, is a lone figure. He has that stooped yet loose frame rappers have. Turning, I see a brush of bright blond hair.

"Crap! Graveyard Boy."

I virtually throw myself into the car's footwell; my breath coming hard and uneven. My fear from the graveyard is quick to clutch at my composure.

I take a gulp of air and sneak a look out the windscreen.

He loiters suspiciously, looking as skaggy as he did in the cemetery.

8

I see a second body, riding a bike, cloaked in a hoodie, approaching. The rider's hunched over the handlebars. He brakes at Graveyard Boy's feet. They make an exchange. Graveyard Boy stuffs something in his pocket and walks off.

Rattled, I lock the car and power walk to the pool. At the counter I show my resident's card.

"Swim please."

"£1.10!"

My disturbed state of mind remains as I undress...as I lower myself into the water...as I swim. I hate tiptoeing around like a scared rabbit. If only he'd disappear off the face of the earth. I don't care how, just when...now!

As my lengths increase, my worries ease. I love the smell of chlorine; inhaling it triggers memories. Right now, Mum and me are laughing in the shallow end; she's Sebastian and I'm the Little Mermaid. My memories warm the water, it's like cinnamon runs through my blood. I blink. Why did I blink! I know how fragile memories are. All I see now is bobbing heads - no Mum.

I swim to the pool floor crossing my legs and holding my nose, knowing with every happy memory comes an unending sense of loss. That when I surface, reality will set in and my parents will be dead. Nothing I can do will bring them back. Ever.

I skip the steam room. I'm too emotional.

I drive towards a detached house in leafy Harrow: my counsellor's office and residence. The roads are free-ish, but I keep to the speed limit. Through the windscreen I see families everywhere. I should stop living in the past and move on; it's what my parents would want.

Diane opens the door. She's a posh Mrs Weasley.

"Phoenix, how lovely to see you."

I follow her to the office. Slipping off my shoes, I grab a soft bouncy cushion and curl up on the floral couch.

You look tired, Phoenix."

"I'm shattered, Greenmead's broken me. I'm sharing a room with a gobby, mini Golem."

"You mean Mercy."

"Is that her human name?

"How are you feeling?"

"It's been stressful."

"You look as if you've lost weight."

9

"Not intentionally. I'm swimming more; it's somewhere to pass the hours."

"Exercise is good. How's your concentration?"

"Crap. It could be the noise and distractions at Greenmead or maybe it's me. I get my laptop out, my books, make a cuppa, sit at my desk and type rubbish."

"How do you feel about Claire being back in your life?"

"I swing between suicidal and murderous. Every time she opens her mouth it's blah,blah,blah and she throws shade at everything."

Diane smiles and leans forward.

"All I can say is, it's not for long."

I laugh knowing Diane wants Claire dead too.

"Tell me about Henry?" she asks.

"Yes, the mysterious Uncle Henry who I've never heard of but has suddenly appeared just as I need help."

"You sound sceptical?"

"It's hard not to. He's a man my parents ghosted. Isn't that odd?"

"Only because we don't know their reasoning."

I squeeze the pillow tightly...it bitterly hurts knowing they kept Henry from me.

"But you are going to live with him?" Diane asks, like I've a choice.

"Yeah! He's family," I blurt out like it's a no-brainer. "And I'm virtually eighteen; too old for a kids' home, and I can't do the hostel thing, not with exams. Moving from one temporary accommodation to another isn't an option. Worst-case scenario: me and Henry don't hit it off; I'll still have a room where I can revise. It's only till the end of next September. How hard can one year living together be?"

"Have you considered the impact of living with a stranger?"

"Well, I'm currently living with over twenty strangers."

"Yes, but they're kids. Henry is what, late twenties, ex-Navy?"

"I suppose," I say running my fingers through my loose mass of hair, staring out the window...doing the teenage thing of being unresponsive when I don't like where the conversation leads. "I'm more scared Henry won't warm to me. Unreachable and unsettling, that's why foster parents rejected me. Maybe it's true?"

"Phoenix, it is not true; you've come so far."

"Then why do I feel left behind?"

My chest is painfully tight.

I stand, take a boiled sweet from Diane's glass jar, and walk to the window. My hands shake as I unwrap it.

"This adult thing is difficult. There's a reason 'eighteen' ends in teen. On paper I'm grown up, but in here," I point to my head. "I'm not sure. I'm thinking about my parents again...seeing them...at the school gate, in the supermarket."

"Trish's death has resurrected memories. You're angry your parents kept a secret from you."

"Yes. fuming. An uncle is a big deal! It's not likes he's a long-lost cousin six times removed; he's my dad's brother!"

I want to shatter the pane of glass; throw a fucking chair through it.

"It totally pisses me off. Secrets are weaponised decisions."

I stride back to the couch dropping onto it.

"These past years Henry and I could have been together," I say, my tone subdued. "Maybe they didn't tell me coz they were afraid he'd get killed in action?" I pause to swallow. "I'll never know. I can never ask, and they can never tell. It is what it is."

I wipe a tear away. Crying is wasting water.

"So, why are you still at Greenmead?"

"Exactly! Why? Because Cow Evil is dragging her hooves."

"I'll chase her up."

"Have you experience in herding cattle? I ask."

We smile simultaneously.

I take a deep breath and look down at my trainers.

"It's fun seeing more of Luke."

Diane says nothing.

"I know you think I wasn't in the right frame of mind when I slept with Luke. That I was grieving. Well that was true, but I needed someone, and Luke's always been there for me, so I don't regret having sex." I look up. "I really don't."

***

I pull on a sweatshirt; the temperature has lowered; a chill wind whistles through the house.

The scaffold is erected. The south-west wall knocked down. Tomorrow the windows will be hammered out as glaziers replace old with new. Electricians will rewire, and plumbers will plumb. Tradesmen and labourers will work twenty-four-seven. In a week this house will be unrecognisable. It is Grand Designs on fast-forward. Walking past the open bathroom door, I catch my reflection in the mirrored cabinet. I assess myself. My face is blank; revealing nothing. I'm calm; my heart rate is close to forty beats a minute.

"I'm Henry...Hi, I'm Henry...Henry Whittle."

My tone is neutral – no edge, no warmth. I smile.

"Henry Whittle, nice to meet you."

Descending the stairs, I cross the hallway, step through the lounge and into the gutted kitchen. Grabbing a beer, I stroll into the garden where my bonfire of Whittle's furniture and belongings blazes. I drop to the ground resting against a tree. The dark expanse of landscape emphasises my isolation – it is beau-ti-ful. I stare into the flames as they greedily consume Whittle's past. Gazing up at the night sky I spot one distant star.

"That's me."

A second star twinkles.

"Bastard."

Then another until the night sky is alight.

***

I climb wearily up the ladder; a woman in a child's bed.

It's school tomorrow. English, Maths, Physics and Bullying; it's a compulsory subject, listed under InHumanities. Mercy is looking forward to it, sleeping comfortably without a care in the world. Bully or be bullied, is Mercy's coping mechanism. Below, I hear snuffles and snores. She's probably dreaming about the new kids, Year Sevens, in stiff, pristine uniforms, excited and enthusiastic about starting secondary school. So many would-be victims. Her school bag is packed, her uniform out. Tomorrow Mercy will be on fire...and so will the science lab.

I turn in bed.

"Squeak."

I punch the pillow.

"Squeak. Squeak."

I settle on my back and wonder what a marine is like. I'd seen 'The Lucky One' with Zac Efron. I remember how sudden bursts of noise spooked Zac. Would Henry be nervy and easily spooked? I'd watched Saving Private Ryan in History. It would be unthinkable if Henry had been wounded or tortured. Does he have all his limbs? It would be typical bovine behaviour for Cow to omit something important to sabotage my first meeting with Henry. I need to prepare myself for Henry having a disability or a disfigured face. Will he look like Dad?

Gazing up to the night sky, I spot one lonesome star. That's me; so solitary that the expanse of my emptiness is infinite. Drifting into a semi-sleep a second star twinkles.

"Hey Henry. Don't worry, regardless of scars, burns or amputations we'll be ok."

Drowsily, I watch the two sparkling distant planets and am comforted I'm no longer alone. Another star appears, then another, until the night sky is alight with a family of incandescent bodies.

GRAVEYARD BOY

Six am. Vans of tradesmen are parked the length of Whittle's house; my house. I press shuffle; Post Malone plays. I raise the volume to block the noise of the kitchen floor being fitted and the bathroom gutted. I want every trace of Whittle obliterated. It's a shame he's dead; I'd like to kill him again.

***

Walking towards my office, I'm thrilled by the 'Detective Inspector' before my name on my office door. Day two of a new life and a new job. I place my latte and chocolate twist down. My desk is bare: no files, notes or crime scene photographs; nothing pinned to my incident board. I have empty folders, coloured trays, sticky notes, highlighters, you name it; everything required to work a case except a body; more specifically a person dead under suspicious circumstances. I've had a few false alarms; suicides and a heart attack. I should be thankful my patch isn't running amuck with mass murderers and enjoy the pay cheque.

Opening my drawer, I take an emery board from my make-up bag. I file my nails whilst perusing the personnel records of my inherited team.

Beyond the glass-partitioned wall of my office reside a collection of old-school coppers. I watch their grey, balding heads bob like buoys weathered by the sea. I've no allies; I'm not here to make friends, but a boss is only as good as her team.

Tom Brady is a ray of hope: a sergeant at thirty-two, very forensically aware but possibly sour grapes; he'd applied for my post.

I find myself lingering on my other sergeant's photo, Andy Jensen. A transfer from Wales, only a few days ago. Ex-military. He'd seen plenty of action and worked some complex, high profile cases. He'd be a good second.

To understand murder...I mean really understand it...you've to experience what it sounds and smells like. Jensen's as near to that as I'm going to get. How many officers have witnessed a person disconnect from their body like a power cut? Or been on the other side of the door when the police come calling.

When you're a child you think in similes and metaphors: the blood was as red as a ruby, the killer was a wild wolf, and it's true. No one describes death better than a child. All the colours so vivid in their head.

I look up toward the detective knocking on my door.

"Ma'am! We've a major incident."

I pick up my latte and pastry.

"Brady, we're up," I call to my sergeant. "Enjoy," I say passing my sugar burst to the constable.

***

I've been awake hours and it's still only 7am.

I stare at my birth certificate - Phoenix Harriet Whittle.

Fourth of September, eighteen years ago, was the day my Mum first held me in her arms. My heart and throat burn with an agony that's trapped inside me. Nothing dulls it. Thinking about my parents, missing them, is killing me...then I die a second time as I cross the school gates.

I blink. Wave upon wave of kids whoosh across the playground. Jade spots me first and a smile of pure evil spreads across her face, as she bitches into Amy's ear. I feel powerless. I can't stop the trolling; a clap back would lead to a slap back.

I step over a rucksack. The ground is littered in them. I carefully move between brands; jostling with students, getting elbowed, when Alex ploughs into me.

"Look where you're fuckin' going."

"You bumped me," I say weakly.

"Fuck you Whittle."

***

Driving down Kings College, my eyes dart left and right to the large stretches of land: Ruislip Rangers football grounds, Kings College Café, the Cricket Club, skateboard park. Turning left before Ruislip Woods, the silence in the car speaks volumes of Tom Brady's disappointment. I understand the frustration of being looked over for Inspector, but we can't let professional jealously impact on the case.

On Park Avenue, I pull in past the running track to an area of long grass, part of which has been cordoned off. Opposite is a row of houses, easily hitting the £750,000 bracket.

It's too early for vultures to circle and too damp and miserable for the general public.

I hastily step into overalls, cover my footwear in forensic socks and pull on gloves, passing spares to DS Brady.

We walk across the sludge of a football pitch, into wild, straw-like grass with tall thistles, onto a pathway by the edge of River Pinn. We duck under a cordon to join two constables.

I look around the grassland. Shit! Sweeping the area for forensics is going to be a nightmare. Foot and pawprints are all over. My heart sinks knowing the original crime scene is long gone. However, there would be a clear view from the houses opposite; someone must have seen or heard something.

"Who found the body?"

A finger is pointed towards a female in running clothes.

"Do we know if she touched the body?"

"No Ma'am, she saw the body from a distance."

"Good, take a statement then get her driven home."

I squat beside a young male, 14-18. He's a mess. Vomit rises. I can't lose face in front of Brady, so I swallow. I'm fine with blood; fine is poor word choice: I'm familiar with blood. This is brutal in a different way, a teen, naked, every contusion revealed, his youth and beauty grotesquely altered; he'd be unrecognisable to his parents.

"Shit!" I shout lurching back.

"Dead bodies convulse; it's just gas."

Brady's tone is condescending. Still, I check for a pulse. My thumb pressing against the boy's wrist. I shake my head.

"Basic rule; don't touch the body," says Brady snidely.

I hate to appear a rookie, but I feel the teen's neck. Nothing…I press my fingers more firmly.

"Get an ambulance here now!"

I sprint to my car, charging back with foil blankets, covering the boy, talking to him, comforting him, until a paramedic ushers me aside.

I'm angered that this farce might reflect badly on me; perhaps indicate to those above that my control over the case is already tenuous. I want to step back into the ranks, not head up a team, but I can't let a screw-up define me.

I inhale and exhale a few deep breaths.

Guilt rushes me; I'd thought about myself before the boy.

Bodies from the nick arrive; I co-ordinate. As the boy is lifted into the ambulance, I draw the constable, first on the scene, to one side. I'd seen Brady give him a bollocking.

"Ma'am," the constable says meekly. "I couldn't feel a pulse, I swear I checked."

"Will you make the same mistake again?"

"No Ma'am."

"Good. Now step-up and put this behind you. Stick with the boy. Call me the second he regains consciousness."

"Yes Ma'am."

I watch as CSI erect the tent and secure the site. Investigators branch out searching for evidence. I look towards a short, white suited figure.

"Can I help you detective? Your silence is affecting my concentration."

"We can't have that."

A deep chuckle breaks up our bleak setting.

"I heard there was a badass, newly appointed DI in town," he says looking at me over his shoulder.

"Long time no see, Neil," I say ruefully.

"We'll go into that one later, say, over a wee dram."

"I'm up for that. I'm back to the nick now, it goes without saying I need the report yesterday."

"Detective, you'll get the report when I'm certain no stone is unturned. Time taken now is well spent. You know that Kate."

I simply nod. It's true. When I catch this monster, and I will, no error is going to let the perp walk. I'll be meticulous with procedure, ruthless with officers who undermine me. I will never watch a killer walk free again.

***

The landscape is grey. I run; towards Kiln Lane, up Priory following the River Pinn. I pinpoint bodies. I reduce my pace. Police have cordoned off the grassland by Pinn Way. Within the blue cordon work white figures; forensic officers examining the area. A lone person stands out. Not because she is a woman. Certainly not because of her stature – she is barely 5'3. It's her bright red jacket contrasting with the bleak discovery of a body. Whatever her rank, she is certainly in charge.

Cutting my run short, I double back – I have a plane to catch. At Heathrow, using a false passport, I will board a British Airways flight to Budapest Ferenc Listz. In the hotel, I will devise a plan to stop the target breathing.

***

Year Thirteen is no different to Year Twelve, except my adversaries are taller, stronger and bullying on full charge. Students are a mix of popular boys fist-pumping, popular girls air-kissing, the geeky gifted and talented, the gym-sluts, the nobodies, the broken and the breakers. I'm an anomaly, I should be in the broken, but I refuse to submit. Being a punchbag half my life has its advantages. Still it's important to stay out of Kirsten Willard's way; she and her gang hate me with relish. I like to think they talk dumb shit, but they're sharply devious; they identify and exploit your weaknesses, whilst taking selfies. I can't wrap my head around their animosity. Ok, back in Year Seven I'd unintentionally made Kirsten look dumb. Big deal. To her it was; she'd initiated a bullying campaign that's ongoing. I thought she'd get bored, instead her loathing of me increases. She genuinely, really, categorically, hates me. A good reason not to have a smart phone: Snapchats, Facebook, Instagram, the potential to cyber bully is immense. Since thirteen, I'd trained in Taekwondo, but it doesn't protect against sly looks, whispered insults or the intentional accident at the top of the stairs. Once falling, you can't fight back. I'm not their only target, but when they corner you, and get right up in your grill, eyes wild, mouths firing insults, you feel overwhelmingly vulnerable. If teachers witness an incident, it's brushed off, inferring we each gave as good as we got. But they're delusional. How do I know? They're teachers!

PE is the scariest. There's something sadistic about PE teachers. Bulldog. Dodgeball. What! Are they! Thinking? These are opportunities for violent teenagers to commit GBH. Teachers not only observe, they praise it. Jesus, it's insane!

I exhale a shaky breath.

My head hurts from the uncertainty of life. It's wearing me down like a giant emery board. Instead of a spray tan, I need hardener for protection. Right now, I'm being slowly chipped away.

"Phoenix! Stop staring at the wall. Get on with the task."

"Sorry Miss."

I check the clock, then the expanse of white; a page waiting to be filled.

"Phe," whispers Clive covertly showing me his workings.

Years back, Priti and I pulled down copies of Clive's school photo, with a giant paper penis pressing against his mouth and 'cocksucker' printed in bold, font 42.

"Cheers," I whisper.

It's horrible how Alex and Frankie make Clive's life miserable, because he's ginger, freckled and useless at football. Why do boys care so much about football? It's just inflated vulcanized rubber, for fucks sake.

**

Walking along the corridor towards the MIT offices, my brain rides a wave of emotion. The battery of a young man; the violence of it. The elation of a real case; something to put my position as Inspector to work.

Nodding to members of my team as I pass their workstations, I stop at Sergeant Jensen's desk."

"Ma'am?" he asks, his voice deep and velvety. A perfect cushion following the harsh reality of a near dead boy.

"We've a body. Not quite dead. Coma. Give me half an hour then gather the team."

Opening my drawer, I find blu-tack. Pulling off a small amount, I round it between my fingers, before pushing it onto a photo which I position on my board.

I step back knowing this boy will stay with me for a lifetime; Bradley Perkins, seventeen.

I slip my fitted red jacket off. Wearing a splash of colour reminds me the world's colourful, not all dark alleys and dead bodies. Considering the preliminary details, I unconsciously ease my fingers beneath my bra, giving my skin a moment's relief. If this kid dies it's murder, not manslaughter, not a robbery gone wrong, or a hit and run, it's cold, frenzied murder.

***

After class, the halls and staircase teem with students. Like a twister they drag wall displays and Year Sevens with them. Cautiously, looking left then right, situation assessed, I deem it safe to join the tail of the hurricane.

"Phe, something's up," says Clive, his shorter strides just keeping up.

I feel it. The air spiked with impending doom. Teachers are outside classes; clipped instructions, tight mouths, stiff bodies; something is very wrong.

"Yeah, an unscheduled assembly; first day back?" I reply.

I don't need to look up to the atrium to know Kirsten and her pack are there. Her laser, Cleopatra eyes sear into my epidermis branding me hers, so others know to stay clear. But for once, Phoenix Whittle is not the main headline of the day - a sixth former from Wensley High has been attacked and hospitalised – obviously looked at Mercy the wrong way.

The hall is a din of teenage sound effects as the police walk the aisles distributing the victim's photo. I'm tense, even before I look at the image and recognise the face of the victim. It's like my head is being crushed; I have the headache from Hell. It'd been dormant, but violence is its trigger, and it can strike in seconds. The rows of chattering students blur, and I want to cover my ears with my hands, but that'd be weird. Priti instinctively glances towards me. Graveyard Boy, I mouth. She shakes her head. Looking furtively around, I sneak out my phone and text. I wait for Priti to feel the vibration. Graveyard Boy, she mouths back astonished. I nod.

My last lesson is Maths. I watch the teacher; her mouth moves, but I don't hear the words. Instead, I see a mean boy lying in a pool of his own blood.

Eventually, the school bell rings. I drive to Greenmead with static in my head. I think about how angry Luke was when I told him about the cemetery. He promised not to get involved. What if his fingers were crossed behind his back?

Walking into the communal lounge, Bradley's school photo fills the tv screen. I plonk down on the couch and watch his parents' plea.

"Phoenix."

I turn from the telly plastering a smile on for Mike.

"How was your day?" he asks cheerily, his tone interested. Mike has the capability to be a great social worker if Cow doesn't turn him.

"Good," I lie. "Umm, smells delish. What's for dinner?"

"A roast, the full works with trifle for pudding. Claire's sick by the way."

"ICS?"

Mike throws a quizzical look.

"Irritable Cow Syndrome?"

"Good one," he laughs.

Drawn back to the telly, I strain to hear the news above arguing voices. The kids are on the rug playing Monopoly. Ben buys 'Mayfair' and Mercy must 'go directly to jail'.

"Phe."

I turn around. Luke looks roguishly cute. His white shirt hangs out of black school trousers. His tie's loosened. He beams a warm smile whilst he slips his rucksack off. He's not bothered seeing Bradley on tv. Maybe it's not such a big deal in the scheme of Luke's life, he didn't get his scar lighting a candle.

"I've A Quiet Place two on DVD. Know you love a horror."

Smiling, I give him the thumbs up.

"That wouldn't be an illegal download would it Luke?"

"Mike, bruv. That's worth looking into. I'll bin it once I've analysed the content."

After dinner, Luke and I lay stretched out, side by side, on his narrow single bed, watching the film.

Later, on the top bunk, sifting through uni prospectuses, obstacles stack up. Even if I achieve the grades, will someone like me get a place? I've no skills; I'm not quad-lingual; I don't play harp; I'm shit at netball; I'm so ordinary - less than ordinary, my dark side whispers. I breathe out exasperatedly. It's hard to rise above everything when I've no one to be proud of me.

Pushing the info to the bottom of my bunk, I crawl under my duvet. Sometimes, like now, I don't get what the point of everything is. Where is the sense in planning, if tomorrow I could die? I need three A's for Nottingham; that's a ton of work and immense pressure. What if I spend my time chasing Nottingham then, over Christmas, I suffer a brain aneurism? My last days would be spent trapped in a school I hate, being maligned by kids who hate me.

I think of my parents; they'd be so disappointed in me. Life is precious, I know, but I don't know how to live it, not properly.

I stare long and hard at Nottingham's uni's site map.

Hours pass.

Mercy has entered, ranted and is comatose.

I'm drifting between consciousness and sleep.

My door creaks open.

A shadowy figure enters.

Luke's fingertip on my lips, affectively hushes me.

"Breaking out bae, and your room's the fire exit. Come with me, it'll be sweet; I know a bruv who'll get us into a club."

I seriously love Luke. I just don't love his friends.

"Next time," I whisper.

"Phe, don't bin me off."

"Sorry," I say. "You know I'm a wet wipe."

Reassuringly, Luke doesn't press me about the club; it's one of the things I like about him – no pressure.

He lifts the window and with one leg in and one on the fire escape, he turns to me.

"Dream about me," he says and blows a kiss.

I don't see Luke, I see Mum.

"Get ready Phe, it's coming, you've got to catch it baby," she laughs blowing me a kiss. I clap the air catching it. "I've got it Mummy," and I put the invisible kiss against my heart. I feel a warmth emanating from it; love makes the impossible possible. "Get ready Mummy, yours is coming." I blow a kiss back; she dives onto the floor grabbing it,

rolling around, wrestling with my naughty kiss. My side hurts from laughing.

The image softens around the edges. Mum loses definition. I jump from the bunk to the window as if keeping sight of Luke will preserve the memory. It doesn't. I've lost her. Now I'm barren; like I've miscarried. An integral part of me is missing and I'm defective without it.

I watch Luke; he's walking towards town. There is barely any light, just a slight hue radiating from streetlamps. Luke walks under the railway bridge where trappers hang on bikes. I wonder do they hassle him? Or does he approach them? Climbing into bed, I lay for a while trying to evoke memories, but they're so fragmented now, it's impossible. I eventually fall into an uneasy sleep.

Much later, waking in a strange room, five feet from the ground, I'm spooked. I've dreamt of the crash again. Sweaty and caught up in the quilt, survivor's guilt kicks in. I harshly cast the bedding off. The metal rungs of the ladder dig into my feet.

The hallway is dark. I flick the light switch - nothing. I shiver in this particularly creepy house with its long, dark corridors where anything could lurk in the shadows. Sucking in my breath, I rush down the hallway making it hard for demons to grab me.

The toilet temp is below zero. I'm drying my hands, bracing myself for the moment I flick off the light.

A terrified scream crackles through the air shattering the silence.

One by one, goosebumps erupt alerting each fine hair on my body. I don't move. Why the fuck would I? My capacity for trauma's at overload...until I realise the scream is Mercy's. Shooting to our room, my feet sliding out of my slippers, I bound in hitting the light switch, to find Mercy cowering in the bed, quilt up to her eyes, huddled in the corner.

I puff out relief mashed with frustration. Luke is an idiot!

***

The risk was worth the reward. Her bra and knickers are old, their colours dull, the material cheap. I smell them. I think about where they've touched. I want to do more than imagine.

***

Morning dawns. I'm shattered. Cow's shrill voice, summoning an emergency breakfast meeting, sharply cuts through my brain fog.

Downstairs she's squeezed her oversized body into an undersized chair.

She stuffs a pastry, nearly whole, into her boa constrictor mouth and gulps it down. Pastry annihilation other than greasy flakes patterning her gaudy blouse. I vote we put a sign up; *'Please don't feed the cow'*.

"I'm perturbed. Last night," she exclaims dramatically, her chins concertinaing like an accordion. "It appears a man may have entered the premises through Mercy and Phoenix's room."

"Whatch-ya' mean 'may'? Some dirty old git fuckin did."

"Mercy! Language!" squeals Cow.

"I'm use'in language, dur, it's called English. Ask her," demands Mercy pointing at me. "It's a pervert Sparra knows."

"Phoenix?" Cow demands, accusation priming her sour face. Didn't she look in the mirror? Her make-up is a hideous mask of dark foundation stopping at her chin and a centimetre from her hairline, totally ridiculous.

"Phoenix! Drop the attitude and explain yourself."

"I was in the loo. Mercy screamed. I ran back. I saw nothing."

"You bitch," yells Mercy, jumping off her chair and walking towards me. "There waz a man! 'E was rootin' frew your drawers, lookin' for your stash. I ain't sleepin' in that room."

I shrug and pour milk over my cereal.

"Phoenix, I haven't finished!"

I don't reply to Cow. I exit and eat breakfast on the top bunk of my cell.

"Luke," I quietly squeak as he joins me.

"I ain't gonna lie Phe, this is some weird shit!"

"It's not that big a deal. Mers doesn't know, otherwise you'd have a written list of demands in return for her silence."

"I ain't Shaggy, Phe, but it wasn't me."

"You're kidding, right?"

"Nah, Phe, I wouldn't bluff, not over this."

I sense a dormant tragedy; a shadow, baiting me.

"Earth to Phoenix Whittle."

"Luke, I've a bad feeling. You know how horrid things happen in threes: Trish dies, then Graveyard Boy, now an intruder. I mean Luke, that's fucking scary. No wonder poor Mers is freaking."

"Bae it's cool. Just some opportunistic druggy."

"Thanks Luke, that's reassuring."

"Phe, window'll get locked, it's cool. Look, I gotta run, already on report."

"I'll give you a lift," I say, though his school's in the opposite direction to mine. I can afford to be late. I grab my bag; fly downstairs and we rush to my car. I vaguely see something on the windscreen. Wow. A beautiful yellow rose tucked under the wiper.

"Okaaay?" I say looking at Luke. I'm a bit stunned.

"Random and cool?" I ask Luke.

"Nah, cringy and stalkerish."

***

I watch how she moves: awkward, all elbows and knees. The pressure in my trousers reinforces how fucking much I want her. I'm so hard, it hurts. Pain, pleasure; for me there is no distinction. The normal me; the me hankering to belong, to be mainstream, feels saddened...but only for the length of time it takes her to get behind the wheel. The compulsion, the hunger, eats its way out, it dominates me. Fighting is fruitless; instead, I embrace it.

***

Driving to school, I spot Priti.

She hops in and we hug.

I'm happy. It's a light spirited emotion that disperses the nearer I get to school. I park and heave my rucksack on my shoulder. My legs are wobbly and my stomach churns. Sometimes life's too much, but I don't tell Priti that. Instead, we walk the plank.

"Lady Macbeth straight ahead," whispers Priti spotting Kirsten. "Let's hang back a few secs," I say, not wanting to start the day with malicious passing glances.

"K. Check my phone," says Priti. "One message: mother, 'chicken biryani for dinner, kerching!'"

"Crap, deputy head coming directly for us," I warn.

Wriggling my hips, I pull the hem of my skirt; still too short. I undo the button and zip, so it falls further down. Better. I grab my lanyard from my bag, dropping it over my head.

"See you in Lit," I say.

"Yeah, remember you're strong; they're weak, you're clever; they're lobotomised, you're cultured, and they're addicted to Botox."

We smile simultaneously, then into the warzone we march.

The register is called. I'm swotting over maths whilst my delinquent form either abuse Mr Edwards or play with their phone. Alex is dropping erasers he nicked from the stationery cupboard out the window. I remember a man was killed by a swede falling from a four-story building. It would be uncomfortable explaining root veg killed your relative.

Clive sits at the back, hunched over his desk, head down. Frankie pulled his trousers down in the line-up for form and he'd been mortified. He'd laughed it off; you have to; looking bothered is a mistake. Mr Edwards was on duty and saw it! Teachers simply turn a blind eye to uncomfortable situations. If they want comfort, they should join DFS. I sneak another look at poor Clive. The life has been sucked out of him, and it's only 9.10. Does a name pre-ordain your status at school? I think the jury would affirm it does, because I'm having a totally shit time too. Right now, I want to reassure Clive, tell him to hold on; just this year to get through and we'll be adults starting new lives.

"Whittle."

I turn to find Casey pushing a note into my hand. I unfold the crumpled paper.

'Give you a quid if you suck my salami at break.'

I look to a grinning Alex, whose tongue is thick in his cheek, as his hand imitates a blow job. Jesus!

A loud knock draws eyes to the door. Cow sticks her snout in.

"Mr Edwards, could you excuse Phoenix Whittle?"

Sniggers and jeers break out.

"Oi, Premium!"

"Premium scrounger!"

"Settle down year thirteen," orders Mr Edwards in a defeatist tone inferring total lack of authority.

I glance at Cow; her lurid pink lips form a sly smile of satisfaction.

Throwing my stuff in my rucksack, I grab my blazer. Passing, I reassuringly squeeze Clive's shoulder and follow Cow to the Learning Support Unit. I watch her massive, helium arse; her trousers fit to burst at the seams, as she totters perilously in her shoes; an oxymoron: Cow and delicate strappy heels.

Sitting opposite, a desk between us, her voice leaks like a tap of irritating, irrelevant, repetitive drivel! I'm desperate to ask about Henry: what he's like, where he lives, where he's been for the past eighteen years of my life!

"Phoenix, you must learn not to interrupt; it's terribly rude!"

My mouth opened, that's all.

A verbal marathon click clacks between teeth that chomp on words like they're pulled pork.

"Uncle...a marine...now a writer...disciplined..."

My eyes strain across the table.

"Criminal records...clean..."

To the form she'd withdrawn from her horse bag.

"Honourable discharge..."

To the area headed: Guardian's address.

"Move in next Friday."

That's what you think.

I'm on the brink of having to be exhumed, when she finally closes her mouth and leaves. For an age, I stare at Henry's address, my address.

A home. Family. I want it so much, I'm giddy. A doctor would diagnose early stage happiness.

***

The superintendent leans against the back wall.

I stand nervously, waiting for everyone to settle, my mouth dry as saw dust.

"Welcome. The team will be bonding over an attempted murder."

I look towards the crime board.

"We've Bradley Perkins, 17, in a coma. I hate to be pessimistic, but indications are he won't make it. He was frenziedly beaten. Secondary injuries were inflicted by an unidentified sharp instrument; either homemade or purchased off the internet. It's cylindrical like a screwdriver, but with a sharp pointed head. There is currently a large market in medieval torture devices, so Stacy I want you to cross-reference the M.E.'s report, when it comes through, with what you can find online."

I point to the incident board

"Timeline. 7.45. Bradley's parents leave for work presuming Bradley goes to school. Not so. Bradley calls absence line stating flu - he's a handful at school, numerous suspensions. According to fellow bunkers, he hangs out at the cemetery or round his estate; the blue roofs on Eastcote Road.

Chris you visit the cemetery; talk to caretakers, ground staff, mourners.

Bill, you work on Bradley's friends. Haul each in with an appropriate adult. Co-ordinate so they arrive at the same time, they might get nervous one might squeal. Bill, remember we are dealing with children, horrible ones but still children, be firm but nothing too heavy."

"Ash, you coordinate the estate door to door."

"Kerry, you collect footage from street cameras: around the cemetery, all routes from there leading to the High Street and then from the High

Street to Bradley's home, concentrating on park routes. We don't know if this attack was planned. The perp. may have had an altercation with Bradley. So, open minds. Work with Penny and scrutinise every single second of footage. Let's form a picture of what Bradley was doing and who with."

I take a sip of water.

"Pete, you're with Family Liaison. Keep your ears open. See what slips from Mum and Dad. We've got tons on, so let's wrap up. I'm expecting twelve-hour shifts. We've a dangerous perp. at large, who hopefully had a grudge with our vic. Otherwise, he may be looking at his next victim as we speak. Thank you."

***

Greenmead is the second last place I want to be, so after school I drive to the High Street. It's busy; McDonalds is the hub for Ruislip kids between five and eighteen. The line of motorbikes with East European delivery drivers outside creates edge. I find a seat in the corner and suck up chocolate milkshake, as I weigh up the need for money with the need to study. I've no parents to badger for cash or extended family sending me money at Christmas and birthdays. A job would take time away from study. It's a dilemma.

"Hey, Minger!"

Oh my God: Alex, Frankie, Jade and Kirsten.

"Shove over."

Frankie's hand on my shoulder forcibly pushes me against the wall. The groupies sit opposite. Meaningful glances exchange like they're the all-seeing eye when they know jack shit about me.

"Is this what you spend your benefits on?" snarls Kirsten, her lip curling in a vicious smirk.

Heat infuses my body; I'm stifled by it.

Frankie snatches my fries; one by one he flings a fry in the air aiming his mouth to catch it. Those around us are like vultures; watching hyenas pick my bones.

"Let me out," I insist, my throat tight, my eyes raw.

"What's the hurry, Premium?" Frankie says sliding his hand across my thigh.

"Get off me," I spit, as my eyes smart.

"Getting fussy? Word has it you went down on that fucking science pussy."

"Shut the fuck up," I hiss, so angry I think I might tear him apart. "Let - me out – now!"

Kirsten knocks my milkshake over the edge of the table. It upturns and pours over the floor. I feel bitterly sick. I want to climb over the fucking table and snap her thin neck. Why is someone so caustic and vile walking this earth when my parents are dead.

"Let's go, sitting near someone so poor is giving me migraine," says Kirsten, her bronzer defining the cheekbones I want to shatter.

"See you soon, skank," laughs Jade swiping up my burger.

"You need money Premium, come see me," Alex says rubbing his crutch, laughing snidely.

"I hear she's got a promotion on – buy one b.j., get one free," sneers Kirsten loudly, flicking her hair as she walks off. I want to rip her hair extensions out.

Alex pushes his face in mine, belches, and leaves laughing. The relief when they go is immense, like a ton weight lifted off my chest. I stare at the table not wanting to meet the gaze of customers. They'd either pity me or think I'm scum. The manager conveniently appears now they've left.

"You need to clean that up or I'm calling the police."

Tears well, but determined not to crack, I stem my fury.

"Fine," I say.

It's easier to comply than get salty.

Mopping up milkshake, a bout of despondency descends. I miss Trish, I miss our home, I hate Greenmead, I hate school. I think I should have died with Mum and Dad. It would have been kinder.

"You've missed some," says the manager. "There. On the seat."

***

Obviously, I want to intervene. To crouch beside her, our shoulders touching, our thighs pressing together. To comfort her. Replace her meal. Sit with her...like girlfriend and boyfriend. Chat about movies and music. Instead, I leave. I follow.

I am helping; my method is more final.

***

It's ironic how I want to sleep forever, yet I can't sleep through the night. Why do I wake when its dark, when the streetlights throw shadows across the wall? I think about school tomorrow, technically today because it's gone midnight. I take my pillow and cover my face. I'm breathing hard. I press it against my nose and mouth and close my eyes. I'm hot and breathing becomes laboured. I could be killing brain cells...starving them of oxygen. I feel the wetness of tears. Frustratedly I pull the pillow away, turn on my belly and cry silently into the mattress. I fall asleep - a girl only half alive.

MY UNCLE

Morning rushes in, bathing me in light because the cheap, orange curtains are paper thin. My usual foreboding is bleached by the idea of Henry. Maybe my luck is about to change.

"Mercy, stop playing dead."

"Fuck off."

"As your frenemy, I'm obliged to get your arse up. You're lucky I'm talking to you. Putting sleeping tablets in my hot chocolate was bloody dangerous. I could have OD'd."

"Obliged? Shit! No wonder you're friendless – what century is obliged from?" Mercy taunts.

"I'm gonna do it," I threaten.

"Do what?" asks Mercy.

"I think you know," I respond not wanting her name to contaminate my voice box.

"No, not her, I'm getting up. Settle down, Sparra. Look, my foot's out."

God she's a mini monster.

I grab my stuff, looking around, making sure I have everything.

I'm not gonna moan, but it's frenzied here. Kids hang around the toilets, bathroom, in front of the mirror; whinging, swearing and heatedly brushing by one another, – chaotically searching for hairbrushes, lanyards and shoes. In the kitchen, over-sleepers and slowcoaches crowd around the fridge, as cereal crunches under foot. Arguing ensues and my senses jangle from overload, as I pull the door behind me.

My car transports me from one hell to another. Whoever decided school days are the best of your life I seriously pity, because their adult life must be shit!

Rushing towards the gate, kids are dragging themselves to form: shoulders rounded, heads down, heavy footed; trying to delay the inevitable. Their dissatisfied babble ruins my positivity as soon as I walk into school. I'm a free, independent young woman one minute, a school child the next. Someone who must ask permission to use the toilet and to take off her blazer. In the real world I'd cared for a dying person. There are lots of us – kids – growing up quickly, coping with parents who are disabled, ill, alcoholics, drug dependent...dead. Once you've matured quickly, you can't switch it off. Society's changed, but not school; they've no idea what kids are up against. Schools don't want you to use initiative or be independent...they want you to obey and study yourself into the ground, to make their stats look good. I'm not the only one who hates school; there are thousands of us, we all wish for a flood, fire, swarm of killer bees – any catastrophe that will close school.

***

At thirty thousand feet; enroute to Heathrow, I am exceedingly agitated. My seat is kicked purposely and repeatedly. A mother and daughter sit behind. 'No', 'boring' and 'what the fuck' are on repeat. The mother flees to the toilet. The brat's feet push my headrest. I lean over. Smiling I beckon her, press my lips to her ear and threaten.

"Kick my chair again and I'll gut you like a fish."

In the passport control queue, the teenager clings to her parent. The mother looks my way. I flash her a smile. The mother flushes and pushes a stray hair from her face before smiling back.

"Honestly Stephanie; I've had it to here with your lies."

***

Plan Henry is happening tonight. I can't concentrate. I skip lunch, not because of Henry, but because it's bloody inedible. How can you get a baked potato so wrong? Priti's potato is dead too.

After school, I drive carefully, aware I'm distracted by tonight's masterplan.

"Today dragged on forever," I moan.

"I know," says Priti distractedly, battling with the car's aging CD player. "Listen to Khair Mangdi."

We shoulder shimmy each time the car is stationary.

"I'm so nervous Priti; what if Henry doesn't like me?"

"Phe, what's not to like. You're adorable."

"True."

My stomach churns. This opportunity is epic. To have someone to share a bag of chips with - it's what my dreams are made of; I've wanted a table for two for an awfully long time.

"Can you believe Cow insisting on handing me over?"

"Bitch! You're not an Amazon delivery. She needs to get a life. Has she a boyfriend?"

"Please, let's not go there. I mean, who in their right mind would want sex with her?"

"People have fetishes. She could be a dominatrix?"

"Pri, is there anything you don't know about sex?"

"I've passed my theory; sadly, not the practical. My virginity's my USP. Unlike someone I know," she says almost winking. She has this mad fantasy of me and Luke riding off into the sunset.

"Tell all about Luke," she demands. She's a little vixen at times.

"Nothing to tell Pri, honestly. We are firmly just friends."

"Does Luke know this?"

I'm momentarily quiet, I mean a nanosecond, but Pri is on it.

"There's been roaming charges; hasn't there?"

"Pri! You are such a whore about this."

I see her cross her arms. She has such a cute scowl.

"Ok, fine. We watched a movie. His hands did casually roam, but I didn't want him to touch my..."

"Breasts!" shouts Priti aghast.

Thankfully we're in the car and not school.

"Exactly. This is gonna sound desperate, but I was just lonely and sad. We both were. There is no me and Luke, Pri."

"Kk, I get it. You used him for sexual gratification."

I laugh, liking her conclusion, it sounds less desperate.

"Oh, my God," says Priti. "Look," she says pointing to a middle-aged Asian man standing in an open doorway of a terraced house.

"Dad's at it again. We're having dinner tonight with a family whose son is going to be a neurologist."

"Good luck with that one Pri."

"You too hon...I'll text you updates when I go to the loo."

I drop Priti off and drive on to Greenmead.

I ring the doorbell. Cow refuses to give me a key; I must earn her trust. I hold my finger down on the doorbell.

She who should be grazing on grass and not allowed near children answers.

"Phoenix, was that necessary?"

"Totally."

"Phoenix, your tone is petulant, revise it immediately. I hope you're not going to behave this way when I accompany you to your uncle's next Friday. He'll be sending you straight back."

Always a threat.

"I can introduce myself to my own uncle without assistance."

Fudge, she's coming out of the shadows; bugger she's under the light. I shield my eyes in case she turns me to stone.

"Phoenix, dear. I have built up a strong rapport with your uncle during our phone conversations; we share an affinity in our desire to help young people. It's not just about supporting you; part of my role is to support the guardian."

"Henry is not my guardian; I'm responsible for myself."

"It's essential I'm present. Phoenix? Phoenix! Don't walk away from me. It's not all about you."

I don't slam the door; the wind catches it. I want to scream. She has a family of her own, unless she's eaten them. I have only Henry, and she is not hijacking him. That's why it must be tonight.

I focus on homework before packing.

"Dinner!"

Stampede time. I rarely participate in this primal ritual. I hang back, let the dust settle and then pray the only vacant seat isn't next to Mercy. Ten minutes later, when the squabbling stops, I wander downstairs, along the hallway to the kitchen/diner. I squeeze between the table and the counter to an empty seat. Twelve kids of assorted ages, ethnicity and religion sit round a large rectangular table all wondering the same thing.

"What is it?" Conner asks unable to identify the meat element of the dish.

"Shit is what it is," Mercy complains.

"Mercy, sit down and shut up for once," says Cow.

"I'm not eating duck or rabbit; if it's in a Disney movie it shouldn't be on the menu," declares Anna.

"It's corned beef," Cow informs, sitting at the head of the table, about to eat our budget.

"Is there gravy?"

"No Chloe, there's beans," replies Cow.

"I hate beans, they make me fart."

"Ben, pass the brown sauce; this is mank," complains Connor.

"For goodness sake, why can't you...you...people be grateful..."

A cooked meal I'm grateful for, but Cow's company is hard to digest.

"Oh, for goodness sake," cries Cow.

Spilt water runs down the table and Ben's gentle features freeze.

"Ben, you dick," shouts Mark swiping his phone off the table.

"It's dripping on me, it's dripping on me," squeals Anna.

Ben wells up.

"It's ok Ben, it's only water," I reassure.

Being closest to the counter I grab paper towels, but am halted in my tracks by Cow's sweaty, fleshy hold on my shoulder.

"Ben. Why is it always you? Well?"

Shaking his head, a tear rolls down his round, pale cheek.

"You're the clumsiest child I've ever had in my care."

"I...I'm...I'm sorry, Claire."

Cow increases the volume.

"Clean it up!"

"Jesus, it was an accident. Don't talk to him like that," I say hating her even more.

Ben remains paralysed by criticism and inadequacy.

"NOW BEN... MOVE!" Cow screeches.

"Ben don't move bruv."

The table falls deadly quiet. We look at Luke. Then Cow. Then Luke. Then Cow. This is prime time viewing. I'm half expecting a Netflix crew to emerge.

"Phe, pass Ben the wipes Bae."

Cow's hoof falls from my shoulder. I lean back in my chair and grab a bunch from the counter passing them over the table to Ben. Conner presses some down on the table, soaking up the water.

"I want you to leave the table," says Cow her words rumbling like thunder.

"Suits me," says Luke standing. "One day, Claire, you'll bump into one of us and we won't be children, maybe you should think about that."

Oh, my God; totally epic. Luke's my hero. All eyes are on him as he walks off. Then on Cow. She's a purple blowfish. Ben remains rooted, but his face is bright with awe.

"Sit down please, Ben."

Cow said please; she's rattled alright.

"Before I leave."

Not Cow, The Sequel!

"The police will be visiting schools asking for information regarding an attack."

"Evans sat on him," whispers Mercy.

Snorting, I spit my food out.

"Phoenix, a boy is in intensive care and you find it amusing. We need to consider having you re-evaluated by your psychologist. Perhaps you're not ready to live with your uncle. Perhaps I'll meet Henry alone and postpone your move in day until such a time as you're more mentally stable."

By leaving tonight I take away her power.

After washing up, I creep into Ben's small box room.

"Ben, are you awake?"

"No."

"Ok, I'd better give these jelly snakes to Luke."

Immediately the side lamp illuminates the room.

Ben nibbles his treat like an otter. I'd seen otters on Country File. I remember sitting on the hardback chair, that doubled as a commode, beside Trish's bed. After a short while my nose would pick-up the sweet, sickly smell of coughed up blood, talcum powder and wee. Her cough was persistent, in fact cruelly unrelenting. There was nothing I could give her, but my company so, with an oxygen mask aiding Trish's breathing, and Netflix, we made the best of it.

I wonder, had my parents lived, would they have taken Trish in? Maybe I'd have a brother or sister? There is so much I don't know about my parents...and now this Uncle Henry business?

"Phoenix?"

I'm staring intently at Ben. Wanting to wrap him in a bubble of love and keep him safe. I know the system...It's not safe.

"Luke was ledge, wasn't he?"

"Yeah, put Cow right in her paddock."

"Will you tell me a story until I fall asleep?"

"Absolutely, tonight it'sssssss Ben and the Enormous Plum...

***

"Gather round everyone," I say bringing the team together for our first evening update. "We've canvassed the homes where we found Bradley and unbelievably no one saw or heard a thing. So, either these residents are all deep sleepers, or our perp is stealthy. Bradly has defensive wounds; he was struck from the front. Probably our perp used the electrical ties at this stage to restrain him, the gaffer tape across his mouth to silence him, and then continued with the attack. It's too early to profile our perp, but Bradley was muscular; he worked out, he was strong. We know he put up a fight, yet he's in the hospital because his opponent got the better of him. So, my guess is perp's male, well-built and emotional. This attack was fuelled by hate. It was not money motivated; Bradley had cash and his iPhone on him when found. There was no evidence of sexual aggression though he was stripped. Probably to dehumanise Bradley. Our guy is violent and, with Bradley in intensive care, potentially a killer.

***

Why do I go from one crisis to another? Mistake number one – riding solo. Mistake number two – forgetting to check the petrol gauge.

Mistake number three – abandoning my car, intent on Finding Nemo. Why am I such a fucking loser.

I zip-up my jacket as a chilled breeze nips at my exposed skin. The sun has set, the cold autumn night creeps in, and I realise how vulnerable I am, unaccompanied, in an isolated area. Fending off negativity, I continue, one step in front of the other.

An owl hoots.

"Shit-twoo," I reply. "Shit-twoo."

I am totally lame.

Trudging along, my rucksack straps dig harshly into my shoulders; it's heavy, although it contains only the basics.

"Basic sums me up – average, one standard issue girl. Jesus, Henry. Where are you?"

Bradley edges into my thoughts. What happened to him was horrendously bad; he'd suffered extensive injuries. It wasn't just a blow to the head. Each day the media reveal new, sickening facts about the attack.

I abruptly stop as my mind processes there is a freak at large. I swallow so hard my tonsils ache. As each minute passes, the night draws near. It's the kind of darkness that, living in town, I'm unfamiliar with. On the plus side, soon I'll no longer see creepy trees with withered arms, tangled veins and knobbly stumps. I think about them moving. Why think such a thing?

I shiver and walk on. It's an ominous September night. Unexpectedly cold and foggy. I exhale deeply, a white cloud momentarily lingers then dissipates. I hear only my footsteps. Nothing else. God, I hope I don't hear a second set of footsteps.

"Just keep swimming Phoenix."

I power walk and worry. Until headlights appear in the distance. I stop. I watch as they dim, disappear, reappear, then glow increasingly brighter as the car travels the hilly lane towards me. I think of abduction. I'm not being dramatic. It's a horror movie waiting to happen. *Saw 13 Phoenix*. So, I throw myself into the shadow of the hedges, camouflaging myself from the passing car.

"Phoenix you are a fucking idiot!"

It's a sick feeling when you realise you've acted recklessly and put yourself in very real danger.

***

Before showering I check the CCTV.

Perimeter – front door, the three-sixty porch, the twelve feet between the porch and the surrounding woods - clear.

The garage – lock engaged, the trackers on each car active.

The roof – sensors on the polyurethane operational, chimney cameras back and front give a clear panoramic view.

Internally I initiate lockdown. I hear multiple clicks as doors and windows engage. Shortly, when works are completed the house will be impenetrable.

***

This house better be fucking cosy, I mean soft, bouncy bed cosy, because my legs are painfully heavy; I can barely put one foot in front of the other without stumbling.

I'm breathing out heavy, laboured puffs of condensation; like the laboured breath of a dying man.

I've lost all hope of finding Henry.

"Oh my God!"

A lighted house, on elevated land, appears.

"Please don't let this be a mirage."

I stop dead in my tracks. My chest is burning from exertion. Fifty-one percent of me is happy. Forty-nine percent of me thinks the house is The Amityville Horror, yet a sob of relief escapes.

The property stands at the end of a long, narrow lane lined by tall trees. If I were to hold my arms up by my sides my hands would touch the sharp briars twisted in the bushes.

"Shit!"

It's suddenly too much: the car, the walk...

"And more bloody ghoulish trees."

Short of breath, I take a minute to calm myself.

"You're so nearly there. Don't break now."

Pausing my emotions, I wait till I comfortably draw breath.

"Ok, let's do this Miss Whittle."

My fingers curl tightly into my palms, as heavy drops of rainwater fall from overhanging branches. As I take a step forward there's a crackle, followed by a snap: rabbits or foxes? Is there rabies in Britain? As my foot squelches down on rotting leaves I fear mass murder of the snail community. There's no time for guilt because, the nearer to the house I get, the black night becomes a patchy darkness and I squint to see through.

A few hurried steps and the lane opens into a large semi-circled gravelled area fronting a sprawling house. It's remote, that's the impression that strikes me; if attacked no one will see or hear. Why think of being attacked? I gotta be rational; imagination has its place, but I need to be calm when I introduce myself to Henry; first impressions count.

I walk towards my uncle's house. My shoes crunch so noisily on the gravel, I imagine curtains twitching. Approaching his door, a glaring security light flares directly at me. I blink uncomfortably, my eyes watering. *All the better to see you with my dear.* I falter; the door's size is intimidating, and I hate the feeling of being exposed. My finger hovers over the doorbell; sensing my apprehension it refuses to press. What if Henry dislikes me? What if I'm not what he expects? How can I explain my early arrival? What if he's out? What if his girlfriend's inside? What if they're having sex? Jesus, that would be s-oh embarrassing. Looking around, I spot a camera. Probably an expensive dummy.

Needing a few minutes to compose myself I sit uncomfortably on the cold doorstep, resting my head against the large oak door.

"What shall I call you? Uncle Henry? Sounds dumb. Henry? Sounds ok. H? Depends if you're cool or corduroy. Maybe H.en.ry? I'll tell you my car's stranded. No, best ease into that."

As my mind turns simple points into complex issues my eyelids grow heavy and my heartbeat slows.

***

One towel draped around my waist, the other rubbing excess water from my hair, I check CCTV. A female Caucasian. It crosses my mind to draw a weapon, a notion I disregard when I reason this is a young woman, a teenager even. Still, Nikita, Electra, Buffy, they'd been teenagers once. Her head is slumped; she is asleep. I rewind to her arrival.

"Fifty-four minutes. Whittle, what the fuck were you up to?"

***

"AHHHHHH."

My head bounces off a hard...floor? Pain alerts me to danger, but I'm too stunned to move. I lay awkwardly, half in a house, half out.

A giant towers over me. Which can't be right; there aren't giants in England. There's Hagrid.

His mouth is stern, his eyes steely. His large hand with its long, splayed fingers reaches out. Hastily attempting to rise I put my hand on the door frame pulling myself up. I'm so nearly standing when my balance waivers under the weight of my rucksack and I stumble, landing on my back; an upturned bug about to be squashed.

He bolts the door. I'm on the inside now! Panic rises from my churning stomach. The man's flat, dull eyes level with mine. They are cold and tombstone grey. There is no volume; the atmosphere is dead flat. He advances. Clumsily, I shuffle back until my rucksack hits a wall. He neither smiles nor gestures. He takes a step closer. My heart is pumping, its beat nearly breaking speed limits. Panicked, my body tries to scramble to its feet. I'm on my hands and knees. I rise, he dips. My head, his chin. Collide. Hard! I throw up.

I want to melt like ice cream and be absorbed into the floor. Instead arms swiftly pick me up, not in a caring way, more like I'm toxic. I'm in mid-air, my eyes tightly shut.

***

I sit her on the toilet seat in the upstairs bathroom then retreat to the doorway. She poses no visible threat, quite the reverse, she's a car crash; a pale girl, hair dripping, in an oversized sweatshirt. She stands unsteadily. Swaying towards me, eyes dark with suspicion, she shuts the door in my face, turning the lock.

I hear her clunking around and filling the bath.

Momentarily I linger.

Listening to a woman bathe is wrong, so I return to the mess downstairs. Cleaning up sick doesn't bother me; I've cleaned up a lot of body fluids in my time.

***

As the bath fills with hot water and steam clouds the air, I approach the mirror fearfully.

"Crap."

I have good reason to be scared. Scraggily, squirrel tails hang limply around my face. My cheeks are smeared with dirt. Scared, sunken eyes, black and beady, stare back. And vomit stains my sweater.

"Jesus! What a mess!"

Tears sting like acid burning my eyes. I'm hopeless. Hopelessly useless. What must he think? What the fuck must he be thinking?

Rummaging in my bag for paracetamol, hands shaking, I press tablets from a strip. I swallow two with tap water.

I recheck the door; it's locked. Twist handle again. It doesn't open. Turn handle one last time: locked, definitely, certainly, one hundred percent. Shit! Imagine if I broke the doorknob. It's a nice door, a rich ivory with a brass lock. I take a minute to settle my breathing, turning around, still too tense to appreciate the luxury. It's impossible to avoid my reflection. Undressing is difficult; my soiled clothes are stiff from cold, while all I smell is sick. I shakily climb in the bath, recline and close my eyes, which makes me feel sicker. My overwrought head is painfully spinning from uncertainty. I need to stop thinking; to shut down my brain, so I submerge. Holding my breath, I hear only the whoosh of water as I shift position. I remain beneath the surface. *My lungs burn.* I hold on a moment more. *A hot pain in my chest.* One. More. Minute. *I'm near the edge.*

I surface, hungrily feeding my lungs, panting hard. They say parental influence defines you. What does that make me? A loser shrouded in death. Am I crying? Or are my cheeks wet from bath water? Laying back, I inhale the aromatic water - it fails to sooth. I can't relax, not whilst wariness fills the gap between me and the man downstairs...Henry, I guess?

Beside the bath is a chrome stand, with products tidily arranged. I squeeze shampoo onto my hands and wash the sick from my hair. There's no conditioner, so I let the shampoo foam up, give it ten minutes and then turn the overhead shower on and rinse. I stand up and reach for a bath sheet; it's super plush, the opposite of my hard, rough, old Frozen towel. I dry off in the bath so as not to drip water everywhere. I've done enough damage for one day.

I pull on my sheep onesie (a present from Priti for my birthday). I saved it for here. Fresh start, fresh pyjamas. It seems stupid and immature now. Maybe I should just re-dress? I look at my watch. It's ten o'clock.

***

"This is a plea for information," I state, my voice steadier than I feel. It's my first press announcement since my promotion to Inspector.

"FLASH!"

Blinking, I'm momentarily stunned. I focus.

"A young man, Bradley Perkins, 17, was brutally attacked in Ruislip on 3rd September. He was reportedly seen with friends in Ruislip High Street at 10pm. It's believed he made his way, unaccompanied, up St Martin's Approach and, at some point, he joined the Calendine Rite pathway, in the direction of Kings College. Here, he was viciously attacked and left for dead. Bradley is in critical condition. We are treating this incident as attempted murder. We need anyone in the area around this time to come forward. The smallest detail can make a significant impact on solving a case. Information to-date indicates this was an unprovoked attack. Should you see anyone acting suspiciously please do not approach them. Instead, call 999. If you were in the vicinity of the attack on 3rd September, I urge you to contact 0800 800 8000; you could be a witness. The number again is 0800 800 8000. Thank you."

I stand, unpinning the microphone attached to my blouse.

"Good job, Daniels," commends the Super, falling in step beside me.

"Thank you, sir. No doubt it will open the floodgates for every weirdo, but we need an early break."

"What's your take on the father?"

I look over my shoulder, to Mr Perkins, he's fidgety, sweating, sniffing, eyes unnaturally bright. He's got form for dealing, but did he brutally attack and leave his own son for dead?

"The level of violence was acute, sir. Bradley's skull was battered so hard it caved in; he has a multitude of broken bones. Someone hated this boy. The father might be a coke-sniffing weasel, but his grief is authentic."

***

About to knock, the bathroom door flies open. A fluffy lamb stands rigidly; staring at me with apprehension, from dark green eyes with spiked lashes from the bath water. It takes but a second to see her heart's covered in defensive wounds.

She offers her hand and I note the hollow of her wrist bone; I think how easy that bone would snap; it's an occupational hazard; identifying physical weakness. She's a bundle of nerves, yet her attire infers a sleepover. Who the fuck is she?

***

"I'm Phoenix...but I guess you know that."

I expect him to say welcome or hug me. But I'm not welcomed or hugged.

"Sorry about earlier."

Not a flicker of response on his face. Not the slightest movement of his body.

"I know I'm a week early. It was rude to turn up, but once I knew about you, I couldn't wait."

I hear my meek voice; like I'm begging; I get a grip.

"Anyways, I'm here now."

He turns. I watch him walk the length of the hallway, towards an end cupboard, averting my eyes as he returns. He thrusts a sleeping bag at me.

"You sleep here."

"Thank you," I say and smile meekly.

He's already walking away.

"Good night then."

I'm left in a doorway. I flick the light switch. No light. I'm in a large, empty room with two tall windows. I look upward; no shade, no bulb; great. No carpet either, just floorboards

I unroll the sleeping bag and sit.

"Well, this is weird."

He's nothing like Dad. No similarities. I'm relieved.

I swallow.

"Crap!" I whisper. My throat burns from vomiting. Fuck! What an entrance.

My phone vibrates in my hand. I drop it like a hot potato, retrieve it and burrow down the sleeping bag.

"You said you'd phone when you got settled."

"Exactly, Mercy."

"Well, its eleven, are you settled or what?"

"It's complicated."

"Whatever," she says sulkily.

"How's things?"

"I'm moving back to my mum's on Saturday."

"That's great news. Why don't you give me your address?"

"So, you can send the feds," she accuses.

"So, I can send a card."

"Will it have money in it?"

"Maybe."

She reels off the address.

"I've no pen, text it."

"Yeah, if I get time…We've got a setting test for maths tomorrow."

"Are you nervous?"

"Of pieces of paper and ink?"

"That's one way of looking at it."

"Sparrow, you're so extra!"

"Whatever. I hope the test goes well. Remember Mercy, I believe in you."

I hear her laughing uncontrollably.

"Fuck, you're jokes; I bet you believe in fairies too."

She disconnects.

In the unsleeping bag I twist, turn and catch my hair in the zip.

"Shit."

Another hour passes. I don't know what I expected, but not this! Weary but wired, I stand, stretch then wander to the window. Outside thick, black dark is everywhere. It shrouds the woods. It's an unnerving landscape. There's not a star in sight. Here there will be no car headlights breaking up the darkness. I don't like that there are no curtains to keep the bad things out.

I tiptoe away from the window...listening. The silence is disturbing. I've never experienced such complete quiet. Admittedly, I've moaned about it, but the mayhem and music at The Institution was reassuringly comforting, even the rowdy drunks from The Fox.

I phone Luke.

"What's happen'in Phe?"

"Everything, nothing. Is it possible to be exhausted yet wide awake?"

"Gimme the deets."

"Luke, this house is nowhere near civilisation. I had no idea it would be this isolated."

"Babe, you've got a motor."

"But I'm in a sleeping bag, on floorboards and my uncle's strange."

"Phe. You caught the man off guard is all, tomorrow he'll be sweet, you'll see," he says softly.

"Yeah, I did surprise him, I guess. Maybe it's tiredness, but today's been like an episode of Lost. Did you give Mike my note?"

"Yeah, my man's cool, but Cow lost her shit; she was frothing at the mouth."

"Mad Cow Disease; I suspect she's a carrier. Jesus, you should hear my tummy rumble. I'm starved."

"Me too, bae. Fucking corned beef!"

"You were epic at dinner."

"I just don't give a fuck. She's a...I ain't gonna say."

"I know what she is."

We fall silent.

"Your voice is smooth and comforting," I say.

"And sexy."

"That too," I laugh.

"Ya not gonna go all bougie on me now ya got Uncle Henry?"

"Nah, I'm still Phoenix from the Flock."

We snigger.

"Girl, you gotta dirty laugh."

A pause. Then a little more seriously.

"I miss you Luke."

"Back at ya Phe. Hang in there, u feel me."

I'm twisting hair tightly around my finger till it hurts.

"Phe? Stay chilled, yeah? He's not a bumlick is all."

"Thanks Luke, you're right. Don't want a bumlick as an uncle."

I feel lonely the minute we disconnect. Right now, I wouldn't mind a bumlick. There are some instances when bumlickin' is cool.

I close my eyes and think of Luke. I remember a few years back; us kissing; it felt warm and easy, but I didn't feel hot and desperate when we touched. Does that even happen, or is it a literary tool to keep the reader interested?

My phone vibrates.

"Priti – thank God."

"Luke said you're freaking out a bit."

"An accurate analysis," I whisper. "Priti, things are awkward, there's no bed, he hasn't welcomed me."

"He must have said, like, hi Phoenix?"

"No."

"Offered you a cuppa?"

"No! I'd kill for one, but I don't know whether to go to the kitchen or not?"

"Course you should. Sorry Phe, my mum has come in my room without knocking, again! She's giving me evils."

"No probs Pri. Catch up tomorrow, yeah. Sleep tight."

"You too honey. Go put the kettle on!"

Confidence renewed, I tiptoe to the doorway, stop and listen. Silence: something I've not heard before. Henry, I assume, is asleep. Beyond my door is a black nothingness; equally dark are the flashbacks of my gruesome past. In theory, the dark shouldn't scare me, I've suffered abuse on a bright Spring morning and under a hot summer sun. So, I step forward, my flat hand sweeping the walls, unable to find a light switch. At the top of the stairs, I hesitate. How many people die falling downstairs? Most accidents happen in the home. Probably because no one can find the bloody light switch. I glance behind me; the space is as dark and ominous as the blackness in front. I descend into pitch black, holding the banister firmly, ready to tighten my grasp should I slip. One by one, I take baby steps, pausing every few seconds to listen, until after what seems an age my foot finds the ground.

"Phew."

My sigh echoes.

Tensing, I abruptly halt. I think momentarily of an entity, lurking silently.

My eyes squint into the dark mass.

My ears strain.

Nothing.

I'm standing in the large square entrance, stage of my earlier humiliation. It's so black, I'm reluctant to leave the stairs. My stomach muscles tightly clench; anxiety or hunger pangs? The dark space surrounding me is endless; I have no borders to gauge the area with. Memories, of nights in foster homes, scared of dark corners in unfamiliar bedrooms, feed my nerves. But this is different. Henry is family. This is my home. So, arms outstretched, I edge forward until I feel an arch. My hands, expectant, don't find furniture to trail over, it's like the room is empty. I fumble my way into the kitchen. I find the fridge. The internal light automatically flicks on. It's ridiculously comforting, as if the fridge light offers protection. The fridge contents are seriously OCD; each food group is represented indicating Henry likes to keep healthy. No cake, no chocolate, no milkshake, no ice cream. He clearly knows nothing about women; no wonder he's uptight. Each opened item is sealed and dated. Who has time to do this, worse, who wants to? Picking up a carton of milk the hairs on my neck stiffen...I'm not alone. I draw a breath; it wedges in my throat. I freeze; easily done in a fridge freezer! Already the blood is rushing to my head and hysterics threaten. Calm. The Fuck. Down! But my heart pounds in my chest; its beat filling my head; its rhythm fast and hard. I can't reassure myself. I can't say it's nothing, when I've experienced...something, a terror unknown to most people. Closing my eyes tightly, I clutch the milk. A presence brushes against me. I can't determine the shape of it. Oh, my God! I'm breathing rapidly, my tight chest burning as I pant out apprehension like it's CO_2. About to scream, light illuminates the kitchen. I find myself blinking rapidly as my eyes adjust.

"You're climbing into the fridge."

It's Henry...He scares the shit out of me, and now he's mocking me. I'm still, unmoving, until I regain my composure. Which could take considerable time. I might even miss school.

Turning to face my uncle, embarrassment silences me. I'm still squinting as the light irritates my retinas. I must seem crazy, creeping in the dark

He doesn't smile. His eyes aren't kind. They're sharp; they take everything in.

"You're killing the milk."

It's true. I'm crushing the carton against my chest; milkslaughter. Fear, my defence.

"I'm thirsty. I didn't want to bother you, and I didn't know where the light switches were, and..." my words trail off; I feel foolish. I turn away; eye contact gives his presence and words more potency. His response is unsettling; I get the sense it's intended to be.

"You scared me."

I hear the tremor in my voice.

"Did I?"

"Yes."

No apology. Why was he acting like a twat?

I put the milk down. The kettle is to my left, a tea caddy beside it.

"Two doors to your left," he says, his voice toneless.

I turn to him, my face quizzical.

"Cups."

He leans against the arch frame, his bare arms folded across his chest. He's wearing loose fitting trackies and a grey, slim-fit sleeveless tee. He's lean, muscled, slim-waisted, broad-shouldered. His hair is cropped, army style. Tattoos inked into his arms disappear beneath his t-shirt. They're not the cliché rose or crucifix. His height is intimidating. Nothing about this man matches my image of him. I saw chinos and brushed cotton. He looks young, and he radiates an animosity that is unexpected and upsetting. Flustered, I turn away and open the wrong cupboard.

"I said to your left," he states.

I want to cry. I don't want the fucking tea now! I swallow my emotions. Two doors left; I repeat silently. His unpleasantness is causing regression. Together we reach for the knob; his hand covers mine. I roughly pull away; I've an aversion to being touched; he is a stranger. No noun has ever been more apt.

Complete resounding silence fills the atmosphere.

I smell him; a mixture of GBO and fading deodorant. He is purposely intimidating me. I glare accusingly. Our eyes meet; his reflect a dark void of nothingness.

"Sit, I'll make tea."

Said the spider to the fly.

I sit because his razor-sharp tone invites no argument and I welcome the distance. I hover nervously at a breakfast bar, not quite on the stool, my body rigid.

Most girls would be sobbing at this stage, especially following the month I've had. I'm not most girls, but my heart feels burnt out, sluggish; it achingly throbs in my chest so I can't relax. His back is to me. I want to say something casual and friendly, but my tongue sticks to my dry mouth and my head draws a blank. I met this man only hours ago and already my state of mind is tilted.

He unexpectedly turns around, his eyebrow raised.

"Do. You. Use. A. Hearing. Aid?" he asks.

"No."

"I've asked you three times if you take sugar."

Had he?

"Yes please, two."

I seriously need sugar.

He places two mugs on coasters. Gay? And two slices of buttery toast in front of me. He leans forward brandishing a large bread knife, rolling it in his hands so the blade becomes a shimmering rod. My eyes jump from the knife to him, from the knife to him. His long fingers hold the toast and the knife slices through its centre, in one clean cut.

"Eat."

I drink the tea, but don't taste it, I eat the toast; it sticks in my throat.

He is sinisterly silent. He watches me the entire time whilst my eyes dart about the kitchen. I've never been the object of such fierce examination; I don't like it. I want to stare him out until he turns away first, but I know he won't.

"Thank you. Sorry about spewing up. My car broke down and I got lost."

I glance up at him. He's disinterested. I stand to go.

"It was rude of me to just show up. I see that now. Goodnight."

I don't think I'll sleep; I'm seriously scared of him. An hour passes, then two; eventually I'm overcome with exhaustion.

***

A person is in my home. A woman. The niece of a man I murdered. It could get complicated and I simply can't let that happen.

THE KEY

I wake confused to hammering, sanding, drilling. A collection of languages float in the air. It takes a minute to remember I'm not at The Institution. I see windows recently fitted, explaining no curtains, beautiful wooden floors, explaining no carpet, and light fittings yet to be wired, explaining no bulb. So, I wasn't being mugged off. I should have waited. I consider how overwrought I was last night and as usual blame myself. Perhaps I'd misconstrued Henry's...Jesus, it's hard to put a label on his behaviour. I shake my head, but despite last night, I enjoy an undercurrent of excitement from being in a home with an uncle. Perhaps Henry has loosened up; he might give me a hand recovering my car.

I dress in the bathroom, in front of a floor to ceiling mirrored wall. My hair shines from Henry's luxurious hair product but the rest of me is tatty: over washed jeggings, and a Levi t-shirt from Scope.

From the landing I see Henry, standing, in the archway below. I smile my broadest, deepest smile. Descending the stairs, a labourer is running up; he's about twenty and wears a 'look at me' confidence that accompanies a gym-body and symmetrical features. His eyes size me up; immediately I stiffen. His grin is predatory.

"Morning, princess."

Two ordinary words, out of a man's mouth, whose inference is sexual.

"Morning," I stiffly reply; my annoyance compounded by Henry turning his back and not waiting for me.

Henry already sits at the kitchen table, long legs stretched out, his feet resting on the chair opposite. Approaching, I see only the top of his head as he holds the newspaper open. In the light of day, I see the kitchen is large, but Henry's presence significantly reduces the scale of the room.

"Good morning," I greet brightly.

No answer. Obviously not a morning person.

"Would you like a cuppa?" I ask.

No response. What should I do? Sit, make a cuppa, do Gangnam Style?

"Cuppa?" I shout.

"No. Thank you."

"There's nothing like the first cup of the day," I declare sitting down, disconcerted to find a pair of bare feet on the chair beside me.

"Midday is perfect for a cappuccino, and a hot chocolate before bed."

The hands holding the paper are strong with long fingers and neatly clipped nails. Capable; hands that could twist a stiff lid off a pickle jar.

The paper lowers, millimetre by millimetre; breathe Phoenix, breathe. Jesus, his eyes are lifeless.

"Are, you, o, k?" Henry articulates with exaggerated precision.

"I, am, not, special, needs."

To my annoyance, he raises an eyebrow indicating the contrary.

"Admittedly it wasn't the best start," I state.

Silence.

"I was nervous, and the corned beef didn't help."

Extra silence for dramatic effect.

"This kitchen is impressive: ultra-contemporary but warm." I look around. "Yeah, the sofas give it that comfortable plushness. Does your fridge have an ice dispenser?"

Still no response. Is he purposely making me squirm?

"Do you live alone?"

"Yes."

"I thought as much," I whisper sarcastically.

He visually appraises me, his expression expressionless.

"Just the two of us then?" I prod.

"So it seems."

Henry isn't as excited about me as I am about him. Maybe he invited me out of a sense of duty. Marines are big on that. It seems they are not big on breakfast. Still, I want to thank Henry and tell him what a huge thing this is for me, but it's clear he isn't ready. He's doing the glare thing again; I'm fighting it, but it's potent. The more awkward and self-conscious I become, the more he commands the room; his presence fills every inch of the kitchen. The high spirits I woke with quickly dissolve. I'm disappointed; down to the pit of my empty stomach. Henry's attitude towards me is unexpectedly cold. How do I deal with him? What do you say to an uncle who doesn't want to communicate? I don't get it? HE wants ME here!

"My car's out of petrol; on Brakespear Road."

An offer of help is unforthcoming...I refuse to ask.

"I might be a while; shall I take a key?"

"No."

I leave exasperated, pulling the heavy oak door behind me.

Standing on the porch, I watch as vans are unloaded and skips filled. It's a bright, warm morning. If you were normal, you'd imagine how amazing this view is when it snows or is covered in bluebells. Me? I'm totally freaked neighbours are nowhere to be seen and there's nothing but dense woodland for miles. Glancing towards the *Blair Witch* oak cloisters, I decide no way, ever, am I going in that direction. I hear a wolf whistle and I know it's Gym Bunny. I push headphones in my ears, click play and Lil Nas X fills my head.

I walk the lane connecting the house to Brakespear Road. Even in the day it's creepy. Little light penetrates the thick, overhanging trees and the ground is a bed of wet leaves trodden to pulp, slug utopia. I shiver and speed up.

On the open road, panting hard, I hike past my abandoned car; autumn leaves crackling beneath my feet, the soundtrack to my simmering disgruntlement. I'm pissed off with having to do everything for myself since forever. I'd hoped for Henry's help, but hope is a dangerous emotion. I pass the Crematorium. Still, it'd be nice to be friends, to be there for each other. Maybe I'm expecting too much, too soon. I take my sweater off and tie it around my waist. The sun is penetrating the clouds and my mood evens out as I take in the scenery. Fields, bushes, flowers; dashes of colour on a green landscape; it's exhilarating. I think, maybe, I'll come to like it.

"Yesss. Petrol!"

I buy petrol, a funnel, Munchies and Pepsi-Max. On a mission I backtrack to my abandoned car. Smiling, I unzip the front pocket of my rucksack.

"That's strange."

The corners of my mouth straighten into an anxious line. I pull the small internal pocket out.

"This isn't right."

Acid rises from my stomach, burning my throat.

"It can't be."

My head clogs with confusion.

"I...I don't understand."

Denial controls me; I check and recheck my pockets hoping, praying I will miraculously find it. I shake my bag erratically spilling the contents onto the grass...no key. I rerun my earlier movements; had I taken it out at any point.

"No," I say shaking my head. My chest is painfully tight. Last night my key WAS in my bag. I've so few things, I'm mindful of them.

I arrive at the only plausible explanation. Henry took my key.

"No."

I want to reject that thought. It's fucking mental. What? Henry – who doesn't know me – sneaks my key out of my bag? It's totally farfetched and paranoid.

"I'm losing my mind then," I declare angrily.

Agitation, doubt, self-blame; my demons whip themselves into a state. I hug myself trying to contain an emotional melt. I can't; I slump between the offside of the car and the privet – sobbing.

***

I pull the key from my pocket. Attached is a smiley face trinket and a photo keyring. Of a family. Care Girl and her parents. The Dad has a strong resemblance to Whittle, except his eyes are honest and his smile warm. The girl is about ten. Her face is alight.

***

The trek home is arduous. I feel pathetic. In his house I lay flat on the floorboards, like a star fish, looking up at a new ceiling, but experiencing old turbulence. The pressure in my head compresses my anxieties together. One worry merges with another and grows out of proportion. I physically stiffen, locking in the panic to prevent it from spilling any further into my life.

***

DINGDONG, DINGDONG.

I open my laptop to see a large woman, mid-forties, out front. She follows a labourer around the back. I watch as a heaving bosom, rising and falling, appears; shortly followed by the rest of the body.

"I am sorry," breathes the woman heavily, heaving her body over my threshold, into my kitchen.

"Ms?"

It's sticky, not knowing if she ever met Whittle.

"Claire, I mean Evans," she replies panting hard, liver pate on her breath. "We spoke on the phone."

"We certainly did."

I stick to generic English. Main thing is, there is no challenge to my identity.

"Is Phoenix here?"

"She is. Follow me."

***

"Look who's here," Henry calls brightly up the stairs.

Really? I descend hesitantly; waiting to be ambushed.

What. Is. She. Wearing? I turn away quickly, trying to swallow a snigger. I glance back. Oh. My. God. My shoulders rise and fall. I glance at Henry, then back to Cow, then back to Henry. Was it a negligee? Black lace? All. That. Flesh! She's a Pussy Cow Doll. I snort with laughter and seconds later my body crumbles giggling. Holding the banister tightly, tears run down my cheeks. I pull an old tissue from my sleeve and blow hard. I th.th.think she w.w.wants to s.seduce Henry. Trying to suppress laughter, I snort. It's beyond my control. My earlier anguish adds to my hysteria. Cow is priceless. She must think she has a chance with Henry.

"Phoenix, stop it, you're embarrassing yourself...This is exactly why handovers matter. Henry...I suspect she's dabbling with drugs."

I shake my head wildly, pressing my lips tightly together to prevent further outbursts.

"Phoenix! The agreement was for me to accompany you. This is very immature and selfish behaviour."

"Yep, it's always about me."

"Tea," says cheery Henry looking at me. "Put the kettle on, you know where the cups are. This way, Claire."

Cow cosies up to a stiff Henry...in her negligee.

Covering my mouth with an oven glove, I muffle further outbursts.

"Sh,sh,sugar, Henry?"

"One please."

I put in six.

Cow spills onto Henry's lap; one of her ample thighs obscures his.

"Sugar Claire?"

She's away with the fairies. I add salt and carry their mugs to the low, square, black coffee table. I sit opposite.

"Henry, how is Phoenix settling in?"

"It's early days."

I glare at him defiantly. The memory of the key; burning hot from the tumble drier that is my head. The one spinning every hurt, around and around, heating it until it's brittle and painful to remember.

"Henry's ordering a bed, a MacBook, iPhone and...a pony."

"Henry you mustn't spoil her."

"No," he denies his voice silkily steel edged, his eyes unwaveringly meaningful. "She'll get what she deserves."

Crap! I don't like the sound of that. If I could siphon out the sugar I would.

Henry takes a mouthful of tea. His eyebrows shoot up and his nostrils pinch. The alteration in the atmosphere is slight yet disturbing. It's like playtime is over.

"I've got to go...um...my car...Priti has the key...towed away." I'm rambling; my words racing ahead desperate for the finish.

"Apologies Claire, she needs supervision. I best drop her down. I see you had your hands full – she requires a lot of support."

It's then it strikes me...Henry hasn't spoken my name. It's Claire this, Claire that...what about Phoenix?

Disillusion is at boiling point.

They stare like I'm an oddity at the circus.

"Even the basics confuse her. Don't they dear?"

I glare, Henry grimaces, Cow nods.

"Got your petrol can?" asks Henry snidely.

"Yes."

"Sure?" he double-checks condescendingly.

"I'm. Sure." I say through gritted teeth.

"This is too short a visit," says Cow. "There's so..."

Henry interrupts Cow.

"So good of you to visit Claire."

Henry bodily ushers the mammoth from the house. We follow. A compliment here, a warm touch there, and she's embarrassingly easy. He likes her hair. For fucks sake, even Gaga would have reservations.

As she drives off, I wonder how her car's suspension copes.

"BLEEP."

I'm confused; Henry's locked his car and is returning to the house.

"Henry?"

He fails to answer.

"Henry!"

He disappears inside. He may as well have kicked me. My mind swims, its liquid consistency unable to form a firm rationalisation. If this is a game; he's winning...but it doesn't feel like a game...it hurts.

***

It's hours later when I hear her wheels on the gravel.

"I'm home," she says wearily, as I let her in.

"THUD. Owh!"

She's fallen climbing the stairs, tripping on doubt.

"I'm fine, no need to fuss," she says without a hit of sarcasm.

***

Day one of my fresh start and it's been hellish.

I drop to the floor like a dead weight. Curl up and rest my head on my rucksack. I'll rest for a tick. Close my eyes for a few minutes.

***

"Dinner!"

I jolt the minute he mouths the first syllable. I hadn't heard his approach; I think he has the power of levitation. He looks casually dangerous. He stares at me with hawkish intensity. His eyes tell me nothing: they have no depth, no light, no warmth.

I follow him downstairs, uneasily.

He pulls out a chair.

My breath stalls in my throat.

Henry's expression is so calm, so still, it could be computer generated. He taps his foot impatiently.

I fly into the chair, pulling it nearer the table, but it scrapes noisily against the tiled floor.

He's behind me. Saying Nothing. Until he places his hand on my shoulder. It's like he's pressing a hot iron to my bare skin. A century passes quicker.

"Enjoy."

The pressure of his fingers lifts.

I breathe again. Nothing, I repeat nothing, affects my appetite. I devour dinner sucking in long lengths of spaghetti whilst minute morsels of bolognaise fly onto my nose. I don't come up for air until my plate is clean.

***

She has an orange ring around her mouth.

"Hen-ry."

My name hesitates on her lips, like it's unsafe to pronounce.

"Thanks for dinner. It was delicious. I mean, the best meal I've had in eight years." She pauses. "Henry, I was thinking..."

I stand. I walk away.

***

I'm a discarded piece of rubbish. I wash up. I'm looking out the window. Night is falling quickly, chasing away the fading light of a September sun. I stand here; I don't know for how long. I'm gripping the edge of the worktop, my mind in turmoil, watching heavy, grey clouds move rapidly across the sky as if a giant had exhaled an angry breath. I'm gutted.

***

I enter the bedroom. She lays on the floor, tightly holding a soft toy to her chest, her knees brought up. She reminds me of the tiny black pill bugs in the garden, rolled up, awaiting imminent assault. How many times have I silently crept to the bedside of a target and held a pillow tightly over their face?

HAPPY SLAP

Monday dawns. Amy Gordon, Kirsten's media shrew, is such a liar! I do not have an STI! Every week she circulates a new rumour to ensure the sixth form population shun me. I'm spitting nails and it's only first break! Lost in moroseness and the conundrum that is Henry, I rush towards Z block. A gentle tap on my shoulder has me turning around.

"Slap!"

The strike is shocking.

"Slap!"

My head snaps sideways, wrenching my neck muscles.

The playground shifts: the background of disinterested students mutates into teeth-baring inciters careering forward. Head after head stretches and strains in my direction. Within seconds, I'm surrounded. Streaks of green and grey; school uniform, quickly become flashing blots of colour. I close my eyes tightly; I don't want to see my attackers.

"Slap!"

"Arghhhh!"

I've bitten the inside of my cheek.

"Argh."

To the side of my head, a whack so hard, so sudden, with an open hand leaves my ear ringing and my eyes watering. The pain and humiliation mounts as shifting shapes dart forward, swinging in slaps. A swooping dizziness strikes. I want the tarmac to crack, to split so wide I can lean back and let myself fall.

"Ha! Yes! F-ight! F-ight. F-ight," Amy incites, and others join in. Everyone. "F-ight! F-ight! F-ight! F-ight!" The whole fucking universe.

I shield my face with my arms and cower. The baying of the crowd diminishing me. A lump the size of a walnut swells in my throat.

"Shit! She's just standing there, she's such a fucking loser," cackles Jade.

The clapping, the cruel, raucous laughter, the chanting, it booms in my ears as I'm pushed and repeatedly struck.

"Melt! Melt! Melt! Melt!"

The whole school hates me.

I.

"HUH."
Can't.
"HUH."
Catch.
"HUH."

My breath. It's stuck in my lungs, crushed by my heaving chest. I want to be nothing; nobody's interested in nothing. My fingers dig deeper into my head as my desperation to not exist peaks.

"Wheeeeeeeew."

The teacher's whistle. Thank. You. God.

The flurry of dispersing bodies is yet another assault as bags are hastily picked up and swung carelessly. I remain Still, until someone's hard shoulder leaves me in a spin.

"Get to class now, or I'm calling the police and getting your backsides arrested!"

Great idea; yes, please, call the police. I jump wearily as warm skin touches mine.

"It's ok now," says a voice.

But it's not.

Hands encircle my wrists and I jerk away, but their gentle pressure pulls my arms from my face.

"Look at me."

Dazed, I register concern in a pair of bright blue eyes; the colour of hope?

"It's over," he says softly.

It's never going to be over; he just doesn't know it.

Attempting to speak my voice cracks. My glottis hangs heavily as it contracts and expands in my throat. Please, Phoenix, don't publicly cry. Is it because I know what a glottis is? Am I such an annoying geek, kids hate me? They must, they really hate me. I swallow a sob. I'm unravelling stitch by stitch. I want to tighten the thread, hold my life together, but I'm so fucking worn out. The temptation to reveal all, to be patched up by healing hands makes me almost delirious. My fragile state must be out there, because his arm, firm and comforting, rests on my shoulders; its strength preventing my seams coming apart.

He guides me to an uninhabited teaching hut. I should be anxious. It's well away from the main school. I should feel vulnerable, if anything I yearn to curl into him. A safe haven. Inside, we say nothing at first.

My pulse pounds in my neck. Shaking threatens, but I clench every muscle.

I look up.

"Are you ok?"

He is so gorgeous I forgive him for asking such a dumb question. I'm anything but ok. I've been assaulted! As the warmth of his hands penetrate my school blouse, I lose the ability to speak.

Many times, I'd fantasised about an attractive stranger saving me from peril. Right now, is my Disney moment. A beautiful man with mahogany hair and sharply shaped stubble rescued me. But I no way resemble a princess. My cheeks smart; they must look horribly red; I bet I resemble an ugly vegetable - a beetroot.

"I'll help you report the assault."

I shake my head madly.

"Please don't, it was a one off and I partially provoked it."

I bend the truth. No good ever came of ratting anyone out.

"Nonsense. Nothing could provoke such a violent reaction. I'm tolerant of many things, but not bullying."

Has he not worked in a school before?

"Sir, please," I plead. "It was cattiness that got out of hand; it happens sometimes. Please don't say anything. It'll inflame the situation. It's fine."

"It's not fine, it was vicious. Can you talk to your parents?"

Henry can't know.

"Sir it was a one-off. I'll get in as much trouble as the others if you take it further. Please...just this once can you drop it?"

This blue-eyed hero gently squeezes my shoulders. Heat charges into my already scarlet face. Comfort is so alien it seems intimate which is absurd because he's a teacher, it's his job.

"Does your face hurt?"

I'm tempted to cave and let him shoulder my problem. As my emotions yearn for one thing, my mouth decides another.

"No. It's fine now."

"What's your name.

"Phoenix."

"Phoenix," he echoes.

I love hearing my name; it's rarely spoken; he says it like it means something. Suddenly I want nothing more than to be beautiful.

***

I roll the trolley through the supermarket aisles: salmon fillets, kale, drowning; grated cheese, mushrooms, poisoning; tinned tomatoes, pistachio nuts, allergic reaction and bananas, fatal slip.

The clone rings; a burner phone; it's set to receive all of Care Girl's data. I listen in on her call.

"Phoenix?"

"Luke, I've had the most horrible, awful, horrendous morning and Priti's doing a mock chemistry ISA."

"Babes, babes, calm. Geography teacher's done a bunk, so I'll be Priti. Let me fix my hair and cross my legs. Go girl."

"Well..."

When the call disconnects, I pocket the clone. Interesting.

***

School drags. That's the way when something horrible happens; you experience the degradation in slow motion: Physics - whispers and stares, Maths - sniggers and pointing. I keep my head down, my mouth shut and my mind on binomial expansion. When the final bell rings, walking through the math block corridors, I ignore the nudges and sniggers. They have a ripple effect; even past the school gates. Happy slap? How about happy blunt force trauma? I put my earphones in, desperate to lose myself in emo rap, to be with artists who know about all this shit!

Parking at Henry's, I don't know what to expect. Before I raise the handbrake, the front door opens and there he is...a daunting figure impatiently waiting. Getting out of the car, my keys fall from my lap to the gravel. Crap! I pick them up, lock the door, then see my rucksack on the back seat.

"Shit!"

I unlock the car, grab the bag and stumble towards Henry. He's in jeans that hang low and a sleeveless gym top. It's hard not to be transfixed by his Fine Art tats. I see his jaw muscles flex. I'm conscious of his breathing, his strength, the salty smell of him. He slows time so my discomfort stretches on and on. It's like I need a password for an underground rave.

"Your face is bruised."

I blush at the idea of him examining me and because I'm about to lie.

"Football at break, a header gone wrong."

"You, play football?"

My eyes dart around.

"Yep, midfield."

He gives me a cynical look that screams 'liar!'

My blush deepens. Jesus, why won't he let me in. A thousand uneasy beats quicken my pulse. He stands aside.

"Dinner's at six. Liver and bacon."

I nearly spew up in the hallway again. Liver? Shit!

Upstairs, I'm glad to close the door and keep the world out. No bed, no soft furnishings, no furniture, but still, the room feels like mine. I look at the beautiful floor and how I've arranged my belongings in neat little piles. I think a couple of new storage baskets or boxes would be cool. I need to make a list of essentials, but first my maths while there's light.

I'm surprised by how easily I fall into homework. Nothing distracts me. When Henry calls me for dinner, I have mixed emotions, but I bury them amongst my textbooks as I pack away. My eyes stray to the window; night has crept in. From my bag I pull two folded A1 sheets of sugar paper. I blu-tack them to the panes of glass of my windows, paper curtain.

Downstairs, I'm conscious of the quiet, still, energy. Henry dishing up looks almost sinister. Cutlery is an extension of his hands. He wields with precision.

We eat in silence until both plates are empty.

"Thank you," I say. "As you cooked, I'll wash-up."

Henry drops his napkin on the table and retreats. Napkins? Undoubtedly gay.

For the remainder of the night, I see Henry only at a distance. He's there; he's not there.

I wonder what barbaric meal Henry will come up with tomorrow. I fall asleep trying to escape the taste of the animal organ I'd force fed myself.

***

I attach the silencer; rock music pumps out of the flat above. I put the muzzle against his forehead and squeeze. I imagine the bullet: burning through his skin, piercing muscle, drilling its way through cranial bone. It's then the real damage occurs; the speed of it tearing tissue and membrane.

A hole scorched in his head; I return the gun to its leather pouch. I feel nothing. Killing close enough for blood splatter to bleed into my clothing, is no harder than killing from a distance; it neither thrills nor guilts me. I am under no illusion about what I do, who I am. I laugh. Who I am. I shake my head at the irony.

HE'S BEHIND YOU

My alarm failed. I was sure I set it. Certain.

Though late for school, I don't exceed the speed limit. My family's car crash is ingrained beneath my skin.

"Shit!"

I realise I haven't put deodorant on. I hate it when that happens. Already tension is building.

Rushing to avoid an 'L' in the register, I bowl through the classroom door into my hero. His hands steady me and my hands automatically grasp his arms. It's totally Jane Austen.

He's muscular; I feel the hardness through his soft mulberry sweater. He doesn't feel like a teacher. He feels flippin' amazin'. Scrambling to my seat, heatedly searching my rucksack for books, Priti nudges my arm. Her face is aglow and her eyes huge and bright. I smile madly.

"Our new teacher - Mr Jacobs," Priti whispers.

At last. Something good.

***

It takes barely a minute to check her belongings. One large, pink plastic box; on it rose gold adhesive letters spelling 'Phoenix'; the 'h' is peeling off. Inside: schoolbooks, dog eared Famous Five, old soft toy, a Peppa Pig writing set, chipped mug printed with 'Mum', a wooden box decorated with shells; inside, diamond engagement and wedding rings. I place the smiley face keyring between the pages of a book. I'm almost sorry for her.

***

In the school library I'm a solitary figure, at a computer, working on my first homework set by Mr Jacobs. I'm so into it. School is epic when it's empty.

"Phoenix dear, it's time to pack up, we are closing."

Ms Baxter is a genuinely caring person who welcomes all to the library. She even turns a blind eye to my cheese and pickle sandwiches. Tuna was pushing it, even I knew that.

"Night, Ms Baxter, have a lovely evening. Mr Baxter's a lucky man."

"Lucky woman," she replies.

"My bad," I apologise smiling.

It's dark and drizzling as I walk through the school gates into a damp, hazy mist. Above ominous, wispy clouds engulf a full moon. In geographical terms it's werewolf weather. I glance behind me; the school stands like an asylum, dingy and oppressive. The caretaker's keys jingle as he pushes the creaking gates closed behind me. I don't say goodnight; he's a creepy sort of man. Then I think of Eleanor Oliphant and turn my head.

"Have a good evening," I say.

"Same to you, love."

My car is ten minutes away - five if I run through the pathways between the park and the garages. Instead I walk towards Eastcote Road. The streetlights are unlit but the house lights from the large detached properties are proof of life. It's reassuring that help is a door knock away.

I walk quickly. The rainfall is heavy and I've the oddest sensation of being watched. I think of the science behind being scared; stress stimulates the brain to release adrenaline and stress hormones, resulting in goose bumps and raised hair. So, there's no boogie man shadowing me, I'm stressed. Of course, I'm stressed, look at my uncle! Yet a distinct uneasiness remains; the instinct that someone, somewhere is observing my every catastrophe. I think of Bradley. He and Luke were friends once. Maybe that's why Luke was so prickly with Cow on my last night.

SNAP!

I hear but ignore.

A pins and needles sensation creeps beneath my skin.

Speeding up, I wish my car keys were to hand.

Rummaging in my bag...

SNAP!

The silence of the quiet residential road is interrupted. I slowly turn around.

Nothing. No one - just me. I pause, listening. Parked cars line the road on both sides. Gardens are dark and gloomy. It's a cat or someone putting out the rubbish.

I catch the slightest glimpse of something - by the park entrance. I don't know if it's real or imagined.

I run towards my car; ready to engage key with lock.

I'm so near to experiencing the relief of being safe when a hand grasps my shoulder and my heart bursts through my chest.

"Arhhhhh."

I'm sprawled on the wet pavement; rainwater soaking through my thin skirt and knickers. I look up angrily terrified.

"Jesus. You gave me a fucking heart attack," I snap.

"Fuck Phe, you look bare scared. Sorry. I figured I'd meet ya what wid Bradley."

Luke pulls me up. Shaken, I rest my back against the car. The feeling of impending threat remains.

"Did you follow me?"

I mean, what were the chances of bumping into each other.

"Nah babes."

"Where did you spring from?"

"Phoenix, chill babes. I came thru Westbury."

His eyes are bright and clear, his expression sincere.

"Babes. Sorry I spooked you."

My eyes still glare.

"Chill Phe. What with Henry being a dick I fought you'd need a friend coz like your week's been shit."

We stand silently, for the first time unsure of ourselves.

"My day's been ok," I breathe out.

"Sweet."

Luke moves nearer. I smell a whiff of Hugo Boss.

"You've been stickin' it on The Perfume Shop girl again."

Luke smiles. His lips frame the whitest teeth.

***

"Boss?"

I turn to my sergeant, who's still, silently cursing I'm DI and not him. Well, that makes him keen. He'll want to prove himself.

"Sergeant?"

"Hospital called. Bradley's been pronounced brain dead."

"Gather the team."

I don't feel much of anything. You can't in this job.

***

The door opens as I drive up to the house. Henry somehow fills the doorway. Concentrate Phoenix. Bag? Check. Key out of ignition and securely in hand? Check. I lock the car, wipe my sweating palms on my skirt and walk to Henry, clearing my throat.

"Have you passed your driving test?" he asks.

"Yes," I say my back immediately up.

"Then your car is more advanced than it appears."

I turn. Horrified to see my car slowly rolling back into Henry's Range Rover. I had applied the handbrake. Had I? I can only watch as the inevitable plays out. If it had been any other car it would have been disastrous but the four by four's giant boot tyre cushions the slight impact. The only damage is to my ego. Henry is laughing at me. His mouth remains a straight line. His forehead doesn't crease. But I know...that Henry Whittle is laughing his socks off.

***

During the night her demons feed on her insecurities. I watch as she thrashes around, deep in crimson dreams.

I find it extremely irksome she's in my home, technically hers since I killed her uncle. Even when she's not speaking, her desire to connect with me is so strong I'm infringed in some way...but she's entertaining...so I follow her to school.

She parks a block away. She moves apologetically, giving pedestrians a wide birth, trying to merge into the scenery. Her school uniform is poor; the blazer sleeves are nearly at her elbows and her legs too long for the skirt. Approaching the school gates, her body language is hesitant. A gang of kids prowl behind her, smirking, taunting. It seems her enemies are widespread. They take out packs of flour which they proceed to tip over her. She hits out furiously smacking one boy in the eye. Another boy headbutts Care Girl and she goes down. Kids walk around her, no doubt relieved not to be the target. One girl, small, dark skin, long black hair, comes to her aid followed by a rounded, well nourished, ginger-haired boy. Care Girl gets up and brushes herself down. She isn't crying or mouthing off, she is reserved. I know her type: internaliser, hard to break.

***

After a floury start to the day, I blow anger and revenge from my thoughts. It's only flour. Yeah, flour today, acid tomorrow. A while back, I'd have crumbled if I'd been flour bombed, instead I'd lashed out. Ok, I've a huge bump on my head, but it sends a message; Phoenix Whittle is a fighter.

I spend six hours on red alert expecting aftershocks. I shelter first in the Art block. Then I take refuge in the shadow of the nearest teacher. I'm twitchy. Every soft step behind me possibly a threat. It's the toilets that disturb me most. I can't keep my legs crossed all day; my bladder's fit to burst. It's the place for catty chavs to swop insults among themselves like it's a kindness. Me? An outsider to the row of pretty maids? Well, I'm asking for it...so I duck into the staff toilets. When the final bell rings, Priti and Clive wait by the gate and fall in either side of me.

"We did it guys; we're another day closer to release," says Clive.

"Yesss," says Priti. "Mondays are the hardest, Tuesdays are depressing."

"Jesus tell me about it," I say. "We'll cope better tomorrow, Wednesday, the half-way point, and it's Mr Jacobs. Disregarding weekends, staff development days, bank holidays and school holidays we have one hundred and seventy-two days to survive – it's doable."

"Clive, what about Bradley?" asks Priti. "Will his family take him off life support or is it gossip?"

Intensive Care, the two most repeated words in school today.

"My mum says the doctors told the parents Bradley's already gone," adds Clive.

"Shit," Priti and I say in unison as we reach my car.

"Anyone need a lift," I offer?

"Nah, I've piano", says Priti.

"Come on Clive, group hug," I insist before we part ways.

I watch as Priti and Clive walk away.

A thought remains with me; a boy my age has been beaten so badly he's on the threshold of death. I'd imagined striking back, hurting him – someone had more than imagined. I picture Bradley: his harsh mouth firing ugly words, blood matting his hair, dark bruising on his temple. For me, Bradley Perkins is more than gossip, he's in my head, half alive, half dead.

***

I consider the concept of being a marine. You know, one day, in the line of duty you will kill. Your enemy will be crouching behind a wall with a machine gun or camouflaged in a forest, a blade held tightly in their hand. They'll be breathing hard like you, eyes darting around like yours, ears listening for the slightest creak, telling themselves to calm fucking down. They will be exhilarated, ruthless, obeying orders, determined to succeed; in short, they are you. You don't know them, hate them, they have not personally slighted you, but you will kill them any way you can - maybe torture them into betraying friends and family. But I'm no longer a marine. I work in a highly specialised sector. I'm deadly, emotionless and insular. I'm not healthy to be around.

***

Bradley's parents requested my presence. Turning off life support is something I've not experienced.

I've no leads. No idea who the perp is. Was it even random? We're clueless, so I can't even offer the Perkins family justice.

I take the elevator instead of the stairs; I'm in no rush to officially end a boy's life. The doors open and the Chief nods at me.

"The Perkins Boy?"

"Yes, totally dreading it."

"Understandably. Still on for dinner tonight."

It's a statement. The lift doors open. Two constables step in. End of conversation.

***

Henry's positioned in the doorway barring me from entering. If this were a computer game, I'd still be on Level One – Mortal Wombat.

"What happened?"

"Sorry?"

"What. Happened?" he queries, eyeing the egg-shaped bump on my forehead.

"Oh this," I say raising my hand to the bump, "dodge ball; I'm not the best dodger."

"So, it seems. Did you put your handbrake on?"

"Yes," I reply, fed up with Henry magnifying my errors.

We stand, Henry inside, me on the outside. I'm just about able to maintain eye contact; I'm building up resistance to his aloofness, his cool scrutiny. When I can, I search for physical similarities between him and Dad, but I can't find any. I think maybe my memory of dad is diminishing. What if a time comes when Mum and Dad are merely two names, six letters, a concept, and I have nothing real to hold on to? I'm losing them…It's fucking crap.

THE DAY JOB

The weekend begins with a shitty note.

Out.

Don't cook. Don't invite anyone over.

"Prat!"

Heating a chocolate croissant in the microwave, I contemplate my situation. Diane is right about me struggling to live with an adult male, especially one so physically formidable. But as sun and shadow chase each other around the kitchen, I relax. It's surprising how at home I am in this house where I'm not wanted. Perhaps because everything is new and devoid of Henry's touch.

Some workmen let themselves in from the garden. Gym Bunny's among them; he's irritatingly sure of himself. Their eyes linger on me. It pisses me off.

"Ding, ding, ding!"

I turn my back on them, lean against the breakfast bar and pick up.

"Hey, Mers."

"You said you'd ring back," Mercy accuses.

"Sorry, things got a bit mental."

"Yeah, I knew once you met someone as boring as you, I'd be out of the picture."

I ignore the dig.

"How's living back home?" I ask chirpily.

"Fine."

"Good. Homework going ok?"

"Why are you still wailing on about homework?"

"It's important."

"Yeah, yeah, I've done it, stop clucking."

"How'd the maths test go?"

"Bottom set. It's not my fault my brain's under-developed coz my mum poisoned it with White."

Five minutes later Mercy hangs up.

In Henry's absence I'm eager to snoop. Either side of a large central window are white, highly glossed, cupboards. Glasses in one; white, plain mugs in another. Tupperware in the next. Empty cupboard.

Empty cupboard. I whizz through the cupboards below. Dinner plates, pasta bowls, sandwich plates, cereal bowls; all white. Empty cupboard. Saucepan cupboard. Cookware cupboard. A gleaming chrome holder with utensils is beside the hob, like at Greenmead, but theirs is covered in a sticky layer of brown grease. Here everything is new?

The kitchen's external walls, like the lounge, are double-glazed bi-folding doors, framing the garden and fields beyond. I press my nose to the glass; my breath forming an enticing drawing board on Henry's glazing. My finger draws a knob. Giggling I continue my reconnaissance. Beside the massive fridge freezer is a door. Hesitant I open it, expecting the door to creek but it doesn't. It reveals a split-level larder comprising floor to ceiling shelving either side of the door. Filled with tinned foods, pasta, rice, bottled water, long life milk. On the top shelves are labelled boxes: candles, matches, torches, batteries, electrical ties, fuses, rope.

I step down into the utility room: washing machine, dryer, ironing board. There is a sleek wet room to the right. Again, conspicuously clean.

Back in the lounge I touch the top of a slim bookcase; no dust. I pull a book from it; no creased pages. I pull another and another – all the same – crisp untouched sheets. In the hallway I go directly to Henry's office next to the stairs. The doorknob won't turn. Crouching, I peer through the keyhole, but the room beyond is in darkness. Upstairs Henry's bedroom is locked; the man has trust issues. The door before mine; the key's in the lock. A large ottoman sits in an otherwise empty room. Checking it out my blood boils. All along Henry had a spare double quilt, pillows and a black throw! I'd no idea snuggly chenille could hurt so much. Why is Henry such a fucking arsehole? Maybe I'd never met my uncle because his older brother knew he was a prick! Angrily I pull the bedding from its plastic, shake it out, and pad out my makeshift bed. If Henry so much as tries to repatriate the bedding I'm taking him down. I wonder where he is. Maybe he's on a date.

**

Female, single, forty-five. I follow her to a little boulangerie in Notting Hill Gate. From there to Waterstones where she purchases a Riley Sagar thriller. She heads for the underground. An Oyster beeps her through the ticket barrier. The station is busy, not frantic but there are enough passengers to ease up to her without causing alarm. She barely notices the prick of the needle as I inject a minute amount of ricin into her bloodstream. On my journey home, I imagine her settling on an easy chair with Final Girls unaware poison is slowly plugging her arteries and starving her organs of blood. In a day or two she'll be in agony; in a week she'll be dead.

***

I've found my car key. In between the pages of a book? He'd searched my bag, stolen my key, let me walk out of his house knowing the anguish ahead? Who fucking does that?

"Aw-right luv," says the youngish decorator winking at me. I'm unsettled. It's not just the key; I'm unused to so many men coming and going. It's hard to change, go to the loo, take a bath. Occasionally I see Gym Bunny looking my way, whispering and laughing with the other men. They don't act this way when Henry's around.

I spend the day working on an English essay. I think about Heathcliff: his intensity, his vindictiveness and I end up with Henry stuck in my head...followed by the car key. Maybe Henry's a total bell end!

***

It's late. There are no other vehicles. I park alongside Care Girl's car; barely an inch away, preventing her from accessing the driver's door. I slip off my trainers dropping them in the shoe basket. In it lay her much smaller, scuffed, black school pumps. I pick one up; it isn't even leather.

The TV is on. She's sprawled half on, half off my sofa, asleep, probably drooling onto my cushion. I survey the room. She's been at the bookshelf. Kitchen: she's gone through the cupboards. Larder: taken a torch. Utility room: no, she hasn't put a wash on. Upstairs: bedding taken.

"Hi Henry."

Our bodies brush. She throws herself down on her bedding. She sits, legs folded, arms crossed, guarding her newly acquired resources. She says nothing further. It is unnecessary. Her eyes shine with defiance.

***

I lay in bed. Listening to Henry next door. I like him near.

"Henry?" It's my Dad's birthday tomorrow. He'd be fifty."

"And?"

"Are you religious?"

"No."

"I like to think heaven is real. That my parents are together somewhere beautiful...I'm sorry you and Dad weren't close...Is that why you don't like me?"

Silence.

CLICK.

He's shut his bedroom door.

SEXUAL HARASSMENT

Monday comes around quicker than any other day.

In my bra and knickers, dressing for school, Gym Bunny barges in.

"Ahh," I shout, jumping out of my skin, before grabbing a blanket.

"Sorry luv, thought you'd left."

His workmates appear, ogling me from the doorway. They snigger like naughty boys and I hate them instantly. Seething, I slam the door and shortly stomp downstairs, leaving the house without breakfast.

I have to fucking climb over the passenger seat to drive the car.

***

"Femi, a word."

The foreman removes his dusk mask, pats himself down and follows me to the kitchen.

"The young apprentice, what's his name?"

"Tyler Lewis."

"Tell Lewis he's no longer needed and walk him off the premises."

"Ok."

"And tell the lads in Lewis' crew to stay clear of my niece."

I want her gone, not sexually harassed.

***

The school day passes uneventfully: I pay attention, I make notes, I sit with Clive at lunch, study in the library until Taekwondo.

I park in the community centre car park. It's small, there's only a few bays enclosed by six-foot hedging. Sometimes, when it's full, I struggle manoeuvring the car out; the space is very tight. The centre is a one-story building consisting of two halls and a waiting area. Sometimes I can't be arsed to come, but tonight I'm in the mood for Taekwondo. I want to punch and kick until my anger diffuses.

"Phoenix!"

I recognise the voice. Irritation fizzles in my head; it's Sex Pest Rob. If he calls me Babe he's going down.

"What's up Babe?"

I grit my teeth. Married men are the worst. I hurry into the dojo. A chorus of hi's are swapped as we settle in our grade rows, bow in, then warm up, before partnering for pad work. I train hard because I face imminent danger. It's inevitable that one day I'll rely on self-defence. Rob's eyes openly stalk me; I hate that I'm in his sick imagination. I think Sensei knows because he walks me to my car after class.

I get kebab and chips on the way home and manage to sneak in as the last builder exits.

Henry's watching Netflix. I stand in the archway wondering what he's watching; The Outsider. I know that he knows that I'm here, but no invitation is offered.

Upstairs I read my English Lit; Emma. I blink and it's bedtime. On the floor, unable to sleep, I shake my snow globe; I watch snowflakes flitter then settle.

Bradley Aldridge, my cemetery tormenter, drifts in and out of my mind. His house was in the papers – a posh detached home with roses in the garden. I have little memory of my house, the one I lived in with Mum and Dad. Now...another family live in our home. They've replaced us; it's like my parents never existed. I shine my torch on the photograph frame, on our three smiling faces. We were so happy. There was never a cross word or a raised voice. Just nursery rhymes, bedtime stories, bubble baths with sticky foam alphabet and mash and beans with a smiling sausage. I know they are in Heaven, but Heaven is still dead.

***

Creating doubt, confusion, frustration is easy. She leaves her purse down, I pick it up. Her lanyard's on top of her maths book, I move it. Her shoes are by the front door, I put them by the back door. Simple measures which play havoc with one's senses and confidence. She is literally stumbling around in circles.

***

My week spirals out of control. I call an emergency meet at Ahimsa Vegan Cafe. I park in Pinner's Medical Centre car park; backing onto M&S, it's constantly busy, but I find a bay. Locking the car, an uneasy sensation wraps tightly around me. I scan the rows of vehicles. People are dotted all over, I couldn't be safer. I enter the narrow walkway joining Marks to the High Street. I hurry and within a sec I come out opposite St. Luke's. I weave between shoppers, passing Nero, and into Ahimsa, the Vegan Cafe. It's a tightly furnished, cool, modern space with a menu of wraps, rice bowls, baked potato and breakfasts. I'm so energised after eating there; all the veggies are a super boost.

Luke's sitting by the window, so chilled, any lingering trepidation is left at the door. I give a little wave before ordering pancakes.

"How's Uncle Henry today?"

"Ruthless, devious, calculated."

I settle opposite and spill my guts.

"It's as if he's got a genetic disorder, like an empathy gene was missing at conception, so he doesn't know how to interact with me. We have fragments of conversation. Everything he says is a fact or an instruction. His tone is formal and he's so scarily literal, it flusters me."

"Phe, Phe, Phe, don't be flustered bubs. It's a Navy ting. One minute he's under attack: mortar bombs, fucking grenades, incendiary devices and then he's trying to converse wid you. He's gonna be clueless bubs. Watch Hurt Locker – you'll see. He's needs more time bubs. He likes you, what's not to like. He's just shit at showing it; he's in emotional hiding, Phe"

"Thank you for that fresh and reassuring perspective, Dr Luke – have you thought about counselling as a career?" I grin.

"Getting paid to ask ladies to lay on my couch? Yeah, I've thought about it."

Through the shopfront window I see Priti and wave.

"Sorry," she says her little cheeks filled out and her eyes playfully darting around. "Anand's tarantula escaped again."

I update Priti regarding Henry.

"You'd have to meet him to get it. He makes the word 'cappuccino' sound like a death threat. I mean, menacing is his trademark. Even weirder, I think I'm being watched."

"Oh, my God, Phe, maybe there's hidden cameras in your room." Priti squeals.

My jaw drops.

"No man zoom-in on my friend's lady bumps," shouts Luke.

Spluttering, milkshake shoots up my nose. Laughing, I clutch Priti who quickly succumbs and rocks back and forth. I don't know what I'm laughing at; nothing's funny enough to warrant my public display of hilarity, but my face needs to stretch and wrinkle and open. I've had a grimace set like cement since Trish died. Luke must need a laugh too because he's fully bent over the table, his back heaving up and down as his foot thumps the floor. The more people look the worse we are. Pedestrians peering through the glass shop front cause further fits of giggles and grunts and quickly our bodies are convulsing.

"Th,th,th,they think we're h,h,h,having a gr,gr,group seizure."

My abdomen hurts so much; like my intestines are being pulled out. Tears run down my face and only the action of blowing my nose calms me. I turn away from Luke and Priti to prevent myself from going off on one again.

"Seriously..."

"No, Phe, please bae, no more Henry."

"I'm not saying he follows me everywhere, but, now and then, when I'm walking, I'll stop and look around expecting to catch a quick glimpse of him. I know it sounds lame."

They nod multiple times in agreement.

"He makes me nervous. I'm jittery around him, and then I make mistakes. Like putting the peas and carrots in the microwave for too long, and them exploding. He's there glaring at me. He doesn't say the word idiot, but I can read it in his eyes."

Luke stands.

"This white man's seriously doin' my head in," moans Luke. "Let's go see a movie."

It seems a good way to pass the time and avoid Henry.

We drive to Harrow and park in St. George's.

The sun is bright, but it's deceptively cold. I link arms with Priti, and we snuggle as we walk.

The Vue is crowded, but I enjoy a sense of calm as Priti and Luke playfully argue their film choices. At the kiosk I empty my purse and my pockets, making piles of copper, silver and gold.

"Fuck, I can't believe you carry around that much shrapnel Whittle. There are over a hundred coins. It's equivalent to weightlifting, bubs. Warn me next time though, so I can disassociate myself."

I squeeze his hand and keep it in mine for a minute.

***

I wash death from my hands. The clothes I'd killed in, lay strewn like a caterpillar's cocoon. I throw them in the incinerator before pulling on a change of clothes.

"You need anything?" Jack asks.

"No." I slip him a fifty. "I'll deal with the car and burner phone myself."

Trust no one. Painful lessons have taught me this much.

***

We hit the food court before the movie. McDonalds serves us individually as we've vouchers. It's my turn to get one Pepsi with two extra cups. The cashier gives me a dirty look. Jesus, it's not like they're her cups.

"Phoenix?"

I'm startled when I hear my name.

"Mr Jacobs, hi."

"Hi," adds Priti, shamelessly moving in on him.

He stands cool and casual, laden down with JD Sports and Next bags.

"This is Luke," I stutter avoiding Mr Jacobs' lovely blue eyes. I don't want Luke to think I have a crush.

"We lived together."

I see Luke endeavouring not to laugh.

"I mean we both lived somewhere, separately…not in the same room."

The hole gets deeper.

"I've moved."

Crimson rises hotly up my cheeks.

"Sounds very modern," he laughs warmly. "You have a good evening. Nice to meet you, Luke. See you tomorrow girls."

We watch Mr Jacobs saunter away; me appreciatively, Luke suspiciously.

"Snide mother fucker"

"Shush, Luke. He is not."

"He's flash, babes. No man buying Next got rights to be flash."

I let it drop. I can't start biggin' Mr Jacobs up.

***

I drive the car to the nearest scrap yard, give the bloke a score and wait and watch until the car crusher flattens the vehicle into a pancake. I use a different scrap merchant each time. Never visit the same place. Never overpay. Never leave a pattern. Keep contact with the public to a minimum. So, I walk the two miles to a tube. Looking forward to Match of the Day.

***

It's late when the film finishes. I drop Luke and Priti home.

Driving up the lane, I realise, even with Henry being weird, I like returning home.

DINGDONG!

I wait patiently.

DINGDONGDINGDONG!

I wait a little longer.

DINGDONGDINGDONGDINGDONGDINGDONG!

I ring continuously till my finger hurts.

"Henry! I know you're in. Please…this is so horrible.

When I get no response, after ten cold minutes, my head heats up, like there's a grenade inside me. Angrily I thump the door, hating I'm in this wretched position. Tiredness, the cold, anxiety; they manifest into hatred for Henry. He is a joy-sucker; everything good about my evening he's remotely sabotaged.

"Henry! You! Are! An! Arsehole!"

***

She makes no further attempts to gain entry. I like her stubbornness - Waking to an empty house - I like her absence more.

I prepare for my run. Let a tradesman in before I approach her car. I see through the windscreen she's asleep. Her head's rolled to one side, her body weight's against the door. It's cruel; I swiftly open her car door.

"Errrrrrrrr!"

She falls hard.

She's up quickly, but disorientated. Stumbling around, she's confused and faltering. She sees me, stares a moment, then shakes her head. Saying nothing she picks her sweatshirt up and locks her car. Abuse is so familiar to this girl she expects nothing less.

***

It's abuse. There is no other definition. I will not be this person. This victim. This sponge soaking up everybody's animosity and frustrations. No! No! Fucking No!

I shower, dress and crunch granola angrily before school.

Leaving, Henry runs towards me. I'm scared, yet in awe of him. His presence, his power; if that rubbed off on me school wouldn't be so dire. Perhaps his behaviour's a form of initiation? That makes sense. Jesus! Why do I still justify his treatment of me? The man's completely physco.com.

Upset, I fumble, drop my book, then find I'm barely an inch from him.

He dips and rises, my book in his hand. I hesitate: the book, Henry, the book, Henry. Do I really need a physics book?

***

She resembles an evacuee; today's wardrobe choice is again poor. A spot's erupting between uneven eyebrows. She blushes easily. No make-up, translucent skin. High cheek bones: one's been rebuilt. Lips? Difficult to judge through scowl. Bitten fingernails; anxiety. Her eyes tell me her optimism is waning. I've disappointed her; well that's a first. I move closer. She flinches. I'm completely conscious of how unnerved she is by my proximity. It's like I'm a grenade; she can barely breathe.

***

Among the pandemonium of students heading to period four, Priti and I find each other. We link arms, walking along the external wall of the main building.

"Phoenix you're so pale; are you ill?"

"Fatal case of Henry-itis."

"Here, eat this," says Priti passing me an Oreo.

"Keep your head down. There's Kirsten and the coven congregating outside the drama barn. Smell Phe, they're smoking weed."

I look across to a gang of nine or ten; all a danger to society. I don't think they carry knives, but they're approaching that level of violence. No other student is in arm's reach, so, there's plenty of room for them to perform.

"Phe, we'd better scoot. Mr Hallahan is on loitering alert. Look! He's got a yellow detention book and he knows how to use it. Catch you at home time, hun."

***

In the laundry room I smile to myself. She'd put a wash on. I stare at the drum door, watching the clothes turning around, watching the loo roll I'd snuck into the drum disintegrate and mix with her clothes. I am looking forward to her coming home.

***

School is the usual blur of mediocre teaching and disrupted classes. Kirsten is my shadow: her barbed tongue tries ripping me to pieces, but I'm too thick skinned and that infuriates her.

This resilience is tested at home. I'll give it to him. This trick is dirty. I hold up my soft black sweatshirt covered in minute pieces of wet tissue. Tights, knickers, tops; the same.

***

"SHIT!" I hear her say, though it's through gritted teeth.

I know it hurts her, but sometimes you don't get a clear shot.

***

Day follows day follows day. Each time I initiate conversation with Henry my blood sugar drops because I've hit a hard, brick, seven-foot wall and can't conquer it.

At night, noises filter into my sleep. I know Henry comes and goes at peculiar hours. I presume it's a girl or boyfriend. Probably Grinder. I know nothing more about Henry than I did the night I puked up. Only that he is not 'the boy next door'.

P.T.S.D

I wait for toast to pop up. There's an estrangement between us and I hate him for it. Didn't he understand that every minute of every day each one of us balances between the living and the dead? That we need to make 'now' priority. Not an apocalypse; if that's what Henry's preparing me for. Maybe he's one of these clever dumb people.

Still, I wonder what a teen Henry was like? Quiet and lonely I presume. What happened to drive a wedge between him and Dad? I can't imagine having a sister and not seeing her for years. I've only lived with Henry two months and already...well...he's ingrained in my memory; nothing will erase him.

I feel the onus is on me to make this work, but Henry is so inaccessible; he should have 'out of service' hanging from his neck. Still I make the effort.

"How's your writing going?"

He looks at me; the intensity of his stare no longer intimidates.

"I don't discuss my work."

Conversation stopper? Not for me.

"My Dad would have made a brilliant children's author. When I was small, he created crazy stories with mad characters. I loved listening; I can't remember his voice. Was it deep, high pitched, smooth, fast? I don't know."

***

Eyes wide open; in them her pain and vulnerability shimmer like ripples on the horizon.

"Do you ever think about my Dad?" she asks timidly.

The yearning in her voice is a desperate static. I can't have interference in my head.

"No."

***

I can't help that I'm still fucked up about my parents.

"Do you have photos of my Dad? I mean when he was young, when you lived together?"

I can't restrain the pleading in my voice.

"No."

"Not one?"

"No."

Silence.

"You're so different. Were you always salt and pepper or did the Navy..."

"Did the Navy what?" he asks almost nastily.

"Um...I mean...Henry, if you have PTSD we can."

"I don't have PTSD. Don't look for an explanation for me. I was wrong to invite you here. It was out of misplaced duty. Your father was a teen when I was born. We weren't close. We didn't care about each other. I can't tell you anything about him because we were strangers. I don't mourn him. Your loss isn't my loss. I don't have feelings for you. We're not connected. You're an emotional teenager with deep-rooted hang-ups who I happen to be related to."

It's like he's punched me in the stomach. I'm so winded I nearly keel over.

Henry stands, and angrily I clutch at his arm.

"You are unbelievable. You think you're complex and fascinating - you're not. Just fucking mental! You should be institutionalised."

I gape at him; my hate is out there.

"You're faulty, defective, broken!"

He must be, otherwise he's sadistically cruel.

"If your book bombs you can dig graves or be a mortician because there's something dead inside you."

I storm off without car keys. Pounding the road, I end up in Eastcote. I've walked miles and I'm gasping. I see a new cafe, TAG, and grab a small corner seat by the window. I slowly stir the chocolate topping into the frothy, milky cappuccino, watching a whirlpool of despondency as I retract the spoon. Scraps of memory from my succession of foster parents bait me further into my black hole. I recall how I tried so hard to be what each family wanted, tolerating verbal abuse and punishments so violent that eventually I shrunk back in fear when any real affection was offered.

"Can I get you anything?"

It's the boy who served me. He's handsome with a warm smile. I know he'd listen; I'm so fucking tempted.

"No. I'm fine thank you, but the coffee here is great."

"Thanks. Erm, here's a card for a free tea tomorrow, we've got a promotion on for Halloween."

I suddenly feel cold, like someone's dancing on my grave.

***

I kerb crawl watching her walk home. As she turns up the lane to the house, I open the gate to the field and drive the track to the back of the property.

Excellent timing. She undresses; pushing her skinny jeans from her hips, down to her ankles and off. She smooths them out and hangs them up. Next, she pulls her top over her head followed by socks, bra, panties; bundling all items in her laundry basket. I envy the material; how it'd hung against the flat of her stomach, how it'd moulded her breasts.

Looking no longer satisfies.

***

Halloween! Instead of bullies covertly terrorising, they openly threaten dismemberment. It's 'The Purge'. Still, Kirsten should be happy, today she's celebrated.

I'm on edge. Class changes are an opportunity for Kirsten to strike. The collective conversation of what happened at the weekend and chats about boys and football does little to camouflage impending doom.

As I think the word 'doom', who do I see?

"What did you fucking call me?" demands Alex, his face a millimetre from Clive's.

We're in a narrow, high traffic corridor. Escape routes are restricted.

"Halfwit, dickass, knobless," I interrupt, placing myself beside Clive.

"Bitch! I'm glad your parents died."

My heart twists.

"Actually, Phoenix, it was Knoblet," says Clive. "In English, small things end with 'let' like piglet.

In a breath; Clive's fear. Alex's angry fist.

I wrench Alex's arm; the motion unbalancing me. I bounce off Clive onto the floor.

Alex heaves over me; a red devil face: white, popping, druggy eyes: cruelly twisted mouth. His knob must be incy to be this mad.

Poof; he's gone.

Mr Jacobs: his back muscles tight beneath his white, crisp shirt: his body blocking Alex.

Clive helps me up.

"Phe?"

My eyes remain on Mr Jacobs, the way his head dips low to Alex's ear. Children stream around us and Alex retreats, lost in the flow of bodies. Mr Jacobs turns his head, and for a mere second something passes between us?

"Phoenix, how cool is Mr Jacobs?"

"Dead cool," I reply as Clive ushers me along.

***

It has been a physical, hands-on day. Rather testing. Some targets' grip on life is tighter than others. I'm nursing an inflamed shoulder, a dislocation I reset myself.

Care Girl's waiting for the kettle to boil, drawing paper hearts on the corner of her homework diary, ill at ease. The kettle flicks off and she pours hot water into her 'mum' mug. She lingers momentarily, tracing its raised letters. If she thinks I'll engage in conversation, she's wrong.

***

"Boss."

I turn to Andy, my sergeant. If I keep repeating 'my sergeant' maybe it'll stop me wondering about his lips.

"Sergeant."

"Body on the tracks Ma'am, at Uxbridge."

"I'll need you on this one, sergeant. It's most likely a jumper but think outside the box."

"Sure boss."

Why does he say 'boss' so fucking sexy!

***

Sleep is elusive. Spending night after night on the floor is a slow form of torture; my body feels bulldozered. I prepare myself for Henry. I'm still angered by his harsh, dismissive reaction to my questions about Dad.

Morning Henry," I say stiffly.

Henry nods. Some flawed morality brought us together, but he's impenetrable, not in a remote way, no, he's always present. His face looks fresh, young, friendly; totally illusory. We're fucked up and I don't know how to fix us. So, I leave.

Driving to school, anxiety encroaches on my concentration. Surely if you're into learning school should be a breeze. Why do those not wanting to learn hate those that do? Why am I letting girls with perfectly arched eyebrows bully me?

Entering form, Clive shuffles me back out.

"Morning to you too. What's up?"

"Quick, sneak behind the rubbish bins." Clive's tone is grave.

"We'll get marked late."

"Phoenix we're adults. We can walk out of school anytime."

I follow Clive down the alley between the history block and the art hut. It's narrow and dark. I look upward; the sky's a sweep of grey. It's an omen. I know this is about blood loss.

"It's Alex...he's dead."

"Dead?"

"Dead like in crushed.

"What? Alex!"

"It's fucked up I know, but it's true."

"How?"

"Suicide or misadventure. He either jumped or fell in front of an oncoming train."

"Fuck!" I say feeling hot. And dizzy. And brittle. "You know this how?"

"I live two doors down from him. News travels fast."

"Jesus. Dead. Are you sure?"

Clive nods slowly. Beneath his freckles he's pale.

My brain is like a smoking oven: I can't think clearly. I can't see how it could have happened. I shift uncomfortably as perspiration transfers from my back to my blouse, making it stick. I wipe the sweat from my hairline.

"Alex is one of those boys that gets away with everything. That's his rep. He can't be dead. Could he kill? Yes. But himself? No. He must have tripped Clive. Jesus, this is horrendous. He was a monster, but this?"

"We'd better get to form, Phoenix."

I nod. My legs wobbly. I want to go home...to Henry. As weird as he is Henry helps me think straight, and right this minute my thoughts are a collection of twisted theories.

***

She enters through the open kitchen. Startled eyes momentarily meet mine before darting away. She's nervy, distracted, almost distraught; not looking where she's going.

"Arhhh. Shit!"

Rubbing her shins, she walks past my large tub of protein and continues upstairs. There's a slight vibration in my pocket.

"Priti, a really bad thing has happened."

"What?" Priti asks in a hushed tone.

"Alex is dead."

"Noooo," whispers Priti astonished "Is this a joke, Phe?"

"It's no joke," I gulp painfully. "He...he...it was a train Pri."

"Fuck!"

"I'm an awful person, Pri; I wished Alex dead and now this. When Mum and Dad died, I questioned why God let muggers, rapists and murderers live but took them. Shouldn't bad things happen to bad people?"

"Yes, and now something has happened to a bad person."

"But Pri, it's odd. There's something unsettling about it."

"Well, yeah, Phe! One minute the boy's ruling sixth form the next he's mangled with a train. Call me a bitch, but that is unsettling."

"I guess...but...I don't know."

"Phe you are alright, aren't you?"

"Yes. No. It's a shock. No way would Alex kill himself, someone yes, but not himself."

"So, what's your theory, Phe?"

"He was pushed."

***

I'm about to roll out the team briefing.

"Just made it, result," says Andy slipping off his scarf and coat. His cheeks are red, not in a ruddy way but a rich blush. Listen to me, I'll be reading Jane Austen next.

Andy joins me at the front. I think pure thoughts, so my colour doesn't match Andy's.

"May I speak Ma'am?" he asks.

"Certainly. Tell us what you've got."

He holds up a disc.

"I've CCTV treasure of the platform where the lad allegedly fell or jumped."

"And?" I ask.

"There's a hand. Nothing more. No head. Or body. A hand among commuters packed like sardines on a platform. That hand is on the vic's shoulder, pushing him in front of the oncoming train."

***

In Shenley Park we discuss Alex for the best part of the night. We'd dragged Clive with us, as he's our source. It's scary, because deep down we know Alex didn't chose decapitation.

We hang on the swings and roundabout, sucking thick banana milkshake up a straw. It's comforting playing on the equipment as if it miraculously shields us from adulthood and responsibility. I want to turn back time so much it hurts. To be ten. Mum and Dad would put Wensley instead of horrid Hatfield, as my first choice of secondary school. We wouldn't be driving to Parents Evening that night. Or on the road when the drunk driver lost control of his car. My parents would be alive. We'd be completing my uni application together, in our house. I wouldn't be this abused, unloved, reject AND I wouldn't be living with HIM.

**

I watch and re-watch the footage. There's no doubt in my mind. We're looking at a second unlawful death. It seems absurd...two murdered teens in the space of six weeks.

**

When dark falls, we huddle on the horse. I've prime spot in the middle, so I get warmth from Luke's body and Pri's.

"How's Uncle Henry," asks Luke.

"A complete dick as usual."

If not for Priti and Luke, my heart would be crushed, my confidence splintered, and my identity transformed into dark energy drifting further and further into space. Together we have a laugh; it's like an interval at the theatre. I've drama before and after but for a short period of time I'm a kid again. If only Priti and Luke could meet Henry. Their impressions might help, but it's pointless asking if my friends can visit when he barely tolerates me.

CATTY CONFRONTATION

In Ruislip High Street I browse the charity shops for thick blankets; who knows when a bed will materialise. Outside the shop, with my hands full, I hear her whiny, corrosive voice.

"Oh, my God, look who it fucking is."

I'm face to face with Angela Wilson, Kirsten's bff and my mtt: most tenacious tormentor. I think it's tempting fate, calling a child a name, with angel embedded in it.

"It's Phoenix, the attention whore, who's so lame her parents died on fucking purpose. Then her aunt croaked."

Angela stands, hand on hip, in high-waisted jeans, an echo hoe either side. Clones: all blond, pouty and skinny with big boobs and dirty mouths. A limited edition: Mean Barbie.

Angela stares at my shopping.

My heart pounds, but the thunder of it fails to evoke a killer me. I'm so fucking weak.

"Look girls, she has her own label; NSPCC: **N**o **S**hit **P**hoenix is a **C**harity **C**unt."

Laughing ensues. I'm hilarious, me.

My eyeballs dry up with contempt. She's covered in fake tan thicker than marzipan. I wonder if I pull her hair will extensions come away. I do nothing.

"You - are a spiteful, slutty slapper with thinly plucked eyebrows and jellyfish lips."

In a flash she shoves me hard with the flat of her hand, her full body weight behind it. I topple backwards; till I rebound off someone. Dropping my cushion, Angela kicks it aggressively onto the road. A car brakes, the driver honking aggressively. Running to the road, hand up in apology, I grab my cushion. Passers-by gasp in shock and disapproval. I'm overheated and breathless and my peripheral vision blurs.

"Stupid bitch," the driver shouts.

Is everyone on earth horrible?

People stop, stare, comment, film. No one helps

Angela feeds off my despair.

"Are you his bitch, Phoenix?"

My mouth, dry as a sandpit forms no words. I'm conscious of onlookers, distressed to be the centre of attention.

"Oh, I get it. You sleep rough; you're a real fucking tramp. What do you do for money? Oh, my God," she shrieks looking at her friends.

"Phoenix is a fucking prostitute."

Pedestrians bow their heads, walking steadily on, entering shops they have no intention of buying from.

"You're indescribably cruel. Now get the hell out of my way or my fist will find your fake fucking orange face."

She swishes her hair and takes a step nearer.

"When you least expect it, I'll fucking jack you, you welfare loser."

Angela and her sidekicks strut off. I remain. In pieces.

My pulse drills in my ears. I'm gulping mouthfuls of oxygen as cruelty threatens to smother me.

"You alright, love?"

In my personal space stands a dusty builder with a McDonalds bag.

I nod.

It's like he's pressed my reset button. I walk unconscious of direction. Instinct guides me to Wenzels. At the counter pre-crying shudders are imminent. I order a cinnamon swirl instead of a Belgian bun.

Perched on the bench outside, I put my mis-cake in my rucksack. Slowly, I consume my sausage, cheese and beans melt; scared I might choke, because my tongue feels thick and my airway narrow.

My eyes strain from the pressure of unshed tears; my dry eyeballs unable to rotate.

I fumble inside my pocket for Mum's crumpled flowery cotton handkerchief. *Tuck it in your sleeve honey,* she said as she'd leant over from the passenger seat pressing it into my outstretched hand. Once more, I stifle a sob. Blowing my nose, I squeeze my shoulders together trapping the internal tremors. *Tuck it in your sleeve honey*; the last words my mum said to me.

I refuse to cry. I'm not wasting tears on bitches.

I sip coffee, holding the polystyrene cup to my lips like a soother. My phone rings.

"Phe, what's up girlfriend?"

"Every...thing's up. It's...it's hor-ri-ble," I stutter trembling.

I stare at my hanky. *'Tuck it in your sleeve honey'*. I want to hear mum say it. I can't remember her tone, only that it was sing songy. On the brink of a full flood, I lock my free arm round myself to prevent an overspill of emotion into the general public's domain.

"It's ok, Phe, take a breath, then tell me everything, I mean everything."

"I c.collided with An.gel.a and she was so hor-rid. She scared me Priti, she threatened to...k.ill me. I know it's farfetched, but she said she'd." I take a moment as my jaw aches with tension. "J.jack me up. Oh, Priti, I'm exhausted, and everything is going wrong; it's like I'm on a runaway train."

"Listen, Phe, that girl's Paranormal Activity. She's the Evil Dead. Block her from your mind; school's nearly finished, and you'll be off to Birmingham, or somewhere amazing, and she'll be on remand."

"Henry hates me, Pri."

"No, he doesn't, Phe."

"He does! He's scary Pri. I don't know if I can go back."

"Of course, you can, hon. He can't be worse than Cow."

"He is!" I gulp another tear.

"Phe, your emotions are all over the place, what with Trish dying and finding out you've an uncle. Forget Angela and don't take everything Henry says or does to heart."

"You're right, it's been an emotional time."

I smile weakly. Priti is skilled in hostage negotiation and calming.

"Henry's gay," I add trying to lighten my mood.

"How so?"

"He labels his food."

"He might have special dietary requirements."

"He's got candles in the bathroom."

"He likes to relax."

"He's got coasters."

"No."

"Yeah."

"Phe, I've gotta go; family are here. We're off to Venue 5 for Mum's birthday, but text me updates."

"Have fun, bitch."

"Phe, I'll hit you later, k?"

"Don't worry, Pri, I'm all good, promise."

On the bench, I sip coffee. My breathing slows and my eyes no longer feel like stress balls. Priti is the best. She's incredible at talking me down from a melt.

***

Gay? Her voice: a mixture of cracked words and fractured sighs, is evidence she's struggling.

87

***

I watch. Sometimes I spend hours watching. I'm a patient man. The girl is with her gang. A collection of mass-produced wannabe bitches: dyed hair, acrylic nails, collagen lips and foul mouths – their only ambition to sucker a footballer into marriage and be on reality tv. Give me time and they'll be headlining.

They sway along, breasts jutting out, skirts short, a flash of buttock only a gust away. They barge through parents holding children's hands, butt the elderly aside, block mobility scooters. It's all about them and how they look as they walk, like they're being filmed.

I watch them perform in the park. Popping pills, downing alcohol, smashing bottles, berating anyone who crosses their path.

I sit behind them in the burger bar. They bitch, glaring at every female, pouting at every male. They viciously dismantle the waitress; she's tearful. I smile reassuringly as she passes and leave a good tip, she smiles cutely, but I'm spoken for.

They abuse as they walk the length of the road, letting a stink bomb off in KFC. Double backing, they drop lit matches into rubbish bins.

The police come cruising. The little shits disperse in the darkness. I follow the most vicious; towards the park. My brain runs through the logistics: it's dark, the park is empty, I've duct tape, electrical ties, a hammer in my satchel. I like to think I'm fun; spontaneous; skilled at improvisation.

And so, it begins again; the line I walk for love. I wolf whistle.

She turns.

I whistle again

She laughs, waiting and I jog up, smiling.

"Hey." My voice is smooth, calm, practiced. My looks draw her in. Someone as gorgeous as me couldn't be dangerous.

She smiles, hand on hip. She's confident, I like what I see.

I get out a splif. She takes it. I strike a match, and as she leans in, the smell of sulphur lingers between us. She takes a long drag. She licks her lips. She's acting out a series of moves she studied in the mirror at great length.

"You got money?" she smiles. I want to slice the smile off her face.

She leans closer and touches my crotch. Un-fucking believable! This isn't some worked street corner. She blows in my ear followed by the word job. Playful. Wonder if she'll enjoy the games I play.

"Give you a helping hand for £30," she barters.

Business acumen, I like it.

"I'm worth it," she smiles rubbing her hand over my jeans. Jesus! Who pays for something they can do better themselves! I take the cigarette from her mouth and extinguish it on my skin. A small murmur of unease escapes her lips. I pull her against me and kiss her roughly. She tastes of fag ash.

"How much to go all the way?" I ask.

"Hand therapy only," she says a tinge of anxiety edging her words.

"Hypothetically: sorry do you know what hypothetically means?"

She stiffens.

"Yeah, I'm not an idiot."

"How much for a screw? How much are you worth."

This is my favourite part. The moment they know. When their brain registers danger.

"I need to get home," she declares pretending she has control over our situation. The shakiness in her voice, the slight breathlessness accompanying fear has my cock painfully pressing against my jeans zip.

I pull her back, kiss her softly and for a moment her fear is neutralised...until I bite her lip and taste her blood.

"Ow, you freak, that fucking hurt!"

She attempts to step back, but I have a tight hold.

"Really? Ok, won't do it again. Promise," I whisper. Only to add, "You taste fuckin sour!"

SLAP!

She cowers on the grass whimpering; no attempt to run, no fight in her, but that's bullies for you.

***

It's gone six am. After pulling an all-nighter I've hit a wall. Drinking coffee and eating my Sub, I take a break by running through a missing person just passed on. I pause at the file of Kathy Aldridge, seventeen, reported missing by parents at two a.m. Four hours already passed and the first twenty-four are crucial. In her school photograph she looks pretty and young. No angel though, she's known for minor offences. Missing persons only become my baby if significant evidence points to abduction or murder. Those upstairs have decided this is such a case. They want it explored promptly, due to the Bradley case. I cut and paste her details into a new file. I hate to be pessimistic, but this girl feels dead already.

***

Eight-thirty, ten minutes before bell. Pri and I are strategically placed near enough to see Kirsten, but far away enough to belt it.

"What's Kirsten fake crying for now?" I ask.

"Alex was on the news, didn't you see?"

"Pri, I haven't a telly."

"With all what's going on, you don't need one. You were right Phe; Alex was pushed. 'Unlawful death', they said on the News."

We momentarily watch Kirsten and her crew; they are savage; teachers know to stay well clear of the courtyard during movement breaks.

"Pri, can you see Angela?"

"No. Bunking probably."

My relief unclenches the muscles tightly strangling all 5 ft 7 of me. I tilt my head towards the sun, needing solar power.

"Jesus Pri, being afraid, worrying about what may happen is exhausting, I want school over. Forever."

"It is for Alex," says Priti solemnly.

We catch sight of our Adonis leaving the staff room. Mr Jacobs strides as good as Darcy, his satchel on his shoulder, handouts under his arm. We fall in line a few feet behind him.

"Phe, Mr Jacobs has theee best arse."

"Priti! Whisper," I whisper, knowing she's trying to lighten the mood. Who needs fake friends when I have Priti.

"Sorry. It keeps popping into my head," she whispers. "It's a real bummer."

"Oh my God Priti, your jokes are getting worse."

Walking up the stairs behind him, we are given a real treat.

"I reckon I could pull Mr Jacob's arse out of a line up," I say.

Priti giggles.

"Would the arse be vertical or bent over?" she sniggers.

In class we sit at the front; it's safer. Mr Jacobs welcomes everyone; it just so happens he's looking at Priti and me and the fifteen kids on our side of the room. His shining eyes match his shining hair; the fringe falls forward and he casually sweeps it back. He is beyond gorgeous. Love Island material – easily. Priti nudges me and giggles. Pushing my shoulders back, I sit up straight, ready to learn.

"Phe," Priti whispers raising her textbook to cover her mouth, "Bet you wouldn't mind extra curricula activities. Huh?"

I roll my eyes, but Pri's right, his uni should never have let him graduate; he is way too lush to teach.

Compelled to watch, sitting enthralled, Mr Jacobs rests on the front of his desk smiling and gesturing. I listen intently, make notes and think filthy thoughts.

As the lunch bell rings, kids bung stuff into bags and tear from the room towards the canteen. Mr Jacobs wanders over.

"Was that helpful?"

We nod in unison, bright smiles fixed on flushed faces.

"Yes, we wrote your points down, didn't we Priti?"

Priti is struck dumb.

"She's still in the zone," I say nudging her.

"Girls, head off and feed your brains."

My eyes linger, barely a second, but I know he notices.

Priti links my arm as we head towards food.

"Oh, my samosa! Still in the zone!" Priti repeats mortified as we queue for lunch.

"It just came out. I had to say something. You'd gone goggly-eyed at him."

"Maybe he's married. A girlfriend at least."

"Yep, he's the epitome of smouldering."

"Phoenix! Epitome! We have a chilli-hot teacher and you're extending your vocabulary. Get real! I've got Economics next. I'll replace The Chancellor of the Exchequer with Mr Jacobs. Maybe that'll help my understanding of the budget."

In between mouthfuls of lunch Priti smiles away to herself.

"What is it? Go on. I know you're thinking dirty."

"Chancellor of the Sexchequer," she squeals her shoulders convulsing with laughter. I join in, we are silly together, we can't help it. We know it's uncool.

I chew, I swallow; Priti spots trouble.

"Don't look up," Priti whispers. "Kirsten's mounted her broom. Bugger she's landed behind you."

My body tenses and my head shrinks into my shoulders.

"Can you smell something?" Kirsten asks before she's even dismounted.

"Yeah," they all respond.

"It's stale curry."

"Yeah, it's stinking curry," Jade repeats.

Jade is Kirsten's echo; she doesn't have the brain power for original thought. She's the muscle. I've the bruises to prove it.

Priti and me, our eyes lock, we know this'll end badly.

"Yeah, it smells of charity shop, too," Kirsten goads.

"An Indian charity shop," Amy sniggers and they all laugh.

"Fuck! It makes sense; it's charity case and her fugly frAsian," Kirsten spits loudly and students at other tables snigger. We are suddenly dwarf pygmy gobies in a goldfish bowl.

"Let's go, Phe."

We rise. Attempting to pass their table, Kirsten stands, blocking us.

"I hate you both. You smell of curry," she bitchily points at Priti. "You smell of charity."

She's so close I see the thin blue veined lines of her eyelids. I could slap her till her teeth fell out, but I'm scared. As usual, teachers are scarce. The dinner ladies scuttle, their backs turned, pretending to be busy.

"Owwwh."

My hand shoots to my temple. A two pence is on the floor.

"Hey, FrAsian."

"Ahh," Priti yelps.

My whole body collides with Kirsten's as I ram her to the ground. She hits it hard. Good! She is a freaking monster. Instantly I'm dragged off. Jade has me in a headlock, while I'm punched punishingly in the face by a laughing Amy. I stagger around, unaware of the Deputy Head.

"You! Outside the Head's office," he bellows at Kirsten as spectators quickly disperse. "You!" That's me. "My office now!"

I look to Priti; she's pale and shaking. Behind her, Mr Jacobs. He lays a reassuring hand on Priti's arm. I'm glad he's there for her, but I hate he saw me like this. The angry me. The me, full of hate.

Outside Mr Grady's office, I write my account and sign it. Mrs Crosby's evil eye settles on me. I don't look away; I'm not ashamed of standing up for myself. This school, and everyone in it, totally sucks! I remember how excited I was to start secondary school. I'd felt so grown up. Mum had sewn the school badge wonky on my blazer, which was way too big. *You'll grow into it, honey, and, if it's nippy, there's room for a cardy.* I still wear that blazer. I can't bear to replace it. It rested on mum's lap, her fingers holding the badge steady as she sewed; us laughing. I can't remember what was funny. I hate that my recollection of her is disintegrating, like the loo paper Henry stuffed in my wash. What happened to our things? In our home? Cow refuses to say. Jesus; it's my stuff, my memories, they were my parents!

What would they think of this? Of me? Dad loved quoting national statistics, how newspapers revealed: 1 in 4 people will commit violent crime, 1 in 3 will mug, 1 in 5 rape. In my form alone, there are hypothetically ten muggers, six rapists, three paedophiles and a murderer so I should be prepared for nasty things to come. I mean, these criminals don't just happen overnight; school is their training ground.

My head jerks upward. Henry! I try to make eye contact to relay a message of 'sorry' but he looks through me; he is incredibly unreachable. Wearing baggy, soft green cords, a homely jumper and glasses? He looks chillingly cosy, but I know he's pissed! He strides past and into the Deputy Head's office.

I catch Mrs Crosby eyeing him up appreciatively as he passes – cougar!

***

She's black-eyed like a panda, half child, half woman, all trouble. The dick head, I mean deputy head, wants her suspended for a week. I insist on viewing the CCTV footage. He denies access, I threaten, we watch. Care Girl is clearly the victim. I mention pressing charges and seeking compensation from the school for not providing a safe environment for my niece. He agrees Care Girl can return tomorrow.

***

Henry slightly inclines his head indicating we're leaving. I trail behind like a naughty child. As we walk across the playground, I see faces pressed to glass scrutinising us. I like that Henry attracts attention and that he's with me, well, sort of.

"You're going the wrong way," says Henry sharply.

"My car's this way?"

"Pick it up tomorrow."

"Am I suspended?"

"No."

Crap. My life's on a loop: sleep, school, abuse, repeat.

I sit uncomfortably in Henry's deluxe BMW. It's slick, black and gleaming. I can't help but be impressed.

I close my eyes; the left lid is swollen, heavy and aching. I wonder what went down in Mr Buckland's office, but Henry is his usual uncommunicative self.

"I'm sorry. Things escalated. I didn't deal with it well. Kirsten brings out the worst in me; she should be charged with incitement, racism and GBH; she's a criminal. Henry, please say something."

The pause stretches long enough to grasp he won't answer.

"Oh my God! Henry why won't you speak? This is ridiculous! The school shouldn't have called you. I'm eighteen. Did you come out of a sense of duty? That 'never leave a man behind' stuff. Is that even a Navy motto? Or army? Hollywood?"

"Could you NOT talk," Henry asks.

"Jesus don't O.D. on sympathy."

"The objective was to prevent your suspension."

"Super-lucky me. Didn't it occur to you I might want to be suspended? Huh?"

Conversation has peaked. It's like I don't exist - Phoenix, a mythical creature.

We arrive home. I run to keep up with his long strides. He opens the door, gesturing for me to precede. It's comical; Henry thwarts me at every opportunity, yet when it comes to manners, Henry is always the gentleman. Deflated, I walk dejectedly upstairs; my feet heavy, my knees stiff.

My room: no table, no chair, no bed, just a crappy sleeping bag and a crappy me. Henry has driven the nail into the coffin; he's confiscated my quilt, throw and pillow. My personal things remain. Dropping to the floor, I pick up my 'parents in a cardboard box', held together with a green elastic band. Inside: their marriage certificate, photographs; proof of life.

My history is fucking with my head. I phone Priti, but it goes to voicemail, so I phone Luke.

"Bubs, are you alright?"

"No. I've been in a fight."

"With Henry?"

"No...Kirsten...it was horrible."

"Fuck! Are you hurt?"

"A bit, mainly my eye. It's swollen."

"That's fuckin shit bubs. Fuck, I've gotta do some dumb shit presentation, Phe."

"I'm fine Luke, go bring it."

"Nah babes, I'll..."

"NO! You'll do your presentation; I'm not going anywhere."

I ring off. I'm the opposite of fine. My eyes smart like I've lemon tear fluid. Shakily, I drift to the bathroom. In the mirror my reflection transports me back to a time that haunts me. My foster dad drunkenly caught me with a plate above my eye; I'd needed stitches. I broke the rule; I'd told the nurse the truth, so I was punished; the cigarette burns hurt more than the stitches. I blink my twelve-year-old self away.

My face pulses with pain; it's badly swollen. The skin surrounding my eye is raised and bluish. My lip is split, and I've smeared blood from it across my cheek. I'm ugly. I am, I am, I am; I fucking am. God, I hate crying.

Henry's serious face reflects above mine. I seem to manifest Henry unconsciously. I close my eyes.

"You weren't bailing-me-out for me. It was for you. You can't bear me near you," I whisper.

I open my eyes. Henry's reflection remains. Even in my imagination he ignores me. I touch the glass as if this will banish him. His soulless eyes continue to penetrate my thick skin; searching for vulnerability. I turn to him, this phantom form making my life impossible. I reach out, expecting my hand to fall through him...but it doesn't, it feels hard muscle. I stare up at real Henry...I will him to hold me. I'm so sick of being lonely; I think I might die from it.

***

The bathroom door is wide open; she's a mess. An inclination to comfort her springs from nowhere. Marine down repeats in my head. True enough, school is a war, but she's not Alpha team. In the car she'd curated her attack. My hold on the steering wheel tightened as I replayed Care Girl launching herself at her provoker. She was wild, there was a beauty in it, a strength I'd miscalculated. She reaches tentatively out and touches me. There's two layers of cotton between us, yet I swear I feel her.

***

My school skirt, bloodied blouse and torn tights lay in a heap; ripped from my body like how I wanted to rip the heart out of Kirsten. Dragging my pjs on, I crawl into my unsleeping bag. Putting headphones on, I press play on my CD player. Listening to Isaac Gracie, Henry drifts around my mind. Different lyrics resonate and wrap around Henry, and his essence expands until he's too much to cope with. I hide in my sleep.

PRIVATE LESSONS

"Wake up."

My foot is being firmly kicked. I look at my mobile and groan at the time; this man is sadistic. Disorientated my eyes settle on Henry who looks annoyingly crisp. I wonder if I'll ever be worthy of a smile or a kind word, instead of Henry's impassive salutations and measured responses. I search his face watching for his features to soften, to reflect an inkling of empathy. I'd wait an eternity; Henry is completely unburdened by my troubles.

"Breakfast. We leave in thirty."

"Ten four," I say groggily.

Henry's expression bores into me; it could literally erode a person's features if they allowed it.

"Roger that," I add.

Henry's mouth thins. From nowhere this burst of warmth infuses my body and riling Henry is its trigger.

"Copy that Henry."

His face is cold stone.

"Code three, I repeat code three; Henry is unarmed, he has no sense of humour."

I'm laughing and Henry is staring almost interestedly. So, I have to keep chipping away, identifying weakness in his empathy-field.

I hold three fingers in the air and subtract.

"Getting up in three, two, one."

Henry walks away; he's good at that.

I pull the cushion over my face. Fuck school! Do I want to live today? No. Not especially. Looking down at my arm I pull up the sleeve to reveal the lines sliced there; though completely healed they act as a reminder of how unbearable my life was. Now's not the time to wallow in emotion. So, I thud downstairs in my onesie; it irritates Henry and I like being irksome and getting under his beautifully moisturised skin. There is something too perfect about him. Ok his uncle-ing skills are poor, but there is something else, something I can't put my finger on.

Henry's in-wait at the table. He doesn't acknowledge me. There's a second plate of sausage, egg and bacon.

"Thank you. That's kind."

I sit and eat The Last Supper. Without thinking, I cut my sausage into small slices and make a happy face from them. My sausage smiles at me. I smile back. I see Mum; her heart slips into my consciousness, then cruelly recedes. My parents' death is like a pulled thread; the pain of it continues to unravel.

The journey is silent. I pray for a flat tyre or a roadblock. Approaching the school gates, sheer dread grips, and in my head, I see Alex – his painted face, his devil horns, his broken body.

Henry parallel parks in two manoeuvres. I turn towards him to beg a stay of execution, but he's looking straight ahead. He wears distance like a panther wears black.

"Do you hate me? I can't tell."

He swiftly leans across me, so rapidly he steals the air from my lungs. Opens my door and I all but fall out.

Kids openly turn and stare; I hear whisperings and judgemental fingers point. Looking back to where Henry had parked, the space is filled by another car. Henry doesn't care, he is that callous.

Priti is waiting in my form. I note her hoppity walk as she approaches. I'm positive one of her legs is shorter than the other – an observation I'll not verbalise. We wrap arms around each other. Her body is warm and welcoming. The contact nearly pushes me over the edge; I never want to let Priti go...but one fact after another tumbles from Priti's mouth.

"Oh my God Phe, I was so worried you'd be expelled.

Kirsten's on a two-week suspension.

You look like you've been mugged.

Mr Grady phoned my dad.

I'm grounded.

Unbelievable!"

I don't want Priti to talk; just to hug. Anger, resentment, frustration bubble hotly like molten lava beneath my surface. If I don't calm down, I'll explode and cease to exist. I've internalised my emotions far too long. I imagine my body, stripped bare of skin: apprehension seeping into my arteries, anxiety constricting my lungs, grief catalysed by pain diffusing into my cells. I am sick, so sick, maybe I'll die.

"Phe, are you ok, you're scaring me, say something," Priti begs.

The form bell shakes me from my morbidity.

"I'm fine Pri. It's the painkiller. Gimme one more squeeze."

I love Priti so much. She's my sister.

"A double with Mr Jacobs next," she says enthusiastically. "See you in twenty," she shouts above the incoming group of rowdy students.

Otis ploughs through 13E form members, throws his thick head into my breathing space and straight away I see he's high.

"Die bitch!" he laughs. Two words of pure hatred and I'm shaking.

I turn to flee, but Frankie's coming in.

"Girl I missed you. Come here and talk on my reefer," he grins.

I give him the finger just as Mr Edwards appears.

"Phoenix it's that kind of communication that gets you into these scrapes. I'd like you to reflect on yesterday and accept responsibility. What do you have to say?"

Bollocks!

"Reflection? Good advice."

The teachers are guilty, too, of picking on the easy target. Where is the protection? It's a word printed on paper; in mission statements, welfare documents. Just a fucking word.

Clive catches my eye. Are you ok he mouths? I shrug. Sitting down I think of Henry; my conundrum. I'm grateful but confused by the neat pile I'd found at the end of my bed. My uniform: washed, pressed and folded neatly. I guess uniform is important to a marine. He'd even managed to wash blood stains out. He's probably an expert on blood. What awful atrocities had he seen? What had he done? Maybe Henry is sick too?

I sit on the edge of my seat, ready to leg it. The bell rings signifying the end of form. Kids file out of classes. Corridors buzz with the noise of students. Some drag feet, some check mobiles, others abuse. Amy barges into me; I fall into Shelly who aggressively shoves me off.

"Fuck off you freak show dyke!"

Amy sniggers like a mean hyena. I hate how kids thrust their faces into mine throwing evil comments and accusations at me like they have the right. Ironically, bullying posters are tacked the length of the wall.

Filtering from the crowd into English hope surfaces. Mr Jacobs looks up from his desk. I smile and he smiles encouragingly back.

"Quiz today, folks, no groans. Let's start with a game. I'll give you a line from a famous writer and you'll have to guess the book or poem. This will not be a hands-up exercise; when I say game, I mean fun. Everyone on my left is team one, everyone on my right team two, I'm giving each person on the left a letter that corresponds with their counterpart on the right. The game's in alphabetical order so the minute

Left A or Right A knows the answer they must run up to the white board and write the answer. Got it? Great let's go."

It's organised chaos; kids darting to the board, getting it wrong, right, being slow or being idiots. I'm next. I stare at Mr Jacobs' mouth; it's a great mouth.

"Some kill their love when they are young,"

I fly, toppling my chair. Frankie's foot pushes a bag into the aisle which I anticipate and jump over. Throwing myself at the whiteboard I scribble Oscar Wilde, The Ballard of Reading Gaol.

"Well done Phoenix," Mr Jacobs cheers patting my back as the bell rings.

"Priti, Phoenix may I have a moment please?"

I want to tell him he can have an hour, a day, possibly a night.

"I'd like you both to come for tutoring on Thursdays. We can work on personal statements, extension questions, mock interviews. It would be a Gifted and Talented class. What do you say?"

"That'd be amazing sir, thanks so much," I respond excitedly.

"I'd love to sir, but I study Mandarin on Thursdays."

The disappointment in Priti's eyes nearly makes me cry.

"That is a shame, can you change nights?"

She shakes her head miserably.

"Shame. It'll start Thursday at four. Don't let me delay you."

As we leave the classroom, Priti turns to me.

"I hate my parents right now…what good will Mandarin be unless I live in Japan or have a job where I work with Japanese."

"Maybe you'll fall in love with a Japanese Tom Hardy."

She raises her eyes.

"I'm sick with jealousy Phe, but I'm glad for you; it will be good, take your mind off Henry, give you somewhere to hang for an extra hour."

I hug her. It's a bummer, but my spirits lift, in fact they take off.

***

She barges in from school; flips her cheap pumps off her feet missing the shoe basket and leaves her frayed, dirty rucksack on the sofa. Now she's in the shower. I hear humming; her tone's cheerfulness is disturbing.

***

I slip into PJ's with little pigs on, new feels like a drug. I'd gone to Primark, Harrow for a new black school skirt; no way can I sit with Mr Jacobs in my three-year-old, rough nylon, crap. I added some cute Brazilians, matching lacy bra and a chemise. Part of me feels responsible for some of the shit I get. I could invest in a better uniform, but I'm saving every penny for uni, because that's where I see my life starting. Still, my skirt is one of those stretchy ones, I can wear it weekends too.

Henry is out. I take my banoffee tart, from Patisserie Brione, from the fridge; it is worth every penny. I make a cappuccino with Henry's coffee maker, settle in front of Netflix and binge watch Sex Education. Life's not so bad, I smile; my black eye hardly hurts...unless I blink!

The evening turns into night. The night turns into a fitful sleep.

At breakfast he rises to leave as I enter the kitchen.

"Why do you leave the room when I walk in?"

It's fucking painful, yet he doesn't raise a hand. I want to tell him about the fear creeping under my skin like itchy pollen, but he wouldn't understand. I guess in relation to the Taliban it's insignificant. None of it matters, he's already gone.

So, I drive to school. Reply 'here' to the register. Struggle in Physics. Excel in Maths. Dwell on Henry.

Walking from the Maths department, I stumble into a disturbance. Instead of lessons, students are shooed into the hall. I hate sodding assembly: sitting cross-legged on a dusty floor like an infant while the teachers lord it over us on chairs.

Mr Jacobs smiles in my direction; I blush. As I smile back, I wonder how grumpy my previous expression was.

I watch as Miss Stewart attempts to make conversation with him, she touches his elbow and leans into him, but Mr Jacobs is distracted. I don't blame Miss Stewart; there's no denying Mr Jacobs is hot. It's odd that I don't think about him outside school. Shouldn't I spend hours mooning over him? Isn't a crush more passionate when it's forbidden? Shouldn't I be all atremble when we are alone?

The hall is brought to a quiet hum as teachers hush students. Complete silence falls when a petite, shapely figure in a Navy trouser suit takes the stage. Frankie wolf whistles. I presume this sudden assembly is about Alex. So far, conversations about Alex are promptly cut short by teachers. I think his body's still in the morgue.

"Good morning. I'm Detective Inspector Daniels of The Metropolitan Police Force; I'm part of Hillingdon's Major Incident Team."

Around me I see admiration, bitchiness, sexual attraction; Frankie James is stroking his groin area – yuk!

"I'm sure you're aware that a young man, Bradley Perkins, was violently attacked near the River Pinn and died from his injuries."

This woman has everyone's attention. Bodies straighten. Heads rise. Necks extend. Violence is a subject that fascinates everyone.

"And you've recently lost a student, Alex Derby, in tragic circumstances, so I'm sorry to be the bearer of further bad news. Angela Wilson, a sixth former at this school, is officially missing."

What. The. Fuck!

Oohs and aahs reverberate around assembly. Upsetting? It's the best news I've heard in fucking years!

"If you've had contact with Angela in the last 48 hours, please see me. If you've spotted anyone behaving strangely, or vehicles that stood out see Sergeant Brady or Detective Constable Atkins. The smallest thing could be relevant to our enquiries, so don't think you're being silly. Now are there any questions?"

A rumble of voices vibrates around the hall.

"Hands up if you have a question; yes, you, third row, fourth person in."

"Is there a serial killer in Ruislip?"

"No."

"How do you know?" asks Zac.

"Presently, we have an absent teenager."

"Was Bradley bummed?" a voice from nowhere asks.

D.I. Daniels ignores and continues

"Avoid isolated areas and routes. Ensure your phone is charged and with you. Also make sure your whereabouts are known."

A pause.

"Thank you."

Teachers hastily move pupils on. Only those needing to speak to the police remain. I decide against telling the police about Angela's threat; it's irrelevant. Ok, I dislike the girl massively. I've fantasised numerous ways to hurt her and now she's missing. I'd never imagined a third party killing her for me. If she dies, will I go to her funeral and make false commiserations. Or will I tell her parents their daughter was a total bitch who made my life misery? My head is all over the place. What about Alex? First Bradley, then Alex, now Angela? I'd be lying if I said it doesn't strike me as unusual. What had they in common other than a shared viciousness and being tacky? They attended different schools, had different friends. Did Luke know Angela? I'd told him what a dick Alex was. And where did Henry go last night? My phone had read one twenty; where would he go, what would he do? I skip the last lesson. I go home. The man himself is bringing in the shopping.

"You!"

"My name is Phoenix, try saying it Pho.e.nix; perhaps it's too phonetically challenging for you?" I shout over my shoulder. He follows me in. The atmosphere is as strong as bleach.

"Has there been another incident?" he asks sharply, running his eyes over me.

The knots in my stomach tighten painfully.

"Why? You don't care," my voice warbles. "If I went missing, you'd be relieved. You wouldn't even report it. Why don't you admit what we both know?"

He says it.

"I don't want you here."

A weighty silence falls as the truth bleeds into my heart. It's what I wanted, what I'd asked for, demanded actually. Why am I such a dick! Why is he so fucking brutal?

"Fine then. Well that's just perfect. Honesty is complete shit!"

Feeling worthless I take the offensive. I step right into him; we nearly touch.

"Something is wrong with you? You're empty and flat and dark." I continue overriding red alert. "It's like you're dead."

I should push my abort button; instead I push his chest with the flat of my hand.

"Or sick."

I push his chest harder.

"You're the biggest..."

And harder.

"Disappointment."

Harder.

"Ever!"

***

"Enough." I draw back. The last thing I want is her touching me. She glares, her lip trembling, her sharp, fiery eyes floating in watery pools. She wavers on the edge of hysteria. Yet she advances

"Enough. Phoenix! My fucking name is Phoenix!" she cries.

I know I'm supposed to do something: give her verbal reassurances, hug her, but I can't, I'm not a liar or a comforter.

She drops to her default position; arms crossed and legs ready to bolt. Her eyes are especially bright.

"Don't. Cry."

"I'm not going to fucking cry," she denies as a single tear rolls out. "Why won't you say my name?" she asks; her tone low and subdued. "What is it about me you don't like?"

Her eyes almost beg for reassurance.

"If you tell me I can change."

"We're done."

***

My Mum used to practice my times tables with me on the way to school. Square numbers were her favourite. She told me I was special, that there was no one like me in the world, and I should never let anyone make me feel bad about myself. I lay down closing my eyes. Eight times eight is sixty-four, five times five is twenty-five, nine times nine is eighty-one.

***

It's late but the Wilson's will be up - sleep eludes frantic parents. I park in front of Tesco's in Ruislip Manor. Beside the supermarket is the dark entrance to an enclosed stone stairway, leading to the flats above the shops. I walk along the shared balcony and knock on their door. What do you say to parents whose daughter is missing? You avoid raising hope because your head is screaming, she's already dead.

ENEMY

Seven thirty am. The flood of bright autumn light flowing from my un-curtained window makes it impossible to snooze back to sleep. That and I'm smarting from my melt yesterday. Still mortified, I bury my head in my pillow. I am such a fucking loser; I really am, and Henry is ruthless.

I drag my lethargic body up. The house is so still it makes every sound unnervingly loud. I inch towards the door, barely breathing so not to rouse Crouching Tiger. I tiptoe from the room and my head jolts as if rejecting the image ahead. Henry, virtually bloody naked, strolling out of the bathroom with the smallest black towel hung around his waist, barely covering his, his...Is that even a towel? I've seen larger facewipes. Oh, my, God. Repeat to oneself I am a modern woman. But I'm not. Sure, I've seen a naked man before on Naked Attraction, but this is way too up close! Henry's like a Viking or a gladiator or Patrick Bateman! I take root, losing all rational thought. Eyes lock on his chest, I daren't look above or below; he stops in front of me. His gleaming wet upper chest and arms are tattooed with intricate designs, all black, covering a series of deep scars. It's as if he's been torn up then sewn together. Inexplicably, the thought of Henry wounded troubles me. He seems indestructible; I can't imagine him threatened or vulnerable. I inwardly shudder.

***

She's drowsy; her face all soft creases of sleep. Today, I'll try a little physical duress. Her sleeping pattern is poor, periorbital darkness circles her eyes, today could break her.

"We're going for a walk."

***

His emotional distance snaps me out of my trance. No good morning, or discussion, he is blunt bordering on rude. It seems we've reverted to our military-like relationship: me the recruit, Henry the drill sergeant from hell. Maybe this is his idea of an apology? A glimmer of hope has me pulling on my trainers.

He presents a commanding figure standing by his car. The passenger door is open. Am I frightened? Terrified. He is unnervingly motionless. I brush past him, into my seat, not realising I've temporarily stopped breathing. He settles in the driving seat, turns the key in the ignition before rotating towards me. I cower; I can't help it.

"Seatbelt," he orders, his tone terse as his jaw clenches.

Immediately, I twist, attempting to pull the belt, but all fingers and thumbs, I clumsily yank it. Fuck it's locked.

He leans over me; I turn in alarm bringing us closer.

***

Her 'don't touch me' eyes relay her history. I pull the belt across her engaging it. She smells like me. Care Girl obviously enjoys my bath products. It's peculiar, her in my car, making indentations in the pristine passenger seat, leaving evidence of her presence. It is essential my life remain unaffected by hers. She's wrong-footed me; it's her transparency; it makes me tense. I don't want to breathe in her dread or observe her anxiety. Like now; she sits as far from me as the car permits; self-conscious and nervous, yet an aura of hope emanates from her. She murmurs along to David Bryne's Psycho Killer. She isn't a Phoenix, she's a Hummingbird.

***

Angela Wilson was abducted. I've no evidence, but my gut knows it. We've two dead teens and one missing. That's not coincidence, that is a spree.

***

I drive towards a wood with steep hills, slopes and rough terrain. What had begun as a bright day is now grey and damp. It won't be long before the forecasted heavy rainfall. Perfect for the sickener I've planned.

"It's remote," she observes.

I remain silent.

"I'm not very outdoorsy, but it's exciting trying new things. Thanks for bringing me."

Outdoorsy? Her thanks will be short-lived. She's sadly bewildered. She has a mouth longing to smile, I have an idea it will break into one at the slightest kindness or invitation of friendship, yet in an hour or two she'll hate me.

***

I fucking hate him. My heels burn from erupting blisters. I've a stitch in my side, like Kirsten's jabbing my effigy with a pin. Gasping; my chest burns from exertion. I want to beg him to stop, but I don't, even though salty sweat runs down my forehead, stinging my eyes. I'm covered in the crap. I hate sweating. I'd rather have frost bite than sweat. Breathing hurts; my throat's like sandpaper from inhaling cold air. I am in real, genuine, authentic pain - where are endorphins when you fucking need them?

***

Andy is busy on the train fatality. Tom is reviewing the Bradley case. I'm enroute to the Wilson property.

***

I try to enjoy the scenery; I really do, but it's tree, after tree, after shitty tree. On the verge of cracking, the sky opens, and rain falls hard. Releasing a deep breath; I tilt my face towards the ominous clouds, my mouth opens, inviting heavy droplets to hydrate me. A hundred metres later, comfort converts to despair as torrential rain soaks me and hail painfully pelts my face. Henry is barely visible.

"Henry, slow down."

Slipping and sliding on mud, my worn trainers are useless against the fluid earth. I can't keep up and the gap between Henry and I steadily increases.

"Henrrry."

Desperate not to lose sight of him, I throw myself forward. I'm tripping over rocks, I'm catching feet in tree roots, but worse I leap forward, miss my footing and fall hard to my knees.

"Shit!"

As mud seeps into my trackies, I feel the muscle around my knee swelling. Staggering, I stand, my eyes darting everywhere?

"Henry."

The rain is like a curtain between us.

"Hen-ry."

Panic wells up inside

"Hen-ryyyyyyyy."

The man I hate, I'm now desperate for.

"Hen-ryyyyyyyy," I catch my breath. "Where are youuuuuuu?"

***

I scan Angela's room; a keeper of secrets; every teen has them. I hate the invasion of privacy but I'm here to dissect every aspect of this victim's life. Her walls are covered with eye candy. Her bed unmade. The carpet strewn with clothes and, on her desk, a collection of vodka bottles. I'm amazed how teenagers understand technology but can't hang clothes or use bins.

Her drawers are filled with makeup, hair straighteners, fake tan; the usual stuff.

"Obviously not a nerd," says a CSI.

"Nope. Final year and not a textbook in sight."

"Guys bag up the tech first and get it to the lab. Be meticulous; I don't want any corrupted evidence."

***

Probably only minutes pass but they're the longest minutes on record.

Rain drips from every edge and curve of me. No longer running, I quiver from cold as my sweat turns to ice. I wrap my arms around myself tightly and peer hard through the trees, but the rain distorts everything.

***

I lift carpet, pull out furniture, shake pillows, upturn handbags.

"Got ecstasy here, boss," says the CSI.

I examine the pills: insufficient quantity for dealing; just.

"I've got her diary," I inform.

I seal it carefully in a labelled evidence bag. Downstairs the police liaison officer explains procedures to the parents. Their lives could change irreversibly; some monster might make them redundant, no longer parents, never to be grandparents.

If we find a link to Bradley or Alex, it'll confirm a serial killer. A shudder runs through me. Keeping calm, thinking logically and not emotionally is essential. Still, I take a minute for myself to absorb the fact that two young men are dead. Then I continue invading a missing girl's teen life.

***

Stay put or move? I don't bloody know. I stretch my stiff fingers; my knuckles are white from cold. I see a crow; the companion of witches. I spin around searching agitatedly for Henry but see only grey trees in a bleak wood. Shit, a magpie; vultures will circle next. Another icy shiver ripples through me. I listen; hearing only the moan of the wind and the rain splattering hard on the ground...until a branch snaps. An anxious fear rises from my toes to my teeth which are nervously grinding together. There could be boars or wolves. Do wolves roam wild in England? No, idiot.

SNAP.

Don't go anywhere isolated, the detective said.

CRACK.

Someone is there, in front of me.

"You think you're so clever, Henry, but I saw you."

Silence.

"I thought marines were meant to be elite."

Silence.

"Henry! You're not funny."

Silence.

"You're bloody immature."

SNAP.

"I'm not scared."

I'm fucking shitting bricks.

"Henry, stop being a dick. I want to go home."

What if it's not Henry?

My whole abdomen twists with dread.

SNAP.

Oh God. Turn around and walk Phoenix. Don't. Panic. It's a fox, yes definitely foxy. My breathing is shallow, my heart thumps in my chest and despite the wrenching pain in my gut, I move. Urgently, but carefully. One foot in front of the other, my mind endeavouring to disregard what my eye had seen. Phoenix! Be mature. Stay calm.

CRUNCH.

I bolt, mindless of direction, dodging trees, scattering leaves. My heart pumps violently, injecting panic through me as I plunge further into the wood. The trees get denser, the light dimmer, my fear so fucking much firmer. Whilst briars catch me with sharp claws, snagging my top, tearing the cloth as I yank free. My body weight jerks forward, and I skate haphazardly across wet leaves, my upper body undulating to maintain balance. Boot thuds! Heavy! Near! Catching up! My lungs are on fire, but overwhelming panic fuels me.

"Ahhhhh."

My shoulder's grasped; I stagger backward. My arms and legs jerk erratically as I twist my body painfully away. Slipping out of its grasp, I barely put a foot forward when I'm brought down...hard enough to wind. The pain in my chest is staggering, but still I kick out until unseen hands restrain my feet. Panic froths over. Manically, I'm threshing and twisting, but substantial weight pins me down, forcing my face into the wet, cold mud. I'm inhaling dirt water, it's filling my airways, I'm choking on it.

"Stop struggling."

The voice is hard. Cold. Void of emotion. He's speaks in letters put together, delivered with abruptness and impatience. I cease grappling with the undergrowth. My energy depleted, my will sapped, I lay face down, eating dirt, sobbing.

Henry's weight eases off.

I cover my head with my arms, but there's no hiding my misery. I want to sink into the dirt, to burn up in the earth's core, to stop feeling this fucking shit.

"Get up."

I continue to sob. It's simply too much to cope with. An eternity of suffering runs from my eyes into the mud. My parents are dead. It's permanent. I want to dig them out of their graves and breathe life into them but it's futile. They are gone.

I am oblivious to Henry until tears no longer flow, until my hands no longer grasp at the ground and my feet stop kicking holes in the soil. I was a wild thing in a wild place and Henry saw. I turn my muddied face sideways, so he can hear my words.

"Why are you doing this to me?"

Exhausted, disorientated, covered in slush I attempt to rise. Henry's hand encircles my upper arm, but I wrench free.

"Don't. You. Touch. Me." I scream, slipping in the sludge, landing hard on my arse. My anger plus embarrassment equals a burning hatred for him. I struggle to stand in the ooze; I'd rather go to school than accept his assistance. He doesn't intervene until I slip again; hoisting me out of the mud, kicking and screaming.

On firm ground I glower up at him furiously.

"You're crazy. Completely mad. A nut job. A lune. No wonder Dad never talked about you. I wanted us to be best friends but right now I. Absolutely. Hate. You!"

"Keep up," he orders, turning in a direction to run as I stumble straight over a stone, landing flat at his feet. He sighs impatiently as he yanks me up and I push him off. I don't want to follow him; he's detestable, but I can't get out of this dark and thorny nightmare alone. Scared of being abandoned, I follow. I will him to turn and say, '*sorry Phoenix, let's start afresh,*' but his back is not for turning. We've barely jogged minutes when I stop. My tongue treacherously mouths.

"Henry."

He breathes out irritation. His body language reflects his opinion of me – I'm a burden he's been saddled with. Well, sod you! Henry! Whittle!

I ignore Henry's sharp stare. He wants me weak and broken; I know that; I won't give him the satisfaction. I nod to him and we continue. Like gusts of wind we blow angrily between the trees and across the woods. I haven't felt this wretched since my parents' death. I don't understand why Henry, his words and actions, have this huge impact on my emotions. I hate him, but I don't.

Eventually, the car appears in the clearing. I no longer hurt; I'm anaesthetised by Henry's bitterly cold detachment. The boot clicks open. Henry pulls his t-shirt off. As he stretches, his muscles ripple tightly. I see black armpit hair. His track bottoms are covered in mud from wrestling me to the ground. He drops them; my eyes shoot upward.

"The same," he orders steely eyed as he holds open a black bag; wearing only Calvin Klein's. The muscle slut! What is it about this man and getting his kit off? Yeah, your body is amazing, but your personality is shit.

He walks towards the driver's door. I satisfyingly give him 'the finger'.

"I saw that."

Furious, I sit in the passenger seat, in underwear stained from seeping mud. Every part of me feels his presence down to the cells in my blood burning with animosity. His enormity fills my head, he is everything: devious, calculated, inscrutable, super clever and dangerous. Yeah, he'd been a marine, but there is something else, something almost sinister.

He turns the radio on. A Years and Years track plays, but it can't comfort me; the damage is done. I'm spiralling into that place in my head where I don't value myself, where I blame me for the crap that comes my way.

I covertly look sideways. He sits so straight, so still, his body rock hard, his mind - fuck knows what goes on up there. Whatever his agenda, I know one thing for certain...I sit next to the enemy.

***

She exits the vehicle and leans her head in the window.

"I'm having a shower. If you think this stunt gets you out of Christmas, you don't know who you're dealing with. We are family and we are doing this!

***

Indoors, in the shower, resentment burns in my head short circuiting my emotional cut-off. I simply can't get over this morning. I think maybe my hate will wash off and swirl down the plug hole along with the mud, but it's deep like the dirt beneath my fingernails. Henry is a total bitch and I so badly want to slap that condescending smirk off his face. I'm angry and aggressive and Henry is to blame but, the cruel thing is, he's my Dad's brother and I nearly love him just for that. Except now, I'm questioning what sort of family my Dad came from.

***

My conscience was silent until today. She's a damaged young woman, dealing with bereavement and a pack of bitches systematically abusing her. It needs to end. It's cruel.

***

I hand round a box of Mars bars and Monsters as the team come together around the incident board.

"I know we're stretched to our limits. We have three incidents which may or may not be linked, but we don't want to miss any red flags. Each of the victims were known to us for petty offences, all local kids, attending local schools: Bradley dead, blunt force trauma; Alex dead, collision with train and Angela, missing. Andy, tell us what you know about Alex Derby."

Andy sits on the edge of the desk nearest the front. I think I'm adjusting to having him in my line of sight.

"An unpleasant lad, neighbours say he was more than a handful. Drunken fights, intimidation, minor drug deals, the usual anti-social behaviour. Your girl?"

"Her diary is revealing. We know where she scored her drugs, who she'd had sex with, how many victims she'd terrorised; they are unnamed; she used initials; one stands out – P."

The static in the room is palpable. No one wants to be the first to roll the words out.

"I can't stress how crucial it is that every line of enquiry is followed up on. Three majors, all teens, within the space of a few months, has everyone speculating about a serial killer. Should that become fact, we will be under the tightest scrutiny, not just professionally but personally. So, think clever. No pubs local to the station. No gambling. No hot affairs. No on your phones driving. We need to be cleaner than clean. Do not make me come down on you, because I will, and you'll hate me for it. Right now, I'm grabbing a few hours. Sergeant," I say looking at Andy. "I've set an alarm for four hours, but if anything new comes through wake me."

I close my office door, slip my shoes off, lay on the camp bed and fall hard into nothingness.

"Ma'am."

I hear a distant voice, a shake on my shoulder, a whiff of aftershave.

"Kate!"

I jerk up, confused, my office, Andy, shit! I check my watch; I've slept less than an hour.

"Ma'am. We've a female body."

"Where?" I ask groggily.

"Ruislip Woods, Kings College."

"Angela?"

"Affirmative."

"Shit!"

"Yup!"

"You drive," I say.

***

I look at the clock it says four forty-four. I hate when that happens, it's such a bad vibe. One eleven is the creepiest. I often wake at two twenty-two; maybe that's the time I was born.

Today, I've decided, is a good day. No more plodding around, sorry for myself. I'm putting yesterday's train wreck behind me. In fact, having a good cry seems to have lessened my load. Henry is still brutal but he's gotta do him and I've gotta do me. I snuggle back down. Yeah, today's a good day to be alive.

***

I stand beside my sergeant, above a body that's undoubtedly Angela Wilson's. She's a mess; the pick and mix of violence. The preliminaries done I leave the crime scene team do their thing. The priority is getting Angela to the morgue, autopsied, cleaned up and officially identified.

"Watch yourself."

"Thank you," I say to Andy for preventing me from falling over a tree root. His hand falls from my arm and I realise I liked it there. Too bad. Andy Jensen is off limits.

"There's a café here. Great breakfast. Shall we?" asks Andy.

I check the time. Six sixty-six. It's weird when that happens.

"Most certainly, plenty of time before Briefing."

***

Priti and I are Primark shopping. It's manic, but I manage to get some joggers and tees. After, we head for a burger. We instantly fall into gossiping about Amy's trout pout.

"How gross were Amy's lips?" I'm stating the obvious.

"So gross. It was impossible not to stare."

"Do you think her lips will stay like that forever?" I ask.

"I hope so, collagen's brilliant. What about her forehead?"

"She's definitely had Botox," I say.

"Definitely. It's so smooth she's like a jelly alien. Shit, I'm such a bitch, but those girls bring out the worst in me. Anyways tell me, how's Henry?"

I shake my head. Where to begin?

"Sparrow!"

We turn; our eyes searching through the crowds. It's Mercy, out on temporary licence.

"What you two bitches doin?"

"Priti, is someone speaking?"

"No, I didn't hear our names."

"Shit, you two are so proper...properly boring."

We ignore the annoying voice until...

"Ok, we'll play by your rules. Sparra...Priti."

"Hi Mers," Priti and I say simultaneously. We do sound prissy.

"What you up to?" I ask lightly.

"Just hanging, you know, lookin around."

She scrawny and her clothes tatty. I wonder if I look this rough. It's hard being a poor kid. School conversations orbit around how you look, the clubs you attend, the cars your parents drive, where you holiday. Mercy has an absent Dad and a mum with a serious drug habit – Columbia is the only country Mrs Andrews is interested in.

I look at Priti, who reads my mind and gives me the green light.

"We're going to McDonalds, want to join us?" I offer.

"Why would I want to hang out with you losers?"

"Cos we're paying," I add.

"I like that reason. Let's go bit...I mean bff's."

Uxbridge McDonalds is smashed. You need your wits about you; it isn't for the faint hearted. Luckily, Mers secures a table by baring her teeth at a mum with toddlers.

With three meal deals and three apple pies on a tray, I surge against hostile queuing customers. Until I see the headline in The Evening Standard.

"BODY OF MISSING SCHOOLGIRL FOUND."

Precariously balancing the tray, I grab the paper from the rack. I've broken out in a sweat. I feel suddenly suffocated by the customers brushing against me and the drone of multiple conversations.

"Phe, your face is like you've seen Kirsten or are they out of apple pies?"

"Way worse, quick, grab your stuff so I can get rid of the tray."

"Which one's strawberry?" asks Priti staring at the milkshakes.

"The one that's not chocolate," sneers Mercy.

Throwing Mers a dirty look I put the paper centre table.

"It must be Angela," I state my tone hollow.

Priti reads aloud.

'A murder enquiry was launched this afternoon following the discovery of a body in Ruislip, Hillingdon, Middlesex. It is believed to be missing schoolgirl, Angela Wilson. D.I. Kate Daniels will make a full statement this evening.'

We sit silently, huddled together, consuming our meal. No one speaks. What is there to say? A girl is dead.

***

Her wheels crunch the gravel. Opening the door, she wobbles in wearily. No wisecrack forthcoming or attempt to rile me. She's ultra-pale with no light in her eyes.

***

The whirling as the external world rotates unstably, makes me nauseous. My hands cover my ears, attempting to block the hammering in my brain. Don't crack Phoenix, not in front of him. I close my eyes...only to find my opponent staring stony faced into them when they reopen. I stagger forward, the ground beneath my feet unstable. Blood crashes around my body, its pressure burning my veins. My wooziness adds to the drama, but Henry's hands encircle my upper arms...and maybe if I think of him, if I can isolate Henry from the panic, I'll be ok.

"Look at me."

An order from a distance. Henry is forever out of reach.

"Look at me. Breathe.

His voice is the antidote.

"I can't catch my bre...

"Yes! You can. Breathe with me."

Slowly inhaling and exhaling, I focus on his fingers on my skin. The even pressure of each one connecting me to Henry. Everything around me is distorted, everything, but Henry. I'm scared I'll throw up on him, like my first night here in this hallway.

"Stay focused on me and breathe."

You have no idea Whittle how focused on you I am. As the chaos around me recedes I glory in being his focus. All his attention is on me.

"Ok?" he asks.

It's not possible to detect a hint of concern in two letters. I assess his perfectly shaped shoulders and chest; encompassing and protective; I could sink into him if he cared.

Henry makes a clinical visual assessment and releases me. What would he do if I cried? Or if I threw myself at him? He is so near to caring. I am adept at recognising 'so near' states, like I am so near to cracking. I am so near to taking one of Henry's Stanley blades and slicing my wrists. Could things get worse? Yes. In my world there is no cut-off point. Things could get better though. What if, in time, Henry cared?

***

Once again, I find myself with bereaved parents; this time in the morgue's viewing room. As senior ranking officer on the case it's only right I take this responsibility.

There are four of us in a cold, impersonal, square room: me, Mr and Mrs Wilson and Angela. The lighting is low, for which I'm thankful. I recommend we stand behind the glass partition, but they want to be near.

"Are you ready?"

Stupid question. How can they possibly be ready, but they nod.

The Technician pulls the sheet down revealing Angela's face. I hear their sharp intakes of breath. The facial bruising is soul destroying. Mrs Wilson cries - loud gut-wrenching sobs. Mr Wilson pulls his wife to him; she's near collapse. I give her time before I officially ask.

"Is this your daughter, Angela Susan Wilson?"

"Yes, that's my daughter, Angela," croaks Mr Wilson hoarsely. "Pull the sheet down," he insists.

"Sir, I'd advise against that," I say knowing what's seen can never be unseen.

"Down," he says firmly.

The technician looks to me for confirmation. I nod.

"That's not Angela's underwear," Mrs Wilson murmurs, so quietly I'm unsure I've heard correctly.

"Sorry?"

"I buy Angela's underwear; what she's wearing isn't hers."

"How can you tell?"

"She never had a white bra, not even a pastel. She liked colour; she said white was for boring virgins."

***

The tall, rusting, metal, school gates are a shrine of teddies and flowers. I hate that Angela is going to be immortalised as a victim.

I duck into the toilet to escape the cold stares that collectively turn me ice cold. I'm throwing water on my face when she walks in. I want to pull the sink from the wall and crush her head with it. Her sly, evil smile erupts. Kirsten is no way as beautiful as she thinks.

"Phoenix, how lovely," she says creepily.

The slap stinging my face comes from nowhere. It's so powerful my head bounds back hitting the hand dryer and unwanted tears spring, but I blink them away.

"Why does someone as plain and poor as you live, when Angela is dead?"

Attempting to brush past she pushes her face violently into mine.

"You're nothing, worthless; why don't you just end it. No one cares."

"Ahhhhh," I groan, doubling up, trying to recover from her fist in my abdomen.

The toilet door is firmly pushed open.

"On your way, no loitering here," says our Head of Year.

My stomach burns as I join student traffic. I pass girls who blubber pathetically, whipping themselves up into hysteria; wondering what outfit she's buried in.

Kirsten makes it about her - how Angela was HER best friend - how hard it is for HER to deal with losing Angela.

The boys are freaks. They plan to break into the morgue to see dead, naked Angela.

Me? Jesus! I'd wished her dead and now she is.

"Phoenix, the answer?"

Sniggers erupt.

"Sorry?"

More sniggers.

"The answer to question three. What is going on in your head?"

**

The team view hour upon hour of CCTV footage. Ninety percent of it is irrelevant, but the other ten percent could lead to a breakthrough. Angela had heated dialogue with a girl identified by the school as Phoenix Whittle; the persecuted P? The school denies knowledge of Phoenix being bullied. The staff say the same; Phoenix is a loner, she doesn't integrate well, she lashes out. It worries me when six people give the same statement.

**

"Phoenix," smiles Mr Jacobs. He's leaning casually against his door frame, wearing black trousers with a black belt; its buckle shiny and a pale pink shirt and tie. For a moment, I want to crumble. He turns to me like he's pleased to see me; thirstily I lap it up; his welcome gives me a glimpse of what it's like to be wanted.

"Today is essay techniques. I'll make a brew first. One sugar?"

"Please," I reply. I want to wrap my arms around this moment and hold it tight against my heart.

"What do you think of Drake's new song?" he asks brightly.

"I love it."

"It's ingenious how you buy a track then it downloads immediately to your iPod. Technology is a marvellous thing."

"I wouldn't know," I laugh. "I'm bringing my Walkman to Antiques Roadshow."

He comes from the English store cupboard with two mugs and biscuits, and I imagine him shirtless in pyjama bottoms. God he'd be the perfect boyfriend.

"You look a little tired, partying I suppose or is it raving?"

"Clubbing."

It wasn't completely a lie - I do go to Taekwondo club.

"You moved in with your uncle recently, I hear?"

"Yeah." What can I add? Me and Henry – we aren't normal.

"When Penny moved in, it drove me mad how she contaminated the jam with the butter…sharing a home takes time…"

An awkward silence follows. I sense Mr Jacobs wanting me to open-up about Henry, but I can't.

"You know Phoenix. If there is anything on your mind, you'd like to share, I'm a good listener?"

A moment lingers between spilling my guts and bottling up. My shields remain as I keep my bitter past and chaotic present private.

"How about a chocolate digestive, then we'll get going?"

We sit heads together, consuming biscuits between essay techniques. He jokes we laugh; his knee touches mine. It feels like a knee against a knee - nothing more; not like when Henry touches me. I want to feel a spark of excitement that me and Mr Jacobs are alone, but nothing ignites. It's for the best, what with him being a teacher and older, except that having a school crush makes turning up every day bearable.

"I'll walk you to your car," Mr Jacobs volunteers. I don't argue, life's a hell of a lot safer in his inner circle.

A shiver runs through me. I think of Alex and that time with Mr Jacobs. As if sensing my consternation, he smiles. Fuck he's fit.

I don't know what we talk about as we walk; I keep smiling and nodding and agreeing.

He waits whilst I unlock the car and get seated.

"Enjoy your evening Phoenix. Penny and I plan to watch SAS; Who Dares Wins. It's rather entertaining; you should give it a go."

"I will Sir; thanks."

As I drive off, I see Mr Jacobs in my rear mirror

Arriving home in darkness, the lit house is a welcome sight. As Henry opens the door, I feel the distinct uneasiness of being watched, but how many films have I seen where the enemy is on the inside?

***

Phoenix is glorious naked. Even seventy metres away I harden at the sight of her peeling off her clothes. The distance frustrates me. Binoculars are fun at first; the thrill of those first illicit sightings, but now I want to touch, to hold, to enter.

THE FUNERAL

The day of Angela's funeral, sixth form is closed. We assemble in the playground, walking in a procession to St Lawrence's. Sitting in a pew, I glance around. It's wrong, these young faces instead of a sea of senior citizens.

The detective's here and she looks at me; not a glance, but a purposeful assessment.

In the front row Angela's parents sit rigidly; their eyes averted from the white coffin. I pick up an 'Order of Mass' pamphlet entitled *'A New Angel in Heaven'*. Oh, please! She was the ante-christ.

Mrs Wade gave the Eulogy, it was a complete misrepresentation of Angela.

"She was a guiding light."

No, she fuckin was not.

"A young woman of great promise, a friend to everyone."

No! A bitch to everyone.

My mind is cluttered with negativity. I shouldn't be here; I don't mourn her. Even in death Angela thwarts me. Yet a sadness so deep has settled on me like a second skin and I can't brush it off. I'm being haunted by an eleven-year-old Angela with spindly legs skipping across the playground. My head is running out of space for dead people.

"Life is a glorious gift, one that should not be discarded lightly."

The killer doesn't share Fr McIntyre's sentiments. Did Angela's murderer record her last moments; does he rerun them in his mind, like I replay my Mum's death?

"Can we ever know the depth of another's suffering?"

How bad had it been? What had Angela endured while imprisoned? Had he shown mercy and killed her swiftly or been cruel? I hope death was quick.

"All sins shall be forgiven."

No. You can't extinguish a life and be absolved. Thou shall not kill. It's bloody rule number one!

The remainder of the mass is foggy; I'm there but I'm not. It's a small period that I refuse to form into a memory. I don't hang about.

At home, I'm restless, unable to eat or settle down to homework.

He's been in his office all day and evening. I bet his book's bloody boring. I think he's avoiding me until I hear the tv between the floorboards; Match of the Day.

It's a code red; my stomach is cramping aggressively and my bum aches from sitting on floorboards. As mental strain burns behind my eyes, I drop my Physics book into my lap and rub my forehead. I'm totally pissed off; with myself, with him. It had been my turn to cook; partridge! Who even eats partridge? Nobody fucking normal, not in this century. I couldn't face another drama, so I googled - partridge was doable. I'd concentrated on the bird then the mash, whisking it till it was lumpless. I hadn't realised the Brussel sprouts were frozen until, attempting to pierce one, it hurdled off the plate. He'd also found my Peppa Pig knickers in his wash and hung them from the chrome ceiling rack, next to the omelette pan. He's evil. I want to dig up his newly-laid lawn with a spoon and dismantle his house screw, by nut, by fucking bracket...with a chisel.

I plod downstairs, my bloated stomach pushing uncomfortably against my waist band. He stretches on the sofa. He may look relaxed, but this man is alert, he's the ultimate predator. I stomp through the lounge and into the kitchen: opening drawers, banging them shut, running the tap on full, putting frozen fruit in the smoothie maker; that was peak. I sneak a looksy around the arch. He's wearing a white t-shirt and grey trackies, stretched out so casually you'd mistake him for normal. The sofa is custom-made to fit his six-foot something height, his feet are bare as usual, he's on his front, a cushion squeezed tightly beneath his head, his eyes on the football. I throw myself noisily into the armchair opposite and crunch loudly on ice. I decide on the direct approach.

"What's wrong with you?"

"I'm watching football."

"Are you always like this?"

"Yes."

"So, you've been diagnosed with pathological grimness then? Are you medicated?

Silence.

"I think you're emotionally challenged and socially stunted. You compartmentalise: biscuits in the tin, shoes in the basket, feelings in the...you don't have feelings, do you? If you attended school you'd be statemented. Actually, you wouldn't be enrolled in mainstream school. Not because of your condition but because you're evil...No comment? Ok, this conversation's peaked; let's play a game then."

"I'm watching football."

"It's half-time. It's a five-minute game. I'll stay till you do."

This is the pushiest I've been with him and this is the most communicative he's been. I need to prolong this.

He sits up. I invite his wrath, his impatience, anything but this disturbingly frosty remoteness. I'm losing him.

"I used to play this game with my father...your brother. We'd do girls' or boys' names, sometimes animals, always in alphabetical order. It's fun. We'll work through each other's personal traits. This way I'll understand how you perceive me and vice versa. You start?"

"Ladies first."

"Fine."

We're a mirror image as we sit upright.

"Arrogant," I smile.

"Agitating."

He's grasped the game.

"Boring."

"Bitchy."

His eyes fix on mine. It's the first time in days he's so much as glanced my way. They're grey eyes. Cold, soulless, but beautiful. How had I not noticed before?

"Cunning."

"Cat-ty," he emphasises.

We've advanced to the edge of our seats.

"Deceitful," I shoot.

"Dependent."

"Egotistical."

"Erratic."

"False."

"Foolhardy," he jeers.

"Grim."

"Geeky."

I'm proud to be a geek. 'Erratic' no I bloody am not!

"Horrid," I spit.

"Hormonal," he laughs.

How dare he use mother nature against me! How fucking dare he. Furious heat courses through my body. He's still laughing. I want to slap his face...very fucking hard with a wet flannel. How does he whip up crazy reactions?

Unconsciously, I rise. Only when Henry stands do I realise we've taken an aggressive stance. As pins and needles tingle in my feet our mouths run ahead of our bodies and insults continue to fly.

"Immature."

"Irritable."

"Jerk," I snap.

"Jinx," he retaliates.

I falter. It's a silly word, a kid's word, so why does Henry using it hurt? Because it's true.

I leer at Henry...fuck what he thinks? But realisation dawns that I care a lot.

"Given up?" Henry goads.

"Kooky," I shout but my breathing is short, and I feel asthmatic.

"Klutz."

"Loser."

"Loon."

We're unstoppable.

"Manipulator."

"Moody."

"Nasty."

"Nuisance."

I'm on tiptoe, Henry's looking down, our eyes lock in battle.

"Obssessive!"

"Overemotional!"

"Partridge!" I shout. What the fuck?

"Paranoid!" he sneers.

"Queer!" My evidence? Coasters and Napkins.

"Quarrelsome."

"Ruthless!"

"Rude!"

"Sinister!"

"Suspicious."

His eyes are now so dark I could lose myself in them.

"Treacherous!"

"Temperamental!"

"Unreasonable!"

"Unstable!"

"Violent!!"

"Virgin!!"

"I'm not a virgin; and if I were it's not a fucking disability! At least I've someone who wants to have sex with me."

I shake from embarrassment and hurt.

Henry's a statue; if he feels anything his features don't relay it.

I should retreat, instead I rock; Henry's hands fly to my wrists.

***

I feel the unsteady beat of her pulse against my finger. How this slight contact disturbs my skin.

***

His touch is so light, I wonder, if forensics dusted me down, could fingerprints be extracted. His hands move lightly up my bare forearms. They steady me yet I feel unstable. Bewildered, I grudgingly pull away and Henry immediately switches to neutral. He's good at that.

***

I see them through my telescopic lens. Her uncle is a challenge -not your average relative that's for sure. There'd been other girls of course; I've been around; experimented somewhat. Admittedly, my tastes are rather bold, but Phoenix is a quick learner. She'll be reticent at first. Bad habits, well, they'll have to be dealt with. I think there's fun to be had...yes. The more I think about it, the quicker I come.

WICKED GAMES

I come down for breakfast, my emotions so conflicted I don't know how to be around him. I turn the 'word game' inside out in my mind and it gives me a bangin headache. Nothing makes sense anymore. Something about Henry affects something in me. It's complex and I don't know if I can handle complex.

I glance at him covertly.

***

I catch her eye. Time to try the softly, softly approach.

"Can I get by," I say, brushing my body against hers. It's a dirty move knowing she's attracted to me.

"I'm making a protein shake. Want one? It's chocolate?"

"No thank you," she replies meekly.

"Ok?" I ask gently. Fake concern. I can't afford any other. "I'm jogging shortly; care to join me?"

I expect her to remember the woods and say no, but hope swims in her eyes. She smiles - so deep, so wide. Her optimism is her calling card.

***

The wind is hostile and the grassy, sloping ground is sodden and break-an-ankle slippery. I cast my eyes downwards; the stream which usually babbles is dark and choppy, its level threatening to break the bank.

"Alright?" he asks.

No, I'm not flipping alright numbskull! I give the thumbs up as I continue to slip and slide. We've run for about thirty minutes. I'm losing steam. Henry bears left, towards sprawling willow trees that line the bank; their withering branches trailing into murky waters, like bony witch's fingers reaching out. As quickly as Henry sweeps long, drooping branches aside to clear his path, he lets them fall...into mine. Their spindly twigs with saw-toothed leaves snag my hair. I imagine bugs, suddenly dragged away from their colony, harbouring on my scalp. We cross a footbridge but continue along the wooded riverbank to where another brook flows in from the left; its water rushing by with its off-white, foamy crests. The reason I've joined Henry on this crazy, senseless sprint is to be with him. I must have Stockholm syndrome.

I'm relinquishing myself, more accurately endangering myself, to gain Henry's approval. I let him pick me up and put me down at will, as if I've no defence against his intermittent interest in me. Henry slows his pace allowing me to catch up. I'm rewarded; we run in unison. Turning to him I smile. Henry remains stone; I'm saddened. I run on; that's what you do when you have Stockholm syndrome.

***

I keep one eye ahead and the other on Care Girl. Strands of hair blow about her face, which is red from exertion. Her eyes shine, she looks alive; it's a good look, it suits her. The river is pushing hard downstream dragging loose sand, stone and litter with it. Its murkiness hides nests borrowed by sand martins and the deep sections formed from worked-out gravel pits.

I sense her alarm.

Slipping with the loose ground she hastily shifts her weight towards me. She reaches out; a scream caught in her throat as further rubble gives way beneath her. She's slipping, her fingers almost reaching me.

"HENRYYYYY."

She hits the water hard. Her arms flailing to keep her head above water. She's choking, swallowing water, spitting it out, calling me.

Where is she? Shit!

***

Henry, agile, strong, capable, with the reflexes of a cheetah was a three-toed sloth. Yes, he'd saved me...after he'd put me in danger. The man who knows everything: when to hang the clothes on the line, what queue to get in, what roads are closed, suddenly plays dumb? No! We ran today for a reason. To scare me.

***

I thought after this morning she'd be running for the hills. She was never in real danger, I fished her out easily enough, ok, she spluttered and coughed for a few hours, but it spooked her...just not enough.

***

Friday night I dream. A nightmare. I lose myself in it; dragged into its murky, painful tide of visual contradictions, emotional turbulence and personal history. I wake drenched in sweat, the nylon of the sleeping bag stuck to me. My eyes fix on the door, until exhausted and distraught, another wave of night-terrors claim me.

The following day I remain in my room. I have nothing to say to him. I have no appetite. My concentration deserts me. I am simply alone with my thoughts which are dangerous company. Part of me wants him to seek me out. Surely that can't be normal? I don't know if he wants to scare me or kill me. I pretend his heart isn't in it, but if Henry was MRI'd the scan would reveal he has no heart – he's an anatomical anomaly.

The night repeats; bad dreams absent for years return; they've altered to incorporate recent fears. One o'clock, three o'clock, five o'clock I jerk awake terrified. Grabbing my torch, I flash first at the Sherlock chair – empty – then into the room's dark corners. Too scared to fall back to sleep I shake my snow globe and wish my Mum and Dad were alive.

Morning follows night. Unfortunately, that's how things work and so Monday begins. My crap life cannot be wallowed in because I must drag on a uniform, get registered, learn and be tormented. I don't think Priti or Luke realise how fragile I am.

"Phe, hurry up, it's Mr Jacobs, we don't all get one on one with the hottest teacher."

I move from lesson to lesson. At lunch I sit with Priti and Clive. I listen to them dissect tv programmes. I haven't watched telly since Pointless with Trish.

My shoulder is poked, and a folded piece of paper is dropped on the table in front of me. I open it:

'Suffocating is easy. Pull a plastic bag over your head and tie it at your neck. If you're too pussy, we'll do it for you.'

"What's it say Phe?"

I force a smile.

"Nothing. A library overdue notice."

"You hoggin Fifty Shades again?" laughs Priti.

I should bin the threat. I don't. I refer to it at intervals. It feeds my darkness.

At home, Henry opens the door. My head scrambles. Was he unbearably near or far? Why does he look at me that way, like he can see right inside me: through skin, bone, head, heart, yet not act on it...not a nod, a smile, a casual word. Why does him doing nothing feel like something.

My fist opens and the note falls to Henry's oak flooring.

"Could you at least pretend to give a fuck," I say meekly.

Upstairs, on tiptoe, I enter Henry's room. I withdraw a pillow from his bed and take it to my unsleeping bag. I lay my head on it and breathe Henry in. I don't care that he'll know what a freak I am. We are beyond that.

I dial Luke's number. When you verbalise certain things, they sound immature. With my phone cradled to my ear I try to convince Luke that it isn't my insecurity or my imagination; Henry is dangerous.

"Luke, I am having a crisis here, would you please be you for five minutes.

"Phe? I'm fuckin baff'd. What you sayin, babes?"

"Henry's threatening me."

"Has he chased you round the kitchen wid a bread knife?"

"Be fucking serious!" I snap. "He's subtle. He doesn't want me here, he's trying to scare me into leaving, I'm certain of it."

Luke is humouring me like I'm a crazy, neurotic drama queen.

"Na, na babes. He special forces. He want you dead, you be dead; d'ya know what I mean. How bout we go Wimpy tomorrow?"

"Jesus, Luke, a burger between two bits of bread won't make me immortal," I retort indignantly. "Have you heard nothing I've said! I'm a headline waiting to happen."

I move quickly to the window, knowing Henry's left the house. Not because I heard him, Henry has no audio...but because I have this Henry receptor. I watch as he walks towards the BMW. He stops. Turns. Looks up at my window. I almost jump back.

"Phe, you still there?"

I step away from the window. I check the time; eleven forty-six.

"Phe!"

"Yeah, sorry, erm, look I'm just being a crazy bitch. Sorry Luke, painters in and all that."

"Jesus Phe, no man wanna hear mother nature talkin."

"I know, sorry. I'm just being a tit. It's not that deep."

"Cool. I meant what I said about Wimpy. I gotta go."

My heart is hammering in my head.

I return to the window. I stare into the dark, an infinite void of nothingness.

Where do you go?

I try to relax. I'm tense all over. Realising, I've been chewing on my nails for the last hour, I grab a stress ball and go put the kettle on. I make a decaf and binge watch 'Hanna'; a bit of escapism, but weirdly her dad reminds me of Henry. Ok, now my imagination is running wild.

***

The target is daydreaming. By the time he glimpses me it is too late. My gun has a silencer, but it's a misconception they silence the discharge of the bullet. They merely quieten it; the noise is sufficient to have bodyguards stampeding into the room. A curtain blowing in the breeze at an open window the only indication of how I'd entered and exited.

On the journey home I consider the scrap of paper she intentionally sent my way. I think about it as I shower. I mull it over as I sit in the Sherlock listening to her breathe.

***

Oh my God! I barely slept. I had a massive case of the heebie-jeebies, and there's no time to recover before school. So, through the gates of hell Priti and I walk. Crap! Kirsten's waiting for me. Channelling Henry I give her a dirty look. She draws her index finger across her neck, smirking. I blasély pass her but once out of sight I bolt to form. Mr Edwards informs us that some year thirteens will be interviewed in connection with Angela, possibly Alex. More than once I'd considered telling them my uncle is a fake. How do I know? Easy – he's shit at being an uncle.

"Phe what's that?" asks Priti as I take out my English folder.

"An official letter addressed to Phoenix Whittle's guardian."

"Really?"

"A police interview; I can bring an appropriate adult."

"Henry?"

"There's nothing appropriate about Henry, Pri."

"Cow then?"

"Uddely, out of the question."

We laugh; the noise is as precious as fairy dust.

"Why do, you think, they want to see you?

I just shrug.

Later. Alone. I tear the letter up.

***

I should be piling on the pressure, pushing her buttons, forcing her out. It should be easy. Should.

***

I've Physics work coming out of my ears, but my concentration is a floor below. I'm clockwatching; waiting for the minutes we share the same space.

***

We eat dinner. She talks for both of us. Smiling. I reckon this is the last time I'll see the corners of her mouth rise. Admittedly the problem of Care Girl has been a challenging one, but I believe tonight will be her last.

"How about a game?" I ask.

She hasn't a choice, she's playing.

"It's a slight of hand game."

"Like magic?" she asks curiously.

"No."

"What's it called?"

"Oops."

"Playing would be a mistake," she jokes.

I don't respond.

"Do you get it? Oops."

No reply.

"Ooookay."

She complies because she's compelled to.

"How do we play?"

Her gullibility is so loveable I nearly stop.

I hold up my steak knife.

"Put your hand, palm side down, on the table," I encourage, but her hand fails to move.

"I'll pass; I've homework to finish," she says too breezily.

"What about being together?"

"It's just..."

"Do you want to be pals? It's not complicated."

***

He doesn't raise his voice. There's no need...the chill coming off his tone is like a freezing agent; it renders me motionless. He takes my hand and I let him; his is unexpectedly warm. Is it weird to be terrified, yet enjoy the sensation of his skin against mine?

"Spread your fingers."

I know what's coming but can't bear to lose his interest.

"Keep still; don't move a millimetre."

My fingers already shake.

He begins. Stabbing the knife in the spaces between my fingers. Slowly. I can see where the knife spikes the tablemat. Faster.

"Henry!"

Faster.

"My fingers are gonna move...I can't keep them stretched...Oh my God!"

Faster.

I scream.

"Dessert?" I ask, casually turning away.

CRASH!

The plate misses me by millimetres. It seems shooting in the back runs in the family. The plate splinters into pieces; gravy splashes and peas roll. It's very Jackson Pollock.

"You're a psycho, a loon, a freak, you're unbalanced. IIIIII hate you!"

Randomly grabbing cutlery and condiments she hurls them wildly whilst slinging every synonym for '*crazy*' at me. Diving behind the breakfast bar I consider how to restrain her before she trashes the place.

That's not her plan.

Care Girl runs from the kitchen, through the lounge, out of the house and down the lane in the dark, in her onesie. Fuck, she's impulsive.

***

I walk, my strides long, my arms swinging rigidly, heading in a direction going nowhere. The man I live with is not Henry Whittle. I try to pinpoint when I subconsciously knew this. The woods? Maybe earlier? It had been out there if I'd looked closer. His youth. His distance. His resistance to my presence. The attempts to make me, his only family, leave. No resemblance to Dad. And the house: no photos, no memorabilia, everything new.

***

My headlights pick her up.

I drive alongside her, lowering the window.

"Get in.

"Fuck. Off!"

"This is easily rectified. I'll support you getting settled elsewhere."

"Are you deaf? I said get fucking lost!"

"You've nowhere to go?"

Silence.

"You're being dramatic."

Silence.

"You're dressed as a lamb without shoes."

"Sheep don't wear shoes, you dick."

"I'm losing patience."

"Oh, my golly! We can't have that."

"Be reasonable."

"Reasonable? You fucking arsehole! I don't give a fuck about reasonable. I'm living with a stranger who hates me. A man who can't say my name. You couldn't even make it through one day without being a complete wanker!"

She does a one eighty.

Breaking and turning off the ignition, I follow and approach cautiously. Lightly touching her shoulder, she violently arches away. I've had experience in calming trauma and grief, but an overwrought young woman I've pushed to the edge is a first. In the beam of the moon her pale skin reflects a glacial blue overlay. She is dangerously cold. I pull her firmly to me. She is almost feral, but I'm too strong for resistance to be effective. She pulls and twists in my hold until emotion depletes her energy.

"I don't deserve this. You're a vacuum, empty and blank."

"Calm down."

Lesson – never speak these words, together, to a woman. Incensed, a renewed momentum fires in. She ferociously punches, slaps, kicks. I consider knocking her out...the me before her would. Instead, I hold her at arms' length until she goes limp, until her head flops forward; her damp, stiff hair sticking to my bare arm.

"We're walking to the car," I say gently. I'm half anticipating further resistance, but she has a distant look in her eye. On autopilot she buckles up.

***

He sits me at the kitchen table. A blanket is pulled around me; his hands firmly run up and down my arms and make circles on my back. My treacherous body welcomes the contact. It's been so long since I was comforted, I nearly beg him not to stop. Hot sweet tea is placed in my hands. He fills a wash basin with warm water and a capful of disinfectant, grabs cotton wool, a towel and kneels at my dirty, bloodied, frozen feet. I don't care they're hideous. He pushes the cuffs of my onesie up to my knees. He may as well have slipped my top off my shoulder; it feels that intimate. While I drink, he cleans my cuts. His skin shimmers in the glow of the light; had he been this beautiful at the beginning?

"Take a hot shower. I'll get you one of my t-shirts, your..."

He is looking at my onesie.

"It's damp."

He turns on the shower, setting the temperature then leaving. As hot needles of water warm my skin, I slide down the shower. I've lost Henry; that's the single conclusion that releases the tears aching to roll. I sit in the shower basin, my knees pulled up to my chin, sobbing my lungs out. I have no family. Nothing. That fake, him, he doesn't belong to me, I have no hold on him, no reason for expectation. I want to hate him with a vengeance, but I don't. I'd willed him to follow me, bring me home...show me an ounce of sympathy or kindness...and he had...Henry had cared for me, but it's a mirage, a smoke screen because Henry doesn't exist.

***

If it's possible to cry yourself to death, she'd be in a coffin. I leave the items on top of the vanity unit and retreat. In my office I pour myself a rum; the familiar burn of it relaxing me. I consider her...me...us. My plan has misfired dismally. I need to regroup...I need to achieve my goal without causing her further damage. She can't take any more and I can't bear to dish it out.

As I lock up, I hear her approach. There she stands, in my tee which falls off one shoulder and drops to her knees. She's pale, her creamy skin like alabaster, her green eyes, usually flashing or sparkling are a subdued midnight tone. Her hair, darkened by water, is sleekly brushed back, fully revealing her face, with its fractured, dead beat expression.

"I am not leaving; I know that's what you want. I'm not giving you what you want, you don't deserve it."

She is impressively resilient. Inside her busy brain, revenge is being hatched and fire burns. Perhaps? No. There could be no perhaps, unfortunately not.

POLICE INTERVIEW

The workmen are finishing off. I worry about how I'll get in the house after they go. Henry is unreliable. A whim might strike, and I'll end up sleeping in the car. I've only seen him at a distance since...that night. Suddenly I'm tearful again, like I'm close to something amazing but I'm too slow, or too late or too unlucky.

"I'll be off then."

"Ok."

"Fine."

That's how it's been. So, when interview day arrives; I'm reduced to bunking. I've never skipped school in my life.

I spend the day in the library. I don't anticipate repercussions.

The minute I spot her pink mini I want to reverse down the lane and never stop. I park centimetres from her driver's door.

The front door opens.

Cow's face is uglier than usual; anger distorts it. She tries to squeeze past Henry to reach me, but Henry's solid body holds her off. I think about Henry's body. He's combat-fit alright. He'll be pissed I've brought trouble to his door.

"You stupid girl," she spits.

I wipe projectile saliva off my face.

"You devious little liar. I've done my best, really Henry, I have, but she's such an attention seeker."

I expect Henry to nod; why does he never do the expected! Frustration and anger claw to freedom.

"Shut! The Fuck! Up! Drugs are trouble. Violence is trouble. I'm eighteen you brainless twat. Stop harassing me, you're like some pigmy sumo stalker...and stop finding excuses to drive by to ogle Henry – he's not yours, he's mine!"

***

I knew an attack was imminent; I am relieved not to be the target. This is the perfect opportunity to ditch Evans. I slip my arm around Care Girl's shoulders, pulling her near. I've wanted to touch her for some time; now I have a legit reason. I pretend to myself it's a casual show of unity but lying to oneself is dangerous. She feels slight beside me, like a sudden bitchy outburst from Evans will sweep her away, so I tighten my grip. Her body responds pressing into mine.

"Leave," I ask.

"But Henry, you heard her, the vile lies she's spreading about me."

"I asked you politely to leave."

"But Henry."

I open the door. I bend to her ear and whisper "HA1 2BZ."

Her body stiffens. On opening the door, she throws herself off the porch, stumbling to her car. Evans is forced to heave her body across the passenger seat to reach the driver's seat. Inwardly, I laugh at Care Girl adopting my move.

I close the door. Turning, I'm caught up in the power of her gaze. It's bursting with hope and longing.

"Do you remember the night I vomited on your floor?"

"It's not easily forgotten."

"Before you, I was hollow, like every happy memory had been painfully scooped out. I needed someone on my side, to watch my back."

Looking at me, her face unguarded, the story of her sad life's there for me to consider. I could be that someone. It's an insane thought.

***

Henry protected me. Ironically, now I know Henry isn't my uncle, I feel less threatened. It accounts for much of his weirdness.

I look for answers in his eyes. There are none.

I know what it is, to be a spider in the bath, caught up in a whirl of water, drawn towards the plug hole and the unknown beyond.

***

I hold an evidence photograph of a thirteen-year-old Care Girl taken by a school nurse. Her bare back is to the camera, it is covered in significant bruising and multiple burns. I pick up the medical report: broken ribs, arm, nose and cheekbone. I raise the x-rays to the light. My body tenses.

The clone beeping is a welcome distraction.

***

"Priti! I've had the most awful confrontation with Cow."

"Tell me everything."

Which I do, including my other problem.

"Sex Pest Rob's at it again: standing too near, breathing into my ear, touching unnecessarily; he's so irritating. Honestly Pri, he's spoiling Taekwondo."

"What a dick! Have you told Henry?"

"No. It's a bit unsettled between us."

"I'm sorry, Phe."

"It's fine: we'll muddle through."

***

She is spread out, on the floor, on her stomach, her CD player plugged into her ears. She is totally 1999. What is she going to reveal to the police? Could she implicate me? She looks up and pulls her earphones out.

***

"Tea," he says taking a cushion to sit on, and placing a tray down. "Who you listening to?"

"A$AP Rocky," I say wondering if this is an olive branch.

I shuffle near offering an earpiece. We sit. Shoulders touching. Knees touching. I'm nearly sick with excitement.

"Like it?"

"Yes, I like it," he says.

His tone has an unfamiliar richness to it. His eyes are piercing. I'm confused. Are we talking about the song?

"Listen to this, Black Coffee," I say, wanting to keep him near. "It's weird, you might like it."

"Someone still has a sense of humour."

My cheeks burn. I note the slight pressure of his body against mine. I notice everything about him. I imagine us naked. My colour deepens. Shit! I seriously need to see Diane. This must be a psychotic episode.

"Ducking police; I didn't think it through," I admit.

I take a bite of sandwich.

"It was another reason for you to reject me."

Then another bite.

"I'm not keen on the police. Must I go?"

"Yes, tomorrow." He says standing. "I'll take you. Say the minimum; it'll be a challenge, I know."

My spiralling heart is so fast I'm woozy.

"Got that?"

I nod. The edge has returned to his vocal cords. Could Henry be the brutal attacker of my enemies? He...oh God...what if he is the Ruislip Avenger; so named by the press. My eyes jump. He is swallowing a mouthful of coke. His eyes peer over the can, black as ink, staring at me. Is this Henry bad? I think he has the potential to be.

***

As arranged, I pick her up from school. I note the pink flush warming her skin as she climbs in the car. I swallow hard. I'd seen behind enemy lines, yet here I sit, next to a teenager, scared I'm in too deep.

In the interview room we sit side by side; I have no idea what is going to come out of her mouth? She is a bird in a cat's garden; twitchy, eyes darting around, ready to take flight. At ten-minute intervals she blurts out a random fact, like 'male kangaroos flex their biceps to impress female kangaroos' and 'eating chocolate improves the brain's ability to do mathematics'. My favourite is, did I know that in Alabama sex toys are illegal? You need a doctor's prescription to own one.

"Ready for this?" I ask.

"Not exactly."

I know she's mentally strong. She won't break under coercion, but does she want to make things difficult for me?

***

I'm rattled and he's to blame. Of all the times to play nice, it's now; doesn't he realise how unnerving this is. I need consistency, even crappy consistency. He'd paid a midnight visit to my room. It bothered me, but it is typical Henry behaviour. My issue was with the pillow he'd slotted under my head and the throw he'd tucked around me. There is more; my pens and pencils had been returned to my pencil case; my schoolbooks were neatly piled in alphabetical order. Perhaps he intended to OCD me. My journal lay beside my bed. I'd got sloppy. Routinely I put it in my rucksack, which I use as a pillow. He knows everything - how I hate him, how I don't. He'll jump to the conclusion I'm obsessed.

Why is my life so disastrous? Who the hell is he? And what's happened to the real Henry? I look sideways, meeting eyes that reveal nothing. But it's obvious. Uncle Henry is dead.

***

Daniels enters accompanied by her sergeant, Tom Brady. He's short, stocky and sandy-haired. Wearing a slim fitting suit, he resembles Dermot O'Leary. Daniels appears younger in person, attractive in an organised way: neat bob, expensive black suit, lime green shirt. Her choice of clothing complements her frame: narrow shoulders and wide hips.

Brady remains standing. Daniels sits neatly opposite, a pink notebook on lap. Pink. I like it, it says I'm a woman - so what.

"Phoenix, Mr Whittle. Thank you for coming. I'm sure you're aware of the recent murders; Bradley, Alex and Angela."

Phoenix is listening intently; leaning over the table like she might miss a crucial point.

"This is an informal meeting, but if you have no objection, I'd like to record it."

"That's unnecessary," I comment. "As you say, it's informal."

"Fine," she replies curtly before firing her first bullet. "It must be difficult having an adult thrust on you. You didn't have much contact with your niece prior to her moving in."

"Is that a question, or a statement?" I ask.

"Both," she says confidently.

"No. It's not too challenging, I'm used to shared accommodation, the house is spacious, my niece is very education driven."

"So, you left the Navy."

"Honourable discharge."

"Did you know Angela Wilson?"

"No."

"You seem sure?"

"Certain."

"Did you know Bradley Perkins?"

"No."

"Your neighbours said you run every day."

Fucking neighbours.

"Yes. Routine. Navy training stays with you."

"Bradley was found by the River Pinn. Angela in Ruislip Woods. Do you run there?"

"Occasionally."

She nods.

"Phoenix, would you mind if we speak to you alone?"

"I prefer Henry with me," she responds.

I find myself warming to that concept.

"We find your age group speak more openly without a guardian present."

"I find Police coerce vulnerable teenagers without a guardian present," I respond.

"Is Phoenix vulnerable?"

"We're all vulnerable, Inspector."

Daniels' lips thin; her eyes narrow. She takes my response as a threat.

"Phoenix I'd like to ask you a few questions about Angela Wilson."

"Ok," Phoenix replies cautiously.

"You had a heated exchange with her the day she went missing."

Phoenix nods.

"Did you threaten her?"

"A little."

"What did you argue about?"

"It wasn't an argument, just a string of abuse, that's her game."

"What do you think happened to Angela?"

"I don't know, or care."

"You're not upset about Angela's death."

"School's a safer place without her."

"We have her diary. We know she was terrorising numerous students; one initial repeatedly appears – P. Phoenix, are you P?"

Phoenix shrugs.

"She's so dumb she'd think my name began with 'f'.

"WAS dumb," corrects DI Daniels. "But she bullied you?"

"Yes."

"Regularly?"

"Yes."

"Would you say you hated her?"

Under the table my hand covers Phoenix's trembling hand.

"You're leading her detective," I interject.

A pause.

"Angela was vicious, wasn't she?"

"Yes." Phoenix's tone is wary.

"Would someone punish her?" asked Daniels.

"That's risky. She's part of a coven."

"Did you know Bradley Perkins?"

"No."

Phoenix's a good liar, no twitch, only the barest elevation of her tone.

"But you know Luke Lawrence?"

"Why are you asking me questions you have the answers to?"

"You seem a little on the defensive, Phoenix."

"That's because the police have a habit of stitching me up. Or is it the black kid you're pinning this on? Luke has nothing to do with any of this."

"Sure, about that, are you?"

"I'm positively certain."

"You're close. Intimate at one point I believe?"

"You sound a little desperate Inspector," I interject before standing. "I think we've sufficiently shared for today."

Phoenix stands but adds...

"Angela Wilson was evil. Honestly? I'm relieved she's dead. For years I'd swallowed every dirty word hurled at me, keeping it deep inside until it festered and threatened to poison me. I was twelve when I turned up at my local police station. You have no idea the courage it took to walk through those station doors: to approach the counter, to tell the sins of one adult to another. I was accused of lying, of being an attention seeker. My self-harming, obviously a cry for help, went ignored. It was a whole year later before I was taken off them. A year of being abused: degraded, knocked-about, burnt, cut, locked-up, no food. I remember standing on the school roof: leaning over, wandering how painful it would be to let myself fall. So, no, I don't trust the police."

Phoenix is clearly distressed. Am I bothered? Yes.

"I apologise if my questions upset you Phoenix. You are not a suspect, but a line of enquiry. I'm aware of your history; I apologise for the conduct of those involved. I understand your lack of trust in the profession, but please come forward with any information you recall."

We drive home in silence which normally I'd appreciate, but the atmosphere is suffused with dread, creating an almost tangible tension.

I open the front door; she shoots upstairs.

BANG!

I listen. She rustles about in her room. Her room; is that what I consider it to be?

At dinner the atmosphere is subdued. Phoenix sits pushing peas around her plate. I consider how I will operate under the watchful eye of Daniels. This person...Phoenix...has made life complicated.

"If you're not going to eat it, leave it."

We glare.

"You're the one who wants to live here," I almost accuse.

"And you're the one who invited me. God, you're so childish. I can't believe I thought we could be friends. You're emotionally incompetent. You're a pretty boy on the outside, but what's inside? Nothing – you're hollow, you're Mr Hollow man. You think you're so smart, that you know everything, but you don't. The police think one of us is a murderer. You could be because you're heartless and you're not...," she hesitates, "you're not..."

Her eyes, huge with dread, dart everywhere. Her lips shape words, but no sound transmits. She stares at me, not with her usual condemnation or hopefulness, more like, who the fuck, are you?

**

He knows I know. I had the perfect opportunity to disclose his crime to the police. To make myself safe. I haven't even told Priti or Luke. Why? Because - it's our secret – mine and Henry's.

***

I should view Care Girl's realisation as a serious vulnerability; yet I don't feel compromised. I'm sure numerous men, taken down by women, felt the same. I've no option but to let this thing between us play out.

Right now, she's squirrelled away, spinning all manner of scenarios in her head.

My feet take up position at her closed door. We're complicated. She's a kid, on the verge of university; a huge adventure. She's not in need of any ties to London. I should remember that.

***

I look at my watch, another seven am briefing. They keep coming and we keep sifting through hundreds of snippets of info.

"Boss, everyone's gathered, ready when you are."

My eyes take in the tray of pastries I'd brought in. Turning to my young pc, I pick the last apricot one.

"Pop that on my desk, please."

I suck my abdomen in as I approach the crime board.

"Angela is on camera leaving friends in the High Street around ten – no further sightings. We've checked camera footage on every road leading off the High Street. By process of elimination, Angela entered the park, which has four official entrances, three camera'd, one not. He knew that, so he's CCTV aware, making the abduction pre-mediated."

"Obviously," interjects Phil, undermining me. "Who carries electrical wires around?"

"I've a dating app for people into that," laughs Penny."

It's good for team moral to interact. It's my job to maintain focus.

"*Obviously* is a dirty word in my department. Its definition is: officers who take the easy option. We are detectives, so we will detect even if the outcome is the obvious one. So, evidence points to a planned abduction, but Angela going to the High Street was spontaneous."

I point to the map.

"She could have walked home a handful of ways. In fact, she was regularly warned by her parents not to take the park route home. So why did he park the car there? He couldn't have known she would walk that route. He didn't even know she was going to the High Street."

"What do parents know, hey?" says Laura, shaking her head, herself the mum of a teenager. "Maybe, he'd been watching her for days, following her, becoming familiar with her routines. He knew there was a good chance she'd take the park route home, so he parked there."

"Deadly stalker?" asks Tom.

"Maybe," I say. "Or he was opportunistic. He knew the park was off-camera. He intended to abduct someone; Angela was unlucky. Maybe Bradley was an abduction gone wrong? It could be that after failing to abduct Bradley he needed an adrenaline shot, so he pushed Alex in front of the train. We must consider every possibility no matter how unlikely. If he's clever, he won't be doing the obvious. Is everyone clear?"

Heads nod and there's murmurs of confirmation. Phil's head is down. I continue.

"The tech team found no suspicious chat-room activity, no red flags on Angela's devices."

"Mistaken identity?" asks Tom.

"The level of violence, both ante-mortem and post-mortem, was so extreme it had to be personal," I say. "It's puzzling: three dead kids...and the circumstances of their deaths different. My gut tells me we've one perp, but let's put the work in. All findings we group text immediately - NO delays. Read emails as they ping. Daily briefings at 8am, 1pm, 8pm. Bodies at desk by 7am. No one leaves before 10pm without authorisation. No one leaves till every point relating to their enquiry is logged on system in full detail. Got that?"

A chorus of 'yes gov' ends the briefing.

***

As I leave for school Henry enters. We pass each other; two pieces on a chess board – me a pawn – obviously - him the king. No greeting – just an undercurrent of resentment mixed with longing.

Henry exudes energy and power; he could light up The Shard. It's not engineered; this current is in his DNA. He totally owns it; oozing lethal threat one-minute, sexual attraction the next, in between putting on a non-coloured wash. I yearn to hate him, in my head I do, but once face to face I don't hate him, not even a smidgen. What am I thinking! Of course, I hate him.

***

I grab my shower bag and fresh clothes; I'm literally living in my office. Enroute to the female shower room I find Henry Whittle on my mind. He's a cold fish that one. In my experience psychos are rare, usually motives for murder are simple: love, hate, jealously or revenge. Whittle's niece is being victimised and he sits back? Me thinks not.

***

It's Taekwondo. Anger swirls around my head, whipped up by sexist, creepy comments from Sex Pest Rob. Without coercion, I partner him and spend the next thirty minutes striking him repeatedly until my fists are red and he sweats heavily from every pore.

NO, I don't need him to walk me to my car. NO, I'm not joining him for coffee. NO, I'm not meeting him at a bar. Jesus, no means bloody no!

Driving home, I bristle with anger. Rob is a prick and Henry is...impossible to label. As usual he's at the front door. I look up at him. He's a man, I know, who'd never harass a woman. I run upstairs before my thoughts lead me further astray. He's the enemy, Phe, remember that.

"Dinner."

His curtness travels up the stairs. He doesn't have to shout; his tone is so flat it glides into my room. I thought I'd choke on food cooked by him, but it's irritatingly delicious now organs are off menu. How does someone so sour cook so sweetly?

He washes up; I dry. We don't converse. I continue living in a world of sad silence. Upstairs, I settle in my unsleeping bag watching Teen Wolf on my laptop, until sleep pulls me into darkness.

At some point I'm disturbed. I'm accustomed to it now; Henry's strange, nocturnal activity. If he's not hooking up, then what the fuck's he up to?

***

The span of my hand fits comfortably round his neck. He's a scrawny man, a heavy smoker, he passes out quickly. He's spared the horror of the plastic bag pulled over his head and the electrical tie that fastens it around his neck.

***

Not, again. It's five fifty-five am. I must have fallen asleep reading as I'm slumped in the Sherlock with The Cruel Prince.

I stand and stretch out, my skeleton stiff from being pinched in places. Outside a layer of frost covers the landscape. It sparkles in places from the moonlight. I think wistfully of Christmas. If Henry eased up just a little more it could be amazing. I ponder this predicament further, as I hear the house breathe: its water pipes, its creaks, its tiles. It's like it's telling me it wants to be filled with holly and baubles. There is only one thing for it.

***

"Henry."

She's in my doorway.

"Henry," she calls a little louder.

I ignore hoping she'll leave. She's turned on the light. Christ she's shaking me.

***

He's bare chested which phases me. Suddenly, the air is too hot, the light too sharp and Henry too near.

"What?"

I know he's going to be difficult.

"Well?"

And hostile.

I sit on the bed, forcing him to sit upright. The quilt falls around his waist. I stare at the headboard like my life depends on it.

"Christmas is coming."

"So?"

"My parents loved celebrating. By now we'd be making paper chains and snowflakes."

"And?"

He's being such a shit again today.

"Why do you make everything so difficult?" I ask agitatedly.

"Why recount your family memories like I'm interested."

It hurt; his snappy dismissal of my dead family.

"I want to call a ceasefire. For Christmas."

He stares like I'm stupid. I should be aggrieved, but his eyes are so sharp like glittering cut glass.

***

With each passing day she edges deeper under my skin. Honestly? I'm getting rather attached to her.

"What's your proposal?"

Bringing her knees to her chest, resting her chin on her hands and her elbows on her knees, she's an owl, all big eyes. She is breathless with excitement.

"We'll go shopping for a tree and decorations. Then a few days before Christmas Eve, we'll stop off at Marks and get a small turkey or a large chicken, all the trimmings, and crackers and Christmas pudding. What do you think?"

I think you're beautiful.

"We'll see."

She leans forward, her face serious, her eyes dark, her words firm.

"We'll see is an answer for five-year-olds. You're so extra! If you're incapable of being a normal, decent, sensible…"

"Ok, no more words. I'm in, but only if you stop speaking."

"Do I need this in writing, because if it's a repeat of the key business I will be so pissed."

"It's not," I say decisively; anything to get her off my bed.

"Promise you won't wake in the morning and revert to your evil alter ego."

"I promise."

"Are you a man of your word?"

"Yessss. Now fuck off."

Her smile is huge. It's like the sun breaking through the clouds.

"You've never sworn before," she grins. "I think we're making progress.

"Turn my light off."

THE VIOLENCE BEFORE CHRISTMAS

It's not like I'm a bumlick, but it's nearly Christmas holidays and Mr Jacobs has been totally cool coaching me after school. He's so easy to be with. I thought I'd feel awkward, but my crush has become admiration. Yeah, he's cute, but he's like the loveliest big brother. Easy going, bantering and he knows masses about love and literature. So, walking by the English department, I pop a thank you card and a 'best teacher' mug on his desk.

My attention is caught. Priti's name, highlighted in yellow, on a semi scrunched up paper in his bin. Glancing around, I guiltily retrieve it, shoving it in my pocket. It's probably nothing, but I'm suspicious.

I don't un-scrunch till I'm in the Taekwondo carpark. The sheet's headed '*School Clubs Pupil List*'. Under Thursday – Mandarin, Priti's name is highlighted. Below the timetable is a handwritten note.

'*Hi Adam, list as requested, regards Sonia, School Office, 1/9/19*'. The date is weeks before he'd asked Priti and I about tutoring.

"He knew all along Priti was busy on Thursday. Arhhhhhhh."

I angrily fling the car door open, so he's forced to jump back.

"Bloody hell, Rob, why are you creeping up to my car?"

"Don't get hysterical. I tapped on your window, is all."

"But why? What are you doing hanging around me?"

"Typical female over reaction."

Wanker.

"There's no typical female; we're individuals."

I storm off – typical reaction of a person who's pissed.

In the dojo, people are taking off footwear, chatting about their week. I'm so caught up in Mr Jacobs, I don't notice people pairing off...till I look up.

Rob winks. I scowl.

Maybe Mr Jacobs forgot Priti was busy.

Rob is looking at my chest...Count to ten, Phoenix.

But why did he ask the office for the list?

"Calmed down, have you darlin?"

Does he dislike Priti? No, he's lovely to everyone. Isn't he?

"What you doing after? Maybe a few shots'd relax you?"

Does he only want to tutor me? But why?

"Ketchup time of the month is it?"

Next minute, Rob's falling to the floor holding his jaw.

"Phoenix!" booms Sensei.

"Sorry Sensei, I thought we'd started."

Giggles echo around the hall as Rob struggles to rise. He's angry and I've seen that type of anger before.

"Sorry everyone." I slip shoes on my feet. "Feelin' sick."

"Sick of Rob," someone whispers, but not low enough.

Between Mr Jacobs and Rob, I do actually feel sick.

Driving up to the house I see Henry's BMW absent. My mood dips. I'm out the car when a vehicle pulls up at speed. I hesitate. That was a mistake. I coulda locked myself in my car, instead of running to a front door I have no key for.

"You bitch."

I'm dragged off the porch.

Dropping my bag, I struggle to escape his hold. My heart isn't racing. I'm not panicked because it's just Rob. But as his grip tightens, I twist wildly, my Gee loosening. The belt drops, I free myself and Rob's left holding the jacket.

"Jesus, Rob! This is mental. Go now and we'll call it quits."

"I want this drink Phoenix. Let's take it inside, say the bedroom?"

"What the hell's wrong with you? You're married!"

He snatches at me and I jump back, but I'm trapped against my car.

"You're such a frigid bitch."

His breath is sour and veins bulge in his neck. He's staring at my sports bra. Things are escalating. I don't know what the fuck to do. His hand is on my arm; squeezing it. His fingers thick, his nails bitten down. His imprint bruising my skin.

"Let. Me. Go," I spit, yanking away sideways, squeezing between him and the car.

"I'm not finished with you."

My legs are weak; he's my violent history...another foster dad.

"Rob, look, I'm sorry, but this is taking it too far."

"Don't think so, sweetheart," he spits. "You've flirted with me all year. Hot one minute, cold the next...well it's your turn to be fucking hot."

I'm charged with adrenaline; my survival instinct is second to none.

"Touch me again I'm callin' the police."

He does...try to touch.

I'm astounded. Blood pours from Rob's nose.

"You. Fucking. Cunt!"

My chest tightens; my airways close. For a minute I think I'll gag. I'm twelve years old, being towered over by a foster dad calling me every derogatory female slang.

Rob roughly wipes his nose with his gee sleeve; blood quickly seeping into white cotton.

"Think about your wife."

A sly smile spreads across his face.

"You're gonna be a dad."

I'm stepping backward, but still I'm cornered by the house, by the garage. I run at him; it's unexpected. It gives me crucial seconds to pass him, but he grabs at my waist, his fingers tightly grasping the elastic of the gee trousers. I'm ferociously twisting to loosen his fingers; I refuse to let this narrative end badly...for me.

A car door slams.

My head snaps in its direction.

A Henry I barely recognise powers towards us.

I shrink back, forgetting Rob and presuming the worst; Henry is done with me.

As Rob turns to see what's shaken me more than him...

Henry strikes Rob hard centre chest.

Rob crumples to his knees, clutching his chest, gasping for air.

"Get up."

Rob is shaking. I think he's having a fucking heart attack.

Henry sharply pulls him up by his gee to slam a punch into his face.

Rob's head rebounds wildly. He sinks back to his knees, folding inward.

"Get the fuck up."

Rob's breathing is audible: desperate and hoarse. Blood runs from his nose and lips. Henry grasps his hand and Rob howls, tears falling freely, as Henry bends a finger back on itself.

CRACK!

Henry doesn't blink through Rob's high-pitched cries of pain.

"Touch her again and I'll break every bone in your body."

We watch Rob crawl to his car and lever himself up on the door. He tries to start it two or three times, revving the engine like it's a beast, before reversing away.

Henry offers his hand. I brace my heart as I put mine in his. It feels incredibly intimate.

"Ok?" he asks.

I nod; not trusting myself to speak without crying. It was shocking; being struck, Henry striking back. I knew Henry was dark, but he has a level of controlled violence that responds so instantly and effectively it's disturbing. I think about the disappearance of my uncle. Has Henry made anyone else disappear? Shivers ripple through me.

"Come inside," he says leading me by the hand to the kitchen. "Sit."

His hand loosens.

"Don't let go," I barely whisper unable to look at him.

He doesn't. Instead his hand captures some stray hair. He feels the strands between his fingers. My eyes are shut tight, I hardly breathe.

"Now I know why you have so many bad hair days."

***

I'm dousing the flame with accelerant. The problem is, I'm acutely attracted to a girl who annoys me. A girl as troubled as she is beautiful; not in a production line way, no, Phoenix is bespoke. But we can't do - whatever this is.

"I'll get you ice."

I turn the radio on.

"The Metropolitan Police are under pressure tonight..."

She's heard enough to withdraw upstairs.

***

Henry is a man completely comfortable with violence. Why am I shocked? He'd been a marine...he'd killed people. It's only now this fact sinks in. Henry has taken a person's life from them. Even in the line of duty, it's pretty fucked up.

***

She's quiet at dinner but the incident hasn't impacted on her appetite.

"I'm away on business tonight," I inform.

She stares at me challengingly. I produce a key from my pocket. On it a keyring of a phoenix; popular with Harry Potter fans.

She turns it around; her fingers examining, like it's a rare gem.

"Are you sure?" she asks with nervous excitement.

It's like I'm giving her my virginity. It's bigger; it's my trust.

***

As Henry demonstrates how to operate the alarm I fixate on his arms. Tightly muscle bound; strong but not bulging. I imagine them around my waist, pulling me near.

"Clear?" asks Henry tersely.

"Erm, one last time?"

I watch his hands. I imagine them on my bare back.

"Got it?" he asks.

Pushing me against him.

"Phoenix?"

"Thanks, I've got it."

Shit! I've got it bad. I want to ask him not to go. It's not a neediness, but a hazy uncertainty about everything. There's something dangerous in the air. I mean, away on business. No further explanation forthcoming. What is Henry's definition of business?

***

Istanbul. The temperature is fourteen degrees centigrade and light rain slightly alters the clarity of my sight. I'm on a rooftop opposite a penthouse. The glass is bullet-proof, but the term is inaccurate; the right gun with the right bullet can penetrate anything and it does. I see the surprise on his face when he hears a dull crack. He looks around confused where the noise originates from. Then he sees it, the fine fracturing of the glass in the window; the cracking transfixes him until the bullet enters his forehead – dead centre.

***

I wake up thinking it's a shame, just as Henry eases up, he's off on a book thingy. It's probably boring. Hopefully he's home after school.

It's funny how quickly people lose interest in events. Two weeks ago, the school grapevine buzzed with theories about Angela. Today everyone's moaning about the manky lasagne. Maybe because it's nearly Christmas no one's arsed about death - only Kirsten: her hate pursues me down the corridors.

Walking towards my car, through an alleyway running from one road to another, I think about my phoenix keyring. I feel warm and fuzzy

***

"Urgh!"

Like popping candy, pain bursts inside my head. There's a moment of pure terror when my brain is confused. I'm hauled up against a wall; my head smashed on the brick and my neck whiplashed. I'm breathing hard, gasping for oxygen, terrified it's the Ruislip Avenger. I cringe in pain as my shoulder throbs from hard brick collision. My mouth eats pebble dash; the stippled surface scraping my cheek. My heart is beating too fast, too loud; straining against my ribs – I'm terrified it'll tear.

"Freak!"

I don't think, I just do. Pushing myself away from the wall, turning my head to alleviate sizzling pain, a large hand bangs my head back.

"Arghhhh."

Its fingers span my face: covering my mouth, crushing my nose. It smells of sweat and piss, a boy's hand. I want to scream, but his palm covers my mouth. It's disgusting that the skin that touched his dick is against mine.

I've learnt my lesson, but they still have something to teach. The hand is withdrawn, released, I drop like a rock, to the stone, cold pavement. I taste blood and panic fills my lungs. In this burst of violence, seconds are an eternity.

"No more, please," I beg.

"Shut your mouth cunt."

It's Amy. It's so Amy. It's totally a bit Amy.

Pain tears through my head as my ponytail is snatched, wrenching my neck back; twisting its muscles; choking me.

Amy's laughing hysterically. I want her dead. I want the Ruislip Avenger to skin her alive.

"This is fuckin' jokes," she says cattily cutting my ponytail.

She kicks me full force in the ribs.

"Urghhhh. H-hur, h-hur!"

I curl up protecting my body. Even when their footfall is feint. I think of the woods. Maybe this is my place in the world, a thing underfoot, to be trod on, kicked at, dug up.

***

I hear her car, then her key attempting to engage with the lock? Her hoodie is up, her head down, as she passes without comment. Her body weight imbalance indicates a blow to the ribs.

I return to preparing veg. It's no surprise I'm bothered by her physical state. As a marine I swore to serve and protect. However, our relationship is deconstructing my personality. I'd be a liar if I didn't admit to resenting her. I like the old me. The me accountable to no one. The me with only myself to keep safe.

I chop an onion.

A rib might have punctured a lung.

Survival of the fittest...or not.

I peel potatoes.

She could have internal bleeding.

I slice carrots.

She could die.

***

I think I've internal bleeding. I am in FUCKING AGONY.

***

I find her slumped against the wall groaning in pain. Her face is badly grazed; particles of grit embedded in the skin's surface. Her forehead is shiny with perspiration. Her ponytail is missing. I smile cruelly; school hasn't changed.

"Step away from the wall."

She does.

"I'm about to touch you."

The low sun outlines her delicate features; she appears surreal. I pull her blouse loose from her skirt and unbutton it. She blows out in pain. She is totally rigid.

"Relax; it's easier for me to examine."

She can't.

I place my hands beneath her rib cage.

Instantly, her hand clamps my arm.

"We're doing this. You may need the hospital."

I take her hand, placing it on my shoulder.

"It'll help with balance. Squeeze when it hurts."

I press each rib, checking its position, working from bottom to top, until my hands rest beneath her breasts.

She holds my shoulder, but refrains from openly sharing her pain. The intimacy of the situation is uncomfortable.

"One of your ribs is cracked. Breathing, coughing, sneezing will hurt, but pain will dull in a few days. There's no advantage going to hospital; x-rays will confirm a cracked rib; strapping might relieve chest pain, but it restricts lung movement."

"Could my lung be pierced?"

"No."

She draws a quivering intake of breath and leans her forehead against my chest.

"Would you help me into my nightshirt."

Pushing off her blouse I'm lightheaded. What the fuck's going on?

"Is your nightshirt under your pillow?"

"Yes," she puffs out in agony.

"Turn away."

With her back to me I unhook her bra.

"Arms up; it's going to hurt."

I see her bare back shake before I slip her hands through and it drops down her arms, covering her.

Kneeling I slip my hands up inside the nightshirt to her waistband. I unbutton, unzip and ease her skirt down.

"I'll get painkillers," I say more cutting than intended. "Your hair...it's...interesting."

***

Henry's touch is unfathomable. As the pressure of his fingers searched for injury, I'd summoned Mr Jacobs. I'd managed to visualise his chiselled features, his conker-brown unshaven chin but Henry's face superimposed – it looked scarily unnatural.

***

She lays on her makeshift bed. Gingerly raising enough to swallow painkillers.

"Lay back."

She looks stricken.

"Relax, I'm not going to tweezer you to death."

"I thought you viewed caring as an affliction?"

"I'm making an exception."

***

I lay unflinching as Henry works away removing particles of gravel from my face. His touch is gentle. His hand intermittently brushes my cheek.

"Tell me something about you and the Navy."

I expect a withering comment or a withdrawal.

"Basic training. Biological and chemical preparation. I entered the gas chamber wearing a protective mask and clothing. The sergeant released a controlled concentration of CS gas. I had to remain calm, lift my mask and give my name, rank and national insurance number then lower mask. I did, then that bastard sergeant kneed me in the groin, pulling my mask off. I fell to my knees, my eyes filling with water, mucus clogged up my nose and lungs - I couldn't fucking breathe. I was glad I'd read up on it. I opened my eyes, real wide, but never touched them. That's a big mistake; it leads to gas penetrating your system further. Open eyes allow fresh air to dissipate the discomfort in minutes. The moral of this memory? Bullies are everywhere. Basic training was like being back at school; it's the same crap."

"Thank you. That means a lot coming from you."

***

I generally don't surprise myself. Telling someone about my past - that's a first. It's also a rats' layer.

***

He lightly applies disinfectant. Henry is exhibiting highly schizophrenic tendencies. Nevertheless, I am drifting, like a fallen leaf, in a river gently, flowing downstream.

***

I think of her upstairs. My housemate. A concept I originally gave no credence. My instinctive reluctance to communicate, she's worn down. Whether they're words of intervention or damage control, she has me talking. Something the Taliban couldn't achieve. Fuck, she's addictive.

***

Pain wakes me. Tablets sit on a nearby piece of paper. Henry has gone Alice in Wonderland on me.

'TAKE THESE'.

I happily swallow; anything to ease this hellish pain. The Sherlock chair is beside my sleeping bag? I use it to pull myself up. Jesus the pain is bloody painful! It seems violence is the trigger to Henry engaging with me. No wonder he doesn't have friends.

I check my phone. Jesus I've slept through the night and half the day. I pull on joggers with particles of degraded toilet paper settled in the fluff. From the kitchen I see Henry in the garden. I feel a warmth like a ray of sun followed by a deep longing. I wrap up warm.

"Hey, Henry, coffee."

Hellos and goodbyes are awkward. I sit on the bench near the patch of ground Henry is digging. Even though it's December, Henry's in a sleeveless tee. I want to look at him: his arms, his tattoos, but instead I stare at the plate in my hands. I worry...about me. Am I becoming obsessed?

"I've got biscuits."

Jesus, I'm talking like he's five. He drops his shovel and sits. The biscuits worked.

"Henry, about yesterday." Speaking directly to him isn't easy. "Thank you for looking after me."

He doesn't respond.

"You were very...very..." Shit, what do I say? "Lovely."

"You'll need to take painkillers regularly for three or four days. I phoned the school, told them you had flu and wouldn't be back till the New Year."

"Cool. It's only a couple of days, and teachers give up teaching in the last week, so I won't miss much."

I run my hands through my sheered hair. I think about what a total mess I am, a calamity, a broken thing...beside perfection. I stand. The last thing he'll want is me talking to him, hanging around, dragging him down.

"Ok then."

***

She's over-thinking. Low self-worth gnawing away. She deserves reassurance, comfort, friendship. She is an open book and I'm Book of the Dead.

"If you're up to it, would you refill the bird feeders?"

Her face lights up and she nods enthusiastically.

"Hang a couple of feed balls on the tree branches for the squirrels."

"Did you know, a squirrel's front teeth never stop growing," she says.

Inside, I'm smiling.

***

I don't like moving this quickly, but a message must be sent.

I hear her scathing remarks to her mother, before heatedly storming off. Thinking about it, I'm doing her family a favour.

I follow and watch. Sometimes for hours. I have a flask of hot chocolate in my rucksack. I patiently wait, conscious that public awareness is heightened because of the last body.

She turns onto a narrow country lane. No cameras. No cars. No properties. No people. No safety.

Her jeans are too tight; they leave nothing to the imagination and her sweatshirt with the slogan *'Kiss me quick'* makes me want to puke! What a slut!

I pull in a few metres ahead of her, jumping out of the car with my map and a little boy lost look.

"Hi, can you help me, I seem to be lost?"

"It's you," she says surprised.

"Yes, it's me," I grin.

We chat, our heads together, leaning over the map. She gives me directions; fuck she's dim.

"Well thanks Amy," I smile brightly, folding the map away.

"How'd you know my name?" she asks like the stupid bitch she is.

"It's on your necklace, sugar," I say warmly. She smiles and poses provocatively. I run my index finger across her breasts underlining the slogan. She is excited. I put one arm either side of her.

"Kiss me quick," I read. "That's no good," I say looking in her eyes, increasing my breathing, so she thinks I'm attracted.

"What's wrong with it," she giggles.

"You, should be kissed slowly, softly, lingeringly."

I lean forward and kiss her. Her tongue is quickly in my mouth. When we run out of breath, I ask...

"You're a local lady, show me in person and we'll do lunch."

"Sure, it's not far from where I live," she smiles.

The sane part of me wants to scream, are you fucking stupid! Never get into a car with a stranger. Never! The monster in me kisses her a gentle thanks. I open the passenger door - cows and sheep the only witnesses.

We have sex in the car. I enjoy it. It wasn't rape; it was consensual. I'm not into sexual aggression. I don't need to control women - just Phoenix.

***

"Pain, pain and more pain," I moan to Luke even though it's been a few days since the attack.

"Phe, I ain't callin' you out bae, but you gotta seriously do something about this shit."

"Luke, pleeeease just say lovely, soft, cushy words to me because I'm on the edge here."

"Phe you're in a shit storm. You can't hide from it."

"I'm not fucking hiding, Luke; it's the Christmas holiday."

"Fuck Phe, I'm feelin' you, but this ain't dumb shit, this is dangerous shit. These bitches ain't gonna stop."

"Luke enough, please," I say close to tears. "Tomorrow I'm seeing Diane, I'll tell her everything. Look I've got to go."

"Hold up. You're not havin a melt, are you?"

"Nooooo!" I blatantly am! "Look, I'm gonna deal."

"Cool."

"I'll hit you letter, yeah?"

"Anytime, Whittle. Love you babes."

Disconnecting, my tight neck muscles twist with tension. How can I even drive to Diane's in this state? What can I say about Henry? The man's a criminal mastermind! Let's not lie about it, yet my feet carry me downstairs, through the lounge, into the kitchen.

I see him through the glass. I love that there's no kitchen wall. That it's a giant window framed only by the roof and floor. I've seen houses like it in Hello magazine. The strange thing is, a while back, a receipt was half out of the site manager's folder. Being nosy I slightly eased it out further; 'polycarbonate and glass laminate' windows costing an extortionate amount of money. I googled them. I'd obviously misread. 'Bulletproof glass.'

***

She looks up as I enter. She half smiles. For a moment we both pause, quietly breathing the other in. I sense her taming her emotions, holding back, endeavouring not to be too obtrusive, but in terms of interfering in my life I may as well have given her a kidney.

***

I need to talk to Henry about Diane
"Henry. Umm," I mumble.
Shit this is hard.
He's still waiting.
"Tea?" I ask chickening out.
He nods.
His fingers reach for the hem of his t-shirt. My eyes leap to the kettle. Until the second, when the garment covers his eyes, then I peek and count each prominent rib as he stretches.
He leans down to the freezer for frozen berries, his skin taut as each back-muscle stretches.
Fluidly he rises, opening the fridge, passing me the milk as he grabs his protein shake. His arm is smooth, no hair or freckles, the strength of it disguised by creamy skin.
My breath burns inside me; so many words, one on top of another. Automatically I pour the tea, hearing the liquid as it flows from the pot to the cups, a slight steam raising. It's like I'm in a place where I don't speak the language. Suddenly I'm stifled, almost claustrophobic. I don't know if I added sugar.
He's leaning close, scrutinising my face; the smell of him is too...too everything.
"You look pale."
My ears roar with blood. His bare arms are reaching for me. His obliques tightening as he turns. I feel...I feel...

***

She slips into unconsciousness. I carry her upstairs, to my bed. She's a vocal whirlwind one minute and a feather floating on a draft the next, yet she stirs something in me.
I lay down beside her.
She's honest, gentle, giving. I'm duplicitous, hard, self-interested. The more intimate we become the less I like myself. Our reality is, I care for

a young woman whose life I've been thrust into. I would never have deliberately chosen to be with Phoenix.

She nestles her back into my chest.

But here we are. Together.

We breathe in unison. Our chests rise and fall as if one motion.

I close my eyes.

Some people count sheep, I count...

***

I wake slow-ly, stretch-ing, co-sy-ing into the pillow. I stiffen. Henry Whittle is in my bed! No...I haven't a bed. I'm in bed with Henry Whittle.

Henry sits up, swinging his legs over the side of the bed. Once again, I'm at a disadvantage, staring at his naked back. At the stitches holding him together. I think about touching one, when he stands.

"You fainted. Carrying you up the stairs exhausted me." he says.

"Ha," I say like it's the most normal thing, waking up in a double bed with this man. I hate that I'm about to complicate things.

"I'm due to see Diane, my counsellor, tomorrow, except I can't drive so she said she'd come here. I said no, but she..."

"That's fine."

I raise myself up on my elbow.

"Really?"

***

"I'm showering, stay, you need to rest up. Your body's taken a bashing; it takes time to recover. See your person tomorrow. Tonight, fancy going for a takeaway?"

She stares at me like it's a trick. I don't blame her.

"It's not a complicated question. Yes? No?"

"Yes please," she smiles tentatively.

"You pick," I say.

"Really?"

"Sure."

"Is there a budget?"

"No."

"Have you any food allergies."

I give her the stare before the cutest giggles burst from her lips.

"I'm winding you up. I get you're a man of few words and I'm a female of too many. Jesus, what are we going to talk about over dinner?"

She's almost laughing, but pain crosses her brow. She has no idea how luminous her eyes are, how they reflect doubt mixed with desire. It's the first time I've really looked at her. Before, had been about intimidation. Today I see Whittle. Where he was depraved, she is innocent, but still, it's like looking into the face of a man I murdered.

***

Washed, dressed and paracetamol swallowed, I grab my phone and purse.

"Ready?" Henry asks as I step into the hallway.

It's that simple. No threat, no dubious comments, no flippant remarks laced with menace. This is unknown territory; Henry communicating directly to me like I exist.

I climb into the passenger seat.

Smooth, tranquil driving; whoever thought it possible. I want Henry to drive and never stop, maybe at red lights and at give-ways, clearly at zebra crossings.

"We're here," says Henry his voice like cut glass.

We turn simultaneously. In under a minute I notice...how small and overheated the car feels...the hint of dark, blunt facial hair beneath his smooth jaw...that there is a centimetre scar under his left eyebrow.

"Phoenix?"

My breath catches; it blocks the next causing me to choke out a chorus of dry coughs. His lips have formed my name. Two syllables he'd previously been unable to join now hang between us. I fight the impulse to touch him. I know he is an advocate of separatism, but I so want to bring him over to the dark side.

My eyes rise from his jaw, past his mouth, back to his irises that are light grey; almost silver.

"Phoenix?"

My cheeks colour; he knows I'm staring, but Henry isn't Henry. He's Mr Topsy Turvy. Will birds fly backwards, will day be in darkness?

"Phoenix, are you up to this."

Jesus his words unglue me.

"Phoenix?"

It's there; in my name. Change floats in the air, I taste it.

***

We're sitting comfortably. I find watching her my new favourite past-time. Since her melt down she's surprisingly at ease in my company.

The waitress arrives with our meals.

"Vegan?" I question.

"You, feeding me animal organs, has left me scarred," she smiles.

It's no ordinary smile, but a bedtime tale of sensuous sentences punctuated with kisses. We're just not sure if we're gonna read it.

"So that's all my friends. Maybe including Mercy is questionable, but I do care about her and then there's little Ben. Knowing what's ahead of him is heart...Shit," she says, her face freezing in mild shock.

***

Her voice has an abrasive edge impossible to forget. She is gaudier than cheap tinsel. Larger than I imagined possible. Make-up good enough for Cirque de Soleil. I nod at Henry. Is he scared? Maybe.

"No. That seat won't do," she complains.

"Madam, I'm sorry, but it's all we have."

"I eat here regularly."

"That's obvious," I whisper.

"As a loyal customer I expect some courtesy. There! That table."

"Madam that table is booked for a large party."

"She is a large party!" I whisper to Henry grinning.

"Then that table."

The one next to us. She doesn't recognise me immediately due to the bruises and bumps. She appears confused. Then. Utterly freaks. I look behind me expecting to see a customer with two heads but there is only a mirror. Her reflection is scary, but she must be used to it by now. Fudge, she grasps the poor waiter with one hand and her other flies haphazardly in the air, like a javelin, landing dead centre in a waitress' tray. Glass shatters, liquids spill, customers throw wobblies and Cow has hold of the waiter. So, when she goes down, so does he.

***

"Home, I think," says Henry.

Suddenly it clicks. It was Henry's reflection. Claire is terrified of Henry.

A slight coldness chills my mood.

As Henry pays, his hand comes to rest at the base of my spine. A warmth emanates from his touch, sweeping away the collywobbles.

I love how Henry walks close by my side and opens the car door for me. His attentiveness makes me feel special, like I'm a unicorn.

In the car, I listen to Henry's music. You learn a lot about someone from their playlist: Die by the Gun, Live or Die, Revenge, Bury a Friend.

We drive down the dark Hillingdon lanes, lit only a few feet ahead by car headlights.

So, what, if Henry scares Claire. If she had a coronary, I'd thank him.

My eyes drift to Henry's thigh, I imagine it naked, next to mine. My eyes rise to the steering wheel, to Henry's fingers. I imagine them, pushing my knickers aside and slip...

"Phoenix?"

"What?" I shout sharply, jerking, like I've been caught out.

"You ok? You were breathing erratically."

"Indigestion."

Henry raises an eyebrow as he parks. He'd be perfect at interrogation. I wonder if he's ever tied a consenting girlfriend up. That is fucking sexy.

I brush Henry's hand as he opens the door for me. He'll know it was on purpose.

"I'm glad we ate before Cow's crumble," I point out: standing gawkily in the hallway, wanting to gravitate to the sofa, but concerned I've overstayed my welcome. "Perhaps the thought of not eating caused respiratory failure."

His eyes are on me. I used to imagine them forming judgements and me falling short. Lately the intensity of his scrutiny feels altered. I'm uncomfortable, yet desperate for more.

"They should have asked for a jumbulance; she'd never fit in an ambulance."

He nods, whilst his eyes remain tight on me.

"I think I'll have an early one. Diane will be here shortly after nine."

"Sleep in my room."

So, here I lay cocooned in Henry's bed. It feels like the safest place in the world. Like nothing can hurt me here. I skip the painkillers. I don't want to sleep and miss out, but within minutes I'm a melted banana, so soft and squishy and sleepy.

THE CHRISTMAS PARTY

I wake, my arms around Henry's pillow, my face buried in it. I make the bed, patting it, smoothing it, reluctantly leaving it for a bath. I think about how fucked up I am right now. As water gushes from the chrome taps into the pristine bath I pour his bath foam under the running water. I think if I drowned in him, I might be happy.

I feel conscious dressing; critical of everything I have. It's either too small, over-washed, bobbly, faded or all the above. As this is genuinely an emergency, I pull on my recently purchased joggers and a pink t-shirt.

DINGDONG, DINGDONG.

"Hey Diane."

"Phoenix."

We hug, then she draws back, her hands holding my forearms.

"You poor thing. What have they done to you?"

"I'm a mess I know." Not wanting a pity party, I link arms and walk her into the lounge. "How cool is this?" I ask.

Diane is impressed; it's some house but Henry's some man.

I make tea; we enjoy Henry's shortbread, but I feel guilty. A secret is a muzzle. My brain is wired to reveal truth, not keep secrets and tell lies. My feelings for Henry already have negative consequences – I can no longer say absolutely anything to Diane. I talk about school; how caustic words burn like acid through my confidence. How each morning I wake up choking on apprehension. How I imagine being in an accident on the way to school. Nothing life-threatening but injured enough to be home-schooled. Yet I keep Henry's skeletons safe. Maybe Henry intends I take them to the grave?

"Phoenix, you're drifting off. Tell me more about Mr Jacobs."

So, I do. I tell her about the Thursday club. I tell her I'm worried he dislikes Priti. Maybe it's a racial thing because she is the only British Pakistani person in our class. I was hoping she'd put forward an opinion to let Mr Jacobs off the hook, but she adds to my dilemma. Diane thinks Mr Jacobs' actions towards me are unprofessional.

***

After dinner Phoenix washes, I dry and put away. She is singing along to the radio. I hadn't thought it possible to sing that badly, but Phoenix achieves the impossible.

At this point, damage limitation is essential. My gut tells me she'd never reveal I'm not her uncle, but my judgement is clouded when it comes to Phoenix. I care for her and that makes me vulnerable. Not a position I choose lightly. Fortunately, I have a voice activated recording system throughout the house. Later I'll assess the situation.

"It's seven and the main headline is missing schoolgirl Amy Gordon, who the police believe to be the third victim of the Ruislip Attacker."

"Did you hear what I just heard?" she asks.

"I take it she's one of your enemies?"

"She sheared my ponytail."

"What goes around comes around is rare; count yourself even and move on. There's no room for emotion in school warfare."

***

Upstairs, I feel physically sick. Sick of the Mr Jacobs' autopsy. Now fucking Amy! Continuous white static between my ears until my mind crashes and no longer buffers; I can't even recall the words to 'Moves like...

CLICK.

What now? What the fuck now?

CLICK.

It's my window.

CLICK.

My phone vibrates.

"Luke?" Where are you?"

"Below you."

"Are you mental. Henry's trained to kill. You can't just creep around; the grounds could be booby-trapped."

"I'm here coza Henry. Phe, it's crazy bae, but Amy's been nabbed, and I know you need downtime; we're getting waved. I'm knockin."

"No! Don't! I'll be out in five."

"I want to see this psycho, boojie uncle of yours."

"Don't you dare, Luke Lawrence."

I have a million reasons not to go, but right now I can't spell the word fun and Luke will, no doubt, knock on Henry's door if I don't appear. If I stay, I'll just drag myself down plotting conspiracy theories, dissecting the Amy nightmare.

I drag a brush through my hair. My reflection is ghostly: my face gaunt, my skin pale. Black is all I have. I look like the creepy girl who wants to kill everyone in school. Crap I am that girl.

Downstairs, Henry is nowhere to be seen. I knock on his office door – no answer. So, I scribble a note and leave it on the kitchen table.

We jump in the back of a waiting van; body squashing body.

"Yo, this is Phoenix," Luke shouts.

My name bounces back at me from a mismatched group of semi drunk teens. Grime or something booms from the massive back speakers.

"Here," says a girl pushing a Bacardi at me.

Luke pulls me down beside him. I feel awkward.

"What's the matter? he asks, sensing my discomfort.

"No seatbelts?"

I bong hard as the van veers around a sharp bend.

"Live a little Phe," he whispers in my ear before kissing my cheek.

Precisely! I want to live. If the van crashes we'll be killed instantly; our bones cracked, our organs ruptured. My parents would be so pissed.

Luke presses another bottle in my hand, passed by a girl wearing a tiny black bodycon dress. I drink steadily, finding alcohol calms my inner turmoil, and like teenagers around the world, the thrill of being bad, of not linking actions to consequences carries me away.

BOOM!BOOM!BOOM!BOOM!BOOM!BOOM!

A continuous beat of grime pumps so loud my brain shakes.

"Where are we?" I shout to Luke who's holding my hand as I jump from the van.

"South Ruislip, some yute's house from college."

Kids overflow from the house into the front garden.

CLINK!

I knock into bottles left in the doorway and fall into a huge, black boy with zigzagged gold hair.

"Hunty," he smiles.

"Fuck off, Jed," says Luke aggressively.

"Bruv, no disrespect," he says, but he's disrespecting, even I see that. He leans into my ear. "Tingting."

What does that even mean. I'm out of my depth. Luke's pulling me firmly through a tight crowd of people.

Music, shouting, laughing; it merges into a thudding drone laced with bitch and nigger. Every expletive mixes with oxygen, carbon dioxide and nitrogen, and breathes out of kids' months like it's essential to respiration. It's scary, but cool, but mainly scary.

Luke tugs me through to the kitchen. Kids do puff, lines, oxy. Upstairs is for the heavies; it scares me that I'm in a house with heroin.

I'm on fast forward. We drink beer, wine, vodka shots. We dance. More drink. I watch Luke do balloons.

More drink. No. I don't do drugs. I dance, drink, dance. I need the loo. I don't want to go alone, but some girl is dry humping Luke. I squeeze past kids. on stairs, snogging and puffing.

A bedroom is filled with boys on PlayStation. I ease open the next door.

"Sorry, sorry, sorry," I apologise, trying to delete the image of one boy giving head to another.

A boy comes out of the loo and I throw myself in it, locking the door. Crap, the toilet-seat is covered in urine. I hover over the seat to pee. Midstream there's pounding on the door. This is fucking horrible.

In the hallway, a druggy looking blond boy, outright measures me up.

"Jer, wanna fuck?"

Oh yeah, I want to do something intimate and special with you too.

My head spins, in fact my world is spinning. I see someone sniffing gear off a hallway bookcase. I don't like this party. I want to go home.

Downstairs, Luke is creeping, his body up against a girl who doesn't care about dating.

Cigarettes and marijuana cling to the air making me heave. Sick and dizzy I need fresh air, but bodies block the hallway. I lurch and tumble. My moments of clarity decreasing by the minute as the room rolls.

A girl with mascara running down her cheeks and smudged lipstick bangs into me.

"What the fuck you lookin at?"

I shake my head.

"Fuckin dumb bitch," she shouts pushing past me - I wonder, does she realise she's not wearing shoes?

I'm too confused to register the change in mood.

Until bodies spiral around me, scrambling over each other and twisting. One body is hurled on another, girls are screaming and crying. Luke is at the centre of it. He has Zigzag Boy pinned to the wall, shouting Fucking! Abuse! at him. Until Luke is dragged off and thrown to the floor.

Why's glimmering glass confetti showering me? Unthinking, I brush the shiny debris off my shoulders and, momentarily, sharp pain causes me to examine my fingertips. Blood escapes through minute slices. I sway; my history leaves me with an aversion to my own blood. Behind me, the internal glass doors have shattered. In front, a mountain of bodies pile onto Luke. My chest feels tight, like we're twins, and I'm being crushed. I might be watching him die, until the heap abruptly subsides, and bodies flee in all directions as police sirens wail. Kids run at the sink and toilets to flush their stash away. One boy remains on the sofa. Dead. No, nearly dead, he retches and retches until a stream of alcoholic vomit spews from his throat. My stomach muscles contract and I taste acid in my mouth. My eyes fix on the carpet pattern; hypnotised by its swirls undulating and expanding.

Escaping bodies, knock me back and forth, back and forth, back and, oh, God. I cling to a wall, resting my forehead on its cool structure. The drill scene thuds loudly, everyone too concerned with the police to mute it.

"Phoenix!"

Turning my head, Luke catches my eye.

"Run!"

***

Driving back from recon., I listen to Phoenix's interaction with her therapist. I regularly listen-in on private lives, however, this feels like an infringement of our blooming friendship, but a necessary one.

Play.

"Heavens, Phoenix!"

Phoenix reveals the full content of her attack. Details she would never share with me. Details I find hard to stomach.

"Tell me about Henry."

"He's complicated."

"In what way?"

"Erm, he's antagonistic, but it's subtle. He has a dry sense of humour, completely deadpan, with a death-stare that is bloody amazing! It scared the crap out of me for ages, but now I think, bring it on, it's peng. We don't argue because that requires emotion, but I've screamed, ranted, insulted and he's pretty much taken it without retaliating. He's good like that: calm, unflappable. He can be unexpectedly caring, but it's like he's incapable of getting emotionally involved."

"That's not uncommon in front-line soldiers."

"He's clever; a marine would need to be tactical, a quick thinker. He's also impatient and judge-y; like when I seared the beef joint on the hob and the dish exploded – Jesus, how was I to know it wasn't a hob-to-oven dish? He didn't say anything, but I sensed disapproval. Henry's

voice isn't loud, his gestures aren't sweeping, yet he dominates every space. He makes me feel safe, which contradicts how scared he's made me. In science terms, Henry is a solid, his emotions are tightly compressed and there's no room for me. Yet," she pauses. "I can't let him go."

Stop, Rewind, Play.

"I can't let him go."

Stop, Rewind, Play.

"I can't let him go"

Play.

"I'm worried."

"About what Phoenix?"

"The way I feel about him."

Stop, Rewind, Play.

"The way I feel about him."

Play.

"Can you explain?"

"I best not."

"How do you feel right now?"

"My heart hurts and I want it to stop. I mean, not beating but hurting. I want Henry to like me. He's been indescribably horrible and I'm like a battered wife, hoping he'll change. I'm worried a pattern is emerging – that I'm seeking out risky relationships."

"Is Henry aggressive towards you?"

"No, he's unnervingly calm, intimidating, quietly threatening, but that's changed recently. I wouldn't say he likes me, but he's tolerating me. I think it's at great cost to himself. I feel that."

Silence.

"I think he was tortured and that's damaged him. He acts weirdly, not in a paedo way, but in an unsettling way. Yet today, right now I trust him. Henry gives me strength; he makes me not want to be a victim. He makes me feel..."

Silence.

"Phoenix?"

"I don't know. I...I don't know. I'm tired and everything is shit."

A long pause.

"Not everything. Henry cares. Which I'm ecstatic about...but what if I made him? What if I've worn him down? What if he realises, he is so much more and I am so much less?

"What do you want Phoenix?"

166

"I want to be a blank page: fresh, crisp, ready to write myself a happy ending. I want to wipe out my past, erase its dirty smudges, draw a line through my mistakes and crumple up my tragic past...I want to rewind to the first day I met Henry and fix it."

Silence.

"If I had a wish, apart from Mum and Dad living, it would be for Henry to like me back."

"He's that important to you?"

"Yes, he's that important to me."

Stop, rewind, play.

"He's that important to me."

I hear the tug of desire in her voice alongside resignation.

"It's been a while since I've seen you so down, but it's to be expected: Trish's death, you're adapting to a new environment, Henry, and the bullying campaign - we're not talking sticks and stones here, it's violence."

"I'm going to report it. I mean, really report it."

"Good! Do you want to talk your dreams through?"

"No. They're too messed up for public distribution...I need to get a grip of things. In the mirror I barely recognise myself. My emotions are erratic: I hate Henry, I love Henry."

Stop, rewind, play.

"I hate Henry, I love Henry."

Play.

"I want to die I want to live. Every day my emotions lurch between worship and hate. I'm exhausted."

Silence.

"I've another problem. It's a teacher student issue."

Interesting.

Being on my mind, I check her phone tracker. She's in HA4? It's past two am? Typical teen behaviour, except Phoenix isn't typical.

***

Stumbling from the house into the garden, the abrupt change in temperature hits me hard. The cold, harsh air invades my nose and throat and within minutes they are coarse. Breathing hard, I stagger over the ground's uneven surface, crossing the garden despite the bracing wind's resistance. There is a wall at the bottom, about six feet high, no four feet, no seven feet. Despite its altering dimensions I take a running jump; my foot hits it and I hurl myself up, scratching my arms, but I don't feel it – I'm Buffnix.

At the top, momentum tosses me over into another garden. I land on spiky privet. We fight bravely until I roll off, falling against a shed, slipping down its rough surface to the grass. Getting my phone out, I stare at it until recollection of how to use it springs to mind. I repeatedly ring until she picks up.

"Priti, you're a pretty Priti," my sing songy voice echoes in my head.

"You sound different. Phoenix, are you...drunk?"

Sweating like mad, I collapse on my back. I lay there, looking towards the starry sky, wanting Henry. I'm a real girl in trouble and not mature enough to call Henry for help.

"Phoenix, are you there? Phoenix, I'm worried..."

Stars disappear and reappear as my eyes lose and regain focus at such a speed my head spins. My eyes unconsciously close, so I stretch my lids wide causing my eyes to bulge awake.

"Don't worry pretty Priti. The grass is nice."

The line goes dead.

***

She's an incoherent, crumpled wreck; totally wasted. Indoors, I slip her trainers off and wash her face and hands before covering her with a blanket. I sit on the Sherlock. I birdwatch.

***

My head is weighted with pain and recriminations. It refuses to lift off the pillow, so I cover my eyes with my arms and fall into a fitful sleep.

Hours later, I wake, my mouth is dry and my head throbs from alcohol abuse. I'm still dressed – thank God. I recall Luke, the van, the house...then nothing concrete. Luke? I feel around for my phone; nine missed calls. Awkwardly, I roll onto my side.

"Shit!"

There's paracetamol and water in arms reach. Henry's my dark angel.

"Luke."

"Phe. Are you ok?"

"No Luke. I am fucking not ok."

"How d'ya get home?"

"No idea."

"Phe, I'z feelin anger here. Don't get ugly now."

"Like what. Upset because you bought me to some trapper's house. There were drugs there Luke, real Top Boy drugs."

"I was fucking waved Phe. I'm sorry."

"Why did you let me drink so much?"

"PhePhePhe. Tings go down at parties, y'know how it goes."

"Drop the gangsta slang, we know I don't. What the hell was I thinking? I'm mad at myself; it was so irresponsible getting into a van, no seatbelts, binge drinking. I'm a stroke waiting to happen."

"Na, na, na babes; it was lit. Come on, instead of youz watchin' life on tv, youz was livin it Phe."

"I don't want to live that life. That life scares me. I don't want YOU living that life."

"Shit Phe, it waz a party, is all. Don't get all out of your pram. Let's do pancakes. I'll say sorry up close."

"Are you flirting? Jesus Luke this is serious. Luckily Henry found me, but I could have been mugged, raped, murdered."

"Babes, babes, come meet me, I'll explain."

"Absolutely not!"

"I don't want tings weird between us."

"What? Like me thinking you're a dick?"

Silence.

"Phe, youz caught up in all your shit and I've got mine. You're like my best mate Phe, I can't lose you."

"Now who's getting all BTEC Drama and Artsy. You've not lost me you moron. I love you. We're friends for life."

"So, we're good?"

"We're always good. Even when we're bad, we're good."

"Sweet."

"I've got to go before I barf over my phone."

I disconnect.

My head pounds, but I need to shower. I can't look like this around Henry and I reek of alcohol. I think I'm sweating it. I open all the windows even though it's minus something.

Downstairs, I'm relieved Henry's not around. I go shower. The spray pulses through my hair, running down my shoulders between my breasts. Breasts I want Henry's hands on. It's sick but true. I want every inch of him on every part of me. As sure as there are ninety degrees in a right-angle, Henry is an imposter, and that's fine, because it makes my feelings for him less taboo.

I wash using his shower gel; the smell of it evokes his presence. He'd rescued me. Split seconds of memories abruptly materialise; how he'd picked me up and held me close. How when my head was a merry-go-round and the room tilted, he'd been there. I rest my cloudy head against the tiled wall. Which one is it Phoenix? Saint or sinner?

169

JINGLE BELLS

Not even a hangover can dampen my spirits. We Jingle Bells onto the A40 and Ding Dong Merrily on High to the garden centre for our first Christmas tree.

Neither of us mention the party. It's sooo awkward.

I sing; to stop myself wondering how Henry found me. Henry's not a joiner-in, but I get my own back.

"How about this one?" he asks.

"Too small, we need a grand tree like at Downton."

"This one?"

I'm testing his patience, but I can't help myself.

"Too wide Henry, it'll block the tv."

"This one?"

***

Enthusiasm bounces off her. She is so easily pleased, it hurts. Even hung over she's incredibly desirable.

***

I take photos, I make a video; I enjoy Photoshop.

It screamed it was sorry, it cried it was sorry, it whimpered it was sorry. I looked at it.

"Who's sorry now?"

***

I'm carrying the tree in when the smoke alarm activates. She's attempting to bake. There is flour in her hair, on her nose, sporadically on her clothes. Fleetingly I think, this is nice. No work. No killing. Care Girl burning mince pies. I quickly come to my senses. I can't be in a situation where I'm thinking of someone else. I can't be distracted.

"How's the Great British Burn Off?"

"HaDiHa. Come scrutinise, I mean, taste one."

***

He walks towards me. It's like the end of The Equaliser when Denzel Washington appears from the DIY shelves, with his nail gun, and the water is teeming down.

"They're rustic," I defend.

"Misshapen," Henry comments.

We taste, enjoying the crumbling pastry, the fruity filling and the heat on our lips - while between us another heat throbs.

"You were there for me after Amy, Rob, the party. I don't want to know how you found me, but I need to know where we're at, and if you intend to blow hot and cold."

***

"Not intentionally, but I can't make guarantees. I'm protective of you, I want good things for you. Why? I can't say; in fifteen years I haven't considered anyone but myself. There is a 'but'. You, will stay out of my business; I, will stay out of yours; we're not interested in each other's worlds; we're not curious about each other's pasts; we're not focusing on the future - we're now."

I steal a look at her; I see a collision of emotion.

***

This is huge, but I can't burn myself out loving a man who can't love me back. Still, I'm feverish with possibility.

We eat mince pies companionably. These are the worst mince pies ever, but equally the best.

"I'm upstairs if you need me."

***

I don't need anyone. That used to ring truer.

Above me floorboards creek. I have an idea; it involves a Phoenix with no clothes. I file the thought under R for risky.

DINGDONG!

"Cheers mate."

Her room. Whether I like it, or not, she's claimed it. In places she'd lifted the edges of the wallpaper and graffitied on the lining paper: *Henry is an arse. Henry's a tit.* Personally, I like *Fuck Henry.*

Upstairs, she's sitting on the Sherlock, under the window, where the light is best. Looking up, she smiles. I want to kiss but juggling razor blades would be safer.

"Hey. What you got there?" she asks as I put the box down by her sleeping bag."

"A good night's sleep. Come gather the bedding and stick it in the laundry basket."

I pull the inflatable bed from the box, attach the air compressor and a few minutes later Phoenix has a comfortable night's sleep ahead.

"Come and test it," I say with fake casualness.

She grins and slips down onto the mattress with a bounce.

"It's heaven, come see."

***

We lie on the inflatable. I think of Henry's mouth; soft and hot and I nearly moan. I touch his hand. His fingers entwine with mine.

"I want to be near you," I say.

"I know."

I'm tumbling down a soft, grassy mound like I used to as a kid. It's thrilling, but I know I'm safe. I lay on the grass looking up at the brilliantly bright sky. I close my eyes.

***

Her breathing is even. She's asleep. I don't know if I can do this with her. I'll hurt her...my world's not her world.

***

I find Henry in the kitchen, marinating. I'm starved; my appetite has returned along with a little feistiness. I stand beside him; as near as acceptable without seeming needy.

"Hi," I say.

"Hi," he answers.

"Smells good."

It's surreal; I'm blocking out a huge twist in our relationship. No more deliberating who Henry is or what he's done with original Henry. Jesus am I being naïve? Phoenix let go, trust. Oh, yeah, trust the man pretending to be someone else. That makes sense! It's certainly a leap of faith, but one I have already taken.

"Vegetable Naverin."

"Is that a posh title for stew?"

"I'll ignore that."

"Can I join you for dinner?" I ask, though it's a given.

"I've set the table for two."

It's what I've been longing to here. It's a Christmas miracle.

"Thank you, Henry. Happy Christmas Eve."

I want to tell Henry a trillion things. Like how I'd wanted to crumble and scatter to the four corners of the world...but that was then.

Now, I'm enjoying posh stew and garlic bread with a man who is an identity thief, at the least. Henry is not his name. Is he a Tom or a Dave? I don't care anymore.

***

We sit together on the sofa.

"Your tv is massive!"

"Tonight, you pick the programmes."

"Really?"

"Really."

"You won't leave if I pick a crappy film?"

Her voice waivers. Her fear of abandonment is so fresh, disappointment will have an indefinite shelf life.

"I won't leave."

The word ever is on the tip of my tongue. I have no idea how it arrived there. I am making a huge mistake; my risk analysis is off the charts, but I'm compelled to form a relationship with this semi-broken girl who is old for her years yet barely an adult.

"This looks good; How to Get Away with Murder," she says excitedly before abruptly changing channel.

"Safe Haven; can't go wrong with Nicolas Sparks."

***

After the movie, we make a thing of straightening the cushions, folding the throws. I feel hugely awkward. I've only kissed Luke. Right now, there is too much time to think about: lips, breathing, tongues. I'm getting way ahead of myself. It's just Henry is easily a bit of me, and I want every bit of him.

"Are you coming to bed?" I ask.

I am such a fucking tit! He looks at me and I start to tingle all over, well mainly my vag, but other places too.

It's like a stand-off. Which one of us will make the first move.

"I mean, I'm off to bed," I say.

"Sleep well Phoenix."

I want to savour every syllable from his hot mouth.

"Night Henry."

I fall asleep content, it's the best night sleep I've ever had.

The morning weather is wild. It's more dramatic because of our wall to wall windows. I press my forehead to the glass. I see the last few crinkled leaves on skeletal trees; their brittle grasp tenuous. Henry is scoring and honeying and forming stuffing balls; he's at ease and content. I've got my wish; Henry and I together on Christmas Day, and I intend to bask in it.

My phone rings; Priti. I rush through to the hallway for privacy.

"Happy Christmas, Pheeeee."

"Happy Christmas, Priiiiiiii. I'm so happy, I'm fit to burst. Henry's doing a masterclass of how to cook the perfect roast. He's talking to me like I matter, we're not perfect but we're together. I'm literally bulging at the seams with happy bubbles."

"Kirsten," says Priti.

One word's enough to open Pandora's Box.

"Christmas Day and fucking Kirsten is on tv Phe! Did you see her interviewed? Did you?" she demands. She can be a firecracker, can Priti.

"No," I say. Doesn't Priti understand it's the last thing I want to hear. "Am I a total bitch wanting to enjoy Christmas and my relationship with Henry?"

"No. You. Are. Not. You deserve a happy Christmas Phe. It's natural to feel angry, but Phe it's weird; all the victims were psychos. It's coincidence obviously, but it's also eerie. The killer must have a list of evil children; maybe it's Bad Santa or Krampus?"

"It could be a parent Pri or maybe it's The Orient Express?"

"What? Different parents working together? Giving each other alibis," says Priti thoughtfully. "One thing I'm certain of is it's karma."

"I'm so glad you phoned Pri, it's just such a crazy time."

"True...but today it's gonna be crazy good...so get your swag on, or get lit, ok? Or even better, munch on food all day."

"Ok Pri, Happy Christmas slag."

"Happy Christmas bitch. Sending you a hug over the phone...got it?"

"Yeah," I laugh. "I've wrapped it around me. Love you lots."

Returning to the kitchen I see Henry, and something stirs.

"Can I help," I offer.

"Did you say hinder?" Henry asks teasingly.

The tone in his voice is warm and my insides melt.

"I may not be a natural cook, but I am getting better."

"True. It's been a week since you melted any equipment."

"That was unfortunate. I didn't know the hob was hot when I put the plastic container on it."

"Why don't you pour us both a glass of wine?"

"Umm...and a Ferrero to keep us going," I decide.

"My hands aren't clean."

I unwrap a chocolate, placing it against Henry's lips. It's only as he opens his mouth, I realise how provocative it is. Charging heat reddens my face. It's such a girlfriend thing to do. I take one for myself and with my wine withdraw. Music. That's what we need.

***

Eating dinner with her is easy. She's vivacious but gently so.

"Strictly Christmas Special tonight," she tells me, her eyes dancing. "On New Year's Eve I'm going clubbing with Luke."

"Boyfriend?"

"Best friend. If I got married, Luke would give me away. If I had a child, Luke would be Godfather."

"But lovers once?"

"I'd describe us more as comforters; we were children, barely sixteen. He's flittered around has Luke. I'm definitely in the Friends Zone."

She takes a sip of wine.

"Girlfriend?"

I shake my head.

"I thought not," she smiles.

***

I am in the Super's office. Not by choice. It's like being ten again; explaining to the teacher why you forgot your PE kit.

"We are running out of possible suspects. Though the victims hadn't been molested, it doesn't mean these weren't sexually motivated crimes. So, we've done the obvious, knocked on doors of known sex offenders, chased down alibis, interviewed and re-interviewed, considered perps recently released from prison."

"Kate, I know the drill and I'm confident you've dotted every 'I' twice, but where do we go next?"

"Sir, we have to ask why now? Reasonable conclusions are it coincides with a perp moving to the area. Or returning to the area, say someone working/living abroad, or a soldier returning home after a tour!"

"So, your money's on Whittle?"

"We can't ignore him. He's the uncle of a girl being abused, while the school look the other way. Maybe he's gone vigilante. He's strong, smart and he has killed."

"There's a difference."

"Maybe not for him sir. I want to bring him in. Get a search warrant."

"Kate, you know that won't happen unless you have probable cause."

"I'll get it, mark my words."

***

I lay on my cosy inflatable bed, feeling light and frothy and warm. Today has been the best Christmas Day since my parents passed. I thought my grief would never lessen. That I'd be wearing it like an iron vest for the rest of my life. I think today was the day I started living again.

***

I edge the basement door ajar with my foot, biscuits in one hand, tea in the other. I breathe in the earthiness of the damp atmosphere. I walk in complete darkness; the tunnels as familiar to me as my face, from padding barefoot around them since childhood.

She's shackled to the wall. A flashback to the first woman I saw chained there disturbs me; my mother. I don't cage or gag this one; that pleasure has passed. As has the begging for mercy...she knows there is none. I sit on the edge of a workbench looking at her but not seeing her. Any appeal to what humanity I have left is passed...she's accepted her role. It wasn't bad luck that brought her here, it was her pathological need to hurt and humiliate.

I pick up the tailor scissors and sheer her hair so near her scalp it bleeds.

I fill a bucket with icy water and toilet bleach and throw it over her...unable to stomach the smell of blood and urine whilst enjoying a chocolate digestive.

She's shaking uncontrollably.

I tuck a blanket around her bruised and bleeding body.

"Shush, it's ok, it won't be long now."

NEW YEAR'S FRIGHT

Painting my toenails, I can't stop smiling.

"I'm off to the supermarket, need anything?"

I rush from my room to the banister, leaning over.

"Can I come?"

"Sure, how long do you need?"

"One minute."

I pull out my flipflops from two summers ago. They're trampy but my toenails are wet.

Flying downstairs, I'm in the car before Henry turns the ignition.

The shops are five mins away.

The supermarket is serious business. Henry drops a bag of salad in the trolley; I put cheesecake. He chooses peppers; me Sensations. He selects lean chicken; me mini sausages. He adds fruit; me Skittles. Him breadsticks, me chocolate twists...And a bottle of pink gin to get me in the party vibe for tonight.

"You've much to learn, Henry Whittle."

The name is natural and fluid on my tongue now, yet it is a lie, a device for a stranger to live beside me as someone he's not. I hate that this is haunting me. The idiot in me says it's not that deep.

On the ride home the silence filling the car is thicker than usual. It strikes me as odd because Henry and I have been getting along so well. I feel the need to squeeze some nouns and verbs from Henry's lips.

"I think the supermarket was good teamwork."

"I forget you're a toddler," he smiles.

"Whatever," I smile back.

Silence.

"You're going out tonight," Henry confirms.

"Yes."

"To a club."

"Yes."

"With Priti and Luke Lawrence."

"I won't jump hedges or lose consciousness in a garden centre."

"A dancing Phoenix. Who knew such a bird existed," he smiles.

***

Thinking of someone else is alien to me. Now I experience a mix of emotions which I resent...but there is no turning the clock back. I'm a new animal, I need to work with that.

***

At eight thirty, I slip into my lace dress. Looking at myself in the mirror my confidence boosts. I'm taller than average, so my legs look like they go on forever. My hair is moussed up into a messy bob. It's the first time I really look at myself and I know with certainly that I'm striking.

Unused to heels I hold the stair rail to descend.

Henry appears at the foot of the stairs. I have grown accustomed to his expressionless face; he is continuously gorgeous. I'm suddenly shy and awkward.

Between us is a space filled with cupid's promise.

"Hen..."

"Pheo..."

"...ry."

"...nix."

"Jinx," I shout.

"The word needs to match for it to be Jinx," says Henry.

"I'm a rule breaker."

"A beautiful slayer of rules," says Henry, deeper than I've heard his voice before.

I'm giddy, my brain's on a fast spin cycle. Out of nowhere I say...

"I haven't worn a dress since my parents' funeral. Cow bought me a black, polyester pinafore with itchy tights. It was too small, and she caught my skin in the zip as she forced it up. God she was horrible...but it was the coffins that gave me nightmares. Two separate coffins. Everything about it was wrong. They'd made vows, lived together, died together and then they were in cheap, separate, wooden boxes; they would have hated it."

Henry steps towards me and gently touches my cheek. A most unexpected move yet I cover his hand with mine. He doesn't quake in his shoes that I've touched him. So, I release a sigh of pleasure. I want to keep his skin next to mine for hours, days, weeks, eternity.

"No make-up," he points out.

I reluctantly free his hand.

"I tried but ended up washing it off. I need practice."

"You're perfect."

I know my face has gone all squishy as I wrinkle my nose, bite my lip and move my jaw side to side.

"Apart from your eyebrows," he adds.

"Oi you, it's not my fault I'm symmetrically challenged. These heels are another obstacle. Going clubbing isn't as easy as I'd thought. I should get Converse."

I gaze. Another Henry is emerging. One that makes my heart flip and my skin overheat. Now that I've brought attention to my footwear, Henry seems to be assessing my legs. I'm not body conscious. I've got all the normal stuff and it works; that's good enough for me. Fuck fillers, collagen and arse squats.

The doorbell rings.

I'm irritated which is irrational because I want to go clubbing, yet now I don't.

Henry opens the door.

Luke is visually unsettled by 'the stare'. Both glance in my direction; Luke grins and Henry is once more unreadable.

His eyes are steely, his lips thinned, his face fearsome. This is more like it. I smile – Henry's exit face no longer freaks me.

He nods and closes the door behind us.

"Fucking hell; he's scary!"

I laugh. I am so over Scary Henry.

***

It's a basement club. Strobe ceiling lights flash to a hard, electronic beat. It's easy to blend in with a pink wig, skinny jeans and floaty top. I intend to soak up the atmosphere and see for myself how my plan pans out. Druggies are unreliable employees. I've made it clear; Phoenix is not to be hurt. Only the boy.

***

I'm back on the carousel of young adulthood: drink, dance, drugs. I crave a different high. One that even the thumping base pounding from the giant speakers doesn't hush. I dance like I'm a wildling; the bass shuddering through me from my feet upwards, pulsating in my ears. Black Coffee alters the tempo. We Dance Again drifts into my head - mesmerizingly. There I see Henry and I'm moving like I'm liquid steel. I've energy to share, to spread across the entire basement. My body's no longer my own, it's seized by a sensuality that embarrasses, but owns me. My open arms undulate and curl and my mind's orbiting Henry; his soft mouth, his cut-glass eyes - until a Garage track is mixed. Grabbing Priti's hand, she pumps it in the air with mine, and we're jumping and springing up and smiling like stupid, crazy kids. Luke is laughing, taking my free hand, his other in Grace's, and now there's a bunch of us crazies, dancing faster and soaring so high to the music. I feel Henry, I mean really feel him, like he's inside my head, freeing me from everything that scares me. I twirl around and around till Priti shouts she's leaving, and we spin off the dance floor together. I'm hugging and kissing and squeezing her goodbye because I love her so much. Then Luke is pulling me.

"Whittle, it's your round."

"Luke, if I pay, would you go to the bar for me?"

"We ain't on the plantation now Missy."

"Come with me then?"

I try ridiculously hard to reach the bar. I'm sardined by sweaty, bawdy, heaving blokes and girls with killer heels and springing limbs. The music vibrating through the floor adds to the discomfort of burning heels and blistering. I am hoarse from repeating 'excuse me'.

"Relax Phe, you're in safe hands."

Luke's strong arms snake around my waist.

"Passing Physics will be easier than this!"

"You get used to it," he shouts in my ear.

"Grace is nice...I like her."

"Yeah, I'm gettin' feelins'."

We laugh. Being together is the bestest. We keep growing stronger."

"Yeah, it's been a great night. The best Luke."

We came with two Greenmead girls, from the year above, who we are close with. Returning to our table Grace, from the perfume shop, takes a beer from Luke and they kiss. I glance away and squeeze back to my seat where Ruby and Katie are busy downing sticky green neon shots. Our table is full of various sized glasses; slipping a drug into a drink would be easy. My grip tightens on my Breezer. To avoid getting spiked I drink all of it in one sitting. It's a reasonable preventative measure.

A boy with a mad head of red wavy hair pulls me from my seat in the direction of the dance floor. Although there's many cute boys, my head won't turn.

Leaving the club, wobbling in heels, a bit lit, I feel young. Like my life's been given a face lift. I'm eighteen not eighty.

"Hey Katy, Ruby," I shout as slim, bronzed legs step into a cab. "See you next week, it's Drake night."

I need to live a little and take risks. Luke has his arm around me; he's looked after me so well.

"Luke, I've put your bad behind me."

"Relax Phe, I'm seeing you to the door. I'll catch up wid my candy later."

"Your candy. Luke Lawrence you are such a pretend bad ass. If you met anyone from an estate, you'd shit yourself."

I kiss his cheek.

"I'm down wid estate kids."

"You're so suited to acting; you live in a world of your own you do."

Our cab is to the left, across the road. We're doing a silly walk whilst singing Frisky; we don't hear the car until it's too late.

***

I'm chopping garlic and coriander for tomorrow's curry when the clone rings. The trembling in her voice as she answers the ambulance service's questions relays the severity of the situation: no, he isn't conscious, no she can't hear him breathing, yes, he's bleeding badly, his head. I lock up, drive to the hospital and wait.

He's rolled out of an ambulance; it's obvious he's critical from the response of the crew. Phoenix steps out; looking frail. At the A&E entrance she hesitates like a vampire unable to cross the threshold or in Phoenix's case a bewildered girl unable to face worst case scenario.

I walk towards her. On seeing me she shakes her head repeatedly in denial. I draw her to me. Unspeaking she slides her arms inside my open coat and locks them tightly around me; her fingers clenching my t-shirt. For a while I'm silent; I don't deal in reassurances.

"Let's get inside," I say eventually.

We wait hours. Her eyes darting each time the swing doors open. Until...

"Phoenix Whittle."

Her tone is revealing. There is no time to prepare Phoenix.

"I'm Dr Kane, I'm a consultant neurosurgeon."

She guides us into a small fishbowl room. My hand is flat against Phoenix's back; her muscles are taut with tension.

"We've contacted the police. They'll be here shortly. You're down as Luke's next of kin?"

"Yes, we're each other's emergency contact."

I am sick for her.

***

It's two am. The team are off duty till six. Other than a few night lights the area is unlit, shadows my only company.

"Fuck!"

I look at the phone, it's ringtone nearly giving me a heart attack.
"DI Daniels," I reel off, then listen...
"Ok. Let her go, we can firm up her statement later today."
I replace the receiver.
"Fuck."
The Whittles. At Hillingdon A&E? Phoenix Whittle involved in a hit and run? I don't believe in coincidence.

***

"Phoenix? We're home."
She's in a trance.
"Phoenix," I repeat, undoing her belt and pulling her slightly. She pliantly follows. The hall light is on. Phoenix sees her reflection in the hallway mirror. Her dress is covered in Luke's blood; it's smeared on her hands and face. She stares at herself. I don't know what to do...I've never not known what to do. The silence is painful to hear, so tightly compressed it fills even my head. She is void of expression and motion until a scream so wounded and desperate splits the quiet. It's hard to see, to hear, to be witness to such deep raw pain. She aggressively shakes off my coat, tearing at her dress, slapping my hands away, punching the wall, scratching herself. I lock my arms across her chest. I recall the woods, how she'd given way to despair. This is different - it's damaging and punishing; she wants to hurt herself; she uses physical pain to diminish emotional anguish. I can't let her do that.

I climb the stairs and lay her limp, unconscious body on the bed. Not wanting her waking up covered in her friend's blood, I remove her torn bloodstained dress. Christ. It's like she's cursed.

It's gone four am. I postpone today's meet, get those involved to stand down. She can't be left. Already my feelings for her are impacting on my life. I can't have emotion in my headspace when I'm on a mission; thinking about her even for a fraction of a second could kill me.

Phoenix sleeps around the clock and more. I'm in the kitchen making tea when she appears. I make hers sweet. She cradles it whilst I make us an omelette.

"I need to phone Priti," she says her tone hollow.
"It's done."
"Mercy?" she chokes out. I put my hand over hers.
"I spoke with her yesterday. She's quite a...character."
"Henry, I'm sorry about...my melt."
"Don't be."
"I know you don't like emotional stuff."

"It's fine, Phoenix."

"Henry," she says almost angrily. "Don't die."

What can I say? My line of work has a high propensity for death.

"Do you feel up to giving your statement?"

She nods.

"Afterwards we'll visit Luke. Coma patients often respond to voices, music, smells. There's always hope Phoenix."

***

I'm a danger to myself and others. Luke is in a coma and I know it's my fault. Oh, I won't verbalise this, or have a strop because I can't make this about me...except somehow it is.

***

The constable guides us to an interview room. Almost immediately Daniels enters.

"Hello Phoenix. I'm so very sorry for what happened."

Daniels sounds sincere but Phoenix stares into vacant space.

"I understand the events last night are raw, but we need to know what happened.

"It was dark. The street was noisy with clubbers. I'd been drinking and Luke was propping me up. It happened so quickly..."

Her voice cracks. I pour her a glass of water. Aware that Daniels watches like a hawk.

"In your own time Phoenix," says Daniels.

"The revving of an engine; so loud. Luke pushing me away."

Silence.

"He thought of me before himself and it cost him. I'd moaned about him not looking after me and now he's dead."

"Phoenix, a coma is not dead. The MRI and CT scan show no brain damage. Luke's chances are even. You are certainly not responsible," Daniels clarifies. "Wouldn't Luke say the same?"

Phoenix shrugs

"For the record, there are no judgements being made when I ask these questions. I need honest answers. They determine the direction of the investigation. Understand?"

I nod.

"Do you use drugs?"

"No."

"Luke?"

"No, he's very body and health conscious. He studies dance and drama."

"The others with you?"

"They dabble, it's recreational."

"Do you recognise either of these men?"

Photographs are put in front of Phoenix. She's breathing hard.

"No. Who are they?"

"Stan Barr and Daniel O'Dowd. Street corner drug dealers."

I feel Phoenix shaking and the impulse to hold her is strong...too strong.

"No. Was it them? Were they in the car?"

Her tone is high; the words quiver angrily on her tongue.

"We recovered prints from a stolen car abandoned in Hayes. We believe it's the vehicle used in your hit and run. Forensics are looking at the car as we speak. These men have past convictions for car theft and drug related offences. Perhaps off their heads, they ploughed into you."

"No! We looked left and right. I remember because the heal of my shoe went down a storm drain. We walked onto the road casually, like we knew no cars were approaching."

"It's surprising how fast a distant car can be on you, especially a speeding one."

"Neither of us heard it. We weren't wasted; the drinks were ridiculously priced. It was more like; it was outside the club and pulled out fast. Without headlights," she says angrily, her voice raised. "No headlights," she repeats softly. "I'm certain."

"Can you think of anyone who'd like to hurt you or Luke?"

"Outside of school, no. Inside school, yeah, but you know that."

"Could someone at school have arranged the attack?"

"No. What would be the fun in that? They're hands on."

***

My recount of events takes a hold in my head. As I follow Henry indoors, I slip my shoes off, make an underarm throw and miss the basket as usual. Henry gracefully bends to retrieve them.

I put my face in his.

"No way. Did that car. Approach. From a distance."

Walking beside Henry into the lounge I step in front, interrupting his stride. I put the flat of my hand against his chest. I feel shaky...he's a lot to take in.

"It pulled out, it swerved towards us, it might have murdered Luke. Henry, it was premeditated."

"Phoenix, that's a leap."

"Henry, I'm right. Please believe me."

I need this. I need Henry to have faith in me.

He removes my hand, I expect him to drop it, instead he slides his palm against my palm and our fingers touch, his long fingers exceeding mine. Henry's quiet. I wonder does he hear the thunder of my heart; pulling away from its arteries, ready to leap into his.

Holding his hand. I press my lips against his wrist. His skin is cool. It's like he's cut from ice.

***

Her lips explore the callouses on my trigger hand. I'm weightless, like my feet are off ground: it's a dangerous sensation: not one conducive to my occupation.

"I'm with you...whatever turn this tragedy takes."

He withdraws his hand. Walks across the glossy black and white tiled floor to the fridge, grabbing a bottle of white wine.

"They'll be cameras. The Police will see for themselves. Someone did try to kill us. Maybe just Luke, or both of us."

Henry puts a glass in my hand, sits and pats the sofa for me to join him.

The tv's off; it's him and me at either end of the sofa, facing each other.

I feel a vibration in my pocket. It's Pri. I dismiss - the first time ever. I take a sip of wine and savour its heat as it warms my throat. I try to be strong. I reach into myself, but I'm barren. As I suffer never-ending grief, I cling to Henry; he alleviates my symptoms. With him the sky is a lighter shade of black. I can't live in the dark again. I just can't.

"Tell me everything out of the ordinary since your aunt's death."

BUSINESS AS USUAL

Back at school, Christmas presents forgotten, Kirsten resurrecta Amy and word's circulates about Luke. So whisperings resurface - she's bad luck, got 666 on her scalp, blah blah blah. Heads turn in my direction like I'm an accessory. It's scary, the influence Kirsten has over others. How people who barely know me are certain I have this strange, evil connection to the Ruislip Avenger. It scares the shit out of me that maybe I do?

At lunch I search Priti out.

"Phe, let's go to the art room; it's not on Circe's radar."

Priti's as emotionally strung out as me but remains unwavering in her commitment as my best friend.

Henry is Henry: uncommunicative, distant and strange, but also tender and caring in unexpected ways; like my lunchbox. I pass a sarnie to Priti.

"Triple decker, crustless, filled with salad and egg mayo – the work of Henry?"

I nod and offer a weak smile.

"So, is Henry gay?" she asks.

"No, not gay."

I pass her the crudities and we dip them in humus.

"Tasty. Homemade?"

"Henry's secret recipe."

With Henry everything is secret.

"Girlfriend?"

"No."

"He's perfect: gorgeous, rich, cooks, says little. Shame your related."

The truth's on the edge of my tongue, but its consequences silence me. As a rule, I am compulsively honest; I've never acquired the art of deception, yet here I am twisting and turning on my bed of lies, the weight of the world on my shoulders.

Who lies to their best friend? WHO!

On the edge of an uncomfortable silence, Kirsten appears in the doorway.

"You fuckin' loser," she spits, her lips curling cruelly. Her diction is excellent, she's not one to drop a vicious vowel or a cruel consonant. Under the light her face seems laminated. She's deceptively strong. An athlete; my height, gym freak. She breaks bones in a blink. I'm scared; not silly teen horror movie scared, but deeply fearful.

"You smell of Eau de Tramp."

As if she'd struck a match, my self-esteem is in cinders, just a few burning embers for her to poke. I choke out a reply.

"How 'bout you slut-up!"

One spitting snarl follows another; her hot, damp breath is like acid on my face. It could give me skin cancer.

Saved by the art teacher.

"You've got a common room. Use it."

Priti is already at ground level; those little feet are lightning. I'm swiftly behind. Kirsten slides down the staircase behind us, turning her head, opening her mouth. The hostile harassment continues. I put my arm round Pri's shoulders. My mind busily filters negative thoughts into my brain's spam folder. This way I'm less burdened by vindictive girls.

***

With Phoenix back at school I balance work, revenge and packed lunches. Phoenix's assailants need to suffer enormously. Do I want to kill them? Most certainly. Will I? I think I will.

***

The girl is a pathetic lump sprawled on the ground, its bones at right angles. I see it holding on to life by a thread. I hate how it's made me do ugly things.

At the table I carefully open my precious delivery. It's perfect; soft and hazelnut brown. I gently place it on my head. I spin around in delight. I touch it, then tuck it behind my ears like Phoenix had. Later I'll French plait it.

***

I park. I rub falling tears away with the back of my hand, blowing my nose with my PE sock. Henry would have a seizure. My grief for Luke needs managing; I have only small pockets of time to crumble. At school I'm strong for Priti, at home I give the impression I'm coping. Me and Priti alternate going to see Luke. I'm relieved it's her vigil tonight.

"Hi Henry, got masses to do, see you for dinner," I say belting upstairs to the bathroom to splash the tear streaks away.

In my room I don't get books out, I drop onto my inflatable bed; so incredibly drained.

***

Early evening, I hear her call out. She's sat on the edge of the bed; her arms wrapped around herself, rocking. Her eyes are haunted, her skin clammy. She bolts past me to the toilet and throws up. Collapsing to the right of the toilet she leans her forehead on the cold rim of the ceramic toilet basin.

"Luke?"

She nods.

"Henry."

"Umm?"

"Have you ever wanted to kill someone? Not in the heat of the moment, but after lengthy deliberation?"

"Yes."

"Me too. I'd wished Angela dead, then she was. That's not all, I lied to the police...I'd met Bradley Perkins."

I crouch beside her.

"Henry, it's Final Destination."

"How so?"

"What if I was meant to die with my parents? What if death is after me and innocent people get in the way."

"Phoenix. That's bollocks. What would Luke say?"

"He'd tell me I was talking shit."

"Up."

I pull her up with ease.

"How is it that, when we get close, you smell of puke?"

Momentarily, I hold her gaze. It's banter, but underneath we know how colossal this thing is. Where my feelings for Phoenix will lead, I have no idea. Well, I know where they lead most people. For both our sakes it would be wise to remain platonic.

I hold three fingers in the air and subtract against my arm.

"Dinner's ready in thirty, twenty, ten. Copy that, Phoenix?"

She's laughing. We're laughing.

"Come on Henry, admit it, I was funny. You wanted to laugh."

"I did laugh."

***

Showered, in fresh PJs, I head downstairs. In the lounge the blinds are pulled, and wall lamps gently illuminate the space. Henry's in the kitchen. On hearing me, he turns around. His expression isn't a smile, yet it's warm. I gravitate to his side, embracing the wildness inside me when he's near. It blocks out the depression threatening to take me on a non-refundable trip. I like how he doesn't fuss or ask a hundred questions. I had a nightmare; it was horrible but it's over. I study the beautiful, long fingers that crafted a perfectly shaped pie, with a pastry P central.

"Chicken and mushroom?"

"Steak and onion," he corrects.

"P for Phoenix?" I ask.

"P for Pain in the arse."

I snigger and give Henry a little knock with my hip. Of all people, Henry in his peculiar way, is my rock. My finger finds the sprinkled, white flour on the worktop and forms a 'thank you'. Unexpectedly, Henry's finger responds with a single kiss. I stare at it, desperate to kiss the kiss maker. Instead I turn to eyes that kill every doubt. My hand raises, hovers, before touching his cheek.

I run my hand along his jawbone.

I have this impulse to crash into him.

My hand caresses the length of his neck.

To feel his lips stripping away my sorrow.

I rub my fingers over his collar bone.

His mouth demolishing my tragic past.

He's capable of anything; he's indestructible; if anyone can shoulder my raging emotions it's Henry.

"B'ding!"

The microwave calls time.

We eat supper. We don't say much. One another's presence and good food are enough to make the moments perfect. Each minute that passes isn't long enough.

"Coffee?"

"Wine?" he suggests.

Desire and Chardonnay could be a combustible mix, but I say...

"Sure."

"What's on tv?"

"Erm, a romcom The Pill. Sounds quirky. Do you like quirky?"

He passes me my glass and a bowl of popcorn.

"I like you, so yeah I like quirky," he says, his half smile teasing. I can't help it; an enormous smile creases my face and the heat of my blush nearly requires calamine lotion. On the couch he settles nearer me than expected; my cheeks are going to be pink for weeks. Jesus! What are my eyebrows like? I haven't plucked them since the club. Henry's thigh touches mine. My insides flutter and a self-consciousness sprouts from my need to be desirable. Right now, I probably have popcorn crumbs around my mouth and a kernel in my hair. Henry squeezes my hand. His touch ignites a feeling in me I'm beginning to embrace. I think he feels it too. We are on the edge of intimacy.

***

I could stop this now. Before she gets hurt. If she knew everything; not the now, but the before. Could she love the before?

***

It's Wednesday; another day waking up remembering Luke is on the edge of death. I throw my pjs off and slip into my towelling robe before heading for the shower.

***

Taking my phone from my pocket I press the photo icon. I scroll from left to right. I twist my nipple ring, enjoying the hot pain. The tilt of her neck. Her high, full breasts. The soft hair concealing her vagina; none of that Hollywood rubbish. I zoom in. I rip the ring free.

***

"I've a plan," he says, catching me on the stairs, heading towards the fridge. My appetite of late is humongous.

"Tell me it doesn't involve trekking for hours over rough terrain and being abandoned in The Hills Have Eyes?" I reply, my eyes zooming in on those mesmerising tattoos. I wonder how uncomfortable sex on the stairs is. You'd probably approach from behind. On your knees.

"Phoenix!"

"What?" I say defensively. This whole attraction thing is embarrassing.

"As you're a permanent fixture, it's time for paint therapy."

"Cool."

I want to ask a thousand questions, instead I follow; my eyes on his peachy butt.

Henry's iPod streams Spotify. He's painting the ceiling white with an extending roller and I'm splashing the walls with duck egg. Henry's wearing a tee and football shorts. Taking a mouthful of Pepsi, I find myself appreciating his long, lean legs. More and more I find myself pondering his private life. Why no girlfriend? Has he ever been in love? What does he do about sex? Would he expect reverse cowgirl?

"Phoenix."

I nod, but I hear only random words. Instead, I wonder what Henry kisses like. Brilliantly I imagine.

"Floorboards…ivory," he says; his voice distant.

Would I have to tip toe up or would he lean down?

"Bed...furniture."

Would I wind my arms around his neck or his waist?

"Phoenix!"

"Yes."

Yes, to everything.

***

Jesus, she is so easy to read. She may as well be holding a neon sign flashing 'you turn me on'. I like it though. Her freshness, her lack of self-interest.

***

"Hey Pri, guess what I'm sitting on?"

"A beached whale."

"A leather bed," I declare unable to contain my elation. "My room's finished. I've got white painted floorboards, duck egg walls, crystal-blue voiles, a clothes rail, a study table and a huge floor mirror, tilted against a wall. It's triple peng. It's peng underlined, in bold."

"Phe that's lit. What's your bedding like?"

"White, with blue and pale green flower heads."

We natter about a tampon advert, avocado, Furious Thing but not Luke; it's too painful. Nothing in our lives will be the same. My knowledge of death is substantial enough to understand Luke might never come back. Unless there's a zombie apocalypse.

***

I want the boy's assailants to suffer. No man is more capable than me. However, that isn't possible with Barr who has quite an entourage. Tuesday is my opportunity, his wife's night out. He doses his kid with sleeping pills and slithers out to hook up with a local prostitute. Each week he walks along the canal and under the bridge – alone.

Routine's a killer.

I park six miles from the bridge.

Pull on waterproofs, trainers, a beanie and gloves; all black, all disposable.

I jog to Barr's housing estate: a collection of terraced houses, all dilapidated. A stretch of green underlines the estate; on it a collection of dumped items: a sofa, kids' toys, a rusting sink. England flags hang as curtains on the street-facing rooms.

I stand in the alley almost three houses down. The wife exits and gets in a white Audi.

His kids are still up. I see the outline of small hands against the flag, trying to find daylight.

I'm a patient man; soldiers are, particularly snipers.

As anticipated, he appears.

I send a text, reporting children abandoned at Barr's address, from a burner phone.

He stands on the green, lighting a splif.

The first time I looked at him I felt anger; an emotion as foreign to me as love. I mean real, pull-him-apart, anger. I enjoyed planning his death; it eased that burning, hot thirst for blood. Now...I'm calm...in the right frame of mind to take his life.

I run ahead, down the stone steps and along the canal; till I'm under the bridge and out the other end, just.

I linger in a shadow, looking up to the lamp post; disabled this morning at first light.

Barr is heavy footed. A consequence of a drug feud in his younger days when he was knee capped.

As he enters the tunnel, I jog towards him. He walks heftily, like his knees will collapse under his weight.

I slip the knife down my sleeve.

His head is inconveniently lowered.

There's a meter between us.

Point five of a metre.

Point two five.

"Barr!"

His head raises.

I draw the blade across his throat; it takes strength; deep into his windpipe, cutting main arteries as I slice from ear to ear.

FALLING IN LOVE

"Morning Henry."

"Morning Phoenix."

God, I could squeeze chocolate sauce over him and let him slip down my throat. My head is obscene right now. I'm taking him all in and I mean all; it's optical sexual harassment. I can't help it; my eyes keep roaming to the soft fullness between his legs. Do my eyes deceive me or has it grown? To prevent myself becoming a sexual predator I bury myself in the newspaper.

***

She hasn't touched her porridge; nor mashed her banana or added honey. When she's upstairs, I skim the articles on the folded page: mugging in Tottenham, the sugar tax, the living wage, body found in Hayes.

***

Stan Barr is dead. It must be 'the' Barr. Luke's assailant. According to the article he was a brutal man, leading a brutal life, so dying a brutal death was not unexpected. I need to put Barr behind me and concentrate on what's important. There's just something too convenient about it. 'A hit' the paper said. Surely, he was too small-time?

I brush my teeth. The routine helps simmer the hungry urges I feel around Henry. He's now surpassed the attraction of Aldi's double chocolate muffin. Luke springs to mind and puts a dampener on my romantic thoughts. The place Luke lives, in my head, is empty. When I think of Priti, Luke follows. His face usually materialises, and I attach an action or thought to him. That's on pause. His space is unoccupied. I want to fill it. It's a completely selfish admission, but I'm glad I fell for Henry before Luke's hit and run. Otherwise I'd question, are my feelings for Henry real, or is he Luke's space filler.

***

I hold a photo of Phoenix Whittle. Her upper arms covered in multiple cigarette burns and bruises. Constable Vickers had been on duty when she'd come in. Three years later he'd been implicated in a paedophile ring the Met took down.

I'm momentarily lost in a time and place where two eleven-year-olds, who'd experienced horror, seem to merge and become one.

***

Tutorials have been tense following Luke's attack - Jesus putting those two words together kills me. Mr Jacobs' need to comfort me is out there but unless he can reverse time comfort doesn't exist. Henry understands this.

"Phoenix, you must taste these chocolates, Penny loves them."

A welcoming smile and chocolates – Henry has a lot to learn.

"Not Hotel Chocolat!"

Dropping my bag I whiz to Mr Jacobs' side; my intention to keep a distance forgotten.

"I've been dying to taste these. Umm. What are we up to today?"

Shit, I've made us sound like a couple. I need to discover if the Thursday thing with Priti is a mix up. I don't know how to go about it.

"We...are up to past exam questions relating to Heathcliff."

"Great," I say, my voice level, my mind working hard not to jump to conclusions. There will be an explanation about Priti. Mr Jacobs' is one of the good guys.

Instead of driving directly home, I spend an hour with Luke, spilling the beans about Mr Jacobs.

"He keeps asking about you, which is kinda getting on my nerves."

I play him French Kisses by ZieZie.

"It's nice he's concerned, but it's like prying."

Then AJ Tracy.

"He tells me about Penny; it's sweet how much he loves her, but still...I don't want you and Henry in the same arena as school...and this Priti thing feels all wrong."

I moisturise his face and hands with Man Cave products. I beg him to wake between new grime artists. I cry a little. I lie beside him.

"Luke, I'm desperate. Please, please, stop pissing about here."

It's my parting plea before kissing his forehead.

I pull my parka around me as I walk across the dark, deserted hospital carpark.

Once I'm driving down Long Lane, I swing from one desperation to another. I really shouldn't be driving - illicit images of me and Henry naked, sweating, in multiple positions is on pause.

Parking the car, handbrake on; obviously! I enter, using my key!

Henry's in the shower. I wonder what he'd do if I joined him? I want to.

I feel a sharp pull inside, between my pelvic bones. It's tight and twisty and vibrates. It's zinging right now as Henry walks towards me. A towel draped around his waist. I eat him up and he's delicious.

He comes within an inch of me and my heart drops to the floor.

"How's Luke?"

"Not chatty," I say with a grim smile.

"If you need anything Phoenix, I've got your back."

That's great but kiss me my eyes plead.

Henry gently presses his lips to my forehead. I hold my breath - feeling every line and crease of his mouth. It's a promising start, there's so much room for development; Henry's lips on my mouth, breasts, between my …

"Phoenix."

A thought crosses my mind. Henry has no expression. Yes, he's strikingly handsome, but if I had to describe him what would I say? His face is symmetrical, no distinguishing marks, no high forehead, or crooked nose or thin lips or bushy eyebrows. He's faceless.

"Phoenix, I think you need to breathe, you look combustible."

"Do you need help with dinner?" I ask.

"You're excluded from helping on medical grounds."

"There's nothing wrong with me."

"It's my health I'm concerned about."

I want to be the ink on his body. To fuse with his skin, to run along the ridges and dips of his torso. I want to know everything about him…his name would be a start.

***

I've had a serious bollocking from upstairs. Working under the threat of having the case taken off me is pressure on pressure. Neither will it make for enjoyable dinner conversation.

The bell chimes. Quickly the door opens, and I am in the arms of a tall, oblong of a woman.

"Kate love, you've lost weight."

I return the squeeze. She's always been good cop. Now to face bad cop. Maggie follows me through to the dining room.

He's standing by the fireplace. We nod to one another. Me the goddaughter, him the surrogate father who raised his best friend's orphaned child. Me the Inspector, him the Super. It's no secret, but at the station our relationship is formal; he's my line manager and he never lets me forget that, his expectations remain high and I continue to raise my game to make him proud.

***

She's ironing in the utility room. Music blearing. In a soft cotton shorts set, she's sway-ing ver-y nice-ly. My eyes lock on her rear and I want nothing more than to ease those shorts off.

"I'm out. Will you be ok?"

"Yeah. Fine. I won't cook...have friends over...Hold on...you've forgotten something."

"No."

She slips her arms around my waist and squeezes.

"It's called a goodbye hug. It's what us civilians do."

I smile all the way to the flat of a man I'm slowly going to kill.

I've had O'Dowd under surveillance. He lives in a high rise in Uxbridge. Familiar with his routine I watch O'Dowd leave. Walking past cameras, head down, hoodie high, it takes two minutes to enter his flat. It's rancid. I pull a chair to the centre of the kitchen floor. The table is covered in takeaway cartons and burnt foils; I tip it and the shit slides off. I fill and boil the kettle. Rooting around I find a meat fork and bleach. I put the items I'd brought with me on the table: two billiard balls and a new, white handkerchief.

I hear the clatter of keys at the front door. Stoned he crashes into the hall. From behind I inject a paralysing agent into his neck. I bind him to a kitchen chair with electrical ties; tight enough to cut. Wrapping the billiard balls in the handkerchief I stuff them in his mouth.

"You're going to die. That's a fact."

I give him time for my words to sink in. I glance out the window overlooking an Aldi carpark.

"You're paralysed but you will feel pain. Talk and it'll be quick."

I show him the meat fork. He's jerks frantically in the chair, his efforts only tightening the electrical ties.

"Let me demonstrate."

I stab his thigh; the prongs puncture two lengthy, narrow entry wounds. His eyes bulge with pain. He's yet to realise this is merely the first strike. I slowly pour bleach over the damage; it fills the wounds, burning the muscle and flesh before over spilling. He's panting, breathing erratically through his nose. His bloodshot eyes float in tears.

"Don't scream," I say, removing the obstruction from his mouth.

He screams.

I shove the balls back in his mouth.

He's gagging; his panic intensifying the pain.

"Don't scream. Nod if you understand."

He nods.

"The hit and run – who paid you?"

His voice is shaky; he begins pleading.

In go the balls.

Mucus runs from his nasal passages.

"I'm not sadistic, merely persistent."

I stab his other thigh; twisting the fork, embedding it deep in his muscle. I give him time to get to grips with his pain. I withdraw the billiard balls.

He retches and throws up.

"The hit and run?"

Tears run down his cheeks. He tells me everything: the email address through his letterbox, the money to cover his drug debt; by doing a hit on some black kid. They never met the client. It was arranged over the internet. A fucking PayPal account. The client made it clear they were to hurt only the boy.

Information extracted, panicking, he lurches on his chair.

I add the silencer.

"He's a kid."

I pull the trigger.

**

Driving up the lane, I note Phoenix's light is off. A part of me wishes she'd bound downstairs and jettison into my arms. That's how I think of her; like an explosion, a high-powered weapon.

Letting myself in I retrieve the firelighters. I undress to my boxers and lay my clothes neatly on top of dead branches and old paper. I watch as the heap catches light. Grabbing the bottle of whiskey from the kitchen I sit at the garden table.

I sense her. She sits beside me. I pass her the bottle of Grouse; she takes a small swig. We sit in silence; we watch shapes dance in the fire. We fall in love.

**

I'd slept soundly. I could easily have stayed put, dreaming of my special forces operative who cooks killer pancakes. Pushing the quilt off, I spring out of the bed. I pull my unicorn slippers on and head for the bathroom. One minute I'm drowsy from sleep, the next my eyes pop like corn. A Henry in black trunks raises himself using a pull-up bar attached to his door frame. It's nothing new, but before, my head battled with suspicion; there'd been no room for getting turned on, and he'd worn trackies! I stare at that tantalising line of hair running from his bellybutton to beneath his boxers. He drops to the floor; lusciously close.

"Your eyes are stunning; I love them."

"I love that you love them," he replies throatily. "I see you're going with the tussled look this morning," he smiles.

"A mess?"

"Totally," he says gently tucking my hair behind both ears. My hunger is a tidal wave dragging me under.

"Phoenix breathe, or I'll be administering the kiss of life."

"It's worth dying for."

I'm breathing hard, my eyes on Henry's lips. Kiss me. Kiss me. If I say it three times will it happen like 'Bloody Mary' or 'Candyman'? Henry who is marble, who's been colder than frost, advances. He could be the Ruislip Avenger? He's murdered your uncle and fed him to the fish. He could be an escapee from an asylum, but he's so fucking a bit of me. I'm so near to stepping into him...but who the fuck is he?

"That looks easy," I say, diverting our attention to the bar. An eyebrow arches, Henry gives me access to his door frame. He'll never initiate. I get that now. Henry knows I'll fold at the first hot breath. He wants me to realise the magnitude of this thing, how fucked up it is. Stretching, I barely touch the bar with my fingertips. A quick glance at Henry and a surge of longing diffuses from my heart gaining tempo as it lowers. All thought of self-preservation melts away. I scare myself because whatever Henry feels, so do I, times a billion. I don't care who he is, what he's done...but I bloody should. Jumping up I barely get a grip on each handle. Confusion affects my agility and I'm dangling awkwardly. Beneath my loose top, my breasts have risen as I stretch up and my midriff is on show. Channelling my strength, I endure muscle burn and haul myself up.

"Yessssss."

Warm hands, on my bare waist, burn through my skin. My breathing's all over the place and my head's empty; it's brainless, I can't think, so I don't know what to do. I lock my grip on the bar.

Henry's breath flutters across my torso and my every nerve tingles. My response is so needy, I'm not in control and that scares me.

"I've got you, let go."

Arms snake around my waist and Henry's blunt facial hair prickles my midriff. I let go...of my reservations. Slowly, millimetre by millimetre my body slides down Henry's until we are eye to eye. The quiet hunger, the silent craving, we both feel it. My pyjama top is bunched round my breasts. Time no longer consists of seconds and minutes but tight, hard breathing and a longing so desperate it stretches infinitely. As Henry's hands move down my torso to my waist the opportunity for this to be a moment passes. Instead his fingers grasp the bottom seam on my pyjama top and gently pull it down. Saying nothing, I turn into the bathroom, locking the door behind me. I rest against the edge of the sink for support. I catch my reflection in the mirror. My face is flushed, my eyes shine like glass. I slip out of my pyjamas. Standing in front of the mirror, I survey what Henry will see.

I jump out of my skin as a knock jerks me out of my sex dream.

"I'll be gone from 1pm, twelve hours approximately, so how about we go out for coffee."

A date. Henry and me out of the house. Together.

"Fantastic."

***

The team works around the clock and every lead, no matter how tenuous, is being chased down. A third victim stretches the budget to a profiler; I resent juggling sums to obtain essential police resources. I sit with the team listening to the expert.

"Male, 17-35, intelligent, physically strong. An only child: isolation in childhood leads to seeds of paranoia planting. Undoubtedly sexually and physically abused in childhood/adolescence leading to gender issues. He's gay or bi but can't come to terms with this. To compensate he needs women to be attracted to him. He'll have erectile dysfunction unless the right circumstance is provided. Not dinner and a moonlight walk, I mean some psychotic fantasy. He's acutely embarrassed by his unreliable penis, he can't blame himself, his ego won't allow it, so he transfers his inadequacies onto women. He's attracted to young women, teenagers, because they're less sexually experienced so less demanding and easier to control. A special someone is the catalyst that begins the cycle of depravity. In this case, a young woman, one he's in daily contact with. In his mind he's created an illogical, gratuitous fantasy revolving around her. Each victim will have some link to his special person: usually friends or enemies. The depth of emotion he feels for his special person is so great it fuels a distorted view, enabling him to carry out depraved acts. This man might be completely psychotic on the inside, but outwardly he is attractive, engaging, someone a teenager has a connection with at first sight. He will make effeminate gestures, but they will be masked by his interests. The only instance where he may break character is when he's in the company of his special person. His speech will be slow and deliberate when he speaks to her, conveying an impression of intimacy. If she's in company and he's not her focal point, he'll slip into his alternate psychopathic ego. His speech will become erratic, he may develop a stammer or perseverate, where he's like a broken record repeating the same word. His body may become agitated; you will see a scratch on his veneer of sanity very quickly. He may get aroused in her presence and rush off to masturbate in some dark alley. If she rejects his sexual advances his punishment will be merciless. If he is unable to get an erection with her, his anger will lead to a ferocious frenzy – she will not know what's hit her. The way to catch this killer is to find the muse, the object of his fantasy. Find her and you've found him

***

In Patisserie Brione, Henry drapes his jacket over a quaint wooden chair before easing mine off. Our attraction is amplified in this compact, intimate coffee shop.

"I'm frightened to ask what you're having," says Henry.

"Cappuccino with soya milk and a banoffee tart, please."

Females furtively glance Henry's way as he orders, then takes his seat opposite me.

"Henry?"

I love saying his name. It's like a dare.

"Phoenix."

His voice is smooth like sea washed glass. Being daring is so worth it.

He smiles the most heart shattering, earth exploding smile. I have to say it, the joke's overused, but so appropriate.

"Oh, my, God! Your face is mutating. It's an allergic reaction to caring. It's spreading! Your mouth's altered beyond recognition – it's smiling!"

***

I sit in a tea shop, in a spot with a view of their table in Brione. I see a laugh, a gesture, a sweep of the hair - equalling an unexpected closeness. She barely knows him. I'm unsure what to think. I'm overheated. I loosen the buttons of my polo. My hand trembles: my coffee overspills, I quickly dab the table with the serviette. I bite down hard on the inside of my cheek.

"Fuck!"

I hear an intake of breath. I taste blood. I bit down harder.

"Fuck," I say standing, knocking a chair over. I'm struggling to understand what I'm seeing. I don't like it. I fucking hate it.

***

It's gone midnight. My contract was messy. The target was unpredictable and arterial blood spray caused a wardrobe malfunction. Phoenix is asleep. I slip into a hot bath glad to ease the aches and pains of combat. Taking out your physical equivalent is always a challenge. Resting my head, closing my eyes, I remain until the water is tepid. Drying, I hear her crossing the hallway. She shuffles in and washes her hands. She doesn't see me at first. She is drowsy, her lids semi closed.

"Henry?"

"It's me."

"Ok. Umm good. Love you."

She isn't fully conscious and that's what frightens me. She had spontaneously revealed what she genuinely felt.

I'm horrified. She's a sandstorm, a tidal beach, a glacier; beautiful but treacherous. I don't do relationships. Retraction. I didn't.

***

I look at my hands, around her neck, so tight and twisted. Now I've got a fucking body to dump.

***

I wake to find Henry's bed made and a house of silence. We're odd in that Henry rarely fills me in on his plans, his timings, his whereabouts; he's totally elusive. He's a strange fish. Me? I'm this embarrassing, gushing open book. That's why I leave Henry a note with bullet points and side headings. First, I'm visiting Luke, then I'm off to Priti's. As soon as I write her name a whoosh of guilt floods my bloodstream. My head's been all over the place recently and with Priti I've gotta think before I open my mouth. It's frustrating and requires a level of duplicity I'm uncomfortable with. What if Henry comes between us? I know I'd risk anything for him...but my friendship with Priti? Shit, the fact that I even consider it is so fucked up.

I park on Priti's road, knock on her door and hear thuds of little feet.

"Phe," she squeaks giving me the squashiest hug.

I follow her upstairs to her box room. We just about fit in it together. Her bed is against the wall, we manoeuvre her pillows so our backs curve against the flowery wallpaper.

"Phoenix show me your room," she says her hand out for my phone. "This is the coolest room on earth," she enthuses, swiping through my photos.

"I know, I nearly cry every time I walk in."

"What shall we watch?" I ask.

"Random Attachment."

"Pri, we've seen it so many times."

"I know, but it's the best."

"Ok but waxing first. Don't give me that look, Priti Chatterjee, you made me buy the strips."

"I have a very low pain threshold."

"I've worked that out Priti. Come on, let's do this, then we can celebrate your birthday in style at The Red Onion in Ruislip High Street. Honestly Pri, their vegan cakes are amazing."

***

Her key opens the lock. Her feet are light on the stairs. It seems she needs alone time. Later she knocks lightly on my bedroom door. Her silky pyjamas gently cling to her curves as she wanders in and lays restlessly on my bed. I lay beside her.

"You seem a little subdued," I comment.

"Tonight, was the first time Priti and I've been out since...since Luke."

She pauses.

"I'm almost resentful her memory of him is happy, which makes me feel shit about myself, because it's so selfish. At school it's more natural because Luke doesn't belong there. Then there's you, us; usually I tell Priti everything."

"The Vegas rule," I affirm solemnly.

"What happens in the house stays in the house. I know."

She blows out a shaky breath.

"At night, when I first close my eyes, the moment of impact flashes in my head. In the morning, I wake, and there's a fleeting instance when Luke's normal and then I remember...I dread those moments."

Rising from the bed, I say nothing except hold my hand out to pull her up. She takes it.

"O'Dowd is dead," she says her eyes looking for answers in mine.

I gently run my hands up and down her arms.

"You need a dressing gown you're cold."

"Then why do I feel hot?"

It's the stillest the house has been, like we're a frame shot, a moment captured in time.

Sorrow and sex; it needs detangling.

"I know you sit in your car and cry. It's unnecessary. I want you Phoenix, entirely, tears and all."

"I want you too."

And so, our desire is validated. It is out there.

***

His phone beeps three times.

"The cherry pie's ready," he says, so intensely I wonder if there's really a pie in the oven or is it a metaphor.

"Perfect," I say. "Are we having custard, ice-cream or squirty cream?"

He pulls my hand, holding it till we're in the kitchen.

"Ice-cream," he says as he removes the most amazing pie from the oven and covers it with a fresh tea towel.

He slips my hand in his again. It's so natural.

"Come find a romance with me," he says, dropping to the sofa. I stand rigidly unsure where to drop myself.

"Phoenix, if we're doing this, you need to relax."

"You're not the easiest person to relax around."

"I'm working on that."

He moves diagonally across the sofa and pats his chest.

"Here."

I hesitate, the fox and the gingerbread man. A sexual relationship with Henry? It's like diving into white water rapids.

"You know we both want you to," he grins.

My heart flips. Instead of sitting gracefully, I bounce into the space. Henry's arm immediately pulls me into his body. It's alien to me; a man's muscles and ridges and weight. With Luke it was rushed fumbling in the dark. It wasn't intimate, just necessary. I sort of curve into Henry but don't know where to put my hands. I worry he's uncomfortable, so I avoid leaning too heavily. 'Kissing Booth' begins, so I stop overthinking and flop. The more romantic the film gets - the more I wiggle in and fit my body cosily against Henry's. As the film ends my awkwardness resumes. How do two people who'd snuggled say good night? A kiss! Surely!

"Tea?" asks Henry.

An hour later we're in bed – our own! Doors ajar.

"Henry?"

"Yes?"

"I like you."

I wait, my ears as pointy as a chihuahua's.

"I like you back."

A moment's quiet.

"I think I'd like you kissing me."

"Umm, I'd like that too."

"I'm lonely in here."

Silence.

"Are you lonely?" I ask boldly.

Silence.

"Henry?"

His laughter floats in the air. Smiling I plump up my pillow. I close my eyes. Umm. I see us naked; I think it would suit us; I think we're ready.

***

"Ma'am, do you have a minute?"

No, but it's Andy so I'm all ears.

"Thought you might be interested. It's about O'Dowd, the second perp in the hit and run involving Phoenix Whittle."

"Yeah?"

"He was shot, execution style."

"Go on..."

***

Since Luke, I've been picking up Priti for school. First, because I felt traumatised driving. Now, because I'm scared to walk into school alone.

"Put Kiss on, Phe. Yeeaaaahh Drake. Tom Hardy wants to call me on my new iPhone. AJ Tracey wants to call me on my new iPhone."

"Pri, you are so annoying," I laugh joining in.

I park, the music cuts off as I remove the ignition key.

"Phe, eerie, isn't it, that somewhere Amy is being held by a freak."

"Um."

"I mean right this very minute. While we are having fun, she might be enduring torture. I bet he stalked her," adds Priti.

"Maybe."

"What if he's chosen his next victim. What if right now he's watching her."

I'm creeped out; nauseous in fact. I try to keep it light.

"There's a sinister side to you Priti Chatterjee. You're scaring the shit out of me. You know Henry's away."

"Sorry, it's just that Amy must be so scared, wherever she is. Maybe she knows him, maybe we know him. Phe how creepy would that be?"

***

As blood from my hands spirals down the sink's plug hole I look to the target. At the deep gash in his thigh. His femoral artery. Once punctured I had only to suppress his rocking and bucking until he bled out.

***

Horseplay, Mr Jeffries called it. Foolhardy, said Mrs Scott. Why can't they see things for what they are: fucking violent? It was only water poured over you, said Mr Jeffries; harmless. Not if they tell you it's lighter fluid. Not if five girls light matches. My situation is progressively deteriorating; the abuse is a degenerative disease weakening me. It's insidious, yet teachers are blind to it; but it's building momentum and I'm seriously scared.

So, it's no surprise I'm squirrely home alone. Dinner's pasta with a quantity of grated cheese Henry would have kittens over. I immerse myself in Atonement to distract myself from Henry's absence. I look up from my desk towards the tall window; I'm still to adjust to the thick shade of black the night brings. I listen to the complete absence of sound; it's disturbing. Pri's words sneak up on me. I step back from the window. Grab my pjs and change out of my uniform in the hallway.

In the kitchen I wash up my solitary pasta bowl. Without Henry to fill it, the kitchen seems unnaturally empty, like it's a stage. How I imagine the MasterChef kitchen to be when the set lights go out. I scroll through Netflix and do a really dumb thing. I watch Slenderman. Halfway through I'm so tense I've eaten my way through a large bag of popcorn. My eyes are peeled on the screen when I see...

I launch myself off the couch, my eyes leaping from corner to corner. My heart is careering into my lungs because for a fraction of a second, I can't breathe.

I don't know how long I've stood here, scared stiff, unable to move. Long enough for my heart to reduce speed, for my breaths to even out, to doubt there'd been a reflection in the tv screen, of someone or something.

I turn the tv off. I ignore the unsettling silence. I'm being a dick!

Ascending the stairs, my brain registers vulnerability. I'm further from the door.

I check every room, including Henry's. A sign of how far Henry and I have come; he leaves his room unlocked. My room's last. I take time to look, really look. My laptops there, my purse, my snow-globe. I blow out a gust of relief.

I set the house alarm, feeling a fraction safer when the piercing beep emits. It's state of the art. Intruder proof.

I thought a restless night would ensue, but sleep comes easy.

***

I detest disposing of the body; it's risky and holds none of the fun of the chase. I don't bury her; it's too much effort and she isn't worth it. Towards the end she'd given up on life, she'd been weak and pathetic. It hadn't been a pleasant stay for her, but then she wasn't a pleasant girl.

I'd been unmoved by her parents' plea for her safe return. They said she was a caring girl, she had a huge heart, everyone loved her – they were liars.

***

I wake up with one glorious thought; Henry is back today.

"Yessssssss!"

I jump out of bed and run around the upstairs for the hell of it, jumping on Henry's bed, dancing with his pillow, snogging it like I'm fourteen.

In the shower I dock my iPhone and set my music to shuffle. LaLaLa Y2K fills the space. The shower is so fucking fab, when I think of Green... I stop before memories of Luke rush towards me. Instead I exfoliate my t-zone and condition my hair. I clean between my toes with body scrub and shave my legs, I...

...Breathe Phoenix breathe.

My eyes stall.

I shut my eyes painfully tight

"It's not there. It's not there."

Sh.i.t it's there. A heart, on the shower screen, breaking the continuity of the steam.

Fear rushes my head; its beat loud, its vibration booming.

I fall out of the shower, arms flailing in the air, feet slipping to the right as my body weight pulls me left. Dripping madly over the tiled floor, my eyes dart everywhere, whilst grabbing a bath sheet.

I search for a weapon. Upending baskets.

Air freshener.

My finger hovers over the spray button. I grip the towel. My eyes dart back to the shower screen; I see an uninterrupted sheet of steam. No heart.

I blink.

"What the fuck."

It isn't real. I'm scaring myself. Like last night. Amy's abduction is in my head, baiting me. I press my hand against the screen staring at my imprint. Had I imagined it? I want to believe that, to laugh at my idiocy but I don't feel like laughing.

I move through the utility area. The door to the kitchen is closed.

My heart jerks.

I don't remember closing it. I never close it.

Had I?

I stare at the door handle. It turns.

***

Her scream is jarring. I catch her towel in time to preserve her modesty. I can't make out what the hell she's saying; she's petrified. I place my hand on her arm, but she shrugs it off.

"Jesus Henry. What the fuck's the matter with you? I thought we were friends; that we'd got past you scaring the shit out of me."

"What's happened?"

"Don't you dare pretend!"

She's going to cry.

"Phoenix tell me what's spooked you."

"Fuck off!"

She pushes passed me, running upstairs, leaving a watery trail behind. I hear the shower spray. I turn it off. The floor is covered in water.

***

My head is whirring so chaotically, I sit. I'd missed him so fucking much and now this madness. Why can't things be simple? Why is my life a series of fucking Stranger Things?

***

What made Phoenix flee the shower? I check CCTV.

A minute later I bound upstairs to find Phoenix sitting on her bed, still in her towel, unmoving. Seeing me, she stands.

"I'll let you get dressed."

"No!"

I turn my back and hear her rapidly throw clothes on.

"Thanks. I'm done."

I turn. She embraces me and automatically my arms enfold her.

"I know it wasn't you. I'm so sorry for swearing. I just lost it."

I want to kiss her. No, it's more serious, I need to kiss her.

"It seems ridiculous now. I, sometimes I see things, when I'm stressed. I used to see my parents...after they'd died. I'm not ...my life's a car crash lately...I'm sorry...my head's a mess."

"What did you see?"

"A heart formed on the shower screen, in the condensation. I blinked and it was still there, then I fell out of the shower, turned back to look and it was gone."

She's spooked. I lift her hand studying her palm like I can read her future. To an extent I can. I run my finger across her lifeline. A relationship with me and that line could shorten.

***

For a long while I'd been a landscape untravelled. My skin was simply there, ignored other than to cover in sunscreen. Now, it fascinates me.

***

She's staring at her hand.

"Phoenix?" I say gently.

She looks up, her eyes bright. It scares me; the responsibility of another's emotions.

"It wasn't your imagination. It was a labourer, that young flash git.

"Oh my God. He saw me naked!"

"Christ Phoenix, it could have been a lot worse. My arrival cut him short. He got in the kitchen window."

"Shit!" she cries. "There was a moth trapped by the sink, so I opened the window an inch for him."

One minute I'm thinking what a twat I am and then I wonder.

"Henry, what will you say to him?"

A moments silence, so loud it's deafening.

"I hear the kettle."

***

Downstairs Phoenix takes a cookie from the jar, a sign she's stabilising.

"Henry."

She still speaks my name timidly; like she's practicing.

"I'm sorry I turned on you."

"You were scared."

"I should have trusted you."

"You were stupid."

***

I throw evils at Henry. He laughs. My heart wobbles...but deep down, in its pointy end, tragedy edges up.

KISS NOT KILL

Running with Henry is the best start to a Saturday. Not as good as waking up in bed with him I imagine or eating breakfast in bed with him. Ok running isn't exciting, but we are together and I'm breathless so it's a start. A couple of miles into our run we reach a kissing gate. For someone so literal, Henry is missing an opportunity. He motions to take a break. The grass is dry; I sit, and Henry drops beside me.

***

"Tell me about your parents."

She is momentarily stunned.

"What's to tell? It was dark, the road icy, the collision head on."

"Did your parents die instantly?"

A moment's silence.

"Dad did," she says breathlessly, like it's a relief.

"Not Mum."

Two words; so taut and strained they almost choke her.

"She was covered in blood and struggling to breathe. The front of the car was crushed, and she and Dad were merged with metal; there was a lot of pressure on her chest. She couldn't turn to me. The effort, her desperate sounds; they broke my heart.

I released my belt - I still hear the click of it. I leaned forward and held her hand. She squeezed mine. I think it took all her will. Her laboured breaths echoed round the car. I'll never forget that last minute; her struggle to stay. She wanted to stay with me so bad. Then silence."

"What happened next?"

"Nothing; for a while. We crashed on Cuckoo Hill, where the River Pinn's visual on one side and seven-foot brick walls on the other."

"I know it. Then?"

"Police, ambulance, fire brigade, sirens, saws. First, I was scared nobody was coming. Then it was an onslaught, so much noise I wished it were just us again."

Embedded in her words is a deeply sad resignation.

"I was freed."

She picks at a blade of grass. A fleeting focus to quell her inner struggle.

"I didn't see Mum and Dad until the night before the burial. Cow dragged me to the funeral parlour. I didn't want to go. They were in a reception, in open caskets and she wouldn't let me leave till I'd looked at them; she's a cruel bitch! There were no windows to the soul just dull eyes, set in waxen faces, staring at me. They weren't Mum and Dad; they were empty bodies; no love inside, no memories, no plans, no me. Cow insisted I say goodbye, but I couldn't – I didn't want to speak to dead people. It was horrendous seeing my parents as corpses. For a long time, I thought they'd come back to life; because they loved me so much, they'd find a way."

Her voice cracks: she takes a moment to steady herself; her trauma still raw. An eleven-year-old, trapped in a car with dead parents.

"We had a trailer tent for camping. Dad loved the outdoors; cooking sausages on the gas ring and playing cards till dark. Always, first night, we'd sit on a wall by a promenade - the wind bracing, the waves crashing - eating battered sausage and chips wrapped in paper. Dad teasing Mum over how she nuked the sausages at home. Even now the smell of seaweed is on the edge of my memory. After the accident, I'd recall that image and each passing week their faces faded, and my heart felt like it was fracturing into a hundred pieces. It's still hard to accept my parents no longer exist, well not in any corporeal form. And that my special memories with them can never be repeated. They are one-offs in my sad history."

She tilts her face; I gaze into eyes that long for me.

"I don't visit their graves. What's the point? It's a place where everything rots: the ones you love, your heart, your future, your dreams. A cemetery is acres of hopelessness. I'm sorry; it's morbid and morose but you understand death."

I want to push her back into the long grass…I need a diffuser…

"Look," I whisper, pointing to where the water meets the sand on the opposite side of the water. "A stoat."

"Where? I can't see."

"Shush, there."

Taking her arm, I point it to where the stoat is. While my hand on her waist encourages her closer, our heads rest lightly together, and we study the stoat.

"He's so cute, Henry; look at him brushing the water off his whiskers."

"Yeah, he's an interesting little guy. I've seen a lot of him."

"What other wildlife have you encountered Henry Attenborough?"

"Minks, grey squirrels, foxes; nearly ran over a hedgehog yesterday."

"Noooo, was it injured?"

"Noooo," I echo, laughing. "I spotted a rare bird today," I say, eyeing up her figure. "It had purple legs, a yellow chest, a crest of feathers on its head." I tug her woolly hat. "And it was flying backwards." I laugh and push her playfully. "It's called a Phoenix!"

Giggling, she scrambles to her feet, finds a cone and lobs it at me hitting my ear.

"Crap that hurt," I pretend.

"You are such a wuss, Mr Special Forces," she banters bravely.

Lithely springing to my feet whilst grabbing a fistful of sticky weed, I chase.

She runs in circles, scrambling for conkers.

I could floor her in a move, but I like hearing her holler and whoop. Her face mottled red, her lips blowing out heavy breaths. Her gawky lolloping, with its unique gracefulness, makes her easy to love.

"Quits, quits," she begs as I wrestle her to the floor.

I'm on top, poking her ribs and under her arms.

"Ah, ah, stop, ah, that hurts."

We are suddenly head level, eye level, mouth level. She has grass in her hair and her eyes dart everywhere before resting on mine.

"I'm going to kiss you," I say realising there's nothing I want more.

"The last boy to press his lips to mine is in a coma."

***

His eyes shine a lighter shade; conveying an invitation, a readiness to let me in. But am I ready? I'm beneath a man, confined by his weight, his physique, as his torso flattens my breasts, pressures my lungs. He has the physical advantage and that should terrify me. As if Henry senses how vulnerable I might feel he moves a fraction, shifting his weight so my chest can rise and fall freely. He smiles and his breath blows delicately across my lips which part in a grin. Our deep breaths mingle, his warm and fruity from this morning's blueberries.

Time is tantalising. My eyes beg him to kiss me. His head lowers, our noses touch and gently Henry rubs mine with his. I feel a sense of calm; like this is how it should be. Suddenly his weight arouses, his body's not close enough.

When Henry feels me push my body up to his, his mouth lowers.

Lips gently slide, his kiss soft and fluid with altering pressure. Only our mouths exist. Nothing burdens me; my head isn't all over the place, I'm not the girl who just re-lived her parents' death. I'm a free spirit, a butterfly, a dandelion.

When his lips pull away, immediately I miss the heat and pressure of his mouth.

"I can't remember my life before you," he reveals.

"Is that bad?"

"Not when your mouth is on mine."

***

I want to be authentic with her.

"Me. You. It's unusual," I say.

"Man. Woman. Yeah, it's so contemporary it's nearly futuristic," she teases, then asks. "Are you sorry you let me stay?"

She nervously bites her delightfully formed bottom lip. I want to kiss doubt away. I want my body to convince her of my certainty. But how? When my head is full of reservations and risk analysis.

"I want to be honest."

It's a loaded comment. Too complex for now. Yet I've said it.

"Honesty's overrated," she says quietly. Two words that reveal she's put doubt aside and is embracing the 'now'.

I spring up pulling her with me. Grabbing her around the waist I hoist her over my shoulder. Gangly arms dangle one side of me, legs the other.

"Put me down, put me down," she squeals delightedly. I run to the edge of the river.

"So, you want me to put you down."

"No!"

Christ! What the fuck! I walk backwards, away from the river. A body; caught up in the reeds. I lower Phoenix, keeping her in hold.

"Let's jog back," I say firmly.

"Race you home commando, gimme a head start, count to a mil. first."

***

I'm running, because what is probably casual to Henry is seismic to me. Jesus I'd have made love with him in a public field! My cheeks are wet. I'm crying. It's insane. Henry's kiss has unlocked the supermassive chasm that is my heart. Seven years of no deposits. I was a shadow of a person. My bones dressed in a skin of inferiority formed by abuse. Now I need to breathe in Henry, for him to fill my lungs; I don't care if I choke on him. I'm scared and hurt and cautious, but I can't be Phoenix before Henry anymore. I just can't.

"Phoenix?"

Henry's by my side as we approach the house.

"Hi," I say breathlessly.

"Hi."

Oh, my God his voice is so sexy and warm and delicious.

"Hi."

"You've said hi twice," Henry points out.

"Now so have you," I laugh my eyes taking in every facet of his face.

"You're staring."

"You're beautiful," I respond. "Stop a sec," I command, slightly tugging on his sweater. I take a minute.

"You're still staring," he says his voice so low and deep I want to strip and bathe in it.

"You're still beautiful."

Tilting my chin up, standing on tippy toes, I tenderly kiss Henry. An instant heat frames my heart. It's a lingering kiss, because I want every minute loving Henry to be a minimum of sixty seconds. It needs to be savoured. I lose everything, loves seems to slip through my fingers, so I lean my body hard into Henry's, so I can feel him long after he's held me.

Henry's lips pull on mine, he opens his mouth and tongues touch and a flicker swells into a flame.

I lose my footing on the unlevel ground and Henry crushes me to him as we eat each other up.

"Let's take this inside. Your kisses might lead to heart failure," he pants.

In the hallway I place my hand on his heart.

"It's super-fast, I should take a closer look."

Are these my brazen words, coming out of my wanton mouth?

Henry smiles sexily whilst pulling off his shirt.

"Wow."

I swallow. Jesus this is unreal. My hand slightly shakes as I touch Henry's skin where his heart is. It's a lot to take in. His body is edgy and hard with smooth skin, interrupted by rough scar tissue. My gaze meets eyes cloudy with desire. I wonder how a man so cold can be so hot.

"Your turn," he challenges.

I fumble with my top. Henry helpfully pulls it over my head.

My hands are on his chest, feeling the edges of his military history. My lips follow. I taste him.

"Fuck your delicious."

I see Henry's maleness lift the soft cotton of his track bottoms and I realise how far out of my comfort zone I am. 'Maleness'? I've said 'dick' a million times: in jest, as an insult...but never as a living, moving body part. God. This is real!

Kissing Henry, Henry kissing me; I've never felt so insanely desperate in my life.

"Ahhh. What you doin?" I scream as Henry tosses me over his shoulder walking through the lounge, the kitchen, the utility room, straight under the shower and power on.

"Awww," I scream as cold-water pulses over us.

Henry pulls me down his body until I'm standing.

"We needed cooling down."

"Did we? I liked us hot...hot's good."

Henry places my hand on something very male and very hard.

"Okaaaaay," I concede. "Maybe I'm not quite ready."

"You've gone red, even your breasts."

My transparent bra clings to my breasts.

Henry sets the thermostat to hot.

"Underwear?" he asks.

I blush and grin like he's told a rude joke, but it doesn't feel awkward. I unhook my bra and slip my knickers off. I stand confidently.

Henry peels skinny trackies off wet legs.

"Better turn around. I don't want to frighten you," he laughs.

"I'm not easily spooked," I say shakily; embarrassed but excited.

He slips out of his boxers.

"Shit! That is never fitting."

We grin.

We take a minute; for me to look, for me to be looked upon. It's everything: intimate, revealing, trusting, tempting.

***

My pulse increases. I could stop. Move on. Become a Ted or a Brian. I have unlimited resources. Whittle could be permanently taken off Hillingdon's Electoral Roll. Instead, I touch her cheek and revel in its heat, because there is only one Phoenix.

***

Henry decides we're too turned on to stay in. We can't trust ourselves to play it cool, so we go on a date. I make a huge effort to look beautiful and casual. I wear black skinny trousers embossed with berry roses and high heeled black ankle boots; my legs appear fabulously long. With it I wear a silky, black, long sleeved, sway-cut t-shirt under a short black leather jacket. I want Henry to see me and be blown away. To bring me home and make love. That's my plan.

***

We drive into Central London, parking in an underground carpark familiar to Henry. Will I always be looking for clues. Will secrecy drive a wedge between us? Why am I bothering with 'what ifs' when I have now!

We walk everywhere: Regent Street, Piccadilly, Soho, Covent Garden. We have coffee in one café, lunch in another. We look round Waterstones, it's so pleasurable to just pick a book up, feel its cover, smell its newness. Henry buys me three YAs, my fav authors. He carries my books. We feed the duck in St James Park, walk down Pall Mall, wave at the Queen.

***

Phoenix tilts her head, her eyes enjoying mine, she's laughing; it's a belly laugh. It's genuine and spontaneous and her joy is infectious. My arm is draped around her shoulder, her arm is wrapped around my waist. With each minute together the sensation of 'us' grows stronger.

***

In the car, uncomfortably full of TGI Friday and toffee apple pudding, I undo the button and lower the zip of my jeans.

"Really Phoenix? What? Here in the car?"

"Let's pull over," I tease seriously.

I realise how I'd clung to romantic love and never considered the physical nature of it. In the dark, crying, Luke holding me, is all I know. I realise with Henry I'm willing to get dirty.

As he weaves in and out of the streets of London like he's written the A-Z, I think about our first kiss. I'm tempted to ask Henry to pull into a dark corner, so we can be indecent in his gleaming BMW. But already we're coasting down the A40, past the Polish War Memorial and off at Swakeleys.

"Home," Henry announces as he gets out of the car.

"That's my favourite word; I love the way you say it so dominantly," I interject wearily, resting my head back and closing my eyes. Henry opens the passenger door carefully in case I fall out. His action triggering a giggling fit.

"What?" Henry asks.

"You're a very bad man Henry Whittle," I laugh remembering falling asleep in the car and Henry opening my door. "I don't know why I'm laughing; you were so horrible."

He sweeps me up in his arms laughing too.

"I regretted it the minute you fell out."

"I don't believe you."

"Ok, but I'm sorry now. How 'bout I kiss where it hurt."

Henry carries me to the door.

"Don't look at me like that," he says seriously.

"Like what?"

"Like you want a sleepover."

"I want a sleepover," I say my voice unsteady, my heart shaking between my lungs.

***

Upstairs I stare at the sexy slip I'd bought with this scenario in mind. I pop it on. My tummy is a bubbling hot tub, which I endeavour to calm by sticking to my nightly routine. First clean and moisturise face, then brush teeth, before untangling hair. I see Henry's reflection in the mirror, he's in my bed. God, he's incredibly striking. I surge with desire; it could blow the National Grid.

"Are you naked under there?" I ask.

"Totally."

"Oh my God. This is amazing. Turn the light off. No keep it on! Off!"

In the darkness my slip hits the floor; Henry can undress me tomorrow. He holds the quilt up and I duck in. I lay on my back, blood rushing in my ears, hardly believing I'm in bed with a man...this fucking man!

"You're a mile away. Come closer," he insists. "Lift up."

I lift my neck and his arm slips under. It loops around pulling me tighter into his embrace. My back's against the hardness of his chest, my bottom against his semi erect penis. God, I hope that's right, coz if that's it off-duty, I'm in for a shock. Or a treat. Or a hospital visit. Shit! Imagine if he got stuck. I giggle nervously. I suddenly feel out of my depth. I take a deep breath and wriggle into him, trusting Henry to work round any self-consciousness. No point stressing. Still, my brain streams every sexual mishap from *Sex Education*.

His other arm snakes around my waist.

"Comfy?" Henry asks, a smile in his voice.

"Umm, very, but no peeking in the morning, I intend to wrap the quilt around me like in the movies. I want to save myself for a heated moment when you unhook my very attractive, shape enhancing bra and we fall into a passionate embrace, ripping clothes off each other."

"You've not given making love much consideration then."

"Just a passing thought here and there."

A moment's quiet.

"I'm glad you said *making love*. I thought it might be too airy-fairy, but I hated the idea of you saying *sex*; it's so impersonal."

"Phoenix, are you self-conscious of your scars?"

"Nah. They're confirmation of my strength. You?" I ask.

"No. They're a visual prompt never to trust."

A pause.

"Were you tortured?"

"Yes."

"How did you bare it?"

"You learn coping techniques. You disassociate your mind from your body."

I turn around...my breasts soft against his obliques. I'm about to ruin everything, but if me or Henry die, not saying it would make me the saddest girl on the planet.

"Henry...My heart loves yours."

A minute passes. I can't see Henry's expression. His forehead finds mine. Our noses touch. Then our lips. Slowly, they slide together until our mouths part and our tongues entwine in velvet darkness; leaving me weightless and satisfied.

"Mine loves it back," whispers Henry softly in my ear.

The English language is amazing. I put my hand on his hip, gently feeling its shape. His pelvic bones are prominent. My fingers lightly feel the arch of his back and spread wide across his bottom. He hardens.

"Your bottom is so firm bullets must have bounced off it. Jesus, it puts mine to shame."

"I can vouch for your bottom," he flirts.

"Can I touch you?"

"Yes."

"Lie on your back," I order like I know what I'm doing. "Oh my God," I say huffing out excitement with a hint of disbelief. I shuffle down and rest my head on his chest.

"Your abdominal muscles are so taut and firm, no bounce...Am I talking too much?"

"You could be the audio on sex tapes for the poorly sighted."

I giggle into his abs before moving my hand lower, feeling the fleecy texture of his pubic hair; the catalyst to increasing my pulse. I have no preconceptions about a man's penis; my teenage fantasies have been about me being touched. Yet here I am wanting to know every inch of the man I long to be my lover.

"Any advice?" I ask as my hand trails downwards and encircles him.

"Make sure it doesn't come off in your hand like the other knob."

"That door was faulty," I laugh. "I do not accept responsibility."

And so, my next step to intimacy is taken.

Afterward I lay quietly, my head on Henry's chest, my ear listening to his heart, as his fingers gently caress my shoulder, soothing me into a deep, deep sleep. It's the first night I don't hear the thud of Luke hitting the windscreen.

***

I reluctantly edge away from our spooning. I drive to Denham. On a burner phone, using a voice altering gadget, I make an anonymous call.

***

BEEPBEEP, BEEPBEEP.

My Road Runner ring tone rudely interrupts my snatched sleep. Feeling in the dark, my hand knocks my mobile onto the carpet.

"Fuck!"

It's an unknown number.

"D.I. Daniels."

"Listen carefully...no, don't interrupt or I'll disconnect. There's a body."

***

I end the call. I lose the phone. I know this development will impact on Phoenix at school. A dead schoolgirl is big news.

These predators of Phoenix, how far will they go?

***

I watch police divers suit up, check air tanks, clean googles. Standing on the bank side, my coat pulled tightly around me, I don't doubt for a second last night's tip-off is real. The police divers barely get their feet wet.

"Ma'am!" One of the crew shouts before pulling out a decomposing body.

***

I wake to an empty space. I think about last night and blush. Henry and me sleeping together; it's totally mad. I lean over the side of the bed, claim my silky nighty and slip it on. I wonder if there will be kissing and cornflakes? Will we fall into a routine for making out? Strike that! I have a feeling nothing about Henry is routine.

Shame the weather doesn't match my happy vibe. It's ominous; end of the world conditions. I stand by my window watching the rain pelt down, splashing wide on impact. Trees whip and lash; gusts so strong the woods look almost advancing. Despite the room's warm temperature, a chill ripples through me like someone's walking on my grave.

***

I bound downstairs, an excited puppy.

On seeing me Henry reaches out.

Sexual magnetism is real!

My arms slip around Henry's neck, and magically the space between our bodies disappears.

His breath stirs my hair as his mouth lowers. The smell of him, the hardness of him, flip rational thinking, I'm inculpable, I'd do anything for this man; what's a body or two.

His lips touch mine with a yearning matching my own. To be wanted, desired; the thrill of it pulses through me. My hand strokes his neck, moving upward to his soft skin fade. I can never not have this.

Our mouths moistening, pulling, pushing, tasting; we breathe only when about to expire.

Tentatively my hands sneak under his t-shirt. Intimacy is so new I'm unsure of boundaries; do I touch whenever I want...do I wait for confirmation? I go on initiative and feel the muscles of his back; so taut, so individual. He'd make anatomy in biology fascinating. There'd not be a body part I wouldn't recall. His services to education could be significant.

"What's up? You've brought a new expression to the table."

"You, in your boxers, moving around, muscles contracting and relaxing, sleeping with me. It's surreal."

"Yeah, I'm as astounded as you...but here we are."

"Henry?"

"Um?"

"Am I enough?"

"Yes."

"Too much?"

"Phoenix you're nearly perfect."

"Nearly?"

"Your big toes are squashed; they look like thumbs, avoid flipflops."

"I think that myself."

"See; we're on track."

Smiling, Henry looks young and fresh, almost boyish.

"Henry, in the Navy I guess you had to put a game face on."

"Phoenix, with you, I'm me."

"Good, coz I'm fit to burst with love. Like an ant to sugar I want to be all over you...Oh my God," I laugh as Henry lifts me from my waist onto the kitchen counter.

We're mouth level.

"Brilliant tactical move. You there, me here."

His hand lightly caresses my neck, stroking from my jawline to the base of my throat. Dead centre of my heart generates a desperate longing. Henry's forefinger raises my chin, titling my head so I'm captured by charcoal eyes. They neither sparkle nor storm, but their depth is deceptive; they know how to disarm any heart.

Henry's hand moves upwards, his thumb brushing my lips. It's a sickness I know, because my tummy turns, my heart sizzles, my breathing's harsh. I should stop. Right now. It's madness. But then he leans in. He kisses my lower lip, his tongue tantalisingly running across it. I moan into his mouth; his touch on my skin briefly satisfying, but I want more. I want it all.

***

I crave more. I crave everything. To touch, to taste, to be inside her. So, this is what's it's like. To need someone so much you don't hear the footfall, the gun cock, the bullet speed. I hate it, but I want to hate it forever.

"Let's make breakfast," I say.

I pull her hand and her feet drop to the floor.

To an observer we look the scene of domestic bliss: she cracks eggs, I add butter, she scrambles, I toast. It's so natural it's scary.

***

She sits at the breakfast bar, long legs dangling, her face framed by a wavy bob. Though the event leading to her new hairstyle was violent the bob suits.

She's uncharacteristically quiet, but happily so; she's adapting to me. The dead girl springs to mind.

"Must you go to school? Surely there is study leave."

"I've been thinking that," she says. "What with the Kirsten situation. But won't me being home bother you?"

"No."

***

A taste of being wanted; not just sexual desire, but my company.

"Brill, that's really cool to know. Study leave got the boot a few years ago, but I think I'll slowly withdraw from school. I don't want any beef before exams. Erm, I've got to go today because I've a Physics ISA after

English. It's the best grade out of five and I've completed four, but I want to give myself the best chance. It's my weakest subject; every point counts."

My voice trails off as I watch Henry's muscles oscillate.

"I never thought it possible to love someone more than chocolate," I say playfully.

"It's true; I'm irresistible."

"Everything you do plays havoc with my hormones; you make stirring a cup of tea erotic," I say.

"I'm making tea now. I'm stirring. Umm I'm squeezing the bag."

"Shut up, and say you love me."

"You love me."

"I've just realised how annoying you can be."

"You're slow, I realised how annoying you were after a day."

Henry pulls me to him; briefly lips heat and bodies radiate until Henry returns to eating breakfast and I return to earth. It's hard leaving the man I love, for a place I hate.

***

"Can I drop you off and pick you up.

I beam.

"That would be amazing. I'll revise in the library till you're available. Ooh, it's such a boyfriend thing to do," I say staring into his eyes.

"You're my girlfriend," he states, like he's ripped a plaster off a wound.

"No matter how thrilled I am by this, it's spoken like an affliction," I laugh. "You're so weird. Anyway, I'll get ready for school."

***

If going to school was special ops, I'd call it off, get the lads to step down.

My phone rings.

"Whittle."

"Daniels is making a press statement regarding Amy at nine," my insider reveals.

"Can you delay? Say till late afternoon?"

"Negative."

"Ok. Keep me posted."

I disconnect.

***

"Let's roll," says Henry seeing me at the foot of the stairs. "Your lunchbox," he adds passing it to me, but not letting go.

He tugs it hard pulling me near. His head lowers. His mouth firm. His free hand slips around the back of my neck, increasing the pressure of our lips.

We drop the box - school forgotten.

The sensation of being touched hooks me in fast and hard. I'm engulfed in a fire I never want to extinguish. I don't care if it obliterates me. I'm alive! My life starts now!

"Phoenix," he whispers into my mouth. "We have to stop."

"No," I mumble as my lips urge his to continue. "Fuck school."

"I'd rather fuck you."

"Stop talking about it and do it!"

Henry pulls out of my clinging grip laughing.

"It's not funny!" I say breathing hard like I've survived an alligator death roll.

"You look like you've been kissed," he smiles.

"Do I look kissed here?" I put my hand against my breast.

His grey eyes glint. I move my hand lower and lower and lower.

"Or here?"

"Fuck me," he blows out shakily.

"But you're right," I say dropping my hand. "Education comes first."

"Now I'll be thinking of you all day," he groans teasingly.

"Kerching!"

***

At Uxbridge Coroner's Office I flash my ID to the receptionist and sign in. She buzzes me through and on the other side of those doors Neil and Amy await.

I sit in Neil's office. A minute later he appears with a welcome hot latte.

"Kate, I know you're juggling a wee too many balls, but we must round up the others and catch-up after this case. In the meantime, let's get cracking."

I walk despondently upstairs to the viewing gallery above Neil's lab. I look towards nothing resembling a body. It's heavy enough but the colouring is wrong, the distortion, everything is disturbingly wrong.

***

Driving to school the rain is torrential, like a biblical flood. It screams doom. Maybe that's theatrical...but the vibe's disturbing.

As Henry pulls over outside the school gates, the urge to kiss him is hard to quash.

"I'll see you after school," Henry says flatly.

"Not if I see you first."

"I'll always see you first," Henry says, a smile appearing.

"Maybe I just let you think that, because of your special ops ego."

"Maybe you need to take me down a peg or two."

"Forget pegs, maybe I need to go down on you."

We're laughing. I feel so naughty.

"I can't believe I said that. This is so much fun. I could float up in the air like Mary Poppins."

I look at Henry whose smile is deeply rich and rarely seen.

"With this gale you probably will...Phoenix."

Something in his tone disturbs me.

"Stick near the teachers. Avoid toilets and empty classrooms."

"Affirmative. I love you," I whisper.

I dash from the car, the high wind pummelling me through the school gates. I dart along the main building, looking for an open classroom door. I spot one of the form-rooms open, but on seeing me, a year twelve on the inside, shuts it in my face, giving me the finger.

I'm drenched, my feet squelching in my shoes, as I reach first period - English. Mr Jacobs' head snaps up – he looks? No - my bad – he's beaming and offers a sympathetic gesture as he takes in my soaked state. Taking my seat, Priti pushes tissues in my hand and I dab my face dry. Under the table I squeeze her hand. I'm glad I made the effort to come, I can't leave Priti here unprotected and lonely, I must keep coming.

Kelly, who barely acknowledges my existence, asks for the loo, then punches my arm as she passes. Priti and I shrug our shoulders. We look around. Others glare angrily or nervously. Jesus! What's up now?

"Phoenix, would you gather up the books and return them please."

I nod, relieved to get some distance from the Whittle haters.

It's ten minutes before the end of lessons, so the playground is deserted. Walking away from H block to storage. splashing between the huts, I concentrate on not dropping the pile whilst peering round it to see.

The strike that hurls the books into the air is immense. What follows flashes like patterns you see when you go from darkness to light: pages flap, blurred figures advance, books descend; but it's hazy and blinding and red. Pain; I'm on the edge of it. The first blows pound in succession, knocking me off my feet.

Phoenix up! Henry, I'm up.

Cruel fists slam through my abdomen, into my womb causing me to lurch violently forward. The very core of me burns with agony whilst my muscles swell and my skin bruises. Doubled up in pain, absolute horror jerks me upright. Panting breathlessly, I blink away the kaleidoscope of colours and shapes shifting in front of me. I concentrate - attempting to intercept the next blow.

A body moves; I dive into it, bringing a girl down, kneeling hard on her ribcage, pressing her windpipe to keep her still. It happens in seconds and the rain warps everything. Two words distract me; excess force. Is there really such a thing when you're threatened? I punch hard in her face.

"Crack!"

Blood transfers from her nose to my fist, momentarily transfixing me until it's washed away.

Arms drag me off, but I'm gripping onto the moaning girl, Jade, digging my nails deeply into her skin, until I'm free and spring up.

You're dead if you're down, Phoenix. I'm scared, Henry.

My stomach feels ruptured.

She's coming for you.

Kirsten's fist is a pneumatic drill. I block whilst her minions kick and punch; but Kirsten is the one to watch. She catches me with a hard blow to my chin. My teeth rattle as I fall to my knees. She strikes again. I'm dazed. I can't get up. I'm on my knees, crawling away, as Kirsten kicks deep inside me, sending me sprawling heavily on the unyielding concrete, battered, bruised and vulnerable.

I'm broke Henry; I'm too slow and they're too many.

Flinching and shrivelling with each blow, I'm on the point of losing consciousness.

"Enough, she's pathetic."

Kirsten grabs my hair using it to hoist my ear to her mouth.

"Snitch and you're dead meat, understand?"

Too traumatised to answer, she bashes my head on the ground.

"Do you fucking hear me, you welfare loser?"

"Yes, I hear you, I hear you."

"This is for Amy. Cunt!"

I hear a glass bottle break. So, the searing pain as jagged edges are dragged through my tights, against my leg, isn't unexpected.

"You're lower than shit. You're nothing."

Alone I crawl to the doorway of the MFL Hut. Pulling out my mobile, my bloodied shaking fingers find Henry's number. I press the call button repeatedly. I'm transfixed by my blood flowing from me into a pool on the tarmac, diluting quickly in the rain. A human body is made up of seven percent blood; I'm down to five.

***

Dismantling my L96 sniper rifle I swiftly place each component in its compartment within the small black case. Advances in technology have significantly reduced the size and weight of the rifle without hampering its accuracy; it fits into my rucksack, and wearing jeans and baseball cap, I'm a tourist joining the crowds in Trafalgar Square. A memory of Phoenix sitting on the edge of the fountain breaches my heart, but I quash it. I text 'done', remove sim, snap it and discard one half in one bin and the remainder in another. Walking towards the tube, I insert my personal sim. It chimes the missed call alert once, twice, three times...repeatedly. Missed calls: Phoenix, Phoenix, Phoenix, Phoenix, Phoenix, Phoenix, Phoenix, Phoenix, Phoenix, Phoenix, Phoenix, Phoenix.

I hear her laboured voice begging for help. The final plea, 'please Henry, if you love me just a little,' kills me. As a marine, I'd experienced a level of pain way beyond that endured by civilians. I'd lost consciousness during torture more times than I remember. In a hole, in the ground, in the desert, I'd scratched around for something sharp, scared a time may come when I'd weaken and put men at risk. This thing with Phoenix is boundless, all consuming, uncontainable; a pain so unique and limitless, I have no strategy to combat it.

***

"Ma'am."

My youngest constable is hovering outside my open door.

"Yes?"

"We've had a call from Hatfield High School. There's been a serious incident."

***

At Hillingdon Hospital A&E, cubicle four, she lays: motionless, her complexion pale. A cannula runs from her wrist to a drip. Eight stitches to her thigh, three to her forehead, a dislocated shoulder, multiple cuts and bruises, concussion and blood loss.

***

I think of blood. This is my second transfusion. How much blood in my body comes from my parents? Pint by pint I'm diluting them. I'm the Neapolitan of the haematology club.

I glare at Henry's hand holding mine. Is he asleep? It's impossible to tell, he's an alligator. Like telepathy, Henry's eyelids lift.

"I'm sorry." And I am. "For the whole drama that is my life."

"Shushhh. Never apologise for an outcome that others orchestrate."

Jesus, he's bizarre. He's well lucky he's attractive.

"Feel up to coming home?"

Henry's fingers flutter against mine: lining up, locking. I can't hear my heart. Henry can do that; stop a heart.

"Home it is," I say quietly, caught up in a moment of affection.

I smile weakly, though inside I'm a total mess; one emotion caught up in another, horrendously entangled.

Henry rests my hand down as the nurse swishes through the gap in the cubical curtains.

"We'll get your cannula out and get you ready for discharge."

Though I'm the patient, she addresses Henry, giving him a slutty smile. I say slutty because we're in a hospital for goodness sake. I could be his girlfriend. Stop the press – I am his girlfriend!

***

I step away from the cubicle for Phoenix to dress; after all I am her uncle. Only to re-enter a moment later; to find her sitting on the edge of the bed, a prescription bag in one hand, a discharge sheet in the other. If I didn't know better, I'd diagnose a severe addiction to sadness.

***

The returning nurse draws the bay curtains to reveal DI Daniels. Her eyes are sharp. Her intuition deep. She's a threat, I just know it. My eyes shift to Henry.

"Detective Inspector," Henry says so calmly, so reasonably, that I know he is a man of many faces.

"Phoenix. Mr Whittle."

Long pause. The silence is killing me. I'm on the edge of a splitting headache. Shit! I just want to go home.

"As I said to your uncle yesterday. I recommend you press charges for grievous bodily harm with intent?"

"Yeah." I mumble. "Whatever," I say moodily wanting this circus over.

"I'm told you're being discharged."

I nod and an electric poker pain shoots across my head.

"I'll send an officer tomorrow, save you coming to the station."

"Thank you, Detective Inspector," dismisses Henry.

I watch DI Daniels walk away, out the ward doors. Her firm, sticky-out bottom is perfect in trousers; a bottom women would pay for.

"Shit!" I squeeze out through my teeth.

"Pain?"

I nod.

If a word could ease pain, it would be Henry saying 'home', but only hard drugs ease pain.

***

She's groggy when I lift her from the car. Mumbling as she lays askew on her bed. I grab her pink unicorn throw. Covering her. I think about pink unicorns; never did I imagine them in this house, yet I feel comforted by them. They reflect Phoenix and I want her essence to bounce off every surface in this house.

It's impossible not to feel a dangerous level of anger when I consider the ordeal she's suffered. We're not talking about a scuffle; a few knocks and bruises. Phoenix's injuries are extensive. Christ. They could have killed her. The smallest incision in the right place. A main artery and she'd have bled out.

Downstairs, I pour a rum and turn the TV on, selecting sky sports. I'm watching the highlights of the MANU game when my phone vibrates. Smiling, I put the kettle on.

***

He sits on my double bed. Our earlier intimacy a memory.

"Amy's body was discovered. That's what set them off. Another dead person," I say...more to myself than Henry.

"People die Phoenix...many before they should."

"School will be hell...I had no idea dead people could be a weapon. My history will be raked up and why not...death follows me."

"I see why you think that, but all over the world people die every minute."

"Yeah, but I'm not the common denominator. That policewoman is suspicious. She might start looking into you." I retort before taking a sip from the mug. "You make great chocolate." I pause. "Since the Navy...were you actually in the Navy?"

"Yes."

"Ok, since leaving the Navy, how many people do you know, who have died?"

***

Awkward.

"Zero!" she exclaims.

What can I say?

"Now, in your lifetime," she pauses and the scrutiny of her gaze corners me again. "How old are you?"

227

"Twenty-four," I say truthfully.

She mulls this over before continuing.

"Ok, forgetting you're a marine, how many people do you know who have died of unnatural causes?"

In order not to lie I say nothing.

"See, it's me. Kirsten and her gang are right: I'm jinxed, I'm bad luck. Right now, I could be sucking the life force out of you."

"Why does that sound sexy?" I reply, my innuendo clear - or not!

The penny drops.

"You're blushing. Stop-over analysing."

"Ahh," she squeals attempting to undress, her stitches tender.

"Let me help. Bum up," I say easing her trackies off. Christ, I feel sick seeing her stitches. I've seen men blown up, amputations, suddenly I'm squeamish. She keeps her Moomin t-shirt on. I lose my clothes and get under the covers.

"Get in before I die of loneliness," I order

She clambers awkwardly into bed. I slip my arm around her and ever so gently draw her into me. Her head rests on my chest, my chin on her head. We lay there. After a short while, her breathing evens and slows.

***

The last thought in my head before I sleep is a memory of a little girl standing in front of me, in our form line, on the first day of secondary school. She has mousy hair, freckles, glasses and a warm smile. She says her name is Amy. I thought we'd be friends.

***

Two am. I'm drinking coffee in abundance. The vacated incident room is eerily quiet; Bradley, Angela, Alex, and now, Amy's eyes follow my every movement – I'll never understand how that works.

"Boss."

I turn to see Andy holding a McDonalds bag. I want to fall at his feet and praise him.

"Pull up a seat," I invite. "You're a walking miracle."

We eat companionably; no shop talk, simply two very hungry, exhausted crime fighters.

"So," comments Andy, clearing the table of cartons. End of romantic dinner for two then. "He's moving quickly. Picking them off sniper-like. Only it's not a quick death. We're talking evil here."

"We're dealing with an egotistical, unpredictable predator. The route to catching him is through his mistakes. Look again, Andy, at every piece of information we have. Tired heads make for mistakes, you've an eye for detail, there will be inconsistencies, something odd, a queer comment during an interview. Also, dig deeper on background checks - someone we've interviewed is not who they appear to be."

***

I wake remembering I'm in a relationship with a demi-God. I shuffle off the bed and limp downstairs.

Henry's at the stove wearing only boxers. They fit where they touch and right now, they are touching prime goods. His endless torso makes my stomach somersault.

He glances over his shoulder. Seeing him is always a moment. A moment my heart contracts. A moment my hands tremble. I want Henry so much I nearly self-destruct from longing.

"I'm feeling a little violated here," he smiles.

"How do you do it, I'm on tiptoe," I say, sliding my arms around his waist and resting my head against his bare back. "You smell of Hugo Boss blended with bacon – hmmm."

"What tempted you down? Me or the smell of food?" Henry asks in a voice that could slice a coconut.

He reaches for me and I ease into his arms. His lips are 'home', but what he does with them tastes lustful and intergalactic. It's astounding that this stunning hottie, who I'd thought colder than liquid nitrogen, is now the reason my pulse races and my heart beats wildly.

"Shit! The bacon – no it's fine, just caught it," says Henry.

He plants a kiss on my forehead before plating up.

"Argh!" I groan

"Stitches?"

"Yes," I say grimacing.

"Sit with your leg stretched out."

It suddenly clicks.

"Jesus, I can't complain after what you've gone through. It must have been horrific."

***

"It was."

There. I said it. It didn't hurt. My world's not crashing down.

***

I didn't expect a response, certainly not an admission. It's the most precious thing I've ever been given. I rub my foot against his under the table.

"This breakfast is so good. I feel tons better already. I can't wait to have a shower...Will my stitches be ok?"

"Yeah, I've got waterproof dressings. Just don't stay in for hours like usual, we don't want you waterlogged."

I throw him a 'whatever' stare, screwing up my eyes and mouth.

He crosses his eyes.

"That's wicked!"

I swallow my tea as quietly as possible; Henry's eyes laugh.

"Your table manners have improved."

"Everyone slurps when they drink. You should hear Mercy she sounds like a pelican swallowing a three-foot salmon."

"That's a sound effect I intend to avoid. Did you sleep well?" he asks.

"I fell asleep on you again," I groan.

"Maybe we should make out in the mornings? You seem more energetic," he teases.

"Like now," I say hopefully.

"Like when you've no medical restrictions."

"We'll see," I say. "You sound very matter of fact and unaffected."

"Unaffected? I'm rock hard now just looking at you."

I choke a little on my tea.

Henry eyes me comically.

"Your face. I'm convinced you fell through a wormhole and you're from the sixteenth century. Anyway. I've got condoms in raspberry, kiwi, grape and lychee."

"Are you taking the piss?" I ask happily.

"A little."

"Henry and fun? The doctors told me not to hope."

"Your rape alarm arrived."

"Oh goodie, I've wanted one for ages," I gush in mock tones.

"I hope you never have to thank me properly."

"I'd like to thank you now," I tease, before the TV screen catches my attention.

The news.

I stand and walk towards the telly. Crime scene footage of where Amy was found. My eyes search through the spectators expecting to recognise someone. It's a fact that killers return to the scene of their crime. That they get gratification from being involved in the case. Did he get some sick kick seeing Amy pulled from the water?

"It's exactly the spot we were," I say incredulously. "Oh God Henry." My heart is racing. "That's bare creepy."

I find myself transfixed.

"Phoenix."

"Ummm?"

I lift my head. Henry's mouth urgently covers mine, and I'm swept up in an unexpected more than casual response that addles my brain. Right or wrong Amy is forgotten.

Henry takes a breath.

"Don't stop," I beg desperately into his mouth, my desire so strong I imagine it manifesting into a halo of hearts and singing love birds.

His lips capture mine and gently holds them. Though the heat's low the simmering is rich and full of tenderness.

"You've experienced a traumatic ordeal and there's your statement."

"Shit! I forgot that," I say my mood plummeting.

Henry's arms tighten around my waist.

"I'll be with you."

"That's what I'm worried about. Jesus Henry, I'm not like you, I can't switch us on and off, if they pick up on..."

"They won't. People don't see what they're not looking for."

DINGDONGDINGDONG.

**

I knew it would be Daniels. Ordinarily a constable would take Phoenix's statement, but Daniels has me pencilled in as a probability; an avenging uncle. She's hit the nail on the head with avenging. She's astute but textbook, asking for the toilet to have a looksee upstairs, but I point her to the downstairs loo. I stay in the background, but my presence prevents her from squeezing Phoenix.

**

"Now that's ticked off." I say sexily delighted to close the door behind DI Daniels and limp up to Henry.

Henry's hands gently run down the length of my arms. I'm bruised and tender, only this is good pain.

I gaze into his eyes. I think he sees right inside me, to the grey, black and red, the history I never share. He's a man I'll have no secrets from, because he reads me better than I can.

Our lips pull and press, firmer, deeper till I'm lost in them. Everything I am passes between us, on a breath, a sigh, a moan. I feel so spiritual yet so fucking dirty.

DINGDONGDINGDONG.

"Bugger," I say frustratedly. We hadn't got passed the hallway. I detach myself and answer the door.

"Clive," I say surprised. "Are they for me?" I ask looking at a large box of Thornton's. He nods. "Come in."

"Can't, my brother's with me," he says nodding towards a Toyota.

"Shit Phoenix I'm sorry. I saw them. I could've helped but I was scared. It's my fault you got beat so bad."

His voice cracks, he's on the verge of crying.

I squeeze him; realising how much I like this boy.

"Clive don't get ahead of yourself, remember when you fainted dissecting the frog?"

A slight smile lifts the corners of his mouth.

"Calling the police and the ambulance was helping."

"I should have done more."

"Maybe. Maybe not. It was pretty violent Clive."

"The whole school got to see Kirsten arrested."

"No," I say, gleeful she's got bad press.

"Yeah, she put up a fight, they had to taser her in the end."

"That's brilliant!"

"Yeah, she got done for resisting arrest and assaulting a police officer. Have you heard about your case?"

"My solicitor is pushing hard for no bail. A magistrate will hear the case today I think."

"Good. I hope they hang her. I still see her ugly face; the satisfaction she got from kicking you - sorry you probably don't want to think about it."

I shake my head; I most definitely don't.

"How are you Phoenix?" he asks sheepishly.

"Beat up, but I'll mend. Sure you and your bro don't want a cuppa?"

"Nah. Gotta split. His shift starts soon."

"Better pass me those chocolates then," I smile.

"I'll keep Physics handouts for you."

"Definitely and an eye on Priti?"

"She's not been in since your attack, but yeah."

I close the door, wandering back to the kitchen.

"Ok?" Henry asks.

"Not really. I don't want reminders of school or Kirsten. I want to live in a bubble with you."

"Are we naked in this bubble?" Henry whispers.

A sensation zig-zags in a place I didn't know I had till Henry.

"Clothes are banned. The only way to stay warm is to make love."

Laughing, he slips a hand around my waist and pulls me near. It's a typical boyfriend move made by boyfriends all around the world, yet to me it feels unique and life changing. One emotion chases another in a head already stormy. Jesus, if I become this turbulent over an embrace, making love might kill me.

"Are you laughing at me?" I ask.

"Yes. You're very funny."

I give him a pretend angry face.

"And beautiful," he adds. "I like the idea of this bubble," he says

"Touch me," I breathe into his mouth.

Henry tugs me towards the sofa. I manoeuvre myself down, keeping my leg straight-ish.

"I can't tell you what I've been thinking about us these last few days because you'd go red faced and big eyed," Henry teases.

"Thanks. I sound like a lobster with frog eyes."

"I've unusual taste."

His hand moves under my top, over my ribcage, onto my tits – well my bra - actually my vest. Crap! My boobs are impassable mountains; thank God Henry's a marine.

Anticipation pauses me. I've stopped kissing. I'm not experienced enough to feel and fondle. I'm on freeze frame waiting for Henry's hands on my bare breasts. I'm breathing hard into his mouth. I feel so fucking basic. Henry's hand slowly moving; purposely delaying. Jesus! I knew he was dark, but never this cruel.

"Yes. Don't stop. Up. UP!"

DINGDONGGGGGGGGGG.

"Christ," says Henry indicating a level of frustration as his hands hover over breasts - inflated two sizes and bursting out of my bra.

"Don't answer," I beg. "It's not like either of us has friends."

Henry's mouth returns to mine. His fingers unfasten my bra, he's about to...

"SPAR.ROWWWWW."

"Oh my God...why is this happening to me."

Frustration leaves me tearful and emotional.

DINGDONGDINGDONGDINGDONG.

"Fuck!" swears Henry.

His frustration gives me confidence that he's into 'us'.

Climbing over my body, Henry quickly kisses me before going to the door. Disappointed, I lower my top in time to greet Bellatrix Lestrange.

"Sparrowwwww, how's it hanging?"

"Mercy?"

"See H, she's glad to see me."

***

The target I'd shot last week was an easier prospect than this bad-mouthed teenager.

***

She impertinently leans against the arch wall. It's hard not to feel cheated. I'm unfulfilled and it's Mercy's fault.

"Why are you here, Mers?"

"Heard you'd been in hospital. I was worried."

"Really?"

"Nah, I'm stuck with my homework."

"Can't you ask the teacher?"

"Not if you've told him he's a shit teacher and he hates you."

"Have you tried apologising?"

"For what? It's not my fault he's a shit teacher."

She rudely flings the fridge door open...tutting. Her scowl could wither Kew Gardens.

"So what's for dinner? Kale? Looks nasty. Gorgonzola? Smells nasty. Mince? Depends."

"On what?" asks Henry his mouth stern.

"Whether we're having skanky chilli con carne or tasty meatballs and pasta," Mercy hints shamelessly. "You ain't cookin are you Sparra coz my estate's safer than your lasagne."

I deliver a scornful look, but she spies the Thorntons.

"Show me your maths first. I'll mull it over whilst you're raiding."

"H! You makin' a cuppa or what."

Unbelievable! I shake my head and pain creeps back in.

Considering Mercy's not house-trained, and Luke's situation hit her hard, she's reasonably behaved at the table. She eats every crumb.

"Pudding." she demands cheekily.

After rhubarb crumble and custard Henry drops Mercy home.

I take two green prescribed painkillers, pull the throw over me and close my eyes, just for ten minutes.

LOVE NOT WAR

I wake thinking of Luke; maybe because things with Henry are progressing speedily and I'm guilty of leaving Luke behind.

Henry's left a note that he's out for the morning.

I munch on granola, then take an Uber to Hillingdon Hospital.

I fill Luke in on the attack; sharing fears and pain I don't share with Henry because whatever I've been through it will always pale in significance to Henry's ordeal. Not that he talks about it. It's the storyboard that is his body. The more I touch his scar tissue the deeper my imagination runs.

"Luuuuuke, pleeeeese fucking wake."

He's my best friend. He's dying in front of me and I can't save him.

***

I hear the key in the door. She looks pissed.

"What's up?" I ask.

"Nothing."

Her voice is void of its characteristic warmth and buoyancy.

"Nothing usually means something."

"Nothing means mind your own business."

"Ok."

"Fine."

We both know the definition of fine! Wait for it...

BANG!

Since meeting Phoenix I've learnt that the word 'fine', though short, is complex.

Ten minutes later she reappears standing uneasily at the breakfast bar.

"Hey," she says, her tone remorseful.

"Hey," I say gently.

"I'm so sorry."

"I take it everything's not fine?"

"I feel like a traitor. He's lying there after saving my life and I'm obsessing over getting inside your boxers. I'm evil.

"Phoenix," I invite, opening my arms.

She nestles in like she's staying for the weekend.

"It's hard, Henry. Luke's always been there for me. He should be having the time of his life, acting all bad and boujie. Writing lyrics for his songs. Auditioning."

I hold her close. I don't kiss her yet. She's too sad.

***

Comfort converts to desire.

"Henry," I say my tone coaxing. "Undress me."

His fingers move to my top button.

"You can tell me to stop," he says.

I'm begging for it. Panting for it.

"Don't ever fucking stop."

He pulls the edges of my shirt apart until it's discarded on the worktop. His fingers, lips, tongue: on the crook of my neck, shoulder, the tops of my breasts. I'm holding tightly to his jeans waistband as my nipples strain against the lace, desperate for attention. Henry's merciful: his hand slips inside my bra, covering my breast. It's achingly glorious. My lips pull on his, stretching like elastic, hot like chilli, as we crush together. His fingers find my nipple and my desire is nearly too much to harness; it is so deep that my lips are feeding on Henry's. I nearly devour him until he pulls away.

"Phoenix? You're shaking."

"Am I?"

I don't know what the hell I'm doing. I've never felt so out of control...but my head is pounding. Is it pain or pleasure?

"Do you want to stop?" he asks.

"No fucking way," I say resolutely. "Do you?"

"Christ, no," he reassures, his eyes on mine. "Maybe we should take this to the bedroom...in case you collapse from combustion."

Henry's eyes are soft and shiny, and me? I'm gooey like mushed banana.

I scramble upstairs, aware of my straining stitches but still falling onto the bed with Henry: kissing, sucking lips, touching tongues: it's basic, nose-squashing, hair-pulling love.

I straddle Henry, immediately embracing my position of power. I wildly toss my bra away. My head pain has breached my neck and my shoulders.

My breasts heave up and down.

Boldly, Henry visually appreciates before his hand covers one. My hand is quick to capture his hand, giving it no avenue for escape. I close my eyes and breathe out. Total. Fucking. Heaven.

"Phoenix?"

"Umm?"

"My hand's numb; it's turning blue."

Opening my eyes, I see his twinkling. Taking his hand, I kiss each fingertip.

"Sorry, I've wanted you to touch me so badly, for so long, I'm turning a bit mad."

Henry sits up, my weight no obstacle.

Henry returns his hand to my breast.

"Better?"

"Umm, much," I say, my lips playing around with Henry's lips.

"I think."

Kiss.

"I've been

Kiss.

"Suffering From."

Kiss.

"A Henry Deficiency."

Henry's mouth travels from my shoulder to my breast to my nipple.

"Oh my God," I breathe out. It's the most overwhelming sensation.

"I might need a daily dose of you," I say, trying to dilute the potency of Henry's touch with humour.

"Vitamin H," he says, his tongue circling.

"To be taken orally, twice a day," I snigger.

As his mouth covers every inch of my breasts, my hands pull agonisingly at the cotton covering his shoulders, twisting it, like the tightness in my stomach.

My senses are freefalling into Dante's inferno because my nipples are burning up. Henry touching me erotically; we are so real it's crazy.

I decide to award Henry an F energy rating because following that surge of ecstasy my battery is dead.

"Phew," I breathe out unable to mask my pain any longer.

"Phoenix?"

I almost slump over him.

"It's ridiculous, I suddenly feel exhausted and my headache's unreal."

"Your body's had a shock and you're concussed."

"Sorry," I say deflated. "I'm desperate to make love."

Henry lifts my chin and sweetly kisses my lips.

"I know you are. There's no rush. There's lots for me to get on with. I've a scheduled face time meeting shortly, maybe call Priti over if you're up to it later?"

Crawling under the duvet, my head mentally painful, I have no idea how Henry converts passion to pages in some military manuscript. I'm disturbed and frustrated and he's mulling over semi-colons. To be fair, it was me that conked out. I close my eyes. Resting eases some of the pain and slowly I slip into a calm sleep.

***

Fresh intel has me bringing forward an important contract. If I say nothing I'm not lying. If I write nothing, I'm not deceiving. I'm glad she's asleep as I leave. It's these minutes that I feel unworthy of her.

***

I put a wash on, happy Priti's free after school, but agitated Henry's absent."

I slip into trackies. An hour ago, I'd been a mustard seed in sizzling oil waiting to pop, now I'm doing laundry. The only clothes I'm interested in are the ones I want to peel off Henry. Bugger dropped a sock. As I lean down, I drop knickers. Blast! Concentrate. Programme five. Forty degrees; can't afford a second wash to come out two sizes smaller. One capful of liquid; don't want a repeat of the suds bubbling out of the detergent drawer either. Wash on I potter upstairs, but not before noting Henry's closed office door. It would be so cool to be Mr Fantastic merged with the Invisible Woman. I'd slip beneath his door and finally know what the bloody hell he does in there.

In my room pulling a drawer open, I pop the smallest tablets ever from the Microgynon foil and swallow. I'm about to make love with a man who reveals nothing, not even his name. What's in a name. I know the man. Do I? There is undoubtedly much more to Henry that I've yet to discover. What if the truth hurts? I push the contraception to the back of my drawer along with my reservations.

I settle on the sofa reading the latest Juno Dawson...until the bell rings.

"Oh my God," I gasp almost tearful. We fall into an embrace. She holds me cautiously and I note a lack of squashiness. With my hands on her shoulders, I look her up and down.

"Pri you've lost weight."

How had I only just noticed...because you're a shit friend!

"I know, it's all this drama. Oh my God Phe you look busted up."

"Priti I'm so glad you're here. I'm putting on a brave face for Henry, but I feel dead."

"I'll order us a Dominos, then make a brew. I want to hear everything."

If only! I would love to reveal every sexy morsel. Luckily, there's so much to dissect about the attack that we're still deep in conversation when Priti's Dad picks her up at eleven. It's her school night curfew.

I have a slice of cheesecake and continue with '*Clean*'.

An hour passes and then another, and by one a.m. I'm two thirds through. I put the book aside, looking forward to picking it up tomorrow. I wonder what Henry is doing. It's weird he has this nocturnal writing life. Anyone would think his book was about bats, owls and badgers. He could call it BOB.

Obviously, I think about my uncle. His disappearance. Maybe his death. I can't mourn a man I never met. It's like he was a name on paper. Henry really is Henry Whittle. He's the man I live with, he's my family.

What if one day he's arrested and I'm in court on the stand. How will I explain not going to the police? It's a pickle; that's what Mum would say.

I close my thoughts off. Shut my brain down. I sleep.

I wake to an empty house. Henry's car's absent. I don't panic. He's Henry. No way is he getting mugged.

Feeling much more myself today. I check my emails.

"Ooh."

There's one from Mr Jacobs. He offers to come to the house for our one on one. That's the last thing I want. Since talking to Diane, I feel conflicted. I decide to bail on Mr Jacobs citing a headache.

Instead I get an Uber to Luke. I hate the idea of him alone.

My phone rings.

"Hi," I say; only two letters, but I elongate them with sweet desperation.

"Hi," Henry says, so tantalisingly, like a man who really knows his consonants and vowels.

"I'm on my way to see Luke."

"Good. I'll be home late evening."

"Fantastic! Shall I make dinner?"

"For humanitarian reasons, that'd be a no."

"That's mean. Your expectations are too high."

"I'll make dinner afterwards."

"After what?"

"After I've slipped my hand between your legs and made you come."

"Oh my God." I've literally started panting. "Really?"

"Definitely."

"Jesus Henry! How can I chill when a man, who is expert at everything, tells you he's going to touch you where no man has gone before?"

"Well Miss Whittle, you're in for a treat."

"You had me convinced at 'humanitarian'."

"Shit, you've given me a hard on. I don't believe it. It's like I'm fourteen. What the fuck are you doing to me Phoenix."

"I'm loving you Henry."

***

I smile satisfied.

My rifle rests on its tripod.

"The Milkman is moving." Ed's voice comes through my earpiece loud and clear.

"Copy that," I reply. "ETA four minutes."

"Black limo pulling in," Anna confirms.

"I have a visual," I confirm. "I'm taking the shot."

I lean into it and pull the trigger.

***

I look around the sterile, characterless room for the hundredth time.

"Well, you always wanted your own room. Think it's a bit needy going this far," I say, sitting as close to Luke as the hospital chair allows.

"Luke, I'm gonna tell you something. It's a supermassive deal. You can't tell anyone, not even Priti. Remember what you say? *We've been together since bread and water.'*.

I move from chair to bed, leaning over him, whispering in his ear.

"The man calling himself Henry Whittle killed my uncle and assumed his identity. It's unconfirmed but true. That's only half the secret."

I swallow hard.

"I love him Luke. I love him with all my heart."

I wipe away the tears I didn't know I was weeping – of course I'm gutted I love a criminal. Needing a minute, I flip through my iPod and select Netflix & Chill. I'd rather play Katy Perry, but it's about Luke.

I take Luke's hand, as drugs and money and death and girls stream from the iPod speaker. Kojey Radical and...

I look at Luke's hand...I shake my head. I want it so much sometimes I think Luke moves.

I listen to words far removed from my world, but part of Luke's; 'rebilling, trapper, bunda.'

"I don't love you any less Luke. I'm dying here without you."

I stare long and hard at the screen of the monitor connected to Luke. Hearing that intermittent beep that tells me Luke is breathing. I close my eyes and listen to Luke's grime and sporadically sing along.

I stall. I stare at Luke's mouth. I'm hearing?

"F..."

"Luke!"

My hand is squeezed.

"Luke!"

I must have screamed because the nurse comes running in. Then she's out. Then she's back. Then the room fills, and I'm asked to leave.

***

I get her garbled message. I park at the house and get an Uber so I can drive her car home.

Phoenix's eyes are on me as I'm buzzed through. Her hands grip either side of the chair she's on, to prevent herself flying towards me. I stop at the nurse's station to set wheels in motion before approaching Phoenix.

"I've arranged for Luke to be moved to a private hospital."

"Thank you. I've been here three hours, and I've been told fuck all. I feel sick Henry."

He nods.

"I'm not leaving without seeing Luke."

***

We make it as far as the car. We get in and the façade crumbles. I'm sobbing, shaking, but it's fine because Henry is holding me, and Luke is alive. Though barely able to speak, he made me promise never to sing grime again.

Indoors, straightaway, I fling myself at Henry. We kiss; my nose, his eyebrows, my chin, his cheek. I think about inside his waistband. I push him hard, so hard he steps back. I pull his lips to mine, and without thinking, my fingers unbutton and unzip his jeans. He's massively hard; it makes me feel like some exotic temptress. As my hand moves over Henry, his kisses swallow mine, and I want to be consumed. It's like he's been holding back. This Henry pulls my blouse so forcibly the straining buttons fly. Hands push my bra upwards, freeing my breasts. His mouth captures my nipple, his tongue permeating a heat that charges my bloodstream. I'm not thinking, just feeling and reacting.

My hand is inside his boxers, moving up and down, firm and deep. The skin is so taut I find myself on my knees, momentarily taking Henry between my lips. But I miss his mouth. He roughly helps me up, kissing my neck; his deep suction bruising, before biting and sucking across my shoulder. If I was breathalysed it would read a million times over the sex drive limit. His fingers brush hard across my breasts, back and forth, until he shudders and buries his face in my hair.

"Jesus Phoenix," he says breathlessly. "No...leave your hand there a moment."

***

I lift my head, my breathing erratic. Phoenix looks wild. Her hair is messed from where my fingers have gripped and pulled. Her breasts are raising and falling. Her eyes gleam.

"Was that dirty enough for you?" she asks, grinning.

I laugh.

"Filthy."

Her mobile rings. She ignores it. She's smiling madly and I know I mirror her.

Again, with the ringing!

"I'd better check, in case it's the hospital."

She looks down at her phone then anxiously at me before answering.

"Ok. Sure. Can I come tomorrow instead?" She shakes her head at me. "Fine. Henry will drive me."

The call disconnects.

"Kate Daniels. She needs to talk like now."

Silence.

"This day's been a total rollercoaster. Why can't we just go to bed and make love like normal people," she blows out, her previous glow now a pallor.

"Does anything scare you, Henry?"

"You."

"Really?"

"Really."

"I'm uncomfortable around the police. I'm scared for us, what with, you know."

I gently, slowly kiss her bruised lips resenting the interruption. Her mouth presses to mine, not wanting to lose the earlier intimacy.

"Deception is easier than you think," I say. "Keep your answers close to the truth. You're on dangerous ground with me, but you know that."

I can't reassure her. I don't know how this will play out. I pull her towards the wet room. She peels her clothes off and showers while I strip and shave.

"Times up," I say holding out a bath sheet which I wrap her in whilst enclosing in my arms.

"I love you Phoenix," I whisper in her ear.

"I like you so much better naked," she says seriously

I laugh.

***

I hate leaving the house. Hate we're wearing clothes. But mostly, I'm scared.

***

"Phoenix, I asked if you knew Bradley Perkins; you said no."

"I didn't KNOW him. I'd met him once on the day of my aunt's funeral. That was a bad day for me, so meeting him didn't stand out."

"Surely a gang haranguing you would be memorable?"

"Not if you're harassed daily."

"Didn't he shake a can of beer and spray it over you?"

She nods.

"And that's nothing?"

"No. Of course, it wasn't nothing. My aunt's body was in the ground, I was back in care, and this vicious prick slagged me from the cemetery to the care home. It was horrible, but it wasn't unusual."

D.I. Daniels turns the page in her notebook.

"There's a difference, Phoenix, and you know it. Bradley did not attend your school. Bradley was not one of your regular abusers. So, his verbal attack would have been traumatic for you at such a vulnerable time."

Phoenix fails to respond.

"How do you feel about Amy's murder?"

"I um...I..I'm not sure."

"You're not sure of what, Phoenix?"

"It's complicated. I thought I hated her. She violently sheered my hair off and threatened to kill me; I think she was capable of it."

"I spoke to the children at Greenmead who were at school with Bradley."

I sense Phoenix getting thrown by the quick changes between victims.

"Mercy in particular had a lot to say."

"Look, that laxative thing had nothing to do with me, honestly."

"I'm referring to the man who entered your room; the same night Bradley was attacked."

"Oh, well, I didn't see him, but Mercy was shaken. She spins a wild tale, but I believed her. Then there was my missing underwear, and a rose on my car."

"Yes, Mercy mentioned the underwear. Can you describe the missing items?"

"Plain white knickers and bra – M&S basics."

"What sizes?"

"Size 12 knickers."

"And the bra?"

"36B."

Phoenix is rattled. It doesn't take a genius to guess where this is heading. Sergeant Brady appears.

"For the purpose of the tape Sergeant Brady has placed Evidence Box 13 on the table. I am opening the box and removing pieces six and seven and placing them in front of Phoenix Whittle. Is this your underwear?"

She stares; she's shocked.

"Take your time, Phoenix; we need you to be sure. Pick up the bags, turn them round."

Phoenix looks like she's been invited to prod herself with a hot poker.

"Mine were white," she says.

"These, were, white."

"Wouldn't my DNA be on them?"

"Conditions destroyed DNA."

"What are the stains?"

Daniels' eyes lock on mine.

"Blood."

"Wh...wh...where did you find them?"

Daniels' mind is ticking. I'm attractive enough to entice, strong enough to restrain, confident enough to think I can get away with murder. Could I be the killer? I note a slight shiver run through her.

"Yes, it's my underwear. Where was it found?" Phoenix asks.

Daniels pushes back her chair to address and analyse us both.

"On Angela's corpse."

***

For someone skilled in English, words fail me. I can't construct a sentence to save my life. I haven't a broad enough vocab to reflect how terror stricken I am. It's a horror movie. A slasher. A British version of college kids, being picked off one by one.

We barely pass through our front door when I stumble into Henry, clutching at him, as if I might be wrenched away by a malevolent force.

I'm breathing hard into his chest; mumbling words too muffled for Henry to hear.

"Phoenix. Relax. Deep breaths in, deep breaths out."

Henry is rubbing my back, soothing me, preventing a panic attack. In hushed tones he lulls my agitated state and his hands pacify my trembling limbs, but deep-down terror has taken root.

I follow him through to the kitchen; not confident a cup of tea will fix the dead, mean girl wearing my knickers.

"It's such a mess Henry. A murderer has put my underwear on my enemy then killed her. How fucked up is that? It's sick." I say answering my own question. "What does it mean?"

"You have an admirer who wants to make your enemies pay."

"That's what I thought," I reply, keeping my eyes averted, terrified of what Henry's face might reveal. What if he's schizophrenic? A serial killer? Is revenge the foundation our love is built on?

I pick up a knife to prep food – too freaked to converse.

Henry slices the carrots; I chop the onion. He fries the mince. I boil the potatoes. I feel it; I think Henry does too, the fine thread of intimacy spinning around us. I don't trust myself to speak. Right now, possibly, the Ruislip Avenger, is placing sliced tomatoes and a sprig of parsley to finish off our shepherds' pie.

We eat dinner in silence. It's not an awkward silence - more a dark pit of hissing snakes. Where's your uncle? Is he dead? Who is this man that lies like it's true?

The mood eases with each delicious mouthful until it's replaced by another hunger.

"Leave the washing up," orders Henry.

He's so military, it's seductive. His hand cups my shoulder lovingly. My concerns dissolve and I'm a skittish Phoenix no longer.

Henry takes my hand, leading me to my, now our, bedroom. There his hand curls gently around my neck; the pressure bringing my lips to his. We kiss so hard I barely inhale. Swiftly we lose our clothes, his weight presses me onto the bed. I'm too lethargic to touch back; I've only enough energy to raise my arms over my head, communicating to Henry I'm willing. His kissing is slow and reassuring, his caresses soft and comforting. There's not an inch of my skin Henry doesn't sooth. In a glorious trance, we lay head to head, side by side...until Henry's hand travels slowly down my stomach to the band of my knickers.

"I love you Phoenix."

Running his fingers along its seams...back and forth...then underneath.

"I need your love."

All the way down.

Soon, I understand what all the fuss is about. I'm liberated yet bonded to a man that's an enigma yet home. I close my eyes.

"Phoenix."

I turn to Henry smiling but my mouth loses its commitment. He has an expression I don't recognise. It's a rock face. In his eyes is a sheer drop; blacker than an abyss.

"We can do something?" he says, his words vague.

"What?"

I hear an uneasiness in my voice. Am I uneasy? Yeah, I am.

"It's a game."

"Like magic?"

"A little. Are you nervous?"

"You're making me nervous; you look..."

"How do I look?"

"I don't know," I say, disconcerted by his unfamiliar tone. I guess I'm jittery about making love. He curls my hair around his fingers.

"It hurt didn't it? When Amy hacked it off."

I'm breathing uncomfortably. Stiflingly.

Henry's hand is at the base of my neck. His fingers so cold. I stiffen.

"Don't be scared. I'll make it quick."

I'm on top, straddling him; I don't know how I got here. I will his hands on my breasts, but Henry seems riveted by my throat; his thumb pressing hard on a blood vessel. Turning my head to Henry's mirror I see us naked with Henry's hands tight around my throat. It's chilling. His face is dead, the features of a stranger. His fingers tighten and squeeze. It's my turn.

***

She shoots up, gasping for air, her hands around her throat. I reach out to calm her. She throws herself out of the bed, trying to catch her breath, painful tears escaping.

"Phoenix, I'm turning on the side light."

The minute the light flickers on I see her fear receding. She's curled up tightly in a ball. I pick up a throw and hand it to her. A meter away I crouch down.

"A nightmare?"

She nods.

"Phoenix...was I in it?"

She nods.

"Did I hurt you?"

"Your, your hands were, were around my neck. You were strangling me Henry, but you were a stranger, I didn't know you."

A moment or two passes. We both know I am a stranger.

"I'll make tea."

"Don't leave me."

Her words rush out; fear easily detected at the root of them.

"Do you want to return to bed?"

She nods and climbs in. I sit at the end, giving her space.

"Should I sleep in my room?"

"No. Come back to bed. I'm being mental."

As I slip in, she wraps her arms around me.

"Don't give up on me Henry, will you?"

"We're only getting started."

EASTER ECSTASY

Outside the school gate, Henry's long, lean body rests against his convertible BMW that's as black and sleek as the sunglasses he wears in the bright spring sun. The sight of him never fails to make my stomach clench disturbingly. I will myself to demonstrate restraint; Henry insists on this, so I reduce my speed and stroll towards him. He takes my bag and opens the passenger door.

In my seat I watch Henry as he eases himself behind the wheel.

"You're doing it Phoenix," he says disapprovingly.

"I'm not," I deny.

"I feel it."

"Really?" I ask.

"Really."

"I'm a bit creepy, aren't I?"

"Or I'm exceedingly hot."

"I could rubber stamp that," I say teasing before asking. "Did my car pass the MOT?"

"In a manner of speaking."

Leaning back I close my eyes. No school. No bullies. Easter at last!

Indoors Henry immediately pushes my hair aside and kisses the back of my neck. I lean forward giving his mouth full access. His teeth gently nip my skin and I want it to hurt, to make the impression permanent. His hands grip my forearm and I revel in being held; it's the securest I've felt in seven years, yet I'm tumbling into the unknown. It's uncanny how he readsS my body because he pulls me tight against him, his heart, his erection. My head swims with pure, desperate lust. I turn, reach up and pull him to me. His mouth tastes of adventure. Isn't that what I'm on? Some wild voyage of discovery with a man who is the very definition of risky.

There's no rational thought once our skin touches, only a rushed response to free ourselves of clothes. On the floor: his jeans, my skirt, his boxers, my knickers. My bra? I think that landed in the shoe basket.

"Let's take this to the bedroom," he exhales heavily.

"I'd take it to a broom cupboard."

Henry sweeps me up in his arms, climbing the stairs. I'm shaky, like I'm on the verge of something life changing.

He lays me down and whips the quilt off the bed. This is full disclosure.

"Shit!"

"What? We can slow it down."

"No! It's just the size of you in the size of me...I've broken into a sweat. Sorry, but I've only done it twice, three years ago. It was bloody painful, and I think virginity can grow back."

Smiling, Henry hands gently spread over my breasts and doubts dissolve as his tongue melts me. Henry presses me down onto the mattress. The weight of him feels so perfect I don't care about pain. He moves down my body; kissing my stomach, my hips, my thighs before coming back to my mouth while his hand disappears between my legs. Biting into his shoulder, I am unable to stop myself from orgasming.

"Henry, I'm so sorry, it was irrepressible."

"It's better this way. It'll be less uncomfortable. We don't have to get it perfect, we can have a thousand hot sessions, right?"

I want to tell him to shut up, but he's so sweet and I'm sure sweetness is as new to him as sex is to me. So, I kiss the tip of his nose and then his mouth...and I feel a charge between us...not our earlier ramped up groping and urgency, but a slow, heated, needy desire. His breath is steady and deep as it gently dampens my skin. He strokes my breast, down my ribcage and I feel a tremor in my kiss when he finds me.

As he enters the pain feels elastic hot and it's impossible not to tense. The stinging gradually intensifies until he's inside. I'm holding my breath and clutching onto Henry waiting for the stretching pressure created by him to pass. Our foreheads touch and we're panting though we've yet to move. It's then I realise how intimate this is; how I really can feel his heartbeat, how he's looking at me like I'm precious, and so I kiss him hard before a tear falls. As Henry moves gently, I lay still thinking I'll see where he takes me. Quickly, that first heat that had me relinquishing my body to Henry reignites and instinctively I move against Henry until he comes.

After, we lay on the bed, naked, sweaty, sticky, holding hands.

"You look...satisfied," I laugh.

"That's an understatement. It's been a while," he smiles.

"Was it ok...I mean I didn't move much."

Henry turns on his side so we're facing each other. He's softer somehow; his piercing eyes, the curve of his mouth. I think I'll love him forever.

"Before you, I didn't date, I hooked up. It meant nothing. The agenda was to get off. I couldn't even give you a name. With you...its...like you're in my head; I could come just looking at you."

Henry plants his winding down kiss on my lips and rolls off.

"Don't go," I say quietly.

"I'm getting the quilt," he smiles, pulling it over us before spooning me.

"I had no idea desire could expend this amount of energy."

***

"Close your eyes. I've got you," I say, stroking her hair. She'd asked was I ever frightened, and I said she scared me. It's true. Right now, I'm terrified. If I'd anticipated relinquishing myself so utterly to Phoenix, I'd have pulled the plug, but that time has passed. I need her...it's that simple.

***

I shower, pulling on fresh, lacy underwear and covering it with comfy joggers and a t-shirt covered in cartoon chicks. The smell of dinner drifts upstairs as I ramble down. Henry is at the hob. Suddenly my heart is hammering. I want to make love again – to experience that perfect intimacy that Henry can't hide behind. Henry who maintains control over every aspect of his life can't control us. He is vulnerable and I don't know how he'll handle that.

As Henry turns and smiles intimately, I'm relieved my worries are unfounded. I join him at the cooker where he is using the juices from the lamb to make gravy. He flutters kisses on my temple, so gentle and fleeting, they are nearly imagined.

"Here, put this on?" I smile.

In a fluid motion Henry replaces one tee with another. I catch a sneaky peak of his obliques – god, they're to die for.

"Perfect," I smile looking at an Easter bunny pulled snuggly across his pecs.

"Sorry for sleeping through Good Friday. At least now I appreciate why it's good."

"I liked watching you. I didn't realise you could smile in your sleep."

"Oh yeah?" I ask smiling.

"You're smiling again. You must be a happy woman?"

I take his hand.

"My boyfriend's long fingers have made me a very happy woman."

"I can tell."

"He cocks, too. I mean cooks," I snort, laughing.

"His cock's magic, did you say. Lucky you."

"No, he's stingy with chocolate – a deal breaker if you ask me."

Henry grins and passes the Lindor.

"Umm, you're a keeper," I smile.

We eat our Easter dinner, sipping wine and watching each other in that appreciatively seductive way lovers do.

"I don't get why you were so ante-partridge for dinner," I say keeping a straight face whilst drying the dishes.

"Phoenix and partridge – two incompatible birds. You're dripping water on your top," says Henry, his eye prised on an erect nipple bought to attention with cold water. He tugs me nearer; his hand snakes under my top and cups my breast as his mouth moulds to mine. I feel shaky, but in a good way.

"God, you're so gorgeous I want to cover you in peanut butter and lick it off," I declare.

"Remind me to put 'smooth' on the Tesco shopping list."

My mouth seeks his and my earlier lethargy is kissed away with wine lips and rhythmic hips.

***

The gentleness of the first time is replaced with a rolling, pulling and pushing technique that can only be achieved with prosecco and a highly enthusiastic Phoenix.

Later we slump in front of the TV with a box of Celebrations; we watch How I Live Now. We kiss the evening away, teasing and joking, knowing that in a couple of hours we'll be naked again.

***

I wake late; surprisingly, Henry is asleep. Rising onto my elbow I study him. Dark, almost black stubble covers his jawline. I wonder about Henry's childhood and whether he'll ever share his history with me. I know him, but I don't.

I shower and return to an empty bed. Henry is singing downstairs and literally my heart jumps with happiness.

"Let's do something silly today," I decide, kissing Henry's smooth bare shoulder.

"Umm, don't go," he says.

"I'm getting milk from the fridge," I laugh.

"That's too far."

I lean over his shoulder my arms locking around his chest. I kiss his neck, nuzzling my nose in.

"You smell of Henry and lavender."

"That would be me polishing the coffee table."

"See how I know your smells. Let's see what you taste of."

I run my tongue across his skin.

"Not salty so you haven't been running."

"Ahhhh," escapes my lips as Henry pulls me onto his lap and brushes his nose against mine several times.

"A clue as to where we're going today," Henry says cryptically.

I'm breathing so deep I've found a chasm in my chest that only Henry can fill.

"To see a plastic surgeon for a nose job?" I say grasping at straws. "Gimme that clue again," I ask. Henry rubs his nose against mine. "Eskimo kiss?"

"Warm," he says.

"Igloo, ice, ice...skating!"

"Yep."

"I hope we have time."

"For what?" asks Henry.

I struggle off his lap.

"This."

I pull him onto the cold stone floor. In between hard, quick, kisses he's inside me and within ten minutes we lay side by side, panting like we've run the marathon. Our heads turn to each other, our fingers entwine. It's hard to remember what I was like before Henry. It's not that I'm a real woman now, or sex completes me. It's this new, strange sensation of fusing; like I'm Henry and Henry is me.

***

My jaw aches from a constant smile; it utilises muscles that were de-activated years ago.

***

We shower together, making love again slowly, then sponging each other with delicious smelling foam. With a bath sheet, Henry sweeps me up. Naked he blow dries my hair. He picks knickers from a drawer. I rest my hand on his shoulder as he holds the knickers which I step into. Pulling them up slowly he kisses my thighs and my midriff.

"Maybe we should stay in," I hint.

"There's more where that came from later."

"What if I can't wait."

He picks up a bra. He lowers his lips to one nipple, sucking gently, then the other.

"Now, they have my taste on them."

He's so sure he's in control. Embarrassed but determined, I drop down to his hard-on, free him and, just for a second, I put my mouth around him....then slowly rise.

"Now, you have my taste on you."

I see my happy face in the mirror, and I hate that from nowhere an ominous gloom settles on my cheerful spirit, cloaking it, suffocating it. Maybe it's the fear of losing Henry, like I lost my parents, like I nearly lost Luke, and how, in my silence, I'm losing Priti. I'm so incapable of lying to her, or withholding info, I keep binning her off. It's total crap!

"Earth calling Phoenix?"

"Can you just hold me for a minute, but not ask why."

He's quickly becoming the best hugger, he really is. My head rests on his obliques and his arms go right round me.

"And squeeze."

I reach up and plant a kiss on his lips.

"I'm all good now."

"Ready in twenty?" he asks.

I nod. I love him so much. Anything less than a lifetime together is going to hurt.

***

How can a woman who barely walks safely be a natural? She glides gracefully across the ice, regularly holding my hand or sliding in for a kiss. I've no complaints; in my head is the memory of Phoenix initiating, of her feeling safe and confident enough to touch me so intimately. As music vibrates through large speakers, Phoenix sings along - the right words in the wrong place, but she makes them fit. For a girl who'd arrived with no natural styling skill, she exceeds in looking jaw-droppingly beautiful.

"Henry. Would it be wrong to want another hot dog?"

***

Today was amazing.

After a movie and a coffee, I follow Henry into the bathroom. I'm wearing a mid-thigh strappy, satin slip. I come behind him and rest my head against his naked back before pressing slow kisses between his shoulder blades and over his scars. I want to ask about them, but I know I'm shut out; his military life is not one he's likely to share. I get that, but what about his life now? Or before? I file apprehension with my knowledge of French; it's highly unlikely to be retrieved."

"Are you coming on to me whilst I'm brushing my teeth?" he asks in mock astonishment.

"I can't help that you make oral hygiene sexy."

In a fluid swoop Henry has me sitting on the sink surround. He bunches my slip up around my waist, I'm knickerless and I open my legs to let him nearer. I pull his head to mine and lick the toothpaste froth from his lips, my tongue running along the edge of his teeth as spearmint transfers between us. I love the way Henry's palm cups my shoulder. How he pushes my strap down to expose one breast. How he transfers minty freshness from his mouth to my nipples.

"Fuck me," I whisper into his hair.

I don't recognise my voice, my vocab, the response of my body. Like how it shuffles forward so I'm on the edge of the sink unit. How I wrap my legs around Henry's waist as he enters me; his hands lifting my bottom as he fills me, surging so deep, I tense around him. I don't recognise myself full stop.

***

I wake to her breath on my chest, her leg between mine. She lays half on me, half tucked under my arm. She's THE one.

***

I wake and my bed is empty. The house is quiet. There is no smell of bacon. Downstairs the kitchen is empty. Henry's door is locked. Why does he feel the need to lock himself in? Or is he locking me out? I open the front door; his BMW is absent. In the kitchen, a note.

'Work stuff. Eat without me. H x'.

It's a fucking short note; even by Henry's standards.

Is Henry being muggy? Course he's not!

I'm bitterly disappointed, which is immature. The last thing I want to be is a crazy, jealous girlfriend, but I'm skilled in reading foreboding and right now it's off the charts.

All day I can't concentrate, my brain is scrambled. I'm being totally ridiculous. Exams are on the horizon, I should be utilising every spare minute, glad that I'm not having to cast-off Henry for A' levels.

I heat a pizza and settle on the couch, a tray on my lap. Blast! TV remote needs batteries. In the larder I stand on the step and reach for batteries. They're next to electrical ties. I stall. Electrical ties. Probably a common household item. But what are they for? Tie girls' wrists. Tie girls' feet. I think of Angela. Amy. Followed by Henry's late night and early morning disappearances. Jesus, what am I thinking? This is ludicrous; the Avenger is not Henry!

I turn the telly on and immediately on national news the reader is...is...commenting on Kirsten!

"Released on bail yesterday. The 18-year-old is caught on camera climbing out her window onto a flat roof, then down a ladder, that parents claim was taken from garage. It's believed the teenager prearranged a meeting with a man, that is most likely The Ruislip Avenger. The teenager has not been seen since."

***

I'm 4,753 miles away, in Kabul, Afghanistan. A part of the world I'd hoped not to see again. Yet here I am, because Alpha team, my old unit, walked into a building, based on sound intel. That building was rigged to explode. Following a call in the early hours, I drove to RAF Northolt and flew ten hours, possibly to my death. I think of the blunt note I left and feel sick. If I don't come back from Kabul, it's the last thing she has left of me.

***

My back is stiff and my head heavy from a dense, vice-like pain. I've revised all year, so I'm not cramming, just testing myself; paper after paper after paper – timed.

I don't want to be a woman who spends her life anticipating drama: who predicts the end before embracing the start. But it's hard to ignore the terse note. It's not what it says, it's what it doesn't say. *'You scare me,'* he admitted. Now I'm scared he's reverted to the Henry before Phoenix.

Then there's Kirsten. No Kirsten – No Henry. You do the math!

***

I've spent the last few days desk-bound chasing leads, separating genuine public info from timewasters. I'm flooded with paperwork: forensics, photos, missing girl reports, witness statements – it's endless. I feel narked my suspicions of Whittle are unsubstantiated, but in most cases the murderer is close to home. I've spent hours cross-referencing to see if anyone knew all vics; I drew a blank. I've asked Vice to run checks but nothing to report so far. Shit! It's time for a briefing.

"People gather round. Bodies are mounting up. All we know is there's no pattern here. Why? Because each kill is spontaneous, an emotion activates his kill button. He knows his victims. Maybe we need to concentrate on WHERE instead of WHO. The deaths were violent. His kill room will carry an abundance of blood transference: blood splatter and bone and brain fragments. He requires space, instruments, devices, soundproofing, unless he's totally isolated. Sheila's looking through floor plans of all local detached properties and at the people residing there. I want bodies helping her. Why I'm confident we'll nail this killer, is that covering his tracks is not top of his agenda; punishing his victims is."

"So, he wants us to catch him, make him stop?" asks Dan.

"No – he doesn't ever want to stop."

***

I walk among the crowd, camouflaged, wearing a peraahan tunbaan; over a desert combat uniform. My boots are a giveaway, but the crowd is too dense for footwear to catch the keen eye of a sniper. As planned, I walk past the haggling shopkeepers, towards the market, and detach from the crowd when I get eyes on Latif. I jump in the pick-up.

"Bergen's in the back," he says.

We don't do small talk, that's for camp.

"You know the risks," I say turning to my old comrade.

"Getting sentimental, my friend?"

I think of Frida, his wife, and their child...I think of Phoenix.

"I don't like how exposed you'll be."

He shrugs.

We drive down crude sand-coloured roads. Latif drops me. I pound across mountainous terrain, in over a hundred-degree heat, way up a high sandy slope with a good vantage point.

Looking down at the plains below, I see Latif approaching from a distance. I lay low into the earth as I build my rifle. Two against I don't know how many, but I know the odds of dying are high. I hate that I carry Phoenix's impending sorrow. Is this my future? Fear of death?

I keep the checkpoint in view through the gun's lens. I make out three in the hut. Two smoking by the barrels, one sitting on broken pallets. Two at the barrier. Eight.

I watch as Latif breaks, slowly approaching the barrier. At gunpoint he's forced out and onto his knees.

A possible match semi-emerges from the building, but insufficiently to ID him as the worm who fed false intel to Alpha.

He points a gun at Latif's forehead before worming it into his mouth: tearing lips, jarring teeth. Two other potentials exit the hut. Laughter ensues as Latif is ridiculed and threatened. I check my watch. One minute for dawn to sharpen the scene below.

One of the smokers ferrets around his vehicle.

Just as the sun bleaches the dark another figure emerges from the hut. Walking from shade to light. I ID the target. I pull the trigger; in the instant of impact his body involuntarily jolts. In that time, Latif and I pick off the guards. All are neutralised. Only their blood pools on the dry, dusty desert ground.

***

It's 2am. No word from Henry. I want to phone the police, check the hospitals, do fucking something, but who shall I say is missing?

***

We miss the exit window so hole up in the mountains, till we make comms at first light. Phoenix will be in bits wondering what's happened. The impact on her, of me dying, is a burden heavier than my bergen.

***

It's 2am and I can't sleep.

I wander to Henry's bedroom, cradling my phone, desperate for it to ring. Lying my head on his pillow I mummify myself in his duvet.

I decide to ring him. It's not unreasonable. Being jittery and tired I mistakenly select myself, instead of Henry. My heart lurches in fear as the pillow beside me jiggers and buzzes. I stare at the pillow, my heart beating, thinking there is a giant species of bee beneath.

I slightly lift the pillow. I see a black thing.

"Ahhh."

I fling the pillow, crash out of bed, running to the doorway.

It takes me a moment for my brain to click. I'm staring at something more unnerving than a killer bee.

I walk slowly towards it.

A phone.

Not Henry's pristine iPhone, but a cheap, bog-basic mobile.

With a heavy heart, I select my number. My finger hovers over the call button. I don't want confirmation of what I think this is.

I grit my teeth. Shake my head. I press the green call circle.

The bogus phone vibrates.

I launch myself at it; horrifyingly disturbed.

There's no data on it. Apart from a missed call. My number.

From my phone I call Priti. It rings and I place the secret phone to my ear. Priti's voice is loud and clear.

"Phe, what's up?

"Nothing, I'm just. Sorry, Pri, just ignore, night hon."

"Phe..."

I've cut her off.

257

All along, from day one, I'll bet, Henry has listened-in to my calls. It is beyond acceptable. It is scary and creepy and a despicable invasion of privacy!

I do not deserve this! I do not fucking deserve this! I feel a fury in me that knows no bounds. Compounded because I've been left roasting.

***

I convince myself to tell her the truth; I'm damaged goods; she needs to know that. If she ends us, the consolation will be it will keep her safe; it will keep me alive.

PORNOGRAPHIC

I wake the following morning, between cold sheets, to Henry returning. I race downstairs. When I see him my heart stops; two reasons: I love him and he's fucking dangerous.

"Jesus, Henry, I've been worried...why didn't you text?"

***

"Phoenix I...Look, the thing is...I...Have work to do."

I turn my back on her, step in my office and lock the door.

I'm a fucking tosser! I pour a rum. I pour a second rum. Fuck.

***

He's shuts me out. An action he knows will hurt. Will feed my insecurity. Will resurrect my loneliness. It's like my first night in this house. What a shit!

I know he loves me, but I have no explanation for his behaviour, it's inexplicable. I so want to talk it over with Priti, but it's taboo. I can't lay this on Luke - he's struggling with physiotherapy.

***

I prepare to update the Super. There are whispers around the Station that I'm to be relieved of the case. That a more experienced DI, from another borough, might be the answer.

***

I hear his office door open. By the time I psych-myself-up to confront him about this shitty phone, he's in the garden - killing the soil: cutting into it, turning, cutting again. The trees behind Henry give his height perspective. Nature's expanse of landscape cannot be de-scaled by him. Out there he appears more human, more open to possibility or is that a fool's wishful thinking? I walk towards him.

Henry looks up, his shovel in hand, his mouth sternly drawn. He may as well be digging my grave. We stare at one another like strangers, like we'd met at a party and decided to fuck.

"Phoenix, look, the thing is..."

I lean up and capture his lips. He responds. His words indicate one thing, but his body is giving me a clear message. His attraction still burns. So, if he's not bored with me. Then what? Why is he acting so weird when it's me that should be having a melt?

I pull him towards the shed. His hands are all over me. The shed is dark and dusty. I pull his trackies down around his thighs, kneel and take him in my mouth. His fingers are in my hair, holding my head while my hands squeeze his buttocks bringing him right to me...until he's on the edge of coming.

I stand and he groans with frustration, then pulls me to him.

"I fucking love you," he breaths before capturing my mouth; his teeth biting my lip.

I'm so aroused yet angry; I think I'll explode.

I pull my sweatshirt off along with the tee. I throw my bra off violently.

The roughness of his jawline scratches my skin as he kisses my breasts. He sucks my nipples so hungrily I know they'll be tender. It feels like we're gripping onto 'us'.

"Phoenix, I..."

I pull my knickers off, hitch my jean skirt up and bend over the worktop. It's so hard and fast it's like he's trying to outrun the devil. We come together and our raspy breathing fills the space; like it's mocking us.

***

I pull her back into my chest, breathing hard into her neck. I feel her chest rise and fall. Angry sex, fuck, I hate myself.

She shakes me off. Pulls her jean skirt down and puts her sweatshirt on.

It's Phoenix's turn to lock me out.

She stands her fists tight, her eyes flashing but nervy, like she might need to make a run for it.

"Phoenix..."

"I know about the phone."

***

Seeing her hurt and confused is painful. A psychological coping technique enables me to detach myself and hide out. I'd come here when I'd been tortured. I lay low. I see myself as stone, rock, granite. Then out of nowhere comes Phoenix: the chisel, the pickaxe, the drill.

***

My heart is as stormy as the feet that run across the garden. I wish I could switch off my emotions like Henry who, frustratingly, is in an unreachable place for the hundredth time. I'd like to say it's boring, but it's far too devastating to be classified as mundane.

Our relationship is in turmoil, possible dying, but I'm Phoenix, the Queen of Resurrection.

***

I stand surrounded by senior police officers. All men. All over fifty.

"Sir, our knowledge and experience of serial killers tells us that the time between abduction and murder shortens with each victim. And the way in which he kills will be progressively violent. He's holding a teenage girl. We need to bring Whittle in."

***

Love is a sickness with no antidote. It's a fucking mind game. I'm pacing, sweating, shivering, desperately wanting. Biting my nails, sucking my hair.

I turn at every sound, pitifully hopeful. I want to throw myself at his feet and beg him to lie to me. My heart palpates, it whispers to me, taunting me, stripping me of my self-respect, a total self-betrayal. I know I'd happily drown in his deceit, bathe in his dishonesty, if he'd only come for me. I hear his footfall. When I see him, my battle with myself is as great as the war I wage on him.

***

"Who, the fuck, are you?"

The inevitable question.

"Because you're not Uncle Henry, you're not my Henry? Maybe you're schizophrenic. Maybe my uncle is beneath your hyacinths or maybe he's decomposing in your compost bin. Who the fuck clone's a phone? Only the FBI and perverts. Do you know how sick that is? Listening to my calls. My personal feelings. You've heard everything haven't you?"

"Yes."

"You're not writing a book either?"

"No."

I feel my soul destroying with each truth.

DINGDONGDINGDONG.

He heads for the front door, but my hand grasps his bare arm. I hate the puppet my body's become; how heat swells within me from the touch of his warm skin, the flex of his muscle. High treason and I'm running to the gallows. I look up into those soulless eyes, my beautiful killer. I know he wants me. My head might say good riddance, but my vagina is very forgiving. It's between us, in the air; particles of lust burning. I feel the dampness in my knickers. Evidence of our physical love, but what about truth, honesty, openness?

DINGDONGDINGDONG.

He looks at me like only Henry can, with eyes that see everything.
I automatically go on the defensive.
"What a fucking contradiction you are."
His fingers are on the latch to open the door.
"You don't trust me, yet you're the one listening in."
There's only an inch between us.
"You're a fucking creep whoever you are."

***

She turns away and with each step the chasm grows. I tell myself this is for the best. She needs a lover her own age, who doesn't have a machete strapped to their bed base. Nothing about me is real. Each time I leave the house to execute a contract I'll be lying to her.
I open the door.

***

"Phoenix!"
Half-way up the stairs, I turn.
Mr Jacobs stands on the veranda, with an enormous bouquet in one hand, and an extravagant chocolate box in the other. He beams a smile at me. Internally animosity towards Mr Jacobs rises. He'd lied about Priti; he'd orchestrated spending time alone with me. It seems men are manipulative fabricators. I'm experiencing my Carol Ann Duffy moment. Undeniably I have got the ick for Mr Jacobs.
Neither man offers their hand to the other. Slightly awkward. Worse; neither Henry nor I invite him in. We stand uncomfortably in the doorway. Like he's some bloodsucking vampire we can't ask in.
"Phoenix sings your praises. You've taken quite an interest in her."
"Yes."
I wait for him to say more; to explain, to refute.
"Are you new to teaching?"
"No."
"I believe the theme is love and loss?"
"Yes," Mr Jacobs replies.
"Do you have personal experience in either category?"
"If I told you, it wouldn't be personal," Mr Jacobs says, sneeringly?
Shit! This is uncomfortably weird!
"Quite. Where was your last posting?"
"New Zealand."
Henry smiles, but it isn't friendly. The word 'posting' bothers me.
"I know New Zealand well, what part?"
"Near Auckland," Mr Jacobs responds, but his eyes are on me.

"Where in Auckland?" Henry presses.

"Who bloody cares?" I shout!

Both men look at me.

I shoot an 'are you for real' look at Henry, but he's eyeballing Mr Jacobs. No wonder Henry had no friends. His people skills are atrocious.

"Do you read much, Mr Whittle?"

Thank god, a change of subject.

"No. Fiction is often tragic; the heroine ends up dead or destitute; it lacks originality."

I could counter that argument!

"True. I'm interested in taboo love, like Ovid's Metamorphosis. It recounts the struggles of a daughter who lusts for her father."

A silence filled with secrets – what does Mr Jacobs know?

"Do you like romance, Mr Whittle?"

"No, I like a grittier read with an ending you never see coming."

"Yes. I like when there's a twist."

"Henry, Mr Jacobs has given up a huge amount of time to coach me."

"Indeed. Do you usually work so closely with a student?"

"No, not usually, but Phoenix and Priti are promising."

He's lying. Why?

"But it's just Phoenix and you."

"That right, it's me and Phoenix."

He was so gorgeous and understanding, but the way he stares at me now...it's definitely icky.

"Have you taught in the UK before?"

"Here and there."

"Anywhere local?"

"No."

"Didn't you teach fleetingly at Wensley High School?"

"Did I?"

Why is Henry giving Mr Jacobs the third degree?

"Mr Jacobs?"

"Yes Phoenix," he responds but his lips are tight, his mouth stern. Where is his gorgeous smile?

"Did you arrange the theatre trip?" He is about to answer when Henry barges in.

"Would that be a class outing or just you and Phoenix?"

"A class outing."

I know what Henry's implying; it hurts because he's right. Mr Jacobs and I have become too close.

"It must be hard devoting time to a student you're unlikely to meet once she goes to uni."

"Phoenix?" asks Mr Jacobs.

Mr Jacobs peers at me. His face pointy, his eyes stark, his lips thinner than Kate Moss. I don't know what to say. A shiver unnerves me - I say nothing. I see? What is it I see in his eyes? It's betrayal. Gone is his professional, amiable exterior. He turns away without a goodbye and in a fraction of a minute I dismiss the hottest teacher ever. I'm bristling with anger. Remembering Henry naked doesn't help.

"What the hell's up? You were fucking rude. I wanted the ground to swallow me up."

***

"You wanted Jacobs to swallow you up," I jeer. Hurtfully.

She yanks my arm and I turn more abruptly than intended.

"What's that mean?" she demands furiously.

She's so vulnerable, yet I reply sneeringly, angrily, possessively. Words that immediately spoken I want to retract.

"You're a big girl Phoenix, I think you know."

"You pig, Mr Jacobs supported me when you could barely look at me."

"Mr Jacobs is a letch and a prowler. His ego is built on impressionable girls fawning around him. You knew the after-school class was a ploy to get you alone, that he edged Priti out. You didn't share that with me, did you? You were the last person I'd expected to see cooing at him. You were embarrassed, what about me? Thank you sooooo much, Mr Jacobs."

"I hate you!"

"We both know that's a lie."

She stares accusingly. Hurt, I'm using her passion against her. It is a low move, but I'm out of my fucking depth here.

"Everything is upside down and jumbled; you're responsible and now you're jealous. You need to grow up Henry. Otherwise life will be hell: I'll fail my exams and your book will be a fucking rotten tomato. Oh, I forgot, there is no book...you lied."

"Because I'm the grown up. I'll leave at the end of the month. The house is yours; the deeds are already in your name."

Turning, she pulls my arm.

"I know what you're doing; you're totally transparent. You love me, you need me, and you hate that you're vulnerable, so you're being destructive. It's scary, Henry, isn't it? Loving. But if you can get through torture you can get to grips with love. It's ME that's been wronged. It's ME that should be melting. For some preposterous reason, you're now being an even bigger dick. Ooh, I know why...it's because everything you do, you do to perfection...which means you an amazing dick, the best dick ever there was..."

I'm laughing. I'm genuinely laughing my head off.

"The best dick...Oh my god...amazing dick." I'm hysterical and Henry has cracked up too. I sink to the floor and Henry's beside me; he's reaching for me and I'm turning to him. I'm laughing so hard my stomach cramps and tears are rolling down my cheeks, not funny tears, but really sad tears. Henry wraps himself around me and is breathing words of remorse into my hair.

"I'm so fucking sorry Phoenix. So, fucking sorry."

I'm sobbing into his chest. I can't look at him.

"It's me that invaded your privacy. It's me in the wrong. Arguing; what for, for Christ sakes. What a fucking wanker. Phoenix please don't hate me."

If he thinks his oh-so-special, sparkly eyes are resolving this, they are fucking not. I shift out of his hold and stagger up. I know I look a wreck.

He stands too: looking unsure, his face unguarded.

"I trusted you. You said we were family. I didn't hold a gun to your head. I've got stitches, broken bones, but nothing hurts like you Henry. Was it some sick game? Physically and emotionally torturing me for months, listening in on my pain, then lulling me into a false sense of security. Are you a complete freak?"

"I won't make excuses; nothing justifies how I treated you. I've never experienced a meaningful relationship. I've been alone since forever, then we collided, things got complicated. I should have gotten rid of the phone. I promise I haven't listened in since Luke's attack. At first, I had to find out who you were and what was going on in your headspace."

He perfectly striking, his eyes subdued with remorse, but he's a man of multiple faces.

"Really? For all I know you're warped; you're enjoying this cat and mouse thing between us. I can't be in an abusive relationship Henry, I refuse to be."

"I'll never hurt you again Phoenix, ever, not in any way, under any circumstance."

The edge in his voice compliments his sharp features. He speaks with certainty. But my despair and hopelessness are so fresh.

"Henry a couple of hours ago you calculatedly cast me aside."

"I know; I'm ashamed."

He reaches out his hand and his fingers tentatively touch mine.

"I understand if you can't forgive me but I'm praying that you can."

As he says the words, hurt springs to the surface and hot, itchy tears run down my cheeks.

"Hey," says Henry gently, his thumbs wiping tears away before he pulls me into his embrace.

After an embarrassingly noisy sob I pull away.

"Phoenix."

My name is a gentle whisper. It amazes me how Henry's merest motion stirs the strongest longing.

"You're beautiful."

Delusions; part of his psychosis, but it's a welcome side effect. My hand rises to his chest. His heartbeat slows down time. He kisses my temple; my cheeks and I breathe out releasing the knots that have twisted inside me. I cup his face.

"Do you love me?"

"I love you. Can I kiss you?"

"No! I'm a mess."

"Sounds like a dare."

DINGDONGDINGDONG.

I open the door.

Henry put his hand in my chest, tore out my heart, kissed it better and now we have DI fucking Daniels...Although I could rest my head on her ample chest and sob. Jesus, I wish I had my Mum.

The timing is unfortunate.

"Mr Whittle we'd like you to answer some further questions."

"Come in," invites Henry.

"We'd prefer you came with us, back to the station."

Instead, I turn to Henry.

"I've got your back," I whisper.

"Never doubted it for a minute," he says, his mouth brushing my ear in what appears an ordinary hug goodbye.

"Jacobs is dangerous. Alarm up," are Henry's last words.

***

I wait for the door to shut behind us.

"Jacobs is your perp. Keep a patrol car here. Phoenix is next."

"Interesting. Suddenly you've got opinions on the case."

"Which I'm happy to share once you reassure me, you'll keep a car here."

"Ever heard of police budgets."

"Phoenix isn't safe, and you know that. If anything should happen to her that makes you culpable."

"Calm down Mr Whittle, I'll leave a unit here."

***

I'm skimming through Hello magazine with shaking hands, the TV's on in the background, Kirsten catches my attention. I turn up the volume.

"...*Kirsten Willard, 18, remains missing. There is growing concern...*"

I still can't believe it. Crap! I don't know how I feel. The attack is so vivid in my mind.

Since Henry, I've turned my conscience down. I've intentionally not pressed him about his identity or my uncle's whereabouts because whatever the answers are, I choose Henry.

I quietly eat, I drink tea, I think of murder.

It's Henry or Mr Jacobs. One is the destroyer of my enemies. Bradley? Either Henry or Mr Jacobs was in the cemetery. It's plausible.

I run my shaky fingers through my hair. Will the dead bodies of those who cross me continue to fall in my wake? I'd wished people dead, then they were. If it's Henry, then I'm as guilty.

***

I'm watching the police vehicles. One leaves. One remains.

***

"For the tape, can you confirm your name."

"Henry Thomas Whittle."

"It's your legal right to have representation."

"I've made a call, but let's begin."

"Do you know why I've bought you in?"

"No."

"You're aware your niece is a victim of bullying."

"Yes."

"You don't seem to know much about your niece, or is it that she doesn't trust you?"

"She trusts me."

"I'm not so sure. Phoenix is frightened of you, so frightened that she concealed how threatened she felt at school."

"She's spent the last six years dealing with everything life's thrown at her single handed. She barely knows me."

"All five victims were known to your niece?"

"There's over three hundred other children at my niece's school that knew your victims."

"True," she agrees "but they didn't know Bradley Aldridge."

"I'm not sure bumping into him once for a few minutes constitutes knowing."

"Your niece lost her parents in tragic circumstances."

"Yes. Some kids would have cracked, turned to drugs, opted out – not Phoenix. She's a strong, empowered woman, not a victim or an unbalanced child knocking off classmates."

"She's tall, strong, has a history of abuse, she's isolated, very few friends – not an uncommon profile of a killer?"

"Detective, we all have the capacity to kill."

She raises an eyebrow.

"Let's talk about you. You're an aggressor," she states calmly.

"No. I keep myself to myself. I garden, cook, keep fit and write."

"You've killed."

"In the line of duty."

"I think you've crossed that line."

I say nothing.

"Have you ever killed in one to one combat?" she digs.

"Yes, I've killed with my bare hands," I confirm maintaining eye contact. I see a flicker of fear then hope in her eyes. She wants it to be me. She needs to close the case.

"It says on your naval record you were seconded to Information Retrieval. So, you've tortured your enemy?"

"If you're asking, did I inflict pain on a restrained person, then no," I lie. "That would be illegal."

"You're a menacing person though, aren't you?"

"No."

"The Deputy Head at Hatfield is of the opinion you are."

I let her continue.

"Claire Evans, Phoenix's care worker says you threatened her."

I don't respond.

You're a dangerous man. You scare everyone."

"Are you scared?"

The tick in her eyelid gives her away.

"Luke Lawrence's attackers died violent deaths before sentencing."

"That can happen to violent people."

"It must be hard for a marine, sworn to protect, to see their niece violently bullied."

I say nothing.

"For the school to do nothing."

There's a rap on the door.

"Mr Whittle's brief Ma'am."

A suit appears and takes the chair beside me.

On the table is an A4 envelope; she withdraws photographs placing them before me.

"These are crime scene photos."

They are graphic images of dead girls.

"How do you want me to respond?" I ask. "I've seen nightmares you can't imagine; whole villages burning, children with missing limbs bleeding out. These were adults who made bad choices. You're dealing with a sicko who loses control and strikes in a frenzy; that's not me. Adam Jacobs, teacher at Phoenix's school, has an unhealthy interest in her. He knew all victims."

"Bradley Aldridge?"

"He fleetingly taught in Aldridge's school as an agency cover teacher under the name Sean Flynn. He's been stalking Phoenix. If you want to do your career a favour, arrest Jacobs. Don't go undermanned, he's no teacher, he's ex-military."

"How long have you known this?"

"About an hour. A contact phoned me just prior to your arrival which is why I asked you to leave a patrol car with Phoenix."

"Detective Inspector, I think it's clear that you have nothing to charge my client with," says the suit. "Mr Whittle has shown willing and provided a lead."

"I don't trust you Henry Whittle. If I find out you've sat on any information, I'm coming for you."

She stares at me long and hard...then stands.

"You're free to go, Mr Whittle."

***

"Andy, you're sure Jacobs' alibi checked out?"

"Jen worked the school employee alibis, nothing was flagged, but Tom took a closer look and there's a question mark over Adam Jacobs."

"Right." I look over to Tom's desk. It's super organised, I have a feeling Tom is the sort of bloke to line up his baked beans on a plate before eating. I scan the floor with its ten to fifteen workstations. "Where is he?"

"Gone to check out his lead."

"To Jacobs?" I ask though I know the answer and I feel fucking sick.

"Yeah."

For a moment, I freeze. My mind is a complete blank. I mean it's white, that's all I see in my head; white.

"Kate?"

My name, the familiarity, the dropping of my title, has me looking at Andy and quickly I'm myself again.

"You recheck Adams' alibi and run Sean Flynn through the system; see what comes up, particularly photos of him. If you get any inkling, he's a bad seed, send armed response to his address. I'll head there now."

"What about Whittle?"

"My bad."

***

Upstairs I grab a jumper. It's like I've been dipped in freezing agent. I'm so freaked out, I run from room to room, window to window, checking locks, feeling vulnerable in this rambling house without Henry. In the kitchen I find the tea caddy empty. On the top shelf is a tin labelled green tea. From it I pull a tea bag and spot a tiny bottle like Olbas Oil, beneath the bags?

"Trichloromethane?"

I google it and my heart stops.

"Fuck," I blow out.

Only bad people use chloroform - kidnappers and killers.

"Shit!"

Why couldn't I accept the tea box was fucking empty?

"Chloroform," I repeat.

It's scary.

Henry who are you?

I think of 'Scream'. Sidney's boyfriend had an accomplice. Could Henry and Jacobs be working together?

I shiver.

Henry loves me. Maybe his way of loving is illegal. Fatal.

"Jesus," I scream jumping heavily on the squeaky floorboard.

CRACK!

"Fuck! Fuck! Fuck! Fuck!"

My trainer is half sunk between a coarse split in the floorboard.

"Crap!" I sob.

Tears roll down my cheeks.

My head is developing images of Henry, in another town, another house with another girl. A dead girl.

Jacobs?

They could be brothers? I mean what were the chances of two amazing hotties arriving to town at the same time.

I pull my ankle free.

Extracting splinters from my trainer sock, something catches my eye, something white, something that has been hidden. I reach into the gap in the floor for the plastic zippy bag filled with what looks like photos and medication. I hold it cautiously, at a distance, between thumb and forefinger. It's covered in web. Bringing it nearer, one hairy leg followed by another appears.

"Feeeeeer-uck!"

Yelping, I toss the package haphazardly across the room, convulsing uncontrollably whilst doing the dance of the freaked out.

"Oh. My. God."

My heart is racing. My thoughts are all knotted up. Crap. I'm expecting Henry to bound in, my hero, but of course he doesn't. Hero? Maybe he's the opposite. And now I have a spider lurking.

My curiosity roused, I retrieve the package and wipe the web from it whilst keeping an eye out for Incy.

I roam with it to the hallway and sit on one of the lower steps, that way I can hear Henry's return.

Contemplating opening the package I am filled with guilty doubt; it's prying. Whatever the package conceals, it isn't my business. Unless it's about my uncle or affects my safety.

I examine it.

"Curiosity killed the cat."

I'm not a fucking cat. I open it.

It cannot be, it just can't! Disbelief mingles with disgust and poisons my thoughts. My trust is decomposing, rotting with each second that passes. My hand covers my mouth; my breath expands, blocking my throat. It's like the air's been suctioned out of the room.

The girls are young – the photos explicit.

"Henry?"

Mistrust diminishes me. I am shot down. My chest burning with suspicion.

"No. No. No."

I sharply turn to the front door. He could return anytime. The monster; the paedophile. He's stashed rohypnol and pornographic images of children. He is sick, utterly sick. I've got to call the police. Report him.

Hot tears roll down my cheeks.

I regress to a shell of a girl - a fire blackened ruin.

I don't want to believe it; every particle in my body rejects the evidence, but am I fooling myself? For once my head agrees with my heart, this isn't Henry. Henry is secretive - his office always locked. Henry is good - good at concealment. No! Think about it; everything with Henry is new and fresh, like he purchased an identity. This package is old, covered in web; it could've been here for years, way before Henry became Henry.

Suddenly all is clear – crystal - why my father kept me away from my uncle. Henry Whittle is the paedophile. I'm certain. The relief is like whooshing down a water flume.

My eyes glance at the door. I don't know why. Instinct?

That's when I see it. The alarm. Being cleverly disarmed as I watch. Two more correct entries and the activation button changes from red to green.

About to scream, my tongue sticks to the roof of my mouth; I nearly swallow it. He is here...for me.

"Mr Jacobs," I whisper.

Adrenaline kicks in and I shoot up.

My eyes fix on the latch...slowly, very slowly, quietly turning.

I throw the photos in the air, they fall onto Henry's oak floor - some downside, some grotesquely upside - and small tablets spill everywhere as I turn frantically and dart up the stairs.

As my foot lightly touches the top landing, I hear the door re-engage with the lock – he's inside.

Softly I close my door behind me, he'll be faced with four closed doors. My heart is flipping. There's no obvious weapon handy. I hear my breaths, desperate and hoarse. There's no fucking time. I look out the window; shit it's a long way down. Already a leg is out, and my hand is reaching for the drainpipe. I'm scared I'll drop like a coin in a fountain, my blood splattering on the concrete, but there's no time to think, just do.

I recklessly slip down, landing hard. I'm so near to safety. The police are parked out front. With a radio.

I dart around the corner, my feet pounding the earth, fear pummelling my heart.

I almost expect the panda to be gone. Yes! It's there.

But I'm running in slow motion; for each step nearer, terror pulls me two steps back. Panting furiously, I open the passenger car door and jump in. Pressing down the lock, I scream at the policeman.

"Go, go, go. Please. For fuck's sake gohhh."

The car door lock clicks up.

"Jesus."

I punch it down again.

"Would you fucking drive," I scream.

"Click!"

The locks pop up again.

I look up at the house, the first-floor window.

There he stands boldly. Dangling car keys. Mr Jacobs.

"What the fuck?"

I push the policeman...and my heart seizes.

The neck. The gash. The blood.

***

Of course, there's fun in the chase. Yes, it's disappointing they're never running to you, always from. It's a commitment issue. I'm heavily invested in a relationship from the outset, but they're young; they don't know what's best. It's a lesson that must be learnt and fuck do I like to teach.

***

I'm running; spluttering vomit out. Not towards the lane, I'd be trapped if he drove down after me. I've no choice. I'm running to the woods: choking on sick: spitting it out. It's a nightmare, but worse, it's real.

Instinct draws me to the left perimeter in case it leads to a gap to the main road, but quickly I lose all sense of direction. Trees crowd me. This episode of Phoenix is a repeat. Except Henry won't rescue me. I must save myself.

The forest surrounds me; it gets denser and darker. I sprint and dodge trees, changing direction, trying to be unpredictable. I'm a good runner, sure footed; perhaps better than him. I concentrate on breathing and motion.

To my left, Henry is running with me. We are synchronised. I love him body and soul; I hope he knows.

I hear the crackles and snaps made by me as I plunge forward. Awkwardly I glance behind me. I slow my pace. I can't run much further. A half mile later I stop. A tree shields me. My body is shaking from fear and exertion. The pain in my side is crippling, I'm panting hard, I know the trick is to straighten and breathe in. Henry says it's about oxygen levels.

Henry...if he could see me, what would he say?

Don't make a sound, Jacobs is coming for you.

"Snap!"

I daren't look; I squeeze my eyes tightly shut. My terror so debilitating it roots me. On the edge of hysteria, random thoughts spiral into mind. Is it the shooting season? Maybe it's a farmer hunting game and instead of shooting a pheasant, he'll kill a Phoenix.

SNAP!

Sad, crazy laughter bubbles up inside.

I don't feel the prick of the needle as I rest against the tree.

He'd crept up, like the creep he is.

My abduction plays in slow motion:

Mr Jacobs

His eyes empty and glacial.

Smiling the slippery grin of frogs.

Stored in formaldehyde in the science lab.

I slump onto a bed of red, brown and orange leaves

I'm numb; I don't feel their chill.

Strange how the sky moves.

No, it's me being pulled.

My lips form words.

But my tongue is too big for my mouth.

A tear wells in the corner of my eye.

It's the last sensation I feel.

FOES REUNITED

My oak floor is a sea of pornography and pills. The house empty; Phoenix taken.

Upstairs I open my window, stand on the ledge and reach to the guttering, retrieving a plastic package. I withdraw a fully automatic gun from waterproof wrapping and check the chamber's loaded. Dropping to the floor I pull out a knife, in a shoulder holster, strapped to the bed base.

***

I drive at optimum speed between cameras.

I head off-road into the woods surrounding Jacobs's house; the four by four taking me in as far as practical.

Jacobs is no different from a high-status target, except he knows I'm coming. That doesn't mean I'm knocking.

From under the passenger seat I withdraw and pocket an injection of adrenaline.

I run through the woods flattening the earth. Minute beads of rainwater bounce from the foliage as I drive forward towards Phoenix. To hell with depersonalisation. The more I imagine him dead, the more I feel alive; the more I think of Phoenix, the more I become me.

The house is shrouded in darkness and death. If a location scout needed a spine-chilling house, this is it. It has a greyness that can only be achieved from neglect and abandonment. Phoenix's life depends on me gaining access stealthily.

Utilising blind spots, I disable his alarm and enter. There are two ways of accessing the tunnels, by the basement door, obvious, or by a dumb waiter, which may or may not be sealed at the bottom.

First door, open two inches; dismantle spring gun. Ten steps in - a wire trigger.

It bothers me that a perfume, unused by Phoenix, drifts through the house; Kate needs a few tips on how to creep up on a suspect. It's clear she took the direct route; she'll have alerted Jacobs, putting herself in danger.

One room leads to another. In it a lifeless body is sprawled across the carpet. His pulse is weak...barely there. I dial the police, leaving the phone on his chest. Tom Brady's chances are low. He's been battered - very possibly to his death.

The dumb waiter is narrow, dark and airless. With a torch between my teeth, I climb in, locking my arms and legs to create a pressure hold. The torch's beam ceases ten feet or so; I have no idea how deep the shaft is. Conscious of time I continue, carefully wall-walking deeper down the shaft, feeling for lose brickwork. Light gradually dilutes the dark, confirming an exit. According to the plan it exits into a narrow tunnel: left leads to a room and right is an incline leading up to the house's basement. About to exit the shaft, I hear footsteps. I hold position. What the fucking hell is Daniels thinking?

***

It's dark, thick dark. I know I've fucked up. I feel more than an intimation of dread - it's absolute terror. What a horrendous error of judgement; I can barely swallow the sickly-sweet taste of fear, but I can't go back. I have a torch, but I'm afraid of forewarning Jacobs, so it remains off. I've read the autopsy reports...seen the graphic photographs, so as each second passes, the monster that is Jacobs grows like a bad seed in my imagination to the point where he's the devil.

I feel my way, running my trembling hands against the length of the wall of the narrow, dusty passage. They are here – in my head - the dead girls; their terror lingers in the air. I can't request back up; there's no signal down here. I've been reckless, that's what people will remember me for. Instead of waiting for the armed response unit, I walked into my grave. Tom Brady is most probably dead; my sergeant, my responsibility!

Underfoot the passage winds downwards, leading me lower and lower underground. I am further down than the souls resting six feet under. The air is stale and thickly dry; the more I silence myself the louder my breath; it fills the tunnel, echoing fool. The less I move the shakier my body. So many scenes from horrors snap successively in my brain, deconstructing my composure.

I sense him before I hear him - a stalker in a subterranean slaughterhouse. I am rotating my body to face him, to defend myself when the bullet hits. The crack as the bullet leaves the chamber is deafening in such an enclosed space; my hands ridiculously cover my ears instead of my abdomen.

I don't feel the bullet at first; I'm propelled backwards hard, into the wall. In a split second a piercing light shines in my face; I recoil. I can't see his face, but I know Jacobs is smiling. In the darkness he's leaves me to die a slow, painful death. The pain is beyond excruciating. It is poker-hot, searing inside me. Fuck, it hurts so fucking much.

***

Crouching out of the shaft, I watch Jacobs' torchlight disappear into the darkness. Daniels scratches and pulls at her clothes, already thickly wet with blood. The pain is like molten lava, burning and bubbling inside – I know. My hands cover hers to prevent her damaging her wound further.

"Daniels, it's a friend. Stop struggling, lay still." My tone is authoritatively soothing, I use it on the dying.

"The pain is overwhelming," I whisper, "but you want to live. Keep repeating in your head, I want to live. Panic will kill you, Kate, so you are going to calm the fuck down. Feel how hard I'm pressing on your wound? So hard you feel the pain in your spine? Now I'm placing your hands on the wound; press hard, even harder. You're dying Kate; you're bleeding out because you won't press fucking hard enough...Better. This adrenaline shot will keep you conscious."

Jacobs could return. The shot takes thirty seconds to kick in. I've administered it before; never to a female; there is no room for error, it will cure or kill. I prepare the shot. It would be safer to slowly titrate it into her system but needs must. Pulling her blouse open, I put my ear to her chest, listening to her heart. It's weak. Feeling along her rib cage, I locate the intercostal space between the ribs. The needle is long. I forcefully jab it into the ventricular chamber of her heart. One second. Two seconds. Her body jolts, exhaling what sounds like a dying breath.

"Let's lift you to your feet. Don't faint because you will die. I'm going for Phoenix."

I search Daniels' pockets.

"I've dialled your office; you'll pick up reception once you hit the basement. Keep walking, Kate, until you're completely out of the house. Your team will trace the call and within minutes medical help will be here. You will do this Kate because you want to live."

***

A long florescent light hangs above me, its brightness stinging my eyes. I hear Priti sobbing. Breathe in, breathe out. I think of English Lit class and what a good teacher Mr Jacobs is. Breathe in, breathe out. Oh, God. What a fucking idiot! I'd wanted so much to impress him. Breathe in and out.

"Phew."

In and out.

"Phew."

The paralysis agent has faded enough to turn my head to where Priti is strapped to an upright trolley. Why Priti? She's not the enemy.

Do I see double, no treble? Because there's a multitude of Pritis and Mr Jacobs; in places they merge into a mangled thing. I squint repeatedly. As my vision restores, I realise the walls are mirrored. Red mirrors - is there such a thing?

The stench in the room is unbearable, but I can't raise my hand to hold my nose. I scan the chamber. Jesus. There is blood, a lot of it. On the floors, on the...Fuck the mirrors aren't red. They're smeared with blood.

Oh, God. Oh, God.

The room screams of the demise of girls - lured to their deaths by pretty words spoken by soft lips and a heinous heart.

And Mr Jacobs. There is a lot of blood on him, too.

I don't want to look around, but I force myself. Maybe when I can move, I'll grab something, knock Mr Jacobs out.

Oh, fuck! I knew it. I'm right. I don't want to be right.

Shit...he's a real freak. He's been watching me. My eyes take in an exhibition of Phoenix: outside Greenmead, at the cemetery, asleep on Henry's doorstep that first awful night. There isn't a move I made that Mr Jacobs hasn't captured...even me naked. Sick fuck!

Me and Mr Jacobs. What the fuck? There was no me and Mr Jacobs? I squint to clear my tired eyes. I stare long and hard.

Jacobs' face is glued over Luke's. He nearly killed Luke. It was him.

Fuck!

We are going to die.

Slowly.

My eyes jump to Priti; she seems unharmed, well physically.

Mr Jacobs is between the trolley and a table; his breathing erratic; he sounds excited, which can't be good.

Priti is breathing out horrible deep rasps of pure horror. I follow the direction of her eyes and catch sight of a large sewing needle in Mr Jacobs' hand.

Je-sus!

I can't speak, so I can't beg. The only sounds I make are blurred murmurings as I try to stop Mr Jacobs.

He glances in my direction, smiles and threads the needle with black twine. I furiously attempt to twist, roll, reach, anything - please!

He has the needle in one hand and is squeezing Priti's lips together with the other.

I moan and swing my head. Yes! Yes! Look at me! I want you, you twisted weasel. Yes, keep coming

Priti is experiencing absolute terror and mental torture and I'm responsible. We will probably both die a gruesome death. Oh, Priti, I'm so sorry, please forgive me! I'm so, so sorry I murmur, but my words are undistinguishable, just a loooooooong, slurrrrrrrred grooooooooannnn.

Jacobs bends over me. His nostrils flare as he runs his fingers through his hair, a gesture that now seems limp and weak; I don't know how I hadn't noticed before. He swallows hard, running his thumb and index finger from each corner of his mouth until they meet in the centre. He kisses my lips, his eyes gleaming with disgusting lust, his fingers covered in blood.

I force myself to look at him, to convey to him that he is the centre of my world. I'm scared I will choke on my own vomit I am so petrified. I watch him undressing me in the mirrors, his hands shaking, his vulgar fingers unbuttoning my blouse.

"Silly girl don't be shy. I've seen it all before."

I'm being shifted; the mirrors above reveal he's removing my jeans, so I'm left in my underwear. My eyes must have flinched.

"Phoenix, I'm beginning to question your devotion," he complains sternly before throwing his tongue down my throat. He aggressively thrusts it around, making me gag, before slipping it out.

His lips remain parted, and his tongue slowly runs down my neck, chest, stomach, pausing for his mouth to suck and pull; so little folds of skin are between his teeth. I watch as he leaves bite marks over my abdomen, down to my knicker line.

I feel nothing. I think nothing. He is nothing.

He straightens. I wriggle trying to regain his attention.

"Be patient, you're not ready yet. I want you to feel everything, but I'll fetch our special treat."

All about me are semi-naked Phoenix's, pale and pliant, not one able to change the course of this nightmare. Henry can change it. Please come Henry. Please come, Henry. If I concentrate hard enough, Henry will hear me, he will come, Henry will save us.

I think of my parents; how they never came for me.

BANG!

I don't need to see the gun to know someone is dead.

I see Mr Jacobs' reflection return.

He puts a box down on a table.

He docs his iPhone, music fills the room.

279

His back is to me.

He dances as he removes his shirt.

He is bulkier than Henry.

Stronger? Yes.

I'm shitting bricks. I couldn't feel more fearful than now, but he cranks it up a notch, when he turns to me.

Fuck no!

No. No. No. No. No.

He's naked.

With an erection.

I close my eyes so tightly my brain could burst from pressure.

It's not real, pleeeeese! But it is so fucking real.

There are different types of fear.

There's dying.

Priti dying.

And this fear...right now...of not dying quick enough. Before my body's layers are slowly and painfully infiltrated.

His body's artwork tells the story of my death and it will not be merciful. Mr Jacobs' mutilated skin is covered in etchings. Some deep, others barely break the skin. They age from freshly cut and bleeding, to red raw, to pink and scarred. One word, repeated at different angles, some superimposed. His body reads, Phoenix.

I think of Henry naked, strong and beautiful. Whatever he does; it will only ever be Henry.

Mr Jacobs smiles. He turns back to the table. He pulls something from the box. He places a wig on his head...of my hair. Of course, it fucking is. I've seen enough horrors to know how things work.

He moves ludicrously, scarily, towards me. Dancing and turning, looking at his reflection, then twirling and blowing kisses to his triplets. He's so taken with himself; it would be sad if he wasn't so sick and twisted.

I want to applaud him and call out more, more, encore, anything to delay the inevitable.

He strokes my cheek; he cups my breasts. I'm expecting him to undo my bra, but no, he puts his hands between his legs and smiles at me whilst jerking off. I see his head bobbing up and down as he pants. Then that awful shriek as he orgasms.

If I survive this, I'm never having sex again.

I look away...up...sideways...anywhere.

That's when I see it. A freezer chest. Holes drilled in it. I'm sick to my stomach. And scared. Horribly scared. It's where he'd kept them. Kirsten's body could be there now.

Fuck!

Henry, if you can hear me, I love you.

Pleassssse. Pleassssse come get us.

We don't want to die.

***

The scene at the entrance to the cavern is not for the faint hearted. It is a torture room. A pulley hangs from the ceiling; to hoist and dislocate shoulders. A chain with shackles is attached to a wall. There are trays of instruments, some sparkling, others not so.

Priti is strapped to a vertical gurney.

Phoenix, flat on the tiled floor, unmoving.

Jacobs is currently living out his sick psychotic fantasy to the soundtrack of Ricky Martin? He is between Phoenix and Priti, so no clear shot. Jacobs and I share the same psychological head space, his is sicker but, ultimately, we are both killers, we think alike. If I go in armed, he'll use the girls as shields. So, I'm going back to basics.

I ram him. Our bodies impact - slamming to the floor - hard muscle on muscle - me on top - straddling. My knees digging into his obliques whilst my hands squeeze his throat. Tight. Tighter. I want to crush his fucking larynx. He will never speak her name again.

His fingers claw at me before locking around my neck; his arms are like extendable poles.

I repeatedly bang his sick brain against the concrete floor. Trying to loosen his grasp. I keep going until...he's laughing, fucking laughing! Seeing Phoenix's name cut into his body makes me fucking sick. I pound my fist into his grinning face.

CRACK!

I've broken his cheek bone. Blood pours from his nose, down the side of his face merging with the fluids from his victims.

I've given him too much room; his feet push unrelentingly into my chest forcing our bodies apart.

Slipping the knife into my hand, I slash deep into his thigh as I jump to my feet. He mirrors me. Upright, wig on floor, blood seeping from the cut beneath his jeans, he chuckles. He's feeding off the pain.

"I'll slice you, dice you and fuck your niece," he laughs.

He's pumped.

"You've taken something that's mine and I want her back."

Circling each other, his eyes dart around the room, to the instruments tray, to Phoenix, to me, to Priti.

"I don't think so, pretty boy. You marines - you're so cocky."

Whippet quick he lands a blow square on my jaw.

"You know what, Jacobs?"

I lunge at him, my knife slitting another clean line through his jeans and the skin underneath.

"What's that Henry?"

"I think you like a man in uniform."

He piles into me, frenziedly throwing punch after punch.

I slash repeatedly; sometimes hitting the target, mainly coursing through air. His technique matches mine, and he's powerful, only I have the knife. Until I don't.

CLATTER!

It's only been minutes, but the frantic lunging and punching is brutal. Jacobs isn't fucking tiring. Trust Phoenix to find the one man in Ruislip with the capability to kill me.

"Come on, Uncle Henry," he laughs, spitting out a tooth I'd dislodged. "Keep up."

"Was it your mother? Or is that too cliché?"

His expression tightens.

"It's always the mother. Did she have a special way of tucking you in?"

He runs at me. We're pulling, grappling, clutching. My lungs are a fucking inferno.

"Another hit for team Henry," I laugh, even though my breathing is laboured and fills my head like a hazy heat.

I need to get him away from the girls so I can shoot this fucking bastard.

Fuck!

My back collides with the gurney Priti is strapped to; I fall from there to the instruments tray. The clang from them hitting the cold, solid ground reverberates.

He's losing blood; I'm losing co-ordination.

Jesus, he's lurched to the ground and grabbed a weapon.

"Sweet...let's play," he invites, his face crazed by a deranged smile.

Before I can reach for my weapon, he's on me; his sharp instrument an inch from my fucking face. My grip is losing strength. I headbutt him crackingly hard, practically knocking us both out.

We stumble, dazed by the impact.

I'm disorientated and he's insane; insanely strong and fast.

He targets my injuries: punching and gouging.

My heart accelerates, and as my pain threshold peaks, a small cleaver is hurled forcefully into my thigh. And there it must remain, to avoid blood loss.

I exhale hard, my throat like sandpaper.

"Phewww."

Phoenix.

"Phewww."

Phoenix.

"Phewww."

Her name is my personal pain suppressant.

I've lost all sense of time and I'm living, possibly dying, in the present tense.

"Look darling," he calls to Phoenix. "Isn't it wonderful, the two men in your life have shared interests - we love killing."

Blood, from a weeping gape in my forehead, runs into my eyes. I'm drenched in perspiration. Jacobs is as sweat-soaked and bloody as me. He's also high as a kite. And a miracle – no one can take the punishment I've inflicted and remain standing.

His eyes settle on Phoenix. I prepare to kill him. My vision zooms in and out.

Phoenix.

"Phewww. Jacobs!"

"Not now Henry."

Jacobs moves towards Phoenix.

"Be terrified, Phoenix," he hisses. "I'm coming, sugar!"

I wipe the blood from my eyes and take aim...

"Jacobs!"

"I. Said. Not. Now."

I fire.

Hearing the rumbles of the cavalry arriving I wipe the gun clean. Place Jacobs' fingers around the trigger, then transfer it to my hand. His prints will be beneath mine substantiating the gun as his. We fought and I reached the gun first.

RECOVERY

Henry had come. I'd seen his reflections in the mirrors. Multiple Henries killing my English teacher, not quickly and efficiently, but slowly and messily.

I'm under Henry's arm, against his chest. He's sitting up, his back against the damp, rough wall, one knee bent, his injured leg stretched out.

I barely register Priti being carried out or Kirsten, broken, bloody but alive, being pulled from the freezer.

"Don't look Phoenix. Close your eyes and visualise home."

So, I do, because Henry has the cleaver deeply embedded in his thigh, I'm covered in my English teacher's brain matter and armed police and paramedics are everywhere. It's like the night of our car crash: blood, people, noises...death.

Me, Henry, Priti and Kirsten need medical attention, and so all the players left in the game are enroute to Hillingdon Hospital.

I travel in the ambulance with Henry. I insist. I'm not letting him out of my sight. I'm holding his hand up until they take him through to theatre. I know we're in public, and we're uncle and niece so I held back; it was excruciating.

Now one of the ambulance crew shuffles me to the assessment area. There, on a bed, I close my eyes and lose consciousness.

I wake with a white gown on and a drip attached via cannula - again! It's freaky. Pulling the stiff sheet back, feeling woozy and shaky, I seek Henry out. Wheeling my drip beside me, I read the names of my sleeping neighbours; no one I know – lucky for them – their survival rate just increased. I creep to the empty nurses' station and run my eyes down the board listing patients and their room. Henry is in a single room; K.

"Phoenix," he breathes gently as I approach his bed.

"How did you know it was me?"

"Because it's two am, the ward is quiet until a squeak, shuffle, shuffle, squeak."

He reaches for the night light above his bed. I hold my breath prepared to see a very different Henry.

"Click."

The same gorgeously grim Henry stares at me like I'm angel delight. I bend over, careful not to hurt my soldier and we gently kiss. It's phenomenal; it's a masterpiece. Fuck, I love this man.

"You look irresistibly injured. Only you can wear a bruise better than Ryan Gosling. How are you?"

"I'm feeling pretty cleaver."

Tears fill my eyes and my shoulders shakily shudder.

"Phoenix, I'm sorry, I wanted to break the tension; you know I don't do comedy."

"No, it was funny - cleaver, clever. You're making real progress."

I pause. I sit on the edge of his bed. He's upright, his chest bare, dressings covering stitches. I find a place undamaged by cuts or bruises, near his heart and rest my palm there. I never want to stop hearing Henry's heart. I never want Henry to stop breathing, like my Mum had.

"I don't know how you did it, Henry."

"Kill?"

"No. How you kept going, fighting, what you put your body through, the cleaver."

He raises his hand and gently touches my cheek, a reminder of how tender he is with me. He rests his head back and closes his eyes.

"Henry?"

"Umm?" He responds, opening one eye.

"Bring me home and make love with me...we've gotten so good at it."

"Give me a couple of hours, it's been an eventful day."

I smile, pull up a chair and hold his hand, humming gently. I know how much he likes that.

***

I think of a home, where Phoenix sings out of tune and cooks inedible meals. It's a taste of heaven and I want to be buried in it.

***

I'm on the move; while Henry sleeps. I search out Priti.

"Excuse me," I say, stopping a nurse. "My friend was admitted."

He taps a few keys and searches his computer screen.

"Kirsten Willard?"

"No, definitely not my friend."

"Priti Chatterjee?"

"Yes."

"She's been transferred to a private hospital."

I shake my head. Priti is gone. Tears well in my eyes.

"Are you ok? You should be in bed."

"How can I fix things if she's not here?"

Tears roll down my cheeks, dropping to the tiled floor.

"How can I make things better?" I sob.

Clutching my IV stand, my head resting on a bag of fluid, I cry...noisily. It's like Jacobs has ripped my heart out.

The nurse presses paper towels into my hand, but I'm inconsolable until he talks sedatives.

"I'm ok now. Really. I am."

"Back to bed with you then."

I nod. Enroute I notice a single room with the door's window blind pulled down. Thinking it's Kate Daniels, I push the door open. I hear my name:

"Phoenix?"

I stiffen and turn to leave.

"Please don't go."

The voice isn't harsh or accusing, it's soft, timid, almost broken.

Wheeling my IV stand to her bedside, I stare down at Kirsten. Her face is swollen and bruised, her arm and legs in plaster suspended on pullies.

"Do you hate me?"

"I don't feel much of anything for you."

Which is true. I'm numb after losing Priti.

"My parents died Kirsten. They died. I was a little girl. How could you have been so brutal?"

"You're clever, pretty, sporty. I saw how friends and teachers were drawn to you. Then your parents died, and everyone felt awkward, so I took advantage. Can you forgive me?"

"You're still making it about YOU. Why should YOU feel better? YOU scraped broken glass down my thigh. *'Dead meat'* - remember that?"

She nods and for once tears stream from her eyes.

"Those words, me in a freezer; it was punishment. He said I deserved to die badly, because I'd lived badly. You think I deserved it, don't you?"

I feel no sympathy or animosity. I don't choose death for any of us.

"Like I said, you're not on my radar. But how far would you have gone I wonder?" Her pale face flushes. "All the way, I think."

I turn away, suddenly flagging. The emotional turmoil of the last five minutes has me feeling wretchedly exhausted.

My last visit. She's in bed recovering from surgery. She ashen, all grey and powdery, but I won't share. Pulling up a chair she opens her eyes.

"Phoenix."

"Hi, Kate. Can I call you Kate?"

She nods.

"How bad is the pain?"

"Grim."

We sit in silence, neither one of us knowing what to say.

"Sorry about your sergeant; how is he?"

"Critical."

She looks no older than me without make-up.

"What happens next Kate? I mean, it was harrowing down there. Where did all that blood come from and the smell?"

"Phoenix, are you sure you want to discuss this right now?"

"Priti's gone. Her parents moved her. They blame me; I know it. Nothing can be as dire as that, honestly."

"I'm sorry."

Tears fall again. I quickly wipe them away.

"There are more bodies at the house aren't there?"

"Possibly; teams will dig up the property and surrounding land."

"Was Jacobs his real name? Was he even a teacher?"

"No."

"He'd followed me for months and organised the hit and run."

"Yes...and you may not have been his first obsession."

It's a lot to take in.

"He was like two people...or a better actor than Tom Hardy."

Kate smiles.

"It's probably best not to think about him for a while."

I nod in agreement.

"I accused your uncle of murder."

"He'll get over it."

We grin at each other.

"You'd better scoot, you look wasted. Maybe on the way out grab that beddable male nurse and tell him I need Class A drugs."

"A Detective Inspector?"

I return to bed weary from the twists and turns of the life and near death of Phoenix Whittle.

HOME

It's early evening when I discharge us. I've never felt so relieved, to be home with a breathing Phoenix. I turn up the heating whilst Phoenix turns the lights on.

"Hungry?" I ask.

"No. If anything, I feel sick. I'll have to put a bin beside the bed; I've never felt so shaky and nauseous in my life."

"That'll be the drug you were injected with."

She looks at me; I wonder do I scare her, now she's seen what I'm capable of.

"Jesus Henry; I'm so sorry for dragging you down with me."

"Do you love me Phoenix?"

"Your brain is obviously addled. If I didn't love you, I wouldn't care about dragging you down; I'd just use you for sex."

She sways into the kitchen, to the fridge, to the chocolates.

"We need a sugar rush." She grabs the box. "Come on, bed Mr S.A.S."

She takes my hand, pulling me up the stairs; slow and unsteadily.

"Would you prefer to sleep in your bed – alone?" she asks painfully like the words tear at her throat.

"No. Come to bed and hold me. I'm tired, in considerable pain and I need you."

It's the first time I've trusted someone to be vulnerable with.

**

"I have to shower Henry. I've got...Jacobs on me."

I tuck Henry in.

Downstairs I shower, washing my hair until the water no longer runs red.

Upstairs Henry remains awake. I pull on a soft nightshirt, blow dry my hair a little then clamber into my hero's bed.

"Do you believe in fate Henry?"

"I'm not sure."

"Imagine Trish lived, I went to uni, and had a simple love affair. After a while we'd move on from each other. I'd meet lovers at work or in bars; maybe they'd muck me about, and it would be painful. Maybe, I marry easy-going jobsworth Darren. Could I be happy? Or would I never be happy or satisfied because none of them were you. Or would I be happy because I didn't know better?"

"Do you wish we'd never met?" he asks.

"Absolutely not." A short silence falls. "Were we destined to meet? Would our names be the same? Is that what sparks off conversation; we're both Whittles?"

***

"We can only base decisions on what's real. We met. We fell in love. There was no choice, our emotions decided for us."

"I'm sorry. Ignore me. I don't know what my point is," she admits.

"You're in pain, tired and overwhelmed."

She nods, but a dilemma edges around us.

"What else...I feel there's more?"

"Luke might know. I foolishly shared info, when he was deep in a coma, only for him to awaken around that key time."

"Luke loves you. He'd never jeopardise that. Give your heart and that brain of yours a rest," I say pulling her in tightly. I savour the feel of her in my arms, watching the sun cast shadows across the room. Eventually, worn out, we succumb to darkness.

***

I wake up; my face flat against Henry's back, my saliva on his skin like I want maximum transference. My arm is around his slender waist and like jigsaw pieces we are slotted together in the foetal position.

My last image before I fell asleep was of Henry aiming the gun; my last emotion, total relief. Mr Jacobs couldn't be dead enough.

"Umm, you're thinking loudly again," accuses Henry groggily.

"That's not possible," I laugh before kissing between his shoulder blades.

"You excel in making the impossible possible."

He moves as if to turn.

"Ahhh. Fuck!"

"You stay." I command. "I'm coming." I nearly fall over myself running around the bed, but now I'm facing Henry.

"Good morning Miss Whittle."

"We are so James Bond and Miss Haven'tGotAPenny."

He leans in; his breath blows between my lips. I kiss the end of his nose.

"What are you thinking?" he asks.

"No. You first."

"That we survived something macabre, something others have not."

I nod, unable to think of how close we came to dying.

"You?" asks Henry.

"How I'd be dead if you'd been an optician."

"You'd be amazed by what I can do with varifocals."

It's hard to believe we're able to flirt and laugh. I think about breakfast which is always a sign of recovery.

"I guess I'd better make us some breakfast as the head chef is out of action. This calls for Justrol. Chocolate croissants and cinnamon swirls."

I have another shower and a good cry. I love Henry so much. Too much. Probably detrimental to my health. Who is he? Who clones a phone? Who kills people?

And Priti! Where is she? Why is she even there? She must blame me. Maybe even hate me.

I turn up the water pressure so Henry can't hear me scream in frustration.

"Ahhhhhhhh!"

"Fuck!"

"Fuck! Fuck! Fuck!!"

Drying myself, I view my roughed-up body in the mirror. Jesus, I'm a total state. I pull on black lace Brazilians, no bra just a Henry black slim-fit tee. A flashback of me whisking it off for Henry flitters across my memory, like a pebble skips across a stream. Who and whatever he is, I'm keeping him.

I potter around, music quietly playing in the background, thinking a little here and there, calming my emotions, only to shake at terrifying flashbacks. Boy, have I a lot to share with Diane. She'll be needing therapy.

I decide to make a veg curry. It involves high quantity peeling which is relaxing. Also, you can't get it wrong unless you forget to add curry sauce.

My phone is in my pocket vibrating. Maybe Henry needs pain relief?

"Where are you?"

"In the kitchen?" I reply.

"What are you wearing?"

"Your black t-shirt; it reminds me how amazing your body is."

"How many male bodies have you seen?"

"Tom Hardy, Christian Bale, Ryan Gosling, Zac Efron..."

"I get the picture, but I'm not jealous because we both know it's me you want to fuck, me who touches you in places no one else will ever touch."

"Is this phone sex?"

"Depends where our hands are whilst we're talking; and what our hands are doing. You're blushing, aren't you?"

I laugh.

"You're very Ryan Gosling."

"Cool, tall, good looking."

"Intense and awkward."

"Ha, ha. So, you're wearing my black t-shirt?"

"Yes." I reply breathlessly.

"I see you. You're lying on top of your quilt; I'm leaning over you. Your hair fans out over the pillow. Your deep green eyes drug me. You take my hand..."

"Why have you stopped?"

"We'll continue this conversation later. Who knows, there might be audience participation."

"Henryyyy, you're torturing me. Shit, bad choice of words."

An hour later I make a brew, grab the cookie jar and clamber into bed with my phone sex buddy.

"What shall we watch now we're through True Detective?" I ask.

"The Sinner sounds our sort of thing."

"Our sort of thing, I love that; confirmation we're a couple."

We watch until Henry decides he needs a shower.

"Time to play nurse."

"Are you in pain?"

"Yes."

"Where?"

"Here."

I see where his hand rests.

"Really?" I laugh flushing.

"Your blush is fucking sexy. Come here wifey."

UNCLE HENRY

Lying in bed I watch a naked Phoenix, fresh from the shower, wander around choosing underwear and casual clothes. She's different; more self-assured, sunnier. For Phoenix her fear of school died the minute Kirsten Willard was abducted. It had been relentless, and Jacobs had, in his own twisted manor, protected her. It wouldn't surprise me if, in some small way, she misses him. Not now, but when the trauma is less raw. For a period, he was the constant in her life; there for her when I wasn't – it's warped but true. She catches me watching.

***

"Whittle! You are such a perv."

The memory of the package under the floorboards hits me hard. I turn to Henry.

"How long have you been Henry?"

For a moment the world stops.

"A month before your arrival."

"So, it was the other Henry who invited me here."

"Yes."

"And that Henry was a paedophile?"

"Yes."

"You killed him."

"Yes."

"Because he was a sex offender?"

"No. Although I knew his tastes. I had history with him. A score to settle. It's important you know I wanted to kill him. I enjoyed it. The bullet in my chest, three millimetres from my heart, was fired from his gun. The scars on my body were inflicted when he left me for dead; the Taliban imprisoned and tortured me. When I needed a new identity, his was easy to assume."

"How did you kill him?"

"I broke his neck. It was quicker than he deserved."

"Where's his body."

"Gone."

"You've killed my uncle. I don't know who you are or where you go. You leave the house at strange times. You wear different clothes coming home than those you left in. Your office is always locked. Now, either you don't trust me or there's things in your office you don't want me to see.

Henry, you're filled with secrets and you're...strange, but I love you. It's an inescapable, permanent fact."

"Phoenix I swear I'll love you till death do us part."

***

She laughs.

"Jesus Henry, that's cheery, couldn't you say for always, or forever. Actually, retraction you wouldn't be you if it didn't sound chilling and fatal."

I swing my legs painfully out of the bed and stand.

"Come here," I ask gently.

I engulf her in a hug that's comforting despite the physical pain.

I slightly pull away. Henry's attempt to comfort has me spinning in a whirlpool of sensual sensation.

He tugs me back. His breath blows down my neck, under my t-shirt and the warm pockets of air relax me. I listen to his breathing and mine slows and adjusts to his. He must have felt my body ease up because he nibbles on my ear.

I look up. He bends down. Our lips are tentative, moving gently across one another's. My hands beg to touch Henry. To slide inside his boxers. I never conceived the tight closeness you feel because of intimacy. I only want to exist now, in this moment when Henry and I are perfect.

"When you touch me, I'm safe but lost."

The words douse our longing in accelerant. For a moment a spark ignites; its embers burn inside us both.

I hear Henry wince in pain.

"Let's watch a teen romance on the big screen," I say, not quite ready myself.

We watch a marathon of films; all silly teen stuff, nothing with murder, abduction, torture, contract killing!

Dinner's a Domino's, on our laps.

I remember us yawning. Cuddling up. Gently drifting away.

I wake. It's early. Light barely edges between the blinds. We'd fallen asleep on the sofa.

Wrapped around Henry, I enjoy the heat generating from his body, transferring to mine. His hand is trapped between my thighs. Our physical closeness, Henry out of emotional hiding, we are suddenly real again.

I stretch and Henry's hold tightens. I nestle my face into the crook of his neck and breathe in the unique scent of him. I'm simultaneously filled with contentment and a surge of longing. It is amazing how Henry's scent stimulates this gnawing desire for me to touch him and abandon myself. I think about him sliding between my thighs and immediately I want him so.fucking.badly. Gently my lips nip his neck, all the way up to his jaw and back.

Henry groans, squeezes me tightly and rolls off the couch. He looks at me; his stunning vivid grey irises give me a lazy, seductive once over.

"Afterwards let's go to Café Rouge for breakfast."

"After what?"

"This," he says gently easing my knees apart.

I leave Phoenix sleeping. Our short outing was a little premature; it knocked her out.

In my office I deal with aftershocks. An email comes through from Andy Jensen. Four bodies found buried at the house. Daniels and Brady to make a full recovery; though Brady out of action for some months. Whilst Daniels recuperates Jensen is acting DI, which I'm pleased about. We go way back to basic training camp. It was no coincidence having a contact on the force.

"Knock, knock."

"Hi Henry," she says from the other side of the office door. "I'm making a deluxe hot chocolate and there's spray cream; I hear it's multi-functional."

"Come in," I invite.

"I think I've misheard," she responds.

"No. Come in."

"I wasn't coming in."

I laugh.

"Phoenix, would you please open this door and enter."

I turn the handle like it's wired to explosives. Oh, so very carefully opening the door. Henry sits behind a desk that is an l-shape. The walls are bare, the desk is bare. Henry is bare-chested, his legs covered with soft trackies. Henry motions for me to sit on his two-seater sofa.

"My life, before you, was about me. When it became about us that posed serious problems. I'm vulnerable. You've got power over me Phoenix, and that's hard to accept, but I'm confident in our love. I know you'd never intentionally hurt me. I'm gut wrenchingly sorry for every horrible drama I've put you through."

His voice, so toneless, so linear, yet so rhythmic, has a unique seduction, nothing like the breathy, hoarse declarations of love in my books. His face is flawless; a piece of cool marble; no creases from smiling, no laughter lines, he will age exceptionally well.

"My emotions are affected by your actions Henry, and your actions are inexplicably weird."

I pause.

"This is going to sound so stupid. I can't believe I'm about to ask this. Are you an assassin?"

A long pause.

"No. I work for the British Secret Service."

A longer pause.

"Are you fucking with me Henry, because it's not funny. I know you're new to humour and banter, but this is too far."

"I keep this office locked, not because I don't trust you, but because I've signed the Official Secrets Acts, and I am bound by British Law to ensure only my eyes see information that crosses my path. I do trust you Phoenix. I fucked up. I'm sorry."

Our foreheads rest against each other's.

"I love you so much it scares me," he reveals.

I take his hand, leisurely leading him upstairs. My other hand holds my pjs up. I've lost so much weight; I'm the wrong side of slim. My boobs have deflated. I think this is a good enough reason to ask Henry for cheesecake, or he could bake me his apple upside down sponge.

"You're on the mend. You look like you," he says smiling.

"But do I feel like me? Umm. I need an expert opinion."

I wind my arms around his neck and stand on tiptoe. My heart blatantly pounding and my rush of desire in his arms comforting.

"What are you doing?" he asks a warm smile sliding into position.

"Stretching whilst hugging; it called struggling. Now I'm pushing you back onto my bed. Now I'm unzipping your jeans. With the programme so far?"

"All the way".

***

Her lips crush mine. She's kissing me wildly and I'm desperate for anything she'll give. I'd die for her; this no longer scares me.

"Henry?"

"Umm?"

"Can I make love to you if I'm gentle?"

"Did you say gentle?" I laugh reproachfully.

"I didn't know your finger was broken," she says aghast.

***

"Just be gentle with me," he says, a vulnerability creeping into his tone. I'm intoxicated by this slight exposure – a glimmer of hope that Henry trusts me. I can't deny his truth is heavy, multi-layered, complex, possibly detrimental to my wellbeing.

But the compulsion to touch Henry is so strong it passes through me, like I'm permeable: bone into marrow, chamber muscle into heart. I clearly understand how a person physically aches for another. It's scary how much I care for him - this man who lives a lie. I should challenge his identity!

Henry is like the sea: beauty conceals its perilous unpredictability: you know the risks, but still you want to dip your toe.

He reaches out his hand...and I take it.